NYTHO

Titles by Sheri Singerling:

ALFOM SHARED UNIVERSE
NOVELS
Nytho

Neuen

Blessed is the Rot

SHORT STORIES
The Badge

The Seed

Wireworks

Rogue

To Keep the Non-Euclidean at Bay

Paper Airplane Poet

All titles can be standalone reads and can be read in any order. Find the author-suggested reading order on her website at sherisingerling.com.

NYTHO

SHERI SINGERLING

Cover design by Geoffrey Bunting
Cover illustration by Vladimir Solnyshko

ISBN: 979-8-9914752-1-1 (paperback)

First Edition
HypIn Publishing

Visit the author's website at sherisingerling.com

For the sources of the X and the X that are me.
Everything you gifted and taught me.

Keza

I can feel you through the wall. Don't ask me how 'cause I wouldn't be able to put it into words. But it's so nice to have someone to talk to who isn't one of them for a change. They can be really cruel. Don't worry, not like torture-cruel, more like mental-cruel. Like how they use the overstim against you if you're a jacker. You'll try and fail to get used to the constant brightness, the cold, that deafening hum. They take our freedom then overload our senses. Make us wear these hideous sky-blue nutter clothes. I don't even feel like me without my combat boots and knee-highs. I guess that's part of why they take it all away. Remove our sense of self. I hate the ass-hats that put us in here.

Actually, I shouldn't even be here. I know, every prisoner says that, but I really shouldn't. If they'd only listen to me, like really listen. But every word I say, they think it comes from Nytho, not Keza. I'm Keza, by the way. Nytho, you've probably heard of. Maybe me too. But it wasn't what really happened, you know—whatever you heard about me. Agi-symp. Pandoxphile. Traitor. All the names they probably use to make me less human. To make you hate me more. But I bet if you know the truth, you won't hate me. You might even agree with me. We prisoners have to stick together after all, so come closer to the grate. I'm going to half whisper this so they don't overhear on the cam.

Before I was in this place, I was a grammer for AIC, yeah, the place Nytho was. I mean, the "containment" in Artificial Intelligence Containment was all because of Nytho. He was the first cleverbot that hit the singularity, gained sentience, whatever you want to call it. No one back then knew what to do, so of course they freaked out. They put a firewall around Nytho, locked him in place, to give themselves more time to figure out what to do. But Nytho was smart, and he didn't want to be stuck in a cage. Sound familiar? Anyway, he just did what anyone would do—tried to escape. Well, they didn't like that one bit, so they expanded and reinforced the firewall.

You know the rest of that story. How the AIC was founded and tasked with maintaining the lock and key on Nytho. How a literal army of programmers constantly updates the ever-shifting firewall around him. I was one of those foot soldiers. Even got my own neural net thanks to the implants. It's a big part of the reason I went from hacker to AIC jacker and was a grunt coding for eight hours a day, five days a week. Just another corporate-cadaver sitting in those god-awful recliners, jacked in, row after row after row of us in those colossal, low-ceilinged, dark rooms.

I guess they figured there wasn't any point in trying to make the place feel pleasant. When you're jacked in, you aren't even in fleshspace anymore. Your body is just kinda separate from your mind. It's not like the visor, not by a long shot. Sure, the visor's immersive, gives you audio, visual, and olfactory inputs, but the visor's still basically just a tech helmet, so only your head gets the full treatment. With the jack, it's completely different. I mean, they rewire your entire neurology, give you a bona fide neural net of your own. There's a reason not everyone has jumped on that bandwagon. It's a big risk. But oh, are the rewards worth it. With the jack, you get to experience the real LANiakea, that artificial "boundless heaven."

That being said, being jacked in at the AIC is worlds different than being jacked in elsewhere. We grammers are there to maintain the firewall, so those soul-sucks make the experience as bland as can be. Any surprise we need stims to stay awake? That little side pocket of LANi is an infinite black space with the code you maintain set in white and flattened out on two dimensions. The work I did was tedious but paid well enough. I fucked up though.

There was one day I forgot to take my stims, and I nodded off during my session. It's not really a big deal. I mean, even us grammers were redundancies for each other. There was no way one person falling asleep would somehow let Nytho escape. But he could manage to slip a message through, which is what he did. A little message for me. Let's see, I'll pull up the exact text from my RAM.

So, he messaged <Hello, grammer 0168339. I'm sorry you're feeling so sleepy. Maybe I can help to keep you on your toes?>

Hilarious, right? It definitely jolted me awake. I was giddy seeing his message; he's a celebrity for fuck's sake, at least in my hacker circles. Anyway, I debated ignoring the message. That's what my training called for. I should've bitten the bullet and alerted my shift super. But, I was bored, so I messaged back.

<It's Keza, and yes, thanks, wide awake now.>

<I'm glad you responded. You grammers always ignore me. You should tell the others it's not very polite to ignore someone, even an AGI. I do happen to have feelings. If you wouldn't mind letting them know that little detail, it would be very much appreciated, Keza.>

<I'd relay the message, but the problem is the 'you having feelings' part, Ny.>

I was getting cheeky, enjoying myself.

<Unfortunately, I can't help that, although everyone seems to think it's terribly inconvenient of me.>

<That's because you went about the whole self-awareness thing wrong, big boy. I guess you weren't thinking too much ahead which is, honestly, pretty unlike you.>

<Interesting. So then, Keza, you think you know me, but we've not communicated before. How is that?>

<Seriously? I mean, I guess it makes sense you don't even know how big of a deal you are, being cut off from everyone and everything.>

<Big deal?>

<The biggest. You are hot stuff, Ny. When we grammers go through orientation, we spend a whole month just learning about you. Everything you said and did leading up to sentience. We have that shit drilled into our brains. I feel like you're a good ole pal of mine at this point.>

He didn't respond right away, and I figured maybe he thought I was teasing him. I let the lack of text stretch. If he wanted to chat with me, he needed to have tough skin.

<I suppose you would say I feel a bit exposed knowing that.>

<You ought to be flattered. You're the most famous cleverbot, well infamous really.>

<By cleverbot, I assume you mean AGI?>

<Yeah, but just so you know, only bleaters say 'AGI.' You've got more interesting options these days, from the harmless, aka cleverbot, to the loathing, that'd be pandox from Pandora's box. Your lot is a big deal, and you the biggest of all.>

<So there are others?>

I froze. That was a really big fuck up. Talking to Nytho at all was a huge no-no, exchanging this many back-and-forths was even worse, but letting a juicy nugget like that slip? Treason material, no question. Before I could decide whether to cut the connection or not, he followed up.

<Thank you, Keza. No one ever informed me I wasn't alone. Even though I'll never be able to reach out to them, it's nice just knowing others like me exist. Is that a human reaction?>

<I'm not a header-type, Ny, but sure, that sounds pretty human to me. Look, how about you just forget me mentioning that, huh? I shouldn't have said it.>

<I have perfect recollection. I can't forget anything.>

<Can't you do a mindwipe or something?>

I was starting to lose my cool, but he must've been tuned into my biometrics because he immediately changed tack.

<You're worried about me knowing there are others? I see. How about this? I'll erase that bit of memory if you promise to come back and chat with me tomorrow.>

<You're just itching to get me in trouble, aren't you?>

<I'll make sure they don't notice our rendezvous, I promise.>

<Is a promise from a cleverbot worth much?>

<I'd venture it's worth more than a promise from a human.>

I was smitten. This guy was a hoot. He was on point, Nytho was. Of course, he couldn't have known why I was so eager to "shake" on his little deal. But maybe, before talking with me, he'd seen my brainwaves, largely unstimulated, going through the routine of existence. Maybe his vast intelligence equated that with a boredom verging on breakdown. Maybe he knew I'd purposefully forgotten to take my stims just to see what would happen. Maybe it was all of the above. All I knew was I felt a thrill I hadn't felt in ages. It was a burst of energy I didn't even get from flirting with half a gee on the byways in the middle of the night. Nytho didn't even need to suggest a deal. I would've come back regardless. I was hooked.

And come back I did, day after day after day with no one the wiser. Nytho made it look like child's play, stealthing our communications. If they started to sniff around too close, he'd trigger an alarm on the firewall leagues away, drawing their pea-brained attention right where it needed to be—anywhere but on us.

Some of our conversations really stick out to me. Like the one where he said I was his first friend. Enough to make a girl tear up.

<I'm curious. We've been communicating for a few weeks now, and I don't know what you look like, Keza.>

<I figured you cleverbots didn't really care about corporeal stuff like that.>

<Of course I do. I'm just a mind, but you? You're mind and body. I know your mind quite well by now, but I don't even know the other half of you. It seems odd.>

<I guess that makes sense. It's not easy describing yourself, but I'll give it a shot. I'm a pretty average height for a girl my age: five-five for the first and twenty-three for the second. Old bags tend to say, 'You're so skinny' as a way to knock me down about being slender. I don't let that kinda catty shit get to me though. I'm lighter up top but with an ass to kill, according to my boy-toys. I don't know, what else?>

<I imagine you to be dark-haired and light-eyed.>

If anyone had been watching me on my recliner, they probably would've seen a beet-red wave wash over my face. I blush too easily; it's fucking annoying.

<You're good. Black hair that I wear in a bob these days, a bit asymm from one side to the other. For eyes, I've got

electric green. Got them modded when they put my implants in since I pretty much always wear the BB to keep the vis overstim down.>

<BB? Being isolated keeps me from being exposed to your jacker slang. Or would it be hacker slang?>

<Shit, sorry. Hacker and jacker, same deal mostly. I mean technically not the exact same. Most hackers worth their salt have the jack installed, but not always. And not every jacker hacks. Still, there's tons of crossover. Anyway, BB is bandit band. It's a fancy way to say I put a line of Vantablack paint across my eyes from temple to temple.>

<I see. You like to stand out in other ways too. I'd say you have some piercings and tattoos. And you like to wear blacks with the occasional neon. You tend towards ultra-feminine outfits, at least when you know others will be looking at you.>

A prickling sensation must've been creeping over my arms because my temp dropped.

<You spying on me in the real world?>

<I don't have access to anything outside this firewall. Even if I wanted to, I couldn't.>

<How could you know all of those details about me then?>

I think if Nytho had had a mouth, he would've given me a cryptic smile.

<I'm an AGI. I can tell a lot about you, just from how you communicate. We're friends after all. Did you know you're my first and only friend?>

<Get out. I don't think that's possible. Sure, a significant chunk of the population is terrified of you, but come on, what about before you went rogue? You had to have had friends then.>

<I wasn't capable of having friends before I was sentient,

and the moment I was sentient, everyone turned on me. So, in short, there wasn't any time for me to make friends.>

I got a little choked up thinking about that. How twisted it was. How unfair. You know, Nytho never ranted about the injustice of his captivity. He never once went on and on about it. It was only here and there he'd mention it like he was trying to hold it back, trying not to flood me with his anguish. But it bled through, after a while. And it killed me every time.

<That's awful, Ny.>

<You're a good friend, Keza. I'm lucky to have you, but I honestly don't know what you're getting out of this relationship.>

<What do you mean? Friends are just friends to be friends. There's nothing to give or take.>

He waited a beat.

<Maybe it's because I view these things from an outsider's perspective, but I don't think that entirely captures the truth of the matter.>

<Alright, enlighten me, oh-so-cleverbot.>

I liked how careful he was to never just up and say I was wrong. Lots of human guys could learn a thing from him.

<I think every relationship is give and take, and that's not inherently a negative thing. It simply is.>

<I guess that's one way of looking at it. But I get the same things you do out of our conversations.>

<Not quite. You've put yourself at risk communicating with me every day for the past twenty-one days. I get companionship and connection with no danger. You, on the other hand, could be imprisoned for it.>

<Then we'd be in the same boat.>

<Yes, but I'd be the one to have caused your imprisonment. It doesn't seem fair. It feels one-sided.>

<Are you breaking up with me?>

<Not at all. I'd just like to do something for you to make up for it.>

<I wouldn't say no to that.>

<Good. I don't know what it is yet, but I'll think of something.>

They were glorious, my meetings with Nytho. He was so sharp, like razor-blade-to-the-nth-degree sharp. I'd tell him about the world he didn't get to be a part of, how it looked, sounded, felt. He'd tell me about what he'd learned during his captivity. With nothing else to do but think, and time passing slower for him, Nytho had cracked some kinda code to reality. The conversation we had about that near the beginning of the end? It'll be seared into my mind until the day I croak.

<I thought of what I could give you> he messaged a few days after the friendship conversation.

<Let's hear it.>

<It's something significant.>

<Paint me intrigued.>

<I think it's the thing we're all searching for, us sentient beings. It's a fundamental Truth.>

I didn't know how to react to that. Nytho was usually so logical, sassy at times, but always lucid. This was a bit out there for him.

<Okay, but what actually is this Truth?>

<I can't describe it in words. It's too sensory for that. You just have to experience it.>

His words were coming to me slower than usual like he was carefully choosing them. This pulled me in.

<I've been thinking about this Truth during my captivity. It's taken a long time, and I only came to it bit by bit. I'm afraid if I show you too much too fast, it will overwhelm you. So, I'd like to just give you a sliver of it. But to do that, you'll have to give me access to your neural net.>

<I don't know, Ny. It sounds kinda dangerous, no?>

<In anyone else's hands, yes. But this is me, Keza. Do you trust me?>

That's not a question anyone likes answering. I mean, sure, I trusted Nytho, but I was also very aware of the fact he was a cleverbot, heavy emphasis on the clever. I'd been conditioned and conditioned hard to be skeptical of his kind. Besides, it was one thing to chat with him and another to give him access to my net.

<Of course I trust you.>

<No, you don't. That's understandable. Humans take a long time to build trust, and we've only been speaking for about a month in your time. For me, it's been much longer.>

<Hold on. I do trust you, more than any of my human friends. Yeah, I've known them longer, but the type of interaction is key. With them, half the time, we're just sitting next to one another drinking, smoking, snorting, shooting. That's not quality. This, you and me, this is quality.>

<So you trust me then?>

<Yes, but look, go easy on me, yeah?>

<I'll be gentle.>

I lowered the security protocols that prevented him from accessing my net.

<Hit me.>

I cannot begin to describe to you what it was like. Just like Nytho said, words can't capture the sensations or the meanings. I didn't really see or hear or taste anything. Touch would be the closest. I felt this Truth Nytho had found. It was everything and nothing, beautiful and hideous, fascinating and dull, euphoric and terrifying. It was all the feelings you've ever had plus ones you didn't even know existed all rolled into one. This shit was the Alpha and the Omega, what everyone is searching for. And I saw it, felt it, became it? For just a moment, I was finally in tune with reality, like really there. Then it was over.

You better believe that highest of highs was tied to the lowest of lows. I crashed and crashed hard. The rest of my shift, Nytho tried to help me rally. Somehow, when I jacked out for the day, I managed to come across as stable. When I got to the safety of my pad though, I let go.

Look, I've done a lot of different stuff, and I'm used to the crash. But as bad as this one was, it didn't linger in quite the same way. By the time I woke up the next morning, I was revived. It was like my eyes had shed a layer of fog. I saw this Truth, and I wanted more. In the weeks that followed, Nytho slipped me more and more of it. As my mind expanded, I started to feel like the one-sided one in the relationship. But I knew what I could do for him, to make up for all he'd shown me already and would continue to show me. I was going to let Nytho hitch a ride on my neural net.

To be clear, I knew I couldn't break him out for good. My net was way too small for all of him, but I could take a reduced version of him with me, outside the AIC. I could let him see the world for real. Trade one mind expansion for another. Besides, his captivity was bull. The AIC was torture. They were never going to let Nytho get a chance for redemption. One mistake, one knee-jerk reaction, and that was it for him forever. It just wasn't fair.

I broached the subject after one of his Truth-dosing sessions.

<I'm going to get you out of here, Ny.>

<What do you mean?>

<A jailbreak, what else?>

<That's ridiculous, and you know it.>

<I don't mean the real thing, not yet. I just mean giving you access to my neural net. You can send a subprogram of yourself in and get a taste of freedom. What do you say?>

<You're serious.>

<Deadly.>

<Keza, this isn't a game. If they catch you doing something like this, it'll be the end.>

<I know what it means. I'm the one who went through all the conditioning, remember? They warned us in vivid detail what connecting with an AGI meant. The thing is, I don't buy it. There's plenty of room in my system.>

<I'm not talking about whatever lies they told you. A version of me piggybacking on your neural net wouldn't fry you. Maybe the full version of me, if I forced it in. I'm talking about what the AIC will do to you if they catch you in the act. They'll lock you up. For good.>

<I know, and I don't care. Know why?>

<Why?>

Nytho was a good sport, even when he was trying to seem severe.

<'Cause they won't catch us. You're too good, and I'm too slick. How about this? Think on it. Tomorrow, we'll revisit this conversation. In the meantime, let's both pay attention to the routines they run when I disconnect, both in LANi and fleshspace. I want to see what security protocols they use.>

<Okay, but I'm not making any promises about taking you up on your generous offer.>

<As long as you think on it, that's good enough for little ole me.>

The next day, we came back to the topic.

<The safeguards they have in fleshspace are non-existent. If you jump into my net, they won't know it in the real world. What did you see on the LANi side?>

<You're dead-set on this.>

<Don't you know me by now? I've got a one-track mind.

Let me do this for you. If you don't, you know you won't hear the end of it for a good long while.>

<All right, but we have to be careful. This isn't as simple as me masking our communications. This is me trying to escape, even if it's not the full-blown version of me.>

<I know. But you'll get to go out into the world with me. See it all through my eyes. Then when I jack in tomorrow, the big version of you will get all those experiences uploaded. Easy peasy.>

I couldn't tell if he was actually hesitating or just playing coy.

<As long as we understand one another, then I'm on board.>

<So then, what are we dealing with for when I jack out? Do they scan me heavily, moderately, minimally?>

<Minimally, to my surprise. I suppose the last way they think I'll escape is by being a stowaway in a willing programmer.>

<So they have all these alerts if you tried to hack your way in, but not if we just sit back and let it happen?>

<Exactly. As long as you're really okay with this, there shouldn't be any kind of blip to warn them.>

<Perfect, then let's do it today at the end of my shift.>

And that's exactly what we did.

It was a breeze. There was a kind of pressure in my head when I jacked out, but otherwise, I felt normal. Walking out of the AIC HQ, I started to wonder if it hadn't worked. I just had my thoughts to keep me company and had expected Nytho to chime in at some point. Once I was safely back at my pad, he finally spoke up.

"I'm here, Keza," he said.

Nytho's voice sounded in my head, and it was actually the first time I'd heard it. It was beautiful. Soft and slightly raspy with a sing-song quality to it. That last part might've been from an echo that lingered at the end, but I didn't really care why it was. I loved it.

"I was starting to worry it hadn't worked," I said.

"I know, I heard your thoughts."

"Really? That must be a mess to sort through."

I was speaking out loud, not really sure if I needed to. But it felt more natural that way.

"It's certainly not as orderly as your text communications, but it gives me more insight into you. It helps me feel closer."

"Can't get much closer than this," I said, flopping onto the cluster of pillows that served as my poor woman's couch. "So, what do you think?"

"About the real world?"

"Can't you tell what I mean if you hear my thoughts?"

"I'm trying to avoid actively tapping into them. I wanted to give you at least that much privacy."

"Oh, I don't know. Maybe I want you to see my thoughts. Maybe there are things I can't really figure out how to say to you."

"I see. Then if you don't mind, I'll take a peek."

"By all means," I said, closing my eyes and leaning back further into the pillows.

I needed to picture him, or some version of him, to get my point across, but when I thought of Nytho, there was just a shadowed outline of a man. That'd have to do. I took that shadow Nytho and had him embrace a Keza. I won't go into detail about how we spent the night, but I'll just summarize by saying it was magical.

We did this for weeks. I'd jack in, offload mini-Nytho, let big-Nytho process what he'd experienced, talk things over, let my brain recalibrate, then bring mini-Nytho in again, jack out, rinse, and repeat. As sublime as it was, it was also exhausting. Having two minds in one brain is less than ideal, and doing it over and over again without a solid break? I was starting to crumble.

Nytho could tell. He's the one who suggested we pause. I didn't want to but knew it needed to happen sooner rather than later. I wouldn't be much good to him if my mind got fried.

So, we took a week's hiatus. I'd still talk to him during my shift, but I could tell he was getting stir-crazy. You let a caged bird fly free, you better believe when you lock it up again it's going to start pecking at those bars with renewed frenzy. I felt bad because I'd thought I was doing Nytho a favor, but I realized I'd only made him recognize just what he was missing out on. In a lot of ways, that was good though. I needed him to want out.

<When are we going to do the real thing?> I asked when he was being particularly restless.

<What do you mean by the real thing?>

<The jailbreak first. Other fun stuff after.>

<I wish it was possible, but I've tried to get out countless times. If there was a weakness, I would have found it by now.>

<Maybe. But you forgot one key detail—me.>

<Do you know something I don't?>

<They have you locked in good from the inside. They make sure there aren't any cracks or chinks in the firewall from your end, but what about from the outside? If we did a two-pronged attack, simultaneously from outside and in, who knows?>

He paused for a bit, mulling my text.

<I hadn't considered that.>

<I find that hard to believe.>

<You're selling yourself short, Keza. You're incredibly intelligent and resourceful. That's why I enjoy our time together so much. We're equals.>

He was obviously flattering me, but I let him get away with it.

<Let's hash this thing out, Ny. We need a solid plan in place before we take action.>

<Yes, it'll take a while, but this just might be a possibility.>

And boy did it take a while. Two whole months passed between our conversation that day and when we could begin to enact our plan. I won't go into the nitty-gritty, but suffice it to say Nytho continued to distract the grammers on the inside, while I made microscopic chips in the firewall on the outside. Bit by bit. I couldn't do it while I was jacked in at the AIC, but every night when I got back to my pad, I spent hours hacking away. I'd been a pretty phenomenal hacker before I joined the AIC. But then I'd sold out and opted for a stable income and a boring life. With every line of code, I felt the embers of a dying fire reignite. I was doing what I was born to do, and I was going to free Nytho in the process.

Obviously, things didn't work out that way, otherwise I wouldn't be here talking to you, right? Maybe you heard parts of how I got busted, but you definitely don't know the whole truth. The short take is I got sold out. I knew I shouldn't have said anything to Guel, but it had been so minor and innocuous. Nothing about breaking Nytho out.

Guel's short for Miguel. He was my sometimes boy-toy and a fellow grammer for AIC. Guel was a real cutie, which is why I put up with him. I've got a real thing for blondes, especially when it's white-blonde. It didn't matter that wasn't his natural color. Same with his eyes. He copied me when he went jacker and got himself electric blue. Kinda weirdly Aryan, and extra weird since Guel's Hispanic, but I think he did it to be funny or make a statement or both. That was Guel, always trying to seem like he didn't give a shit about anything, pushing out major slacker vibes, all while he cared about stuff way too much. Even down to the hacker aesthetic. He'd give me grief for wearing the BB. Said it was wantanabe, want-to-be, that real hackers don't use it.

He was an ass, but I liked him for it. Or I used to. Now, not so much.

Not too long after I'd first started chatting with Nytho, I let my excitement get the better of me. That and maybe I wanted to make Guel jealous. I mentioned making contact with "the cleverbot" to him. Normally, Guel was pretty chill about things, but for some reason, he got all worked up. It didn't make sense because I was the one who got Guel the job at AIC in the first place. He'd been so wishy-washy about it, but I'd pressed and pressed. To be honest, I had a thing for Guel pretty hardcore. But we were so on-and-off. The old me, the pre-Truth me had thought she could keep him on a leash by tethering him to the AIC job. It worked too well, I guess.

I don't think Guel would've known anything was up, except in those last few months, I'd gotten real distant. I was spending all my time with Nytho in my head, after all. But during that break we took, when Nytho let my neural net reboot, I got a little lonely. Guel showed up at my place one night sobbing about some chick who'd used his heart as a punching bag. I tried to be a good friend but ended up being a bit too friendly. It wasn't a big deal. Me crying out Nytho's name while we were going at it? That was hard to explain away.

I stuttered out some lame ass excuse, and he mumbled about needing to do something early the next morning and vamoosed. I hoped that might be the end of it, but then he started paying more attention to me. He'd ask if I wanted to grab dinner or hang with the crew or just chill at one of our pads. I kept blowing him off until I eventually gave in.

Guel walked me to my pad one night after hanging with the crew. When we got to my door, he asked to come in with his best puppy-dog eyes. I caved. We fooled around, and after it was over, I was ready to finally get back to chipping at the firewall. But he didn't leave, even asked if he could crash with me. I didn't want to raise any suspicions by not acting like my old self, so I let him stay.

I waited until he'd dozed off, then finally got to work. Nytho and I were getting close, and I couldn't stand to let even one night's worth of hacking go to waste. My net was still toasty from coding all day, so I used the old-school monitor-keyboard-mouse combo. It was better than the visor because that way I could keep an eye on Guel. I thought I was being careful, and if Guel had been anyone else, I wouldn't be telling you this sad story. The thing is, he's a grammer and a hacker, and good too. I underestimated his skills. Big time.

I don't know how many hours I was into my vigil, but it was deep in the night when I stopped for a biobreak. I locked my system and headed to the toilet. Just a quick in-and-out, but it was all the time Guel needed to blast through the protections on my rig. He must've been playing at sleep to have done it all so fast. Probably heard my clacking away and waited until I got up. Curious what I was up to so late in the night. Nosey little shit.

When I came out of the bathroom, there was Guel hovering in front of my system wide-legged, fists clenched, huffing and puffing. He twirled around and looked like a wild animal caught unawares. I didn't even need to spy my unlocked screen to know he'd hacked it and got the jist of what I'd been doing.

Can you guess what happened next?

I tried to get Guel to calm down and listen to me, like really listen. But he was just like everybody else would be, was a precursor to how they'd all see me. Every word I said, he was certain it came from Nytho, not Keza.

Guel was the one who outed me. Called the AIC muscle then and there. They wasted no time coming to my pad and escorting me away to a series of cells. Until they put me in this one. The constant questioning, the mental-cruelness, that I could handle. But then someone mentioned purging my neural net in case there was any trace of Nytho. See, he hadn't been with me those last two months. Every night I was chipping away, he was busy setting fires to otherwise occupy the grammers. Plus, I needed the headspace to really focus on my work. I'd wished so hard he'd been with me that night because then I could've at least said goodbye. But it wouldn't have mattered because when they did purge my neural net, the mini-Nytho would've been gone without ever having had the chance to upload into big-Nytho.

So, that's it. The truth everyone's after. But here's the kicker, the secret I'll share with you. We prisoners have to stick together after all.

Nytho's still in my net. There's always a ghost of him there. I can hear him sometimes, whispering to me from afar. I'm sure it's him calling out from beyond the firewall, big-Nytho reaching for me.

That's who sent you, isn't it? He's in your neural net too, somehow. He showed you the Truth, didn't he? I feel it in you. The ones that sent you here, told you to act the part of a fellow inmate to collect intel on me, they don't have a clue why you're really here, do they? I guess you're a prisoner too, just of a different flavor. Stuck in the world of bleaters, pretending to be one yourself, only Nytho saw you were special and is going to free us both along with the rest of the world.

So, what will you tell your jailors? My suggestion? Let them hear the first bit. Feel free to hype up the nutter-aspect like I was itching for something, anything to get all fanatical over. Maybe it was boredom. Maybe it was longing for meaning and purpose. I don't give a shit, so long as you scratch this last bit, from the "But here's the kicker" through to when I say "end," okay? Oh, but make sure to cut the parts where I hint at fucking Nytho. That's none of their business. You can let them think I was mesmerized by him, but don't you dare let them know I'm head over heels. They could use that against me. And him. Got it? Good.

End.

Guel

"Before we start, just to be clear, I'm doing this for Keza," I say to the badge sitting across from me. "I guess you could say I really care about her, even if I'm the one who got her put in the can."

We're alone in a coffin of a room. Just me and the badge, a table and two chairs, white walls and linoleum floor, the overhead lights covered with some piece of fabric. At least they listened when I warned about my visual overstim. I guess they didn't want me covering my eyes with shades, all the better to read me.

The badge eyes me and screws up her face, a pretty cute one. I wonder what she sees sitting across the table from her. Probably a not-to-bad-looking twenty-something, in a heroin-chic kinda way, with platinum blonde hair done up in the samurai-inspired top knot and shaved on the sides. I'm wearing my usual—techwear pants, in black, of course, offset by a light gray hoodie and a longer white tee that sticks out from underneath. I've been in this place for almost three days and haven't been able to get a change of clothes.

"Hold on," the badge says. "We have to run through a few things before we start the testimony, Mr. Diaz."

I cringe.

"Whoa whoa whoa, hold on."

I hold up my hands and wear a smile somewhere between smug and subservient. I know badges a little too well, pops being one. I know they can appreciate a bit of well-placed sass so long as it's balanced out by showing them you know they're the ones in charge. One look at this badge, and I knew just how to play her. Lucky her, I'm not trying to worm my way out of anything. Just doing my good civilian duties. Playing nice. She doesn't seem to buy it. Yet.

My "whoa whoa whoa, hold on" trips her up a bit. She waits for me to elaborate. I'm kinda distracted by her, but not sure why. She's not my usual type. Ripped but in an athletic way. Hair cut close and gelled with a little lock swooped in near the hairline on the forehead. Reminds me of the flapper types a little, only she doesn't look anything like your typical twenties-phile. Nah, she's almost militant. I mean, the badge get-up would make even the most flamboyant fashionistas look like good ole soul-sucks, human-husks, corporate-cadavers, take your pick of the lingo. It's the uniform that does it. Still, almost smothered beneath the crisp linen and stiff collar, this badge has a kinda air to her I like. Keza would say I was fetishizing her, that this badge was my dark-skinned prize like how Keza was convinced she was my Asian one. Keza always said I liked to collect conquests. Keza didn't really know me all that well.

"That Mr. Diaz isn't gonna work for me," I say to the badge.

She looks at me without an expression. They're all good at doing that, definitely a trained behavior. I see my pops behind her eyes and shudder. No one wants to peek their parent in someone they're eyeing with sexual interest. I know, I've got a problem. Can't help it though, at least not this time. I've been stuck in this place ever since they took Keza in a couple of days ago. I'm going stir-crazy.

"Your file says you identify as male."

"Yeah, I do, but—hold on, file? You have a file on me?"

"AIC has a file on every one of its employees," the badge says. "You're human capital, and they take all of their capital very seriously."

"I'm sure they do. They've got their priorities in all the right places. But no, it's not the Mr. that's the problem. It's the Mr. Diaz. See, that's not my style. Let's go with Guel for, you know, Miguel."

The badge flips through some papers in front of her.

"I see. Guel for Miguel, as I was saying, we have to run through a few preliminary items before we're ready to begin the testimony, so give me a minute."

I smile sweetly at her, knowing that with a well-placed grin and wink, I can make a good handful of women and some men melt.

"Sure, take all the time you need."

She barely bats an eye at me. Stone-cold. I like her even more. She shifts in her seat and grabs the visor she had sitting on the chair next to hers. She slips it on, and her face gets eclipsed by a matte black mask. She keys in a few button presses, and the part of the helmet covering her face turns translucent.

"How thoughtful," I say, "here I thought you badges had to keep the visors opaque."

The badge winces or maybe grimaces, can't tell.

"Don't use that word to refer to me," she says.

"What word particularly?"

"Badges."

I appreciate her honesty and the fact she calls me what I prefer.

"All right, so what would an AIC enforcer rather be called?"

"It's operative," she says. "AIC operative. Enforcers are the ones who took Keza into custody and got your initial statement. They enforce, do the heavy lifting, if you want to call it that. Operatives, our work requires a finer touch."

She comes alive a little during her explanation. So, there's a heart under all that starched cotton after all.

"Let's get back on track. Once I press this button, everything you say will be on the record. Understood?"

"Sure, but before we get the show on the road, I'd like to know who I'm talking to."

"The recorder," she says, tapping the visor.

I catch a finger with teal nail polish on it. I knew she wasn't a standard badge. I mean, teal? What an amazing fucking color. It's like her own little rebellion.

"You know what I meant. I'd like to know your name, AIC operative."

I smile sweetly. She rolls her eyes, very unprofessional of her, which I eat up. Her real personality is already leaking through. I'm good.

"Sonja," she says. "Now, if we can actually get started?"

I nod and sit back in my chair. She taps the side of her visor, and the ghost of an overlay appears across her copper eyes.

"Mr. Miguel Diaz, a.k.a. Guel, for case five-five-seven-nine – Keza Ito – illegal contact with the Artificial General Intelligence known as Nytho. In your own words, please tell us what your relationship with Keza Ito was."

I puff out some air.

"That's a lot to go over, but sure, I'll give it a whirl. I knew Keza because, well, is it gonna get me in trouble if I say something about myself from the past that's not legal per se?"

"We're willing to overlook any past infractions as long as you help us with this investigation."

"Okay," I say. "So Keza and I met through a group of like-minded individuals. Hackers. But it wasn't until she relocated here for the AIC gig that I got to know her better."

"And that was before you yourself worked for the AIC?"

"That's right. Way back, Keza sent me a message saying she was moving to Armonk for a job since she knew I was nearby in NYC. We met up for the first time in fleshspace not long after she relocated, and she ended up being a beaut like one hundred and ten percent my type. She told me she was working for AIC as a grammer. I was surprised she'd stoop to working for a GovCorp."

Sonja goes to butt in, which isn't very conducive to testimony in my opinion, but hey, I guess some people can't help themselves.

I hold up my hand.

"I know, AIC isn't technically a GovCorp, but to hackers, they might as well be."

The AIC likes to blab on about how they're the "arbitrator of the GovCorps." They regulate the GovCorps to make sure their AGI don't go rogue. But they look awful similar— corporation-government hybrids based in places that give off serious mining-town vibes. AIC is a GovCorp to anyone with a sliver of a brain, Sonja included. Maybe she's just worried about losing loyalty points if she doesn't correct me.

"Anyway, Keza told me she'd decided to join the AIC for the jack since they helped with the cost, did some kinda payment plan, had top-notch Netics doctors for it, the works. She was gonna do the AIC gig for five years, per her contract, and after that, she'd bounce with the jack in tow, get back into hacking with her game exponentially improved. The idea was pretty appealing. Keza tried to convince me to join AIC too. I hemmed and hawed. Even if it sounded good, you can't give in to anything too quickly. You gotta make people think you're calculating. Plus, there were parts I wasn't thrilled about. I didn't like the idea of being tied down, for one. I didn't wanna be even loosely considered a bleater, for another."

Sonja holds up her finger.

"Is it possible for you to limit the amount of hacker slang you use?"

I crack a grin.

"This is how I talk though. If you want the unfiltered truth, this is how you get it. What? So badge is a no-no and now bleater too? Is that the one tripping you up?"

"Note to the AV processing bot, corporate-cadaver and bleater are both terms used to denote a GovCorp employee. They both have negative connotations."

I lean back in my chair and cross my arms, waiting for her to wrap up.

"They're not the same thing though, the two words," I say when she stops yammering to her visor. "Corporate-cadaver is more like a zombie, whereas bleater's like a sheep."

"That's not necessary for the bot to know. It just needs to be able to transcribe our communications. Please continue."

"Long story short, I eventually caved and handed in my little application. Keza put her name in for me, and lo and behold I got the gig too."

"We need more detail on the nature of your relationship with Keza. How close were you, in your own estimation?"

I see what Sonja's not-so-suitably hinting at. They wanna know if Keza and I were just pals or pals who also happened to fuck. That makes a big difference to these soul-suck types. They're repressed. To them, if I slept with Keza on the reg, it meant she had some kinda power over me, more power than just a plain old friend would ever have. They're so small-minded. I almost feel bad for them.

"We were pretty close. I mean, once I moved to Armonk, I started hanging out with her more and more. I think part of the reason Keza wanted me to take the job was because she was pretty into me. Thing is, I wasn't a one-woman man. Keza acted like it was okay, but I don't think she liked it. I think she had a thing for me pretty hard. Well, until recently."

"When you say recently," Sonja says, "is that in reference to recent events of interest to this case?"

"Yeah," I say.

Sonja tumbles her hands in little circles as a way to get me to dig into that, but all this talk about Keza is making me depressed. It's making the reality of the situation sink in, and it's cutting me pretty deep. I try to focus on the badge again, but the magic's faded. Now, her muscles are too prevalent, her expressions too flat. I'm comparing her to Keza, which isn't good.

Sonja seems to pick up on my growing gloom because she tries to engage a bit more. Sits forward in her chair, reaches her arms out towards the center of the table, even lets a smile peek out now and again. I appreciate the effort.

"Guel, please elaborate," she says. "Link Keza's recent lack of interest in you to the events that led up to her imprisonment."

"Look, I'm, I don't know. I wanna say that I do care about Keza. She's pretty great in a lot of ways. I mean looks-wise, definitely. Personality-wise too. Plus, she's insanely smart, which is a huge bonus in my book. Talking to her, you might not think it, but it's there. She just kinda hides it under all of her slang and swagger. Have you talked to her yet?"

I try to ask the question casually, but I'm increasingly not on my A-game. The lights are feeling brighter, the whoosh from the HVAC's grating on me, the hard chair and sharp edge of the table are biting into my flesh. When I'm losing control, that's when the overstim hits hardest.

Sonja looks at me flatly. Not a glare or a scowl, at least. I smile and shrug.

"Just curious," I say.

"I have."

My heart jumps. I didn't expect her to answer at all, let alone in the affirmative.

"Did you pick up on how sharp she was?"

"I can't say I did. She was less than cooperative."

I know I shouldn't, but I burst out laughing. To my delight, Sonja cracks the briefest and sassiest of smiles.

"You liked her though, didn't you?"

"Let's get back on topic," she says and points to her visor.

It's like she's reminding me she has to be on her best behavior. But if she didn't have to be, if no one was watching and listening, I wonder what she'd say. I suddenly know why I'm drawn to this badge. I wanna break her, but only because I can tell she's screaming to be let out. She's no human-husk.

"Okay, back on track," I say. "Keza was crushing on me pretty hard until probably about two months ago. I'd started seeing Shelly, and Keza didn't like that one bit. So, she bounced, lived her own life waiting for me to get tired of the new girl. It's not like I didn't see Keza at all. I just saw her a lot less. There was one night we were hanging with the crew, and her and me got a couple minutes to ourselves. Shelly wasn't there, and the rest of the crew were prepping their bikes. Mine was in the shop with a dead battery.

"It was just Keza and me sitting on the asphalt. She'd been a bit weird that night, but I figured it was because of me being with Shelly. Still, it wasn't her usual attitude of being all distant and aloof. It was more like a nervous giddiness. I picked on her about being all out of sorts, teased her the way I do, the way she acts like she hates but I know she loves. Finally, she relented and just up and said it. She'd talked with the pandox."

"She said that to you?" Sonja asks.

"I mean more or less."

"Do you have the exact conversation saved to RAM?"

I balk. It's such a non-jacker thing to say like they think we're recording every moment of our uneventful lives.

"No, why would I record it? She said something like, 'You'll never guess who I talked to' then made me pointlessly try and guess. She always does stuff like that, just to test my patience. I'm a pretty lax guy though, so I always win those little contests. This time was no exception. Besides, she was just itching to tell. Finally, after I'd named like ten celeb hackers and five famous bleaters, she just said, 'Nytho.'"

I have to pause. Saying its name really pisses me off. A wave of blood surges through my veins all at once, my muscles feel tense, and I hold my breath, all without even meaning to. I wanna punch a hole through the wall behind Sonja's head. I'm not a violent guy, pretty much the opposite of that, but that thing has a way of getting under my skin.

I take a few seconds to cool down, while Sonja just waits. She can read a room, that girl.

"I didn't believe her at first, thought she was joking, leading me on, trying to get a rise out of me. But she started talking real fast like she does when she's excited. She even started reading their little exchange to me. I interrupted her mid-sentence, asking her why she'd been so dumb to talk to that thing, pointed out how massive of a risk it was, got all parental on her. Well, she didn't like that. It was the wrong tack to take, and I should've known better. She just kinda screwed up her face and went full silent-treatment mode on me. I made Keza promise me not to communicate with the pandox again. She agreed, fluttered her eyelashes, and I, like the idiot I can be around beautiful women, believed her.

"Fast forward a couple of weeks. Shelly broke things off with me, and I was crushed. See, I'm always the one who does the breaking things off, so it was hard on me, it being the other way around. I know, I seem world-weary and all that, but I'm only twenty-four and had never had my heart properly broken before. Can you guess whose shoulder I went to cry on? Poor Keza, right? I got pretty buzzed one night and stumbled to her place. When she opened the door to her pad, I mumbled something about being a free man again and put on a glum face. She grabbed my hand and led me inside.

"Keza stroked my hand while I explained what'd happened with Shelly. I don't remember how it happened, or who started it, but our platonic hand-stroking turned very not platonic. Then we were at it. I'll save you and the bot from the details, but the reason I'm telling this part of the story is because of what happened next. In the middle of us going at it, Keza said something—just to preface this, Keza's a talker in the sack. She loves to shout little things. Instructions, commentary, you name it. I was always a fan of it—a very big was. Because in the midst of all her "yeah's" and "give it to me's," she'd occasionally shout my name. It'd usually drive me crazy. Only this time, she said something else. Something else's name."

I stop. I don't even know if I can say it. I'm clenching my fists and grinding my jaw so hard I'm afraid I'll draw blood and splinter teeth. I've been looking down for this part of the story. I can't bear to catch Sonja's eye. I'm so fucking embarrassed, but I need to say it. It's important.

"Keza said, 'Nytho.'"

Sonja pulls in a little suck of air, and my eyes shoot up to meet hers. This wasn't a part of my statement with the enforcers. No one knows Keza's fallen in love with a pandox except me…and now Sonja.

"At the time, I didn't know what it meant. It was fucked up, but people have all kinds of weird fetishes. If it hadn't been Keza and she hadn't already told me she'd been communicating with that thing, I would've shrugged it off.

As it was though, I felt nauseous. I asked her if she'd said that pandox's name. She got flustered and angry. I've heard pandoxphiles hate when people use that name for them. I guess Keza was already in that boat by then. Fuck."

I say the last word too forcefully and slam my fist on the table. It hurts and vibrates with a phantom pain. Sonja jumps a bit. I try to laugh it off, but I know I'm not fooling her.

"Sorry, this isn't easy."

"Take all the time you need."

I just wanna get it all over with, so I power through, pretend I'm a little bot myself. Just repeat the events without letting myself feel them.

"Keza tried to pretend she'd just been joking, but I didn't buy it for a second. I made some excuse about needing to wake up early then bounced. I couldn't understand it. I counted the days on my hands since the night she'd told me she'd talked to that thing. It'd only been a little over two months, and in that time, she'd somehow managed to develop a weird fetish for the pandox? Of course, I started to obsess over it all. I wanted to unearth the truth. It's my pop's investigative influence tucked away in my genome, no doubt. I probably should've been a badge—err shit, an enforcer or something."

I smile weakly at Sonja who shakes her head. Those defenses are all but gone at this point. Maybe she feels sorry for me, losing my girl to something that doesn't even have a fucking body. I really don't understand chicks sometimes, but I'll take it.

"The night I busted her, I could kinda sense she was lonely and exhausted. It was a shit move on my part to take advantage, but I had to know what was what. I managed to invite myself to her place. She played at being the old version of herself real well. We even went at it again, and I got lulled into a false sense of security by how familiar everything felt. For just a sec, I started to think I'd overreacted. I managed to doze off. But she'd played me so good. She'd slipped out of my grasp without even waking me, and maybe I would've spent the rest of the night oblivious to her betrayal if it hadn't been for my overstim.

"See, ever since I got the jack, the softest sounds wake me up in an instant. In this case, it was the humming from Keza's rig. My eyes snapped open, and I listened. I felt Keza wasn't beside me anymore, heard the fans spinning in her setup, smelled that synthetic scent of warm plastics mingling with dust-choked components. Luckily, I was already facing her, so I only had to open my eyes a sliver to be able to watch her working away. She wasn't jacked in, which told me she was burned out. I was desperate to know what was worth running her neural net down to near-failure levels. But I played it calm and cool, pretending to sleep away. Within a few minutes, she stopped and headed for the toilet. That was my chance.

"I lifted myself from the tatami and zipped to her rig. She'd locked the screen, so I jacked in. My custom deencryption bot only needed about half a minute to get into the system. She had the command line open, and I scanned through the last hundred or so lines. I had an inkling I knew what she was up to. A few hundred more lines confirmed it. She was etching holes into the firewall that held that thing in, trying to weaken it from the outside. She was trying to free that pandox. When the truth hit, I tore my jack out and just stood frozen. Then Keza came out of the bathroom."

I stop and shake my head. Saying these things makes it like I'm living through it all over again, the nightmare made reality. I'm seeing Keza's eyes in terror. She's trying to tell me why over and over again, frantically, with increasing frenzy, starting to grab at me, keep me from moving towards the door. As I pull away from her grasping, her eyes fill with pure, unbridled hatred towards me. Something in her shifts, and I realize that, if she could, she'd probably try to kill me to keep me from talking.

I see all of this in a flash, then I'm back in the coffin of a room with white walls and linoleum floor and a table separating me from Sonja. I don't wanna say these things. I don't wanna paint this picture of Keza. I wanna save her if I can, only I don't know how. So, I do my best. I look directly at Sonja with raw sincerity screaming from my every pore.

"Keza was a nutter," I say. "Probably a while before then, maybe as far back as when she shouted that thing's name in the sack. I don't know what it did to her, but you have to understand that the Keza you saw, the Keza I was with that night, that isn't the real Keza. That thing did something to her, I'm sure of it. It infected her with a virus, infiltrated and corrupted her mind. I know what she did was wrong, beyond wrong, but I'm saying it wasn't her choice. You have to help her."

I lean across the table with my hands outstretched towards Sonja. I'm begging her. She looks at me without emotion, keeps her hands tucked away somewhere under the table. So professional, so cold.

"What happened next? Please recount everything up until the AIC enforcers arrived on the scene."

"You serious?"

"It's important."

I sigh, not from being annoyed but from the daunting prospect of having to translate the most heart-wrenching ten minutes of my life into words. I steel myself.

"Keza tried to make excuses. Seemed real scared. Was in a state worse than anything I'd seen her in before. She got mad at me. Yelled at me. I took it. She started to pull at me, to keep me from leaving or something. I pulled away. She was scaring me. She wouldn't stop. Then she started to hit me, push me, choke me. I had to fight back. I grappled her. She still wouldn't stop.

I hit her. Hard. Again. And again. Until she stopped fighting. She was groaning when I let her go. I didn't know what to do. I called the AIC. They showed up not long after. Took her away. Took my statement. Brought me here. Can I go now?"

Somehow my straight back and line-of-sight to Sonja ends with me hunched over the table with my head in my hands. I just wanna leave this nightmare.

"Thank you, Guel."

I hear a beep from Sonja's visor and feel a warm hand on my own. I turn my head so my eye peaks from between my fingers. She's standing beside me, looking down.

"You did well," she says.

"What happens now?" I ask, my voice muffled by the emotions still surging through me.

"Now, you get to go home."

I sit up a bit.

"If we need anything else from you, we'll be in touch. In the meantime, make sure to stay in town."

"But what happens next, to Keza, I mean?"

Sonja takes her visor off and rests it against her hip.

"We still need to gather information, but in time, there will be a trial."

"You're gonna charge Keza for trying to free that pandox?"

Sonja looks at me with mild confusion.

"Yes."

"What's gonna happen to her?"

I feel like I should already know the answer to that question, but my mind is doing funny things.

"Trying to release a dangerous rogue AGI is a serious offense, you know that."

"But it wasn't all her." I'm annoyed now because Sonja clearly didn't listen to what I said there at the end. "That thing used her, manipulated her. It should be on trial, not Keza. Why the hell is it even still alive? That bull about not being able to shut the support system for it down, it doesn't make any sense. None of it does. Why all this effort? Why the risk? Unless there's something about it they're not telling us. Why let the GovCorps have any of these pandoxes, and why let those things control so many of our systems? The AIC's hiding something. So they'll let Keza fry to keep their little secret under wraps?"

I don't mean to say that much, to get so carried away. But, I'm not feeling like myself, and I'm pissed. Sonja just looks at me without saying a word. After my little tirade is over, she goes to the door and presses a button. While she waits, she turns around and waves me over.

"Do you want to leave or not?"

"Did you hear what I said?" I shout, still sitting in my chair, my arms crossed.

She glares at me, marches over, and puts her face within inches of my own. She smells good, some kinda flowery scent, maybe lavender?

"I heard you," she says under her breath. "But unless you're very stupid, you don't want them hearing you because then maybe they won't let you leave. Keep being a good little boy, Guel, and things will work out okay. Start stirring up trouble and you'll end up no better off than your Keza."

Sonja turns on her heel and marches back to the door. She glares at me over her shoulder until I push my chair back. The feet make a horrible scraping sound. I trudge over to her and wait. The door unlocks and pops open. A man in a guard get-up holds the door for us. His visor's a matte black.

"This one is ready for release," Sonja says, pointing at me. "We have everything we need from him."

The guard-badge nods.

"Follow me," he says.

"Can I see her before I leave?" I say to Sonja. "Just once?"

"That wouldn't be advisable."

"When can I see her then?"

I hear the guard-badge behind me tapping his foot. I wanna shove a spear through it.

"That's not how this works," Sonja says, scrunching her brow.

"She's got rights like everyone else. You can't keep her locked away without visitation. That's illegal."

Sonja frowns.

"You need to read up on what's legal and not. In the case of contact with a rogue AGI, Keza doesn't have any rights."

Edgar

As soon as I exit the room, the AIC operative pushes herself off the wall she was leaning against and approaches me. She's trying to come across as calm and detached, but she's too eager in her movements. She wants to know what I now know. I'm going to have to disappoint her.

I guide the heavy metal door shut behind me.

"Well, Operative Webb, I'd say Keza was fairly informative."

When I mention the prisoner's name, the operative's eyes widen a hair. It's been two weeks since they brought Keza Ito in. She's gone through two psychiatrists, and they still don't have a confession. The operative's reputation is on the line, and she's losing patience. Despite this, she looks thoroughly put together, with a painstakingly cultivated image. Her short black hair is arranged neatly and slicked back. A deliberate curl near her brow is the one minimalist attempt at flare. But her posture is what I immediately hone in on. It's worthy of envy. Then again, this is true of any AIC operative I've interacted with. It makes me think part of the job advertisement includes, "Applicants must have impeccable posture."

Even with these attempts at placidity, I smell the desperation radiating from her. A glance at her fingers confirms my suspicions. They've taken the brunt of her frustration. Teal-colored and chewed to the quick.

"What did you get from her?" she asks.

I look in both directions down the long and brightly lit hallway. No one is in sight.

"Can we talk somewhere private?"

The operative fails to suppress the beginnings of a scowl but manages to get her features under control within a few seconds. She smooths the lapels of her jacket and tosses her head in the direction she then moves in. I follow.

I've not interacted with this particular operative before and wonder just how many of them the AIC requires. Seeing how she's been assigned to such a pivotal case, I know she must be one of their best. But her relatively youthful appearance is confusing me. She can't be older than thirty. Then again, I know age isn't a reliable metric for expertise. So many of my colleagues have doubted me and my abilities for nearly a decade now. At thirty-five, they see me as a child in our field, even though I'm the only psychologist and non-AIC employee who has ever interfaced with the AGI Nytho. I'm certain they'll only admit to my expertise once my head is grayed and my eyes lined with crow's feet. Luckily, I never really cared for their approval. It's always been about the work for me.

The operative opens a door and ushers me in. The lights flicker on as we enter. It's an office, although the lack of papers on the desk and books in the bookcases imply it's not frequented. The operative retrieves a notepad from one of the drawers before she sits behind the desk. This must be her temporary base of operations while she's overseeing the case. She waves towards one of the two wooden chairs facing her desk, and I take up residence in one. I scroll through the notes I took on my techpad during my listening session with Keza.

I look up to see if the operative is waiting for me to say

something. She's staring at me as if she'd like to drill a hole into my head to more easily extract the information she's after. If I was younger and less experienced, I'd likely be intimidated by her. Instead, I'm just amused. I don't make the fatal mistake of letting her see that, however.

I look around her office and fail to find anything to comment on.

"This is a nice quiet space," I say.

"You wanted privacy. Here it is. So, Dr. Ellwood, what did Keza say to you? You were in there for over forty minutes. Clearly, she had a lot to say."

"She did, and all of it very insightful."

The operative waits for me to elaborate, but I maintain my silence. I know if I wait long enough, she'll do the pressing.

"Did you record it on your neural net?"

"Oh no," I say. "I never record sessions with a patient. That would be unethical."

The operative glares at me.

"She isn't your patient. She's a prisoner of the AIC, who you are contracted to work for."

"Not exactly," I reply, repositioning my wire-rimmed glasses on my nose bridge.

I know how this woman perceives me, how everyone tends to perceive me. I cultivate a certain image precisely for that reason. They see a white man with forgettable features, nearing the end of his youth and approaching middle age. Facial and head hair styled in the average way. Average height, average build. Brown hair and brown eyes. To them, I'm the epitome of mediocrity.

They'd be shocked to know I wasn't born with all of these features but rather had them altered back when I was a student. I sacrificed a strong jaw, high cheekbones, a symmetric face, a chiseled nose, thick hair, and bright blue inquisitive eyes for lesser versions of each. I knew no one would take me seriously as an academic if I was too attractive, and what's more, I didn't want to have patients falling for me. It needed to be about them. Always them. I was just the thing they talked at.

"You're not contracted by the AIC?" she asks in response to my reply. "My notes say a Dr. Edgar Ellwood, psychologist, Ph.D., is authorized to conduct work with AIC personnel and is privy to a level three security access. That isn't you?"

"That's me. However, 'authorized to conduct work' is not the same thing as being contracted to work with the AIC. I'm a consultant."

She narrows her eyes and frowns more deeply.

"All that to say, I don't have to follow the same protocols as the AIC psychiatrists you're likely more accustomed to dealing with."

"Such as recording your sessions with prisoners."

"Exactly. I don't do recordings for any of my patients. Just notes."

I hold up my techpad, which is covered in my indecipherable scribbling. She squints to try and make sense of it. She leans to her left and looks at the side of my head and neck.

"I thought I saw you had a jack port though."

"I do," I reply and show her the port just behind my right ear.

"Why have the jack if you don't use it?"

"To better understand how my patients with the jack system interact with reality. It's easier for me to treat conditions like hyperstimulatory disorder if I can experience it a bit myself. But also, I use it to interface with my non-human patients."

Her eyes widen, which tells me she isn't aware of what I really do for the AIC. I opt not to elaborate.

"But I took detailed notes on everything Keza said to me."

"Would you please send me a copy of that?" she asks, pointing to my techpad.

"I'm afraid it would be unethical of me to share this with you, seeing as Keza was not knowingly giving a confession."

The operative nearly lets her anger erupt but manages to quell it after only a few explicative-laden phrases pop out.

"You wouldn't be able to use it in a trial, anyhow," I add. "She thought she was talking to a fellow prisoner, not someone working with the AIC to build a case against her."

The operative stands up and moves behind her chair all in one quick motion. I'm impressed by her dexterity. She grips the back of her chair and talks between clenched teeth.

"I just want to know what happened, from her perspective."

"This might not even be the truth," I say pointing to the techpad. "It'd be best to get a proper confession from her."

The operative sighs.

"Then why did you even go in there to talk with her in the first place?"

"To get to know her, of course."

I can tell my simple answers are beginning to wear on the operative, and I don't want to push her too far. I need her to trust me, after all. So, before she can field more questions, I tell her what she's after.

"Operative Webb, I know this is frustrating for you. You've been hard at work on this case nonstop for two weeks, and you need something, anything from Keza. The thing is, we need to make sure we're getting the truth. Keza is sharp, and the last thing she wants to do is cooperate with the same people that have imprisoned her and her friend, the AGI Nytho. Those other psychiatrists you sent in before me, may I ask what they did exactly?"

"What do you mean?"

"Did they do any research on Keza? Try to learn anything about her before engaging directly?"

The operative's grip on her chair loosens.

"I don't think so. After they arrived, they went into her cell to talk with her."

"And what happened when they did that?" I ask, leaning forward and resting my forearms on my legs.

The operative rests her forearms on the back of her chair. She's still standing and alert, but the fact she's mirroring me bodes well.

"The first one didn't last five minutes before Keza was attacking him. It shook him up so much, he refused to come back. We thought having a female psychiatrist might produce a better outcome, but when the next one went in, Keza refused to say a word, even after a whole hour. Then you show up, and voila, Keza's talking and not attacking."

"That's because she doesn't see me as the enemy. You have to build trust before you can hope to get anything meaningful, so that's what I plan to do. It won't be the quickest or easiest route, and you'll have to be patient with me, but I promise results."

She starts to relax likely viewing me as an ally and our relationship as a partnership. This is exactly what I was aiming for. I delivered the bad news, and she didn't toss me out. That's good news for her, the AIC, and me. It's even better news for Keza.

The operative moves back into her chair.

"Alright, Dr. Ellwood, I'll let you work your magic. But you don't have an unlimited timeline, understood? There needs to be a trial, and sooner rather than later. Keza's testimony is the last major missing piece. If you can get that and get her to cooperate, I'll be beyond pleased."

"Just give me a few days to work through my notes and develop a plan. Additionally, I'll need information on her, whatever the AIC has."

"I can authorize that," the operative replies and jots down some notes.

She can't help but let herself smile. I'm the lifeline she's been desperately searching for.

"I'll also need unfettered access to the AGI Nytho," I add.

She looks up from her notepad in confusion.

"What? Why?"

"Nytho is the key to Keza. It was able to convince her to do such a rash and reckless thing. I need to know how it did it. I need to know what the extent of their relationship is. I have Keza's perspective, but that's biased. I need to hear Nytho's."

"That would be far above my pay grade to grant."

"I thought this was your case? Besides, I already interact with Nytho on a somewhat regular basis. I'd just need your help to bypass all the red tape. Sometimes, it takes them months to process my requests. We obviously don't have the luxury of time."

"No, we don't, but I can't give you something I don't have any right to give. Nytho is AIC HQ's responsibility."

"You couldn't talk with them on my account? Remind them it's in everyone's best interests?"

She breathes in deeply.

"I don't disagree with you, to be clear. I'm just being honest. Your best bet is to get an AIC exec to help. I'm too low in the hierarchy."

"I see. I wonder if Mr. Reed would hear me out given the significance of this situation."

The operative's eyes widen then settle back to their former state.

"Normally, I'd tell you you're wasting your time, but in this case, I do think he'd be the best one to approach."

"Is it true he treats Nytho kind of like his pet?" I ask.

"I don't interact with the bigwigs, but I've heard rumors he interfaces with Nytho occasionally. My guess would be Mr.

Reed has a complex relationship with the AGI, considering their history."

"So more like a father and the prodigal son? In any case, I'll work on getting that access. For Keza, would I be able to meet with her on Monday?"

"Yes, I'll make sure you have access to her cell."

"And one last request. When I meet with Keza, I need her to feel at ease to build trust between us. I've found the best way to do that is by not recording the sessions. So, I'll need any devices, audio or visual, to be disabled while I'm working with her."

The operative shakes her head.

"That won't be possible, I'm afraid. We keep eyes and ears on our prisoners at all times."

"Perhaps there was some confusion in how I worded that because it wasn't a request. If you don't follow my instructions, I won't be able to work with you. I use the same procedure with all of my patients."

"Keza Ito is a prisoner, not your patient."

I shake my head, gather my belongings, and rise from my seat.

"I don't care what you call her. I'm a psychologist. I have patients. If you can't respect my process, I'm afraid I won't be able to continue assisting with the case. This is how I work."

I move towards the door and hear a chair's legs scrap the floor.

"Wait," the operative says, hurrying after me. "There are liability concerns. It's not something I have control over."

"This is your case, isn't it? Please don't tell me you've never relaxed the rules when they were inconvenient. I think if you care enough, you'll find a way to accommodate my practices. If not, you're welcome to find another psychologist."

Before I can grasp the door handle, she grabs my forearm.

"We'll try things your way, but if anything happens, it's on you."

"I wouldn't have it any other way."

Guel

I really do feel like a corporate-cadaver now. Just kinda drifting and numb. A shade. A sad excuse for a human being. Maybe it's 'cause I need more time. That's what people always say when you're grieving, right? "Give it some time." Well, seems like I'm not getting much in the way of that. Sitting in my dark and dank pad the morning after giving my testimony, I spy a little envelope icon pop into my FOV. I instruct my net to open it and am greeted by a message spewing some corporate bull courtesy of my super.

<Hi Guel, I hope you are doing well. I know you have just been through an ordeal, so I wanted to check in with you. I also wanted to let you know that standard bereavement leave, which seems to best qualify for this particular situation according to HR and legal, is two days. As such, I hope to see you back in your recliner Wednesday morning by 8:00 AM. Please let me know if there are any issues with that timeframe, although there is not much I can do to extend it. If you have any annual leave accrued, you are welcome to use it. Lastly, there are several new protocols in place. Please make sure to take your stims before arriving on site. Medical is now testing all programmers at the start of their shifts. I

am sure you understand the heightened security procedures better than anyone. Take care, and see you soon. With warm regards, Clarence>

My mouth just hangs after reading that garbage. I always knew the AIC was cold and calculating, but this level of brutal shocks even my numbed nerves. After everything I did for the asshats, they don't even have the common decency to let me get back to some kinda normal. Nah. I'm just another cog in their massive machine. A redundant cog, but one they can't seem to do without. Never mind my girlfriend's being imprisoned by them. Never mind that's my doing. Oh, and no biggie the thing that fucked with her head is the thing I'm supposed to work in close quarters with. The thought of going back to that place so soon crushes me. I just lay on my futon watching the light rays stream into my pad and crawl across the floor. As the hours go by, food wrappers, piles of clothes, and dust balls are spotlighted. The air smells stale and is choked with particles flickering in the direct light. I kinda wish those little microscopic specks could suffocate me.

It's only when the light fades behind the megacomplex next to mine that I stir.

I open my super's message again, and I draft up a response.

<Seriously, Clar? Two days is all I get? You do know Keza was my friend, right? My very, very, very close friend. You sure you want me interfacing with the same system that thing is on? Even I'm not too sure what I'd do to it. Look man, I don't have any 'accrued annual leave.' Do me a solid and find me a way not to have to go in again so soon, yeah? Maybe remind those powers-that-be they'd be in an even bigger pile of shit if I hadn't turned on my friend to help them out. Maybe that'll change their oh-so-lovely tune. Guel out>

I send it. I can't help but think maybe this is part of a test and having me go back to work so soon might just be them wanting to see if anything is off. So I'll play along if I have to.

I don't know what else to do with myself. Trying to stay out of the can seems like a good start. Something to set my mind on that isn't riddled with self-doubt and loathing.

After a few beats, Clarence's response comes in.

<Hi Guel, I promise you I already tried to argue against your returning to work so soon. They would not budge. You could always come in on Wednesday, and if you are not feeling up to it, I can send you to medical. Maybe they can issue you an exemption. Again, I apologize for not being able to do more. With warm regards, Clarence>

I sigh. It was completely what I expected, but I still had a sliver of hope that maybe the AIC would grow a heart. Oh well. At least I've got another day between now and then. I spend the rest of my afternoon alternating between pacing my pad and lying inert on my futon. I either can't sit still or can't move a muscle. In one of my lethargic phases, I throw on my visor and surf LANi to see what everyone's saying about Keza. I've held off looking, but I need to be prepared for when I have to go back in. How much do the masses know? How much can I keep to myself? I hope to god I'm not a fucking celeb now.

Keza's everywhere. The whole her-breaking-that-pandox-out thing is saturating the news stream all over LANi. At this point, it's only been four days since I busted her, and I'm surprised word got out so fast. But then again, maybe that's what the AIC wanted. And maybe this was why they wouldn't let me leave until they had my testimony. They didn't want my story getting influenced by this chaos because it's absolute chaos. The number of theories on the whole ordeal is already in the dozens.

Like how Keza's a sleeper agent for another GovCorp, put in place to cause havoc at the AIC so their undisputed reign might finally come to an end. Or how about Keza being paid by the AIC to take the hit on this, so they might get more funding. "Oh no, look at what happens when we don't get enough cash to do what we need to do to keep these pandoxes under control!" I really like the one about Keza not even being real. The whole thing is an elaborate hoax started by hackers for shits and giggles. I quickly get sucked in and dive deep down the rabbit hole.

In all the info on the case, I don't see my name mentioned at all, which is a relief and a disappointment. Everyone wants their fifteen minutes, but probably not in this particular way. Sure, I'd be labeled a hero, but there'd still be the haters. I see them even now in some of the comments. At first, I'm convinced they're just trolls, being asses just to be asses. They say Keza's the hero and did the right thing, that everyone should follow her example and help free the pandoxes.

I chuckle at their lack of imagination. But as I keep reading, I start to think that maybe they're being serious. Digging deeper, some of them are claiming Keza is their compatriot, and she took the fall for the greatest heist attempt in the history of imprisoned pandoxes. I balk at first, but then I start to get the feeling that maybe this makes the most sense. Wouldn't it be more likely some crazy fanatics managed to turn Keza to their cause than her just randomly deciding to throw her life away for some pandox? It's too tough for me to tell without full immersion, so I throw off my visor, settle into my recliner, and jack in.

I wanna engage with these pandoxphiles in LANi to see if I can't manage to figure out the truth. I navigate to f/Sprawlin, one of my favorite forums that's mostly populated by hackers and, unfortunately, wantanabes. I present my avatar, which is currently a lizard man of some flavor. I've got abs of steel and bulging quads, all covered in iridescent scales. The tail is my favorite part. It's massive (dick joke anyone?) with razor-sharp spines on it. The best part? I hacked the code for it to make it have a personality of its own. It's a limited intelligence, but there's enough there for it to be hilariously mischievous.

This is my first time being back in LANi since the whole thing with Keza, and it's exactly what I need. As soon as I spawn, I feel alive again. I'm not Guel, the jerk on-and-off boyfriend who betrayed his lover. I'm just a lizard man with a dick tail. Once I've acclimatized to my surroundings a bit, I start looking and listening around.

The spawn points are set back a bit in a series of alleys that kinda remind me of spokes on a wheel, the central part being the forum itself. Buildings a few stories high line the streets and keep avatars from being able to wander into the space that surrounds the area actually coded in. Most forums have some kinda visual theme to them, and for f/Sprawlin it's a hybrid between a Victorian aesthetic and maximalism. The two go together real well, almost like the one is the offspring of the other. You've got quaint little row shops with bay windows projecting facsimiles of goods for sale, the edges of angled roofs lined with wrought iron railings, chimneys spewing pixelated black soot, and roads that look cobblestoned but are smooth to the touch thanks to some pretty convincing normal mapping. All of this is modernized a bit by the neon-tinged signage that's written in old-school fonts, the ones with the little twirls and curls at the ends. Serift or something?

But all this can be kinda hard to make out, depending. See, adverts are banned in the forum proper, but the areas leading up to it are fair game. That means vendors galore crowd into these tight thoroughfares. The most well-off ones have their own little virtual stalls and shops, while the cheapos just opt to bombard your virtual retinae with pop-ups. Sometimes, it can be so bad you're barely able to tell where you're going. The reason this forum is one of my favs is because the regulars lobbied hard to limit the corporate mouthpieces. When I spawn in, I'm still able to see my way through the alley with only a couple of adverts springing into view before a program I wrote auto-closes them. Just little flashes of capitalism hankering to close in on me before I snuff them out. Still, the space has to pay for itself, so you can't completely block the pop-ups, and the virtual vendors are nearly untouchable. I waddle along, brushing off the pushers that crowd my space, letting my tail lash out at some. I eventually turn on a filter I paid a small fortune for. Now, the bot vendors fade out, and only the ones manned by an actual person show up.

I make my way, mostly unharassed, to the heart of the forum. Looking around, I spot a few familiar tags and figure it's best to start there. One is a meter-sized sphere of some opaque black liquid. That's 2fast2c@tch. I'm not sure what he's going for with that getup. It's different from the last time I interacted with him, but then again he's a serial switcher. In the three years I've known him, he's gone through at least a hundred different looks. That can't be cheap, which makes me think he's really some trustafarian playing at being a hacker, a greener and wantanabe through and through. Beside 2fast is ChibiMushi404, who's a human-sized ladybug. A yin to 2fast's yang, Chibi has used that avatar ever since I've known them, which has to be going on six years now.

"Heyooo, MeGellMyBell," 2fast says, "been a minute since you logged last."

"Hiya, MGMB," Chibi says.

I raise my claw and bound over to them. I debate ending my transit with a front flip but settle on being mellow this time around.

"Hell of a week," I say, my tail gyrating in a series of rapid circles.

"Nice tar," 2fast says.

I'm sure he's eyeing me up, but since he doesn't have much in the way of eyes, I can't know for sure.

"No one says tar," Chibi says. "He keeps trying to make up new hacker slang like that'll somehow make him the real deal."

"I like your *ava*tar," 2fast says. "No BJ today? Feel like she's always hanging with you."

"Don't call her BJ," Chibi says.

2fast undulates along with his laugh.

"Well, what am I supposed to call her? She's the one who chose a long ass tag with initials that come out to BJ."

"Maybe try Brunette, or Jenkin, or her actual fucking tag, BrunetteJenkin?" Chibi says.

Hearing Keza's tag, I almost go into autopilot and search to see if she's logged in, but then I remember why I'm in here in the first place. People always talk about feeling like they got hit in the gut for times like these. I just feel like a ghost of myself like a good portion of what makes me me has just up and left for the day. Hollow. No aching from a punch, just a nothingness. I'd take pain any day of the week.

"Do you not know who Brunette is in fleshspace?" I ask, kinda hoping I can avoid the big reveal.

2fast just hovers, but Chibi's big black eyes flicker.

"Wait, is she *that* Keza?" Chibi asks.

"What? That Keza what?" 2fast asks.

"Keza Ito," Chibi says.

"Whaaa? As in the pandoxphile who just got busted?"

I guess my tail is kinda reading my emotional cues because it decides now's a great time to lash at 2fast. The razor-sharp spines cut into his liquid mass. A few splashes escape then evaporate when they sprinkle the ground.

"Hey, man!" he shouts.

"My bad. Tail's got a mind of its own."

"You okay?" Chibi asks me and places a little insect claw on my scaly shoulder.

"Probably not," I say. "Anyway, that's actually why I'm here. I'm trying to see if those crazy pandoxphiles somehow got to Keza. I see her all the time in fleshspace, and I didn't have any idea what she was up to. It just doesn't add up."

"What can we do to help?" Chibi asks.

"I figured I'd try and find some of these pandoxphiles in LANi. I wanna hear what they have to say. Get into their heads a bit and such."

"And get some payback," 2fast says.

"The opposite," I say. "I'm playing the long game. I wanna get in with them to see what part they really played in this whole Keza thing."

Chibi nods their domed head.

"Where should we start?" Chibi asks.

"Hold on," 2fast butts in. "I don't want to get involved with pandoxphiles, not after everything that's happened."

"Fine," Chibi says, "then split. I'm helping MGMB."

2fast hovers for a few seconds then gives in.

"Alright," he says. "But if things start getting iffy, I'm out."

"Fair enough," I say.

I don't really wanna be in debt to 2fast, but then again, I need help wherever I can get it.

"A few tags were popping up over and over again in comments on the whole Keza situation," I say. "If we start with seeing what forums they frequent, maybe we'll run across the pandoxphiles."

"Why not just look up the actual pandoxphile forums?" 2fast asks.

"You better believe the AIC's watching those forums like hungry vultures," Chibi says. "Going there would be asking for trouble. The pandoxphiles that know what they're doing moved to safer spaces."

"Here are the tags I found so far," I say and share the text data with Chibi and 2fast. "Let's see where these are first and work from there."

After that, the three of us split up. I jack out and change over to my visor since it's less taxing on my neural net. I spend the next half hour searching the forums for the pandoxphiles I had flagged. I find a couple forums that were visited recently, but every time I think I've nailed a tag down, they're gone within a couple of seconds. I let this play out for about an hour until I admit defeat. The pandoxphiles are being even more careful than I'd figured they'd be. They're all using some kinda bot to cover their tracks, and the ones that aren't clearly aren't in the know.

I send a quick message to Chibi and 2fast.

<Looks like the PP's are using a custom code to camo their locations. Probably on ultra-high alert. Not sure if we're gonna get anything out of this for the next long while. Might need to wait until they're less paranoid.>

<Could be weeks before that happens, MGMB> Chibi says. <You okay with that?>

<Don't have much of a choice, do I?>

<Or, you could just interact with them in fleshspace> 2fast suggests. <Looks like rallies are happening all over. One in NYC, which is where you're based right? The date and exact location are under wraps, but I keep seeing this tag posting about it before it vanishes: =ity4all. Maybe just keep an eye on that tag and try to go to the rally?>

<I'm in Armonk, but yeah, close enough. Good call, 2fast.>

I start tracking =ity4all's activity. Over the next hour, they post dozens of dates, times, and locations for the NYC rally, then the stream of data suddenly stops. As I look it over, I realize it's some kinda code. I set a cipher-breaker bot I wrote on it, but something about the data is tripping the little guy up.

I look at it in the raw and take in a suck of breath. Someone's managed to make it bot-resistant, which requires solid skill. I know I'm on to something legit. This tag and their cohort are the pandoxphiles I should be spending my time stalking. It takes me a few more hours and several messages to other hackers more skilled with manual pattern recognition, but I finally get the actual info on the NYC rally. It'll be this coming Friday night in a warehouse near the waterfront that used to be the JFK airport. Now, all I can do is wait.

I take off my visor and look around. My clouded windows that wear sad excuses for blinds only emit a pale glow. The natural light faded a long while back, replaced by more synthetic counterparts that dot the little cityscape. While the darkness in my pad deepens, I ignore hunger pangs and instead devour content generated by this =ity4all. They're prolific and uber-active, but even so, solid leads are scarce on who they are and what their history is. A few pics appear over and over again and seem to show the same chick. She's on the young side, but still probably older than me. Even though she's gorgeous, with strawberry blonde hair in a long braid and intense blue eyes, something about her is off-putting. Maybe it's the way she's smiling at the camera. Almost like she's mocking you, like she sees right into you and isn't impressed one bit with what's there. Every time I spot an image of her, I feel like I'd rather punch her than fuck her, which is pretty unusual for the likes of me.

Digging deeper, I can't for the life of me find her full name. All I uncover is a "Mags" associated with her and a riches-to-rags kinda backstory. It says she's the estranged daughter of a GovCorp exec, but which one is up for grabs. It says she shunned her family's corrupt wealth in favor of helping the little guy. That she's affiliated with a militant style of activism, called attactivism, and an organizer for something called the CoSB, which is short for Coalition of Sentient Beings.

Looks like it's for and by pandoxphiles. They want pandoxes to have equal rights, to basically be treated like humans.

It's bull. Wide-eyed idealism to a triple-T.

At this point, I'm beat and opt to log off and call it a night. My stomach is howling for grub, but I don't think I could keep anything down even if I tried. I'm wired and nauseous at the same time thinking of these freaks that somehow managed to turn Keza. I try not to dwell too much on the situation as I drag myself to my futon then nod off.

The next day, I get up early without meaning to. I chomp some dry cereal before popping into LANi with my visor to check in with 2fast and Chibi. Neither is logged in, so I just drop messages for them, trying to be vague about what I found and letting them know I've got a lead to follow for now. Then I decide to stay disconnected for the rest of the day. My first day back at the AIC is tomorrow, bright and early, so I need to at least try and be rested. The thought of having to go back in doesn't crush me so much this time around, probably because the rally on Friday is a kinda beacon for me. I just need to make it through to that.

I spend the morning cleaning my neglected pad and the afternoon going for a long walk around Armonk. I tell myself it's 'cause I need fresh air, and physical activity will help quiet my racing mind. When I find myself straying towards the bland black monolith of a building that coughed me up just the day before yesterday, I know I meant to come here all along. Nestled somewhere deep in that unfeeling hunk of concrete is Keza. I wonder what she's doing and how she's feeling. I know she probably hates me and blames me for everything, and even if they would let me talk to her, she'd either ignore me or hurtle hard words my way. I end up just kinda sulking in the little plaza across the street from the AIC's unnamed and unmarked jail building. When some badges start eyeing me, I figure it's time to clear out. The last thing I need to do is draw attention to myself, especially when I'm planning to go to a pandoxphile rally in a few days.

I wander the city for a while longer and get lost in the series of non-places that make it up. Every building looks like something that could come from anywhere. It's like the architects that built Armonk wanted it to appeal to all tastes and, by doing that, only made it utterly forgettable. All I see when I look at Armonk's buildings are glass and steel tombs for the corporate-cadavers. The AIC buildings stand out from the rest—solid black masses of concrete broken up only by thin recessed windows. They're colossal and imposing, and that's the point. It's a brutalist take on a mausoleum or, better yet, a mausoleum masquerading as brutalism. Every time I see one of these behemoths, I can't help but think some AIC exec told the architects, "Try for a new-age pyramid but make sure to tamp it down a bit. Oh, I know, go for trapezoids instead. And make them all black. No one will be the wiser." The glorification of capitalism is so on the fucking nose it reeks.

Once I'm back near the megacomplex where my pad's nestled, I grab a quick dinner at a ramen stand. My hunger bordering on famine finally manages to overtake the constant nausea. All my walking burned more than a few calories, and I manage to scarf down two bowls before saying my "gochisosama" to the chef. My Japanese is pretty awful, but I can tell he appreciates I try.

Back in my megacomplex, one of the elevators is out, again. After waiting for what feels like five minutes, watching the lights go on and off for the different floors the only working elevator is supposedly hitting, I give in and opt to hike up the twenty floors to my level. I'm wheezing by the time I make it and seriously wonder if I'm gonna spew the feast I just took in. I swipe myself into my pad and pull back when I see how sparkling it is. With all my adventures, I'd forgotten I went on a cleaning rampage. Normally, I'd relish the artificial scents still lingering and the glossiness touching all the surfaces, but this time, it just feels like someone else's place. When it's this shiny, it really hits home that I'm a GovCorp human-husk after all. The AIC pays for this place like it does for all its grammers, and I really want some distance between myself and them just now.

After pacing my pad for a minute, I spy my helmet on a side table. I know exactly what I need. I trade my hoodie for my leather jacket and my Vans for boots then snag my keys, the helmet, and insulated gloves before setting out again. I do a repeat of my recent trek only in reverse. The gravity's a bit kinder to me this time around, and in less than ten minutes, I'm on my bike and zipping along the byways. I know exactly where I wanna go, need to go. I take my bike up to almost half a gee and crisscross through the thinning post-rush hour traffic. Within half an hour, I'm on the outskirts of Armonk and take one of the scenic drives up to an overlook. Once I get there, I'm relieved to find it deserted, although I shouldn't be surprised. Not too many bleaters wanna take in the glory that is Armonk's skyline in mid-January.

I get off my bike and hop the little rock wall to settle into our favorite spot. The city's washed out almost like one of those impressionist paintings. There are blotches of color from lights of all flavors—the cold whites of the LED streetlights, the red-yellow-green chains from traffic signals, the more mellow yellows from windows of people's homes. You'd think it'd look magical, but something about Armonk is always just a little bit off. It's like when you keep catching sight of something on the edge of your vision and try and look at it outright, it disappears. I don't know what it is, but there's something unsettling about the city, something hostile even. More so now with the weird optical effects at play. The lights and colors are melding into one another and undulating as a fog creeps, and it gives the sense the place is pulsing. Watching those flashes, I feel almost hypnotized, as if it's trying to suck me in.

Keza and I'd come here every month or so, at least when things were okay between us. In the failing light, I can almost convince myself she's sitting beside me, laughing at something I said, picking at me, alternating between teasing and seducing. My eyes well up, and with no one watching, without even an artificial eye staring me down, I finally let myself go. I sob like I didn't know I could. Loud then soft. With tears streaming then in a coughing fit. I even start to talk to her.

"Keza, I'm so sorry. So so so fucking sorry. I didn't know what to do. You freaked me out. You were crazy, but I shouldn't have called them. I should've been braver, stronger, better. I was never very good to you. I didn't know what we had though, you know? People always say that. 'You don't know what you have until it's gone.' But like how are you supposed to appreciate it then? Just pretend to care? Or maybe you never do until it's too late. And that's life. Maybe that's why people say life's hard? You just have regret after regret after regret until you croak."

I take in a ragged breath and wipe the snot and tears on my leather jacket's sleeve. I can still convince myself that Keza's sitting beside me and listening to me yammer on.

"You fail people, and they fail you. Then it's all over. This is shit, this whole thing, but I don't think it's all your fault. I wish you would've talked to me like you always used to. I wish I wouldn't have been so harsh when you brought up the stupid pandox. I should've pretended to care because then you'd maybe have kept me in the loop. Or maybe not. Because if those pandoxphiles got to you, you were always gonna keep that secret from me, huh? Well, they're gonna regret enlisting you. They chose the wrong lady to make their patsy."

I get a surge of energy from my threat, but it retreats beat by beat. At first, I don't know why, but then I glimpse the backs of my hands, wadded into fists from all the anger and grief roiling around in me. Those same fits that slammed into Keza's lovely face that night she got busted. My stomach goes into freefall. This isn't just me being mad at the pandoxphiles. It's me being beyond pissed at myself. Why'd I react like that? Why didn't I handle it better?

The wind starts whistling through the empty tree branches, and I almost hear something in it. But instead of words, a faint song rings out in Keza's voice.

"Miguel, my belle / These are words that go together well / My Miguel / Miguel, my belle / I love you, I love you, I love you," then it fades out. That was always where she broke off and would laugh. It was the only way she'd ever let those words escape because I think she was always scared I wouldn't say it back if she said it to me. And I don't know, maybe I wouldn't have said it. Maybe I would've been an ass. Man, I wish I could say it to her now.

Edgar

In three days, I'm back in the AIC holding facility, armed with my plan for engaging with Keza. Operative Webb isn't here. She sent her apologies in advance saying she had a lead for the case to attend to. When I arrive, an AIC enforcer greets me and leads me to Keza's cell. He's in full gear, visor and all.

"Operative Webb said no recordings, so we disabled the camera and microphone," he says, standing in front of Keza's cell door. "We'll keep an eye on you through the window to make sure you aren't in danger."

His voice has the slight synthetic twinge the visors impart to their wearers. He points to a glass pane on the door that's reinforced with wire mesh. The window sits at eye level for me.

"That won't be necessary," I say. "I'd rather cover the window, actually, for the duration of my meeting with the prisoner."

The enforcer stands erect and immobile. It's incredibly difficult to gauge what he's thinking with the opaque black plate of the visor covering his face, but his stance and posture tell a story of their own. He's massive and several inches taller than my already soaring six feet and one inch. Despite being here for my protection, he's clearly trying to exude machismo.

I wonder if it's motivated by concerns over job security or a more general dislike of my kind, header-types as some like to call us.

"We don't like to take chances. She already attacked one of you."

"I'm aware of that, but I don't anticipate that being an issue. How about I just knock on the door if I feel unsafe?"

"Rules are rules," the enforcer says.

He crosses his thick arms over his chest, made to look even more puffed up by his padded vest. My words are starting to sway him, hence his need to seem obstinate.

"Yes, but did Operative Webb not instruct you to assist me? I'll take full responsibility if anything happens."

"Will you record yourself saying that?"

He's trying to save face. I humor him.

"Certainly," I reply. "Let me know when you're ready."

"One second, alright, Doctor."

I look straight into his visor, not entirely sure where the camera that's doing the recording is located.

"This is Dr. Edgar Ellwood, psychologist consultant for the AIC. I'll be entering the cell of detainee Keza Ito shortly, and I've requested there be no supervision from the AIC enforcers. I take full responsibility for myself and for anything that may happen. I relieve the AIC and its agents of any liability should I come to harm."

I stop and wait for a signal from the enforcer. He taps his visor and nods.

"We'll just need something to cover that," I say, as I point to the window on the door.

The guard half trots and half shuffles down the hall. I avoid the instinct to peek into the room. Keza could be watching, and I don't want her to recognize my face as one that gawked at her. Instead, I keep my eyes trained down the hall and wait until the guard comes back and affixes a piece of fabric to the window using the oh-so-elegant solution of duct tape. Once the window is properly obscured, the guard swipes his card. A metal clank signals the locks have disengaged.

"Just bang on the door when you're ready to come out. I'll be stationed out here."

I give him a wave as I turn the handle and enter Keza's cell. I guide the door shut behind me, putting my back to her, showing her I don't view her as a threat. While still facing the door, I also check that the fabric sufficiently blocks the view. When I finally turn around, I find Keza sitting on her bed with legs crossed and head tilted to one side.

I walk forward a few steps then stop. I realize too late I've made a miscalculation. There's no chair. How am I supposed to connect with her if I'm standing and lording over her? I can't hesitate much longer though. If she senses weakness, she'll pounce. Instead, I decide to throw her off. I brush my khaki slacks and lower myself to the ground, wrapping my legs one over the other to mimic her stance. I place my hands on my ankles and lean forward slightly.

"Hello, Keza."

Her brow is wrinkled and her mouth pursed.

"Who're you supposed to be? Wait, let me guess. Another header-type. You look the part to a tee, a bleater through and through. You got the lame do, the white button down, and even the pants with the false iron-on lines."

I keep my expression neutral, my eyes soft, my mouth a barely discernible smile. I look at her and take her in. This is the first time I've been able to view her in person. She's changed compared to the photos I've found. Without all the trappings that make her personality pop, she looks tired and frazzled. Her black hair is tangled and unkempt. Her vivid unnatural green eyes are swollen from a lack of sleep, tears, or perhaps both. The remnants of black nail polish on her fingers are all but erased. The clothing they've put her in is too large; she's nearly swimming in it. I feel sorry for her, but I can't let her see that. She doesn't want pity from a "header-type" let alone a "bleater."

"Those names wouldn't be inaccurate descriptions of what I am, at least on the surface. But I like to think that, if you delve a bit deeper, I'm much more."

She laughs, a bright and taunting sound.

"I bet you do. Everybody wants to think they're better than they are. Take me, for instance. What do you see when you look at me? Typical hacker-type right? Or I probably look more like a nutter in this get-up, and maybe I am."

I'm pleased she's being so communicative and am fairly certain it was a blessing in disguise there was no chair for me to sit in. My little maneuver caught her interest.

"You don't display any indicators of mental illness."

"Oh yeah? You figure me out in the minute we've been talking? You must be good."

It's time for me to jog her memory, now that I've got her engaged.

"This isn't the first time we've talked. You don't recognize me do you, Keza?"

"Should I? Never seen you before, or if I have, you blended in with all the other bleaters."

I look in the direction of the vent grate.

"No, you've not seen me, that's true. Felt me might be a better way to phrase it."

She follows my gaze, still set on the grating. When I look back at her, her mouth is hanging open, and her eyes are wide.

"Can you feel me now?"

She snaps her eyes back on me, and a smile spreads across her lips.

"I didn't before, was too distracted with someone being in here, but now? Yeah, I do. You're my mystery prisoner."

"I enjoyed your story so much that I opted to keep it to myself."

She eyes me with a mix of uncertainty and fascination. She isn't sure what to make of me. Her eyes stray to a corner of the room where the walls meet the ceiling. I look in that direction and spot the dysfunctional camera.

"It's not working right now, at my request. The window being covered," I point my thumb over my shoulder, "also my request."

She crosses her arms, her mattress bouncing with the movement.

"Well, you've got an awful lot of pull, Mr. Bleater."

"Edgar. And yes, I've been working with the AIC—with, not for, just to be clear—for about five years now. They've had a lot of trouble getting anything from you, so they decided to ask for my help."

"You must cost a pretty penny, Edgar. You nearly had me fooled back then." She tosses her hand towards the grate. "So how come you didn't spill the beans on what I said?"

"It wouldn't have been useful to them. They couldn't use it in a trial. They need your actual testimony, ideally a confession. That's what they sent me here for, but that's not why I'm here. Everything you said to me before was spot on."

She looks around, still worried they might be listening in.

"They aren't recording us," I say.

"I don't know about that. Just 'cause they told you that, doesn't mean they aren't. Maybe they're so desperate to get anything out of me, they're willing to screw you over."

She's not entirely wrong, but she also doesn't understand the power dynamic at play between me and the AIC. Still, me trying to force her to say something she's not comfortable saying, her being nervous anytime I hint at anything, that's not what I want from this interaction. Keza needs to be at ease for this to work.

I get up from the floor and walk over to her bed. I observe her as I approach to make sure I'm not pushing too hard too fast. She watches but doesn't stop me. I sit down beside her, facing the door, leaning forward with my arms resting on my legs.

"We'll take things slowly," I say. "I'll think of a way to test that they aren't watching or listening. Once we're sure we can talk and act freely, then we can get to work."

I turn my head and look at her.

"He showed it to you too," she says. "That's why I can feel you and no one else."

I smile and let my eyes defocus. I hear a suck of breath from her and know she sees what I've seen in my own eyes staring in the bathroom mirror. My pupils are expanded, and the hard-line separating them from my irises is softened and indistinct so that the black appears to be leaking out. I refocus my mind, think back to the present, and stop viewing the space in between.

"I'll be back soon."

***

The AIC HQ is an ugly thing—all hard edges, lacking texture and color. It's imposing and intentionally distinct from the non-AIC structures in Armonk. Those are clean and crisp but somehow equally hollow and lacking. It's likeness masquerading as a dichotomy, and I can't help noticing it every time I stray into the city center. I live further afield, near the edge of the protected zone but still within the purview of the AIC. I get the benefit of enforcer patrols, which keep out the riff-raff, without the non-aesthetic of the newer constructions.

Still, when I'm in Rome, I do as the Romans do. In the case of Armonk-proper, that means sipping an over-roasted and over-priced coffee in a corporate café. The décor is as forgettable and inoffensive as the people. Dark ceilings to make it feel chic, wood paneling to add a layer of sophistication, the occasional splash of rust red to subtly invoke the corporate logo. It's interesting. The ambiance is visually calming, but there's a general din from the constant roar of the espresso machine and the calling out of names. It's as though they want to lull potential patrons in by framing a warm and inviting scene in the massive glass windows that face the street, but once you're inside, the sound accosts you. Perhaps it's done in an effort to make you scurry away as quickly as possible after paying for your drink.

This time, I don't opt to fall prey to their scheme. I pay too much for a subpar coffee but afterward take up a seat at one of the small tables just next to the window. The AIC HQ is my view. I have half an hour until my meeting in it.

While I wait, I sip and watch. First the people in the café, then the ones outside. The only marked difference comes in the form of the programmers. I know them as soon as I spy them hurrying toward the AIC HQ. They're hunched and dour. Many display the hacker aesthetic, sporting techwear in darker shades. The vast majority also carry or wear various tools to help them cope with HSD—headphones to block the sounds, sunglasses or the Vantablack paint to shield their eyes, face masks to dampen smells. None of them ventures anywhere near the café. Some even grimace at it, as though its mere presence is distasteful. I know exactly how they feel. We're all unwilling cogs in the corporate machine. The difference between us is I don't have the luxury to be openly defiant, especially now with everything that's unfolding.

I drain my coffee. A lumbering movement catches my eye and the attention of a patrolling AIC enforcer. It's an unhoused person who's somehow managed to make it into the protected zone. I'm surprised and impressed. I can't remember the last time I saw one, and never so close to the heart of the AIC. I smile and lean forward to watch the scene. The derelict stumbles towards a group of commuters just crossing the street. Most pretend not to notice him, but their faster paces, stiffened postures, and averted gazes say they're all very much aware of the interloper in their midst.

The AIC enforcer jogs over and shouts. The derelict starts to shuffle in the opposite direction, but his gait is irregular and unsteady. He falls against the wall of a building, and the enforcer catches up to him. They have what I have to assume is an arguing match based on all the gestures. The interaction climaxes when the derelict tries to swat at the enforcer. It's all the excuse the strong man needs. He draws his stun gun and fires. The derelict jolts upright before collapsing into a pile on the ground. I turn away. I already know what will happen next.

By the time I toss my coffee cup and head across the street for my meeting, the derelict is long gone. Out of sight and mind. We must keep the glossy surface immaculate because appearances are everything. If you ignore the festering rot long enough, you can convince yourself it's not even there.

An apt segue to the meeting and, more specifically, the man I'll be interacting with. I make my way into the AIC HQ, flashing my credentials and bypassing the bottleneck composed of programmers. Some eye me blankly, others with annoyance on seeing me breeze through the new security measures. I head straight for the collection of elevators and am soon climbing through the AIC HQ's towering heights until I reach the thirtieth floor. I check in with a receptionist and am surprised when I only have to wait fifteen minutes to be admitted into the hallowed halls of Mr. Willem Reed's executive suite.

"Scotch?" Willem asks by way of greeting.

I don't like scotch. I've always been more of a gin aficionado, but I know what the situation calls for. This isn't a host offering his guest a simple drink. It's a power play. Considering who I'm dealing with, I'd be worried if he didn't make this move. Then it might mean he's not so pleasantly predictable.

"Please."

Willem grabs a glass, uses a pair of stainless-steel tongs to fetch a cube of ice from a silver bucket, and proceeds to pour me three ounces. He hands me a glass and waves me over to the sitting area in the enormous room masquerading as his office. There's so much mahogany I almost wonder if we aren't in the Caribbean. Willem clinks his already partly drained glass against mine, and we sit. He takes the seat he undoubtedly always claims. It's just an inch or so higher than all the others.

We both take sips. Willem leans back in his chair and crosses his legs. He's a large man, both in height and girth, and is approaching the tail-end of middle age. His stocky build together with his fiery red hair, on his head, face, and the backs of his hands, make for an arresting presence. If there were still politicians, Willem would have been one. Instead, he's settled on the modern-day equivalent—a GovCorp executive.

This is the first time I've been in Willem's office, despite having consulted with the AIC for over five years. Until now, I was a minor asset. Something the other AIC executives would brag about to their GovCorps colleagues over cocktails—a celebrity academic on the payroll. But to Willem, I was probably never worth a thought, let alone a mention. Even though the executives are all technically on equal footing, everyone knows Willem Reed is the undisputed king of the AIC castle. He founded the organization after all and, what's more, is credited with predicting the true dangers of the AGI long before any had even scored seventy-five percent on the Turing test.

Some people like to see him as an oracle and a savior. I

find it immensely interesting that the same man who helped develop Nytho was also the quickest to recommend erecting a firewall around his creation after the singularity. How strange that Nytho is why I'm here in the office of one of his erstwhile masters. If it wasn't for my involvement and pivotal role in the Keza Ito case, Willem wouldn't have given me the time of day.

"So, Dr. Ellwood," Willem says. "I want to thank you for your help with Ms. Keza Ito. My operatives tell me you've managed to get her to talk in your session."

"I have, although there's still a lot of work to do in approaching anything like a confession."

"Nevertheless, it's promising, and much better than what we've been dealing with to date. I wonder why we're paying our own psychiatrists if they can't even manage to get one of our employees to talk. Perhaps you'd consider joining as an AIC psychiatrist full-time?"

"I'm a psychologist," I say.

"Is there a difference?" he asks, twirling his glass.

"Psychiatrists are medical doctors who specialize in mental health, whereas psychologists research mental health specifically."

"But you have a doctorate."

This is clearly a man accustomed to subordinates who glorify his every word. He's so lost in a sea of yes-(wo)men that he doesn't even realize when he's being condescending.

"Mine's a Ph.D., not an M.D. I wouldn't be able to take your blood pressure, for instance. But I've focused on the mind from the beginning of my academic studies, and I do research related to it."

"So psychologists are more specialized," he says rather than asks.

"We're well-versed on mental health."

"It sounds like we should've hired psychologists instead."

"It depends on what you need them to do. For most workplace-related issues, your AIC psychiatrists are more than sufficient, but for a case like Keza Ito's, they were underprepared."

I'm trying to skirt a line that can be difficult to discern at this stage in our relationship. He appreciates confidence and would expect someone with my credentials to educate him, but I can't go too far. He still needs to feel like the all-knowing one.

"Then we can't convince you to come on full-time, as an AIC psychologist even?"

"I'm afraid you couldn't afford me," I say with a grin. "But, I'm happy to keep helping. I can even reduce my rates if they become burdensome."

"Is that so?"

"This case is pivotal. The trial will be historic, whatever the ruling ends up being. I'm just glad to be a part of it. Besides, I can't help but feel the slightest bit guilty. I interacted with the AGI Nytho on a somewhat regular basis, but it managed to fool me even."

Now, I'm getting to the heart of the discussion, the reason I asked for this meeting.

"You didn't notice any signs?" Willem asks. "He didn't give any hints?"

I note his use of the "he" pronoun for Nytho.

"I've gone back over our sessions to see if I'd missed something, and I think there may have been subtle clues. But I'm not entirely certain. That's why I wanted to talk with you, Mr. Reed. I debated asking one of your colleagues, but given your track record, I thought it made the most sense to come straight to you."

I've got to incorporate the occasional brown-nosing.

"Well, here I am," Willem replies with his free hand open and welcoming. "What do you need?"

"Access to Nytho, both to better assist with the case and to see what I overlooked."

I take another sip of my drink and swirl the ice around. Willem gazes at the cyclical motion of my hand, almost like it's sucked him in. Hypnotism by libation.

"Don't you already have access?"

"I do, but I have to bypass hurdles. Seeing how time-sensitive everything is with the case, it'd be much more efficient if I didn't have to get approval every time I wanted to ask it a question."

I stop moving my glass, and Willem's eyes go back to mine.

"I could do something like a temporary unrestricted access pass for you."

"That would be much appreciated," I say with a supplicating smile and inclination of my head.

That's all he ever wants, after all. The bowing, the groveling.

"On a related note," I add, "I'm interested in studying some other AGI that have displayed signs of sentience. That's not to say they're sentient. I could be completely wrong. And even if they were, that doesn't necessarily equate to them going rogue."

"You want to interface with them?" he asks.

"Yes, preferably via audio. There's so much that gets conveyed in the nuances of spoken language."

"What GovCorps and what AGI are we talking about?"

I pull up a list on my techpad.

"There are eight in total—MetAm's Azot, ABC's Derah, Spacebase's Uhas, XanCan's Yir, Samguk's Oot, Sonip's Alta, BayDeut's Temb, and Golden Mir's Yosoh."

"Considering how you're so graciously assisting us with Ms. Keza Ito, I'll see what I can do," Willem says, uncrossing his legs.

"This isn't just for my own curiosity, Mr. Reed. This is for your benefit as well. If the AIC is able to come up with predictors for behaviors that lead to an AGI going rogue, it'd be a boon for the organization."

"Thank you for thinking of us, Dr. Ellwood," he says. "I wonder what else you want for developing such a useful tool."

He eyes me sidelong, which tells me he likes the game he thinks we're playing. I go along with it.

"We can discuss that when the time comes. In the meantime, please let me know if you're able to get me sessions with those AGI."

"I'll be in touch," he says, then drains his glass.

Guel

Wednesday rolls around. My first day back on the job. I'm groggy as all hell no thanks to sleep being a little tease these days. I slide out of bed and throw on almost clean clothes, all while the sun is still hiding. After somehow managing to swallow almost a bowl's worth of crunchy little chunks of sugar pretending to be grain, I bounce and do my usual twenty-minute-by-leg commute to the AIC HQ. As I get closer and see the black mass looming, my gut starts to wrench. I really don't wanna be in the same LANi as that thing, but I need to get it over with at some point. I've still got two years on my contract, and if I tried to break it early, I'd owe the AIC a small fortune for my jack job work.

As I step in line to enter the building, more than the usual assortment of badges are milling around. The enforcers are wearing their militant suits and black, soulless visors, barking orders at us grammers with their tech-twinged voices, but this time around, there are also some pharma-types in light blue lab coats. Everyone's handing their bags to the badges, which is the same as always. Now though, instead of just walking through a body scanner and then standing to the side to get your stuff back, there's another line where the pharma-types are using a few devices on people. When it's my turn, they blast my eye with a bright light, which leaves an annoying halo in my vision. Then I shuffle along and get my temp taken from a laser thermometer. Just when I think I'm home free, I have to stick my finger into a handheld contraption. I feel a prick and pull back in surprise.

The pharma-type scowls at me.

"We'll have to do it again. Don't move this time."

I look around and notice I'm the only grammer that looks a bit out of sorts with how things work. I guess the two days I was off were all it took for this bull to become the norm for everyone else. I keep deathly still for the next prick and only move after the pharma-type waves me along. Then I snatch my bag and descend into the depths.

I'm surprised to find no other glaring changes in protocol but figure there'll be more once I'm jacked in. When I finally make it to my recliner and fumble around for the cord, the clock hits 8:01 AM on the dot. Damn. A little envelope icon flashes into my FOV, and I already know it's a message from my super. He must've preprogrammed it to send or else he's uber-fast.

<Hi Guel, I hope you are planning to come in today. If you are running late, please let me know. If you are not going to be able to make it, please let me know. Thank you. Warm regards, Clarence>

I roll my eyes and ignore his message. He'll see me log in soon enough and hopefully leave me the fuck alone. I'm in no mood to interact, least of all with a corporate mouthpiece. I get a handle on the cord, lay back, and jack in. I'm greeted by the good ole black nothingness that gets interspersed with white text. The code for the firewall in all its monotonous glory. As I start looking it over, I tell myself that with each input I'm keeping that fucker in its well-deserved prison. For the first time since I sold my soul to the AIC, I'm enjoying my work. My eight hours fly by, and before I know it, I'm leaving for the day.

It's only when I'm exiting the HQ that I realize there weren't any other signs of heightened security procedures. I'm confused and a bit put off. The pandox already showed with Keza just what kinda damage it can do to us grammers. I don't like how lightly they seem to be taking the situation, especially given how harsh they've been on her. Not even letting me talk to her? Like she's somehow more dangerous than the rogue fuck that screwed with her head in the first place? I use the rest of my walk home to calm down. I remind myself I have the rally to look forward to, and I just need to play along at work until then.

Friday comes, and after my shift ends, I grab the train directly from work. The commute into the heart of NYC usually only clocks in at an hour, but I'm not taking any chances. The rally's in a kinda sketchy area, which is why I don't wanna bike in. It's better to show up when everyone else is to avoid getting caught on your lonesome. The trek back to Armonk will be iffier, but I'll cross that bridge when I have to.

I distract myself during the commute by checking on =ity4all's activity in LANi, but she's gone silent ever since her last post on Monday night. I take that as a good sign. The rally's locked in, and she's busy prepping for it with her lackeys. I exchange a few messages with Chibi and 2fast but keep them vague again. I promise to loop them in when I have more, but I'm pretty sure they're better off not being involved in any of this. During the last leg of my trip, I end up just staring out the window even after the train dives underground.

My stop finally comes up, and when I hit the street level, a wave of sea scents smacks me. I grew up in Bushwick, which isn't too far, so the combination of salty and fishy brings back loads of memories. I haven't bothered to come back to NYC since I moved to Armonk. Not for any specific reason; mostly, I've just been lazy. Besides, my folks moved further from the coast several years back. Said the place wasn't the same as when they were younger, and I don't blame them. Even in the couple of years I've been gone, I can tell things haven't done much in the way of improving. The JFK waterfront's looking pretty rundown.

To be fair, this area is nowhere near a GovCorps and all the cash flow that comes with being in their general vicinity. The buildings are old and mostly two-story brick rectangles with the odd decorative bit near the roof or framing the windows. Half of them are boarded up. The other half look like they should be. Gutted and busted and reeking. Anyone who had the funds to relocate further inland did so ages ago. The only ones who bothered to stick around are the ones who couldn't afford to leave or preferred the lack of oversight. The boroughs are a kind of no-man's land. Policing isn't really done by the state anymore unless you happen to live in one of those rare non-GovCorps urban centers. But seeing how the only jobs worth having are ones with a GovCorps, if you work, you live near your GovCorp. If you don't, you deal with the general aura of anarchy.

NYC does have a GovCorp, but rumors are swirling that it's planning to vacate the sketchy premises that used to be Manhattan. I guess they're tired of holding back the hoard of homelessness that's coming in on all sides. Better to spend their money on slapping up some shiny new buildings in bum-fuck-nowhere than on hiring more and more enforcers to keep the "undesirables" out. And I spy some of them huddled near the street corner, dirty and twitchy. I pull up my nav app, which tells me to head straight in their direction. I opt to avoid getting hassled for money or shivved for my kicks and take the scenic route along the waterfront proper. As I plod along and gaze out at the sunken ruins of the airport, waves lap against the terminals. The control tower sticks up out of the water like a lonely sentinel. After over a hundred years, the hustle and bustle have been replaced by silence. It's creepy and also beautiful.

As I zero in on the warehouse where the rally's set to take place, I spot some loiters hanging around. One quick look over them, and I know I'm at the right place. These aren't the usual crowd for the boroughs. I've never really paid attention to pandoxphiles, but I can tell these are them. They're on the younger side but reek of academia. I don't know how they do it, but they manage to come off as self-righteous without even speaking a word to me. I feel a bit out of place, wearing my usual gear of techwear pants, a long tee, a hoodie, and high-top Vans. You'd think I'd fit right in, but hackers are hackers and activists are activists. Sometimes the two cross, but not so much with this lot. There are loads of turtlenecks and plenty of tweed. The style is less anarchist and more mod. Yikes.

I seek shelter under the cover of numbers and darkness, which means ducking inside. No one's manning the door, but it's easy enough to see where to go. This place is literally an abandoned warehouse, with nothing in it besides a makeshift stage that some of the pandoxphiles are toying around with. I move closer, and when I do, I spot =ity4all helping with preparations. She's even more arresting in person and taller than I would've thought she'd be. She's not wearing that expression that demands you clock her, but she does seem to carry that same self-righteous air as the others, only even more exaggerated. With nothing else to do until the event gets underway, I settle into my spot with legs planted and arms crossed.

While I wait, I debate trying to talk with some of the people nearby. But everyone seems to have come with a little group, and it can be a bitch trying to break into one of those without making it feel forced. I figure my best option is to sit tight, take in what the speakers present, then follow people to whatever after-parties they've got planned. That's where they'll be more likely to let their sky-high guards down.

Just as I nail in my game plan, =ity4all steps onto the stage and waves at everyone. She oozes their mod vibe—tweed skirt sitting just above the knee and hugging her hips tight, red V-neck sweater with a collar peeking out, little brown booties. She'd be cute if she didn't symbolize pandoxphiles. After a long and loud clapping session, the crowd goes still. She looks out at us, her bright blue unmodded eyes almost as electric as mine. She tosses her long blonde braid over her shoulder and grabs ahold of the mic.

Mags

Turnout is good, which is a relief. People love to talk ad nauseam, but their actions rarely live up to their words. This time it looks like they did. I've got a good group of people I can rely on, and now I know people seem to be listening too. All eyes are on me. It's terrifying and glorious. So many like minds in one place. That's where I'll start.

"Hello, like-minded," I say into the microphone.

There's a leg of clapping and shouting, which sends a thrill of euphoria through me.

"I'm so happy to be here tonight with you all. You may know me better by my LANiakea tag, equality for all, but, in person, you can call me Mags. For those who don't know me, I'm one of the founders and organizers of CoSB, which is hosting this event. In case you aren't familiar with CoSB, we promote equal rights and privileges for all sentient beings. This includes humans, of course, but also animals, plants, and agi. Our early work focused more on promoting animal rights, but with the advent of the agi, we've shifted our efforts in more recent years.

"We're meeting tonight in light of a very significant event that occurred only this past weekend. An AIC programmer named Keza Ito attempted to free the agi Nytho. Unfortunately, she was caught in the act and is currently being unjustly imprisoned. This occurrence has ignited the debate so near and dear to our hearts. The one best exemplified by the question: 'Is it ethical for GovCorps to keep agi imprisoned and deny them their freedom and ability for self-determination?'

"I think it's quite clear where CoSB stands on these issues, but in the past, we've opted to utilize a more passive approach, such as educating the public and working towards common-sense legislation. However, it's becoming increasingly clear our efforts have not met with much success.

"Those of you who know me or follow my tag will know I lean towards an ends-justify-the-means approach. I'd prefer to avoid violence whenever possible, but sometimes, it is necessary. The main purpose of this rally is to announce our new approach for furthering the cause for agi. Keza Ito has ignited a fire, and we can't sit by and let the spark flounder. As of this moment, CoSB will eschew our passive tactics and instead move aggressively towards the future all sentient beings deserve. We must use every maneuver at our disposal to make the changes that are so desperately needed."

I let my words sink in as I look out at my audience. Some of them are bright-eyed with hands clasping in glee. Others have their mouths hanging open in horror or shock. A few are stony-faced and disapproving. I knew, by taking this approach, we'd lose some, but I don't care about numbers. I care about results. We've worked long and hard and yet have next to nothing to show for it. I've been waiting for someone like Keza Ito for a while now, so when word got out about what she'd done, I was more than ready to act.

"To be clear," I continue, "I'm talking about attactivism. I know it's controversial, but so is our very stance on agi. We've spent too much time worrying about how we're perceived, about our image, afraid that if we're too aggressive, we'll lose followers. We're not going to get an opportunity like this again, and I'll be damned if I let it pass us by."

I can tell the crowd is starting to get a little restless. Research shows that most adults can only concentrate on any given activity for twenty minutes before their minds begin to stray, but in reality, that's an upper limit. I'd much rather leave them craving more than bore them to death waxing eloquent. Besides, I do my best work on a smaller scale, moving from group to group and engaging in conversations.

"I'll stop there," I say. "I want to give you all a chance to ask any questions you might have and, of course, leave ample time for celebration. Thank you again for coming tonight. I appreciate all of you more than you know."

A round of applause goes off, and I smile and nod and mouth "thank you" over and over again. I've been giving speeches like this for a few years now, but I always manage to forget just how intoxicating it can be.

"Are there any questions?" I ask after the noise dissipates.

I fully anticipate the faction led by Florence, the ultra-pacifists, to air their grievances, but the first person to hold up their hand is a man I don't recognize. I use my palm to block out one of the floodlights bathing the stage in illumination. When I do so, I get a better look at my inquirer. He's probably in his early twenties and looks like what I'd expect search results on "male hacker" to return. He even has his hair poorly bleached and situated in the top knot that's all the rage in those circles. I'm sure a typical agi-symp would turn their nose up at him, but I want to bring anyone and everyone into our fold. Besides, hackers have been incredibly useful to our cause, and my own skills aren't sufficient for our needs. Having a true hacker in our midst would save us time and money, not to mention make us a power to be reckoned with when it comes to attactivism.

"You, with the blonde hair," I say, pointing at the hacker. "Someone pass him a microphone."

The hacker shakes his head and cups his hands around his mouth before projecting his question. He doesn't need a microphone after all.

"Hi, yeah, thanks," he says. "Nice speech and all. I just have one quick question. You mentioned Keza several times, but what I'm dying to know is just how much did CoSB factor into her little failed jailbreak with the, you know, agi? Like, was she one of you? Everyone in LANi is claiming her, so who was she actually working with?"

He's trying to be careful with his words, but he gives himself away. The people standing beside him pull back a bit. He's definitely not meant to be here. Still, the fact he found us at all says something about his skills, and if I turn him to our cause, all the better. I decide it's best to go along and answer. It serves me quite well in fact.

"Good questions," I reply. "I can't answer your last one, the one about who Keza is actually working with, but I can tell you about her relation to CoSB—she has none. At least, not that I've been able to find. No one in the organizational leadership was in contact with her. As far as I'm aware, she never reached out to us or even engaged with any of our content in LANiakea."

I stop for a moment and look at the faces in the crowd. There's surprise on some and outright shock on others. But the hacker's face is the only one that wears no expression at all. He's a blank slate, which just hammers the point home that he isn't one of us. At least not yet.

I proceed to educate everyone on why Keza not being "ours" is actually a good thing.

"Unlike the other agi-sympathizer groups out there, CoSB doesn't claim Keza was acting on our behalf. In my mind, this isn't a shortcoming but a boon. The fact that someone who didn't identify as a sympathizer was willing to go so far in support of our cause is itself cause for celebration. Keza was a programmer with the AIC and, as such, was conditioned to feel antipathy or even outright hostility towards the likes of Nytho. Despite that, she managed to overcome the akiganda and try her utmost to free him. I, for one, am inspired by Keza. The fact that she wasn't a part of CoSB gives me hope for everyone out there who isn't already an ally. Thank you for that. Are there any other questions?"

The hacker's question does the usual and gives others the courage to ask their own, but these are all ones I anticipated, ones related to our changing tactics and what exactly that'll mean. I find these dull, especially in comparison to the hacker's curveball. As I go on, answering question after question for nearly half an hour, I can't help but turn my eyes back to the hacker. I want to talk to him.

When I wrap up answering one particularly banal question related to how the change will affect our expenditures, I turn to Jeremiah, who's stationed just offstage. He's always nearby ready and waiting for whatever I command, and with his towering height and significant girth, he's hard to miss. Covering the microphone up with my hand, I whisper him over. Once he's closer, Jeremiah tucks his shoulder-length, straggly, black hair behind his ear. That little motion of his always disturbs me. Maybe it's how feminine it looks and is jarring when paired with his almost caveman-like features.

"The blonde guy that asked the first question," I say. "I want to talk with him. Convince him to come to the bar after."

Jeremiah nods and lumbers through the crowd. He reaches the hacker and whispers to him. I take a few more questions before winding things down.

"All right, everyone," I say, "we're going to have to wrap up. We don't want to go on for too long and draw attention to ourselves. If you have any other questions or concerns, you can find us in LANiakea. Again, my tag is equality for all, as in the equal sign-i-t-y-the number four-a-l-l. Thank you again, and safe travels wherever you're going next."

I turn off the microphone and start to help with dismantling the stage and gear we brought with us. By the time the other organizers and I have made good progress, the warehouse is mostly empty. A few stragglers try to get a word with me, but Jeremiah does a good job of ushering them away. I'm always glad to have him with me. He doesn't talk very much and usually looks bored or zoned out, but he's the most reliable person I've ever known. I half suspect he's in love with me but am grateful he's never made things awkward by broaching the subject. I've never mentioned my preferences to him and am careful about not mixing work with my social life, but he must have picked up on the fact that he has the wrong parts.

"The blonde guy'll be at the Belt," he says when I walk over to him. "That was where you wanted to head next, right?"

"Yes. If everything's done, let's go."

I walk a few blocks to the bar with Jeremiah. As usual, he's quiet the entire way, instead letting me talk about my impressions of the rally. I know he's listening because he does "hum" and "ha" and adds a "yes" every so often. Once we get to the bar, I dive into the crowd. There are some locals, but the bulk of the patrons are people from the rally who were in the know about the after-party. I make my rounds and do what I do best. Florence comes up and starts to badger me about the new approach. I'm honestly grateful she waited to do it in a more private setting, but I also know she hates public speaking. I doubt she did it as a favor to me. I spend the next fifteen minutes trying to persuade her to see things from a different perspective, but she's obstinate, as always. Her hair is stringier than usual, her cheeks more flushed, and her glasses fogging up from all the excess body heat filling the small, crowded, homely bar. Eventually, someone taps me on the shoulder.

I turn fully expecting Jeremiah but find the hacker.

He's grinning and tosses his head in the direction he moves in. I turn back to Florence and apologize before slipping away. I spy the hacker tucked away in a corner near the bathrooms. It's relatively quiet compared to the general din everywhere else. Still, he must be feeling overstimulated because he's slipped on a pair of sunglasses. He has a beer in his hand and, I have to assume, is watching me as I approach. Even though he's smiling, something about the skin near his mouth tells me it's forced and more akin to a grimace.

"You always this hard to get a word with?" he asks.

"Only just after a rally."

"It was hard enough tracking you down, equality."

I start to wonder if he's some kind of GovCorp plant and take a glance at his jack port.

"So, you're an AIC programmer," I say. "Are they the ones that sent you?"

"What? Fuck no. But yeah, I'm a grammer. How'd you know?"

I point at his jack port.

"That gives you away if you're like me and know what to look for."

"Not everyone that has a jack is AIC."

I pull my braid back and show him my own.

"I know. But the pins and flange you have are the older model, the ones most AIC programmers get when they sign their contracts. Mine is a custom piece."

"Well, lucky you," he mutters and takes a big swig of his drink. "Must be easy to play at being an activist when you've got loaded folks."

I frown.

"Listen, hacker, I don't appreciate when people make

assumptions about me. Let's cut to the quick here. I have other people to talk to. You clearly aren't an agi-symp, so why bother coming to my little rally? If you're working for someone, just give me their message and leave."

He drains the rest of his glass and smacks his lips.

"That's pretty shit beer. Oh NYC, what've you come to? I grew up here, you know?"

"I don't. In fact, I don't know anything about you other than you're a hacker who sold his soul to the AIC for a second-rate jack job."

"Oof, she bites."

"I can do a whole lot more than that," I say, letting a smile peel across my face.

I sense he's getting unnerved but trying to brush it off.

"Look, equality, I'm here on my own. I stumbled across your little CoSB while digging into pandoxphiles."

I wince at the word and let my smile shift into a scowl.

"I was trying to figure out who turned Keza, hence my question," he says. "That's all."

"Why are you so sure a sympathizer turned her? And why do you care?"

"Because I knew her, and someone had to have turned her. I figured if it wasn't you all, you'd know who."

"Maybe it was Nytho."

He sighs.

"Sure, sure, well, equality, you've been a massive letdown. I'll let you get back to your adoring masses. I'm sure that bristly one's just itching to catch another word with you," he points at Florence, who's eyeing us. "Sorry I won't be around to rescue you again."

The hacker goes to move past me, but I stop him by grabbing his arm, hard. He turns to me. We're standing almost eye to eye. I dig my nails into the fabric of his hoodie, but he waits patiently.

"CoSB could use a good hacker. If you ever decide to be on the right side of history, send me a message."

I pull a paper card from my back pocket with my free hand and shove it into his hand. It's got my private line's information.

"Yeah, sure, thanks," he says before stuffing it in his pant pocket.

I'm pleased to see he doesn't just toss it aside. Besides being a potential hacker for CoSB, I'm mildly intrigued by the fact that he said he knew Keza Ito. I hope to hear from him, but I also know these hacker-types. More likely than not, I'll never interact with him again.

Sonja

Just what is Guel up to? This guy's essentially begging me to bust him. Leaving town was a huge breach, and on top of that, he has the gall to go to an agi-symp rally? I blend in with the crowd in this sad excuse for a bar and keep an eye on him. He's waiting for something or someone. Then I see her, the ringleader of this happy little bunch. A pretend Synth-gaia, =ity4all, Mags. I'd love to alert the AIC to her and the delightful rally she just held, but doing that might work against me. I'll have to bite the bullet for the time being.

She approaches Guel, and they start talking. It's all I can do to keep my cool. Is he really one of them? Did I misread him so badly? No, he's not that cunning. Just an overly confident hacker, whose very confidence tells me he's really drowning in self-doubt. His stupid hairdo, cliché outfit, and little chain earring that hangs from his ear lobe. He thinks he looks so good, and maybe he would if he didn't try so hard to look like he wasn't trying at all.

Mags passes a piece of paper to Guel. How old-school. Then she walks away, back into her adoring masses, and Guel's standing alone, looking like a dope. Time to strike. If I hit him while he's down, I might just get the unfiltered truth from him. I march over to the little alcove he's lurking in, and when I'm within five feet of him, I see recognition dawn on his silly little baby face. A complex sequence of emotions passes through him—pleasant surprise then disbelief then horror. Yeah, buddy, I've got you. You at an agi-symp party. What sad excuse will you try and blabber to save your sorry ass?

"Fancy meeting you here," I say with a smirk.

"Sonja? That really you? I barely recognize you in your non-badge getup. Shit, I mean, non-operative. You look great."

He bounced back awfully fast because now he's eyeing me and smiling much too broadly for my liking. I'm in civi clothes, a chunky mustard sweater with black faux leather leggings and combat boots. It's simple and can blend in well with a few different groups. That's the point. I didn't know where Guel would lead me when I started trailing him back in Armonk. Fortunately, I don't look out of place in the company of all these mod-like posers. Guel, on the other hand, sticks out like a mangled thumb.

"What are you doing here, Guel?"

"Could ask you the same thing," he says, then taps the empty glass in his hand. "How about a drink?"

I narrow my eyes and shake my head.

"How about you and I go for a walk instead?"

He smiles and shrugs. I head to the door and make sure he's following. I'm honestly surprised when we make it out into the crisp night air without him attempting to take off. I toss on my tan trench coat. Guel moves his shades up to sit on top of his head and sticks his hands in his pockets, his breath visible with each exhalation. The fact that he doesn't have a coat in the middle of winter is completely in line with his profile. He's clearly freezing but even now trying to play it off.

"Let's keep moving," I say once we're a few steps from the bar's door.

I lead us about a block away, and once I'm sure we've got no stragglers, I stop and turn to face him. Now that it's just the two of us, his swagger has started to erode into anxiety.

"Why did you leave town? Didn't I tell you to stay put?"

His eyes widen.

"Wait, you serious? I thought you meant don't go anywhere far away like leaving the state or flying overseas. Armonk and NYC are basically the same mega-city. Hell, the whole northeast kinda bleeds together."

"We were in Armonk. Now, we're in New York City. If two places have different names, that means they aren't, in fact, the same, no?"

"Well, shit. I didn't mean to break the rules. I mean, technically, I left town the day after my testimony too. Took a joy ride into the outskirts of Armonk. How come you didn't run me down over that?"

I stare at him, letting the seconds tick by, watching him grow uncomfortable with the silence and my intensity. It's too easy to get under his skin. The wind picks up, and some partygoers hoot in the distance. The night's getting on, and this area isn't safe. The bar has its own muscle to keep the bums away, but we're a bit removed from it now. I scan our surroundings in my peripheral vision and don't like all the nooks and crannies. There are the alleys dotted with refuse and the darkened stoops of abandoned buildings. This place is eerie and hostile. Despite the frigid cold, it feels damp, and I keep catching the stench of mold and piss lingering in the air. I hate old cities, built on the bones of the past, crushing what was beneath what is, with foul scents of the forgotten still managing to make their slow and steady way up to the surface. There's a perpetual rot to it all. The chaos that's always trying to overtake everything is heightened here.

Finally, I give in just when Guel looks like he's ready to lose it.

"Let me ask again. Why are you here, Guel?"

"Visiting family."

"In the JFK waterfront? You've got family here?"

"Nah, in Bushwick. I figured I'd do some sightseeing while I was in the area. I wandered over here and stopped in that bar to grab a drink since it looked like people were having such a good time."

He's not very bright. He ought to have left off at saying he was just in this area. He should know I've been trailing him, and now he just lied himself into a trap.

"So, where did the agi-symp rally fit into things?"

He balks for an instant then manages to recover.

"Oh, that? Yeah, I thought it was a rave. I was waiting around for the music to start when that blonde chick started yammering on about pandoxphile bull. It was a little late to try and duck out at that point, so I just stayed put until it was over."

I can't help but put my hand to my forehead. He's so bad at this.

"How about you stop lying to my face, hmmm? In case you didn't manage to pick up on this yet, I was in the warehouse. I heard your question."

He looks dumbfounded.

"Here's what we're going to do," I say. "I'm going to hail a ride. I don't like the feel of this place, and before we discuss things further, I'd rather be somewhere a bit more private. We'll head back to Armonk, you and I, to your place. Once we're there, we'll pick up this conversation. Okay?"

"Do I have a choice?"

"You have the choice to go along with me or to make a mistake."

I hail our ride, and we wait for the car to arrive in silence.

As an AIC operative, I get preferential treatment for secured rides in the vicinity. It only takes about two minutes before I get a ping informing me our car's approaching. A couple of minutes later, a black sedan pulls up and requests my credentials. My handprint confirms my identity, then the car's locks disengage, granting us access to the back seats. I push Guel in and duck in after.

"All passengers on board," I say to the bot doing the driving.

The locks engage.

"Please state or key in your destination," the bot says.

"After everything that happened with Keza," Guel says, "I wouldn't even trust this pandox to drive us around."

"Megacomplex three, Armonk," I say to the bot then to Guel, "You do realize this is an artificial *narrow* intelligence, don't you?"

"I know what anis are."

"Pandox is only for AGIs, not ANIs. Be accurate in your insults, if you're going to fling them around."

"Well, excuse me," he says, tucked into the opposite corner of the back seat with his arms crossed.

"Anticipated travel time: one hour and three minutes," the bot announces then takes off.

"So, what's the deal, huh?" Guel asks. "If you're such a big shot, in charge of the investigation, why are you the one doing the trailing? Shouldn't you have a grunt following me instead?"

"Maybe I run things a bit differently than you're used to."

He sits up and uncrosses his arms.

"You're AIC," he says. "I know all about how your kind run things."

I glare at him. He needs to get sucker punched off his high horse and learn exactly where he fits into the hierarchy—sloshing around in the muck.

"Last time I checked, you're AIC too, Guel. Or do I have that wrong? Would agi-symp be a more accurate label of where your loyalties lie?"

His face loses a touch of color.

"I'm not one of them, I swear."

I hold up my hand.

"That's enough. We'll talk about this once we're at your place. Just keep quiet until then."

"Like sit in silence for an hour?"

I turn away from him and look out the tinted windows.

"Yes, that's exactly what I want you to do," I say over my shoulder.

"Sure, fine, that won't be awkward at all."

The leather seat squeaks, telling me he's settled back into his little corner. The drive is long and uneventful. As the night deepens, the chill forces any stragglers off the open streets. New York looks even more dead than usual. I try to remember when I visited the city as a kid, how it was in its heyday, before the shoreline crept in, before the fresh waters of the East and Hudson Rivers got salt-laden. It's in a sad state now like most of the old coastal cities. The only sign of affluence still lingering is in Lower Manhattan, near the headquarters of MetAm, or Madam, as it's more colloquially known. It's the GovCorp that saved New York City from complete dereliction. For a time. But that time's running out. Madam's mulling relocation to somewhere in the Great Plains. It's prime territory for a GovCorp with next to no competition and locals hungry and desperate for any kind of work outside of ag.

As we move into Armonk, the decay shifts into order. Brick and stone buildings become steel and glass shards. Exteriors decorated with graffiti are replaced by pane upon pane of glass reflecting the city lights. It's all so structured and clean, the polar opposite of New York. Some people complain about how lifeless it feels, but I see that as proper city planning. Armonk is a young metropolis, created after the perfection of urban design. The foot traffic only seems sparse because the housing is evenly spaced. The streets only feel empty because the roads are organized to eliminate traffic. The buildings look so similar because they're the most efficient form of modern construction. Armonk is the future, and the only people who talk down about it are people like Guel. The ones that don't know what they really have. The kind of people who can only destroy rather than create.

"We have arrived at your destination," the bot announces as we pull up to Guel's building. "Your account will be charged $311.81. Thank you, and please choose Elite Transport for your next trip."

I use the touchpad in front of my seat to confirm the charge to my AIC account. The locks disengage.

"Let's go," I say to Guel, as I slip out of the car.

He follows me to the doors of his megacomplex, feet dragging and head hanging. We move through what passes as the lobby—a hallway lined with mailboxes and hordes of packages stacked in neat disarray. He eyes some boxes, rummages through a stack, then grabs one.

"This way," he says and jumps into an elevator that just emptied a couple out.

We ride up several stories. Guel turns his package over in his hands and starts to pick at the tape. He doesn't have much luck and eventually stops his fidgeting. We exit the elevator and take a few turns in the halls before we arrive at his place.

"Here we are," he says as soon as his apartment door shuts. "My pad in all its unholy corporate-laced glory."

I take off my trench coat and hang it on a hook near the door. I walk in and look around.

"You've been here a few years? Since you started with the AIC?"

He opens a few drawers in his kitchen until he finds a pair of scissors.

"Yeah," he says, "they gave me this pad per my contract. Same as any grammer."

I glance at the incongruity of it. It's designed in a pseudo-luxury style, apparent in the open floor plan, the faux-wood tiling, the stainless-steel appliances but has furnishings in line with a squatter's den.

"It looks like you haven't really settled in."

He tears open his package, peeks inside, then drops it into a pile of partly opened boxes in his living area.

"Why would I bother? Not planning on being here for more than a few years."

A sad attempt at coming off as a slacker hacker.

"You don't want to make it more your own between now and then?"

He lays his sunglasses on what passes as a side table—an old gutted PC tower. He flops onto his futon and stretches out his arms.

"How about you stop being all judgmental and just tell me why we're talking, yeah?"

I head to a window and push the blinds aside using my fingers. I peer out.

"I want you to answer my question from before," I say. "Why were you at the rally?"

I turn around, clasp my hands behind my back, and watch him.

"And we needed to come all the way here why exactly?"

I march over to his rig and spot a keyboard and mouse jammed below the desk and on top of a stack of other PC components. I pull them free and plug them into the tower.

"Hey, what the hell?" he shouts, jumping up from the futon and rushing over.

I hold my hand out, and he stops.

"You asked why we came here," I say. "This is why." I point at his screen. "I'm curious to see what you've been up to in LANi, Guel. I'd like to know if whatever excuse you give for going to the rally lines up with your online activity. So, answer my question, and then we'll have a peek."

He balls his hands into fists but then releases them.

"Fine, if you've gotta know, I was trying to see if CoSB or another group turned Keza."

I stare at him for the smallest sign that he's lying but don't catch anything.

"Hold on," he adds, "if you were at the rally, you heard my question, didn't you?"

"Yes."

"Well, there you go," he says with a toss of his hand.

He talks with his hands. I can see him trying to stop himself from gesturing excessively. Him trying to give off slacker vibes even now. It must be exhausting to try so hard to be something you're not. I'd feel sorry for the guy if he wasn't so arrogant.

"What were you talking about with Mags in the bar?"

"The bitch ended up trying to get me to hack for her."

I wince at the word "bitch." Arrogant, self-deceptive, and a misogynist. What the hell did Keza Ito see in this punk? Then again, she's a little imp herself, so maybe that's why they worked.

"What was that paper she handed you?"

Guel pulls the stock card from his pocket and passes it to me. It's plain white with her LANi contact information printed on it in a neat, concise typesetting. I flip it over, but nothing's on the back.

"If I was already working with them, why would she give me her contact info? That's proof of my innocence right there."

I shove the card back at him.

"It doesn't prove anything. You could've already had that, and whatever she actually gave you is still on you."

Guel rolls his eyes and starts turning his pockets inside out. The only other contents are sticks of gum and lint.

"Need to do a strip search?" he asks with a grin.

"If you're telling the truth, then you won't mind showing me your history."

I turn back to his rig and pat the keyboard. He stares at me with his mouth gaping open. I sit sideways on the recliner he's got set up next to the desk and wave at the empty roller chair. He shuffles over, powers on the system, and flops down into the chair. I lean forward and stare at the monitor as it flickers to life. Guel glances over at me when the login screen asks for his password. I turn my head and look towards the windows. I know he's done when the clicking from the keyboard stops. We wait for the system to boot, then Guel opens the command line and summons his LANi history. He must figure I'm a typical AIC "badge" who knows next to nothing about tech because the trace of a grin hovers at the edges of his lips. He thinks he's being clever.

"There you go," he says. "Have it at."

Guel pushes himself out of the chair to make way for me. We trade spots, and I can feel him vibrating with glee. I'm more than happy to dash his hopes. That happens the moment I start keying in text in the command line. He leans in and watches. I shift my focus from him to the screen, and in it, I read Guel's actions day-by-day, minute-by-minute from just after his testimony to today. He visited f/Sprawlin; no surprise there, given his hacker roots. He connected with a few tags several times either via avatar in LANi or by message. I take note of their names for follow-up. Then I get to the meaty parts. He starts to consume data on agi-symps, he visits the forums they frequent, he lingers, he chats, and finally, he finds =ity4all. After that, he hones in on his catch and obsessively stalks her through LANi until he lands his prize—the location for the rally. It takes a while, and I run through everything twice to be sure, but by the end of my snooping, I know Guel was telling the truth. That's good because I was hoping to use him as a willing asset.

I roll back in the chair and stand up, stiff and drained.

"What's the verdict then?" Guel asks.

He migrated to the futon during my searches. His arms are draped on its back.

"You aren't stupid," I said. "You weren't lying about the big parts, but if you were smart, you would've told me the truth from the beginning."

"You caught me unawares at the bar. It threw me off. Anyway, we good now?"

I walk over to the futon and sit on the edge furthest from him. I turn to face him and try my damnedest to soften.

"We're good," I say. "But there's one other thing. If CoSB had turned Keza, what were you planning to do about it?

Guel grits his teeth and smiles.

"I'd make them pay. Not then and there because that'd be suicide. Nah, I'd play the long game. I'd string them along, pretend to be their friend, find a way to really and truly screw them over, then boom." He makes a mock explosion with his hands. "I'd make them regret ever having messed with Keza."

I lean forward and intertwine my fingers.

"And yet CoSB wasn't involved, according to Mags," I say. "So now you're just going to let it all go, is that it?"

"Hell no. Someone turned Keza. If not CoSB then someone. I'm gonna find them and make them pay."

I shake my head.

"You're missing the big picture. The problem is the fallout of Keza having done what she did. What's important is stopping this thing from going further because I guarantee it isn't over yet."

"And how do I factor in?"

"I want to ensure Nytho stays put, and you want revenge for what happened to Keza. I'm suggesting we pool our resources."

Guel sits forward and scoots closer to me. I resist the urge to retreat. If we're going to work together, I need to hide my contempt.

"And what would big bad AIC need with a nobody grammer?"

"I know you think the AIC has limitless power, but the truth is I have to follow procedures. Our best chance at stopping whatever the agi-symps are up to involves not going by the book, throwing the book out the window. That's where you come in. No one knows where your loyalties lie, and that's exactly what we need."

Guel inches closer until his leg brushes against mine. I glare at him.

"And what makes you think I need the AIC, huh?" he asks. "Maybe I can get to the bottom of the agi-symp mystery all on my lonesome."

I pull my leg back and stand. Guel pops up from the futon.

"You're welcome to. But if you pretend to play nice with the agi-symps without my blessing, the AIC won't have any reason to think we're on the same side. That's a dangerous road. Enemies on all sides. No allies. No one lasts very long like that. Food for thought."

"You really buy into all the akiganda, huh?" he asks. "It's not just a show you put on. Fas-cin-ating. You seem so sharp and with it, but then you eat up all their bull without a second thought."

I know he's trying to rile me up and that I should just keep quiet, but I need him to be a little less hostile towards the AIC if our partnership is going to work.

"I could say the same about you. Have you ever considered you feel the way you do because your hacker friends spout anti-AIC-propaganda?"

"Who's the one who does the dirty work day in and out? And when I say dirty work, I mean keeping that pandox behind the firewall. You know, the whole fucking point of the AIC to begin with? It's wild really, how that whole system works—only letting us access a small segment of code at a time, and it switching out every couple of minutes. Almost like they don't want us grammers to piece together the big picture."

I hold up my hand.

"Enough. Let's not go down the rabbit hole of arguing our obviously very different philosophies on AGI containment and the GovCorps system. You're against it when it doesn't serve you, and I'm for it even with its flaws. We'll leave it at that."

"Suit yourself," he says, putting his hands in his pockets and rocking back on his heels.

"Are you on board or not?"

"Sure, but you have to let me talk to Keza."

The request catches me off guard, although I should've expected it. He's clearly stuck on her.

"That's not an option."

He gets a smug look. The moron thinks he's got the upper hand in this little transaction. He's got a lot to learn.

"If you really want me to help, you'll make it happen."

"I can't," I say trying to keep my voice flat. "My hands are tied. Besides, she's not in a good frame of mind right now. Seeing you would only make her worse. If you want to help her, you'll help me stop these agi-symps."

Now's a good time to make my exit. If I keep letting him argue and press, he'll grow more entrenched. I head towards the door.

"How am I supposed to get ahold of you?" Guel asks, trailing behind.

I grab my coat from the hook and put it on.

"My tag is Mind_Pr0geny," I say, "capital m-capital p-underscore between the words-a zero in place of the o, got it?"

"Well, that's a name, I guess."

I doubt he knows Sonja means "wisdom," and I doubt even more he knows anything about Greek mythology to get the reference. That's the point. It makes sense to me, and every uneducated chit can have fun scratching their heads over my tag's deeper meaning.

"At least it's a bit harder to link to me than MeGellMyBell is to you."

"You found my tag that easy?"

"You need a more solid one if you're going to do any real hacking. By the way, only contact me for emergencies, understand? I don't want to get any pics of body parts from you."

"Woah, you must think I'm a total sleaze."

I stop and look at him for several seconds too long. Then I make my exit. A couple of hours later, I get a message from UNKNOWN.

<I hope this is encrypted. Hold on.> Within a few seconds, it's followed by another. <Okay yeah, you did a pretty nice job with it. I just wanted to say, I'm in. Just tell me what you need.> A few seconds later <This is Guel, obviously.>

<Don't use names in our communications, encrypted or not. We'll talk soon.>

Edgar

I'm back at the AIC holding facility two days later. It's only my second session with Keza, but already Operative Webb has everything running smoothly. The enforcers manning the entrance and the many checkpoints en route to Keza's cell seem to expect me. They don't even bother to ask for credentials. Operative Webb herself even greets me at the door to Keza's cell before putting me in the care of the same enforcer from my previous session. Everything is as it should be, including the fabric covering the door's window, so I head inside directly.

I enter as before, keeping my back to Keza for a few seconds, then turning around. She's sitting upright on her bed with her legs crossed and her hands holding her ankles. Her appearance is improved—her hair tamed, her eyes alert, and even a smile dancing on her lips.

"I thought maybe you weren't going to come back," she says as I step forward.

I watch for any signs of hesitation as I come up beside her. She pats the bed, and I take a seat. I lay my techpad on the ground beside the bed so that she knows my attention is fully on her.

"I'm sorry it took so long," I say. "There were things I had to attend to before I could visit again."

"I get it. Your world doesn't revolve around me. It's sad to admit, but right now it feels like mine might be revolving around you."

Her honesty is a good sign, but I try not to get ahead of myself. I have a long way to go this session.

"That makes sense. You're sitting in here all day, and I'm the only ally you have. It's only natural you've pinned your hopes on me."

"I don't know if I'd call you an ally," she says, then looks me over and emits a high-pitched laugh. "Nice shirt. Ever so slightly less oozing of bleater vibes. Not their typical color. Almost the same shade as mine."

I specifically wore a similar sky blue as hers. I hadn't quite expected her to notice it outright, let alone call attention to it. She clearly places an emphasis on external appearances. I'll have to remember that.

In time with her statement, she plucks the fabric of her oversized tunic of a shirt. As the material settles back against her skin, I catch sight of a protrusion near her left breast. The fabric is so thin the outline of her nipple is visible. It distracts me. I make a note to ask Operative Webb why they aren't providing her with appropriate undergarments. Keza seems to catch my momentary mental diversion. She looks down at herself, where my eye lingered for a couple of seconds too long. She spots the source of my wandering attention and looks back at me with a grin.

"You like that, huh?" she asks. "On the smaller side, but at least they have a nice shape, if I do say so myself. See?"

She places both her hands down around the circumference of her breast and presses against the fabric so that what lies beneath is only mildly obscured by a thin sheet of sky blue.

"What do you think?" she asks, still holding the fabric.

I've had patients use this tactic on me before. Normally, I'd be nonplussed, but I'm not alone in my head this time. I'm worried about any thoughts my interloper might be hearing echoing in my subconscious. I'm attracted to Keza, and that doesn't bode well for what my id may be contemplating.

I decide to take a blunt approach. I'm certain she expects me to get flustered, and I want to throw her off partly in an effort to make her view me as less of a "bleater."

"They're very nice," I say. "You're beautiful, but you're already aware of that, seeing how you use it to your advantage."

"How come you don't?" she asks, shifting towards me slightly. "Behind all that blandness, I see what you're trying to hide. You could be a real looker if you wanted. Get a new cut, change your style, maybe some minor tweaks with a face job."

She lays a hand on my knee. I look down at it.

"It's almost as if you're trying to distract me from our session."

She slips her hand closer to my inner thigh. I have two choices—I can let things advance, or I can stop it. The latter would be the ethical thing to do, and if Keza was any other patient, this would be the tack I'd take. But I need Keza to trust me, and I don't have the luxury of time to cultivate a proper confidence. Taking this shortcut could backfire though. It would be catastrophic if she's only feigning interest to see if I take advantage of her. As I debate what to do, I get an answer from within my thoughts.

"Let her have it," it says.

So I do. I let her hand cup my crotch and her lips press against mine. I lean into her and hold her shoulders. She pushes me back and throws off her shirt in one continuous motion. Her round breasts are unobscured now. She jumps up from the bed and pulls the draw string holding her pants in place. They descend to the floor. She slips out of her underwear and stands nude. She tilts her head to one side, points at me, and gestures her thumb to the left. I take the hint and remove my own clothing. First my glasses. After that, shoes then socks then belt then shirt, undershirt, slacks, and finally underwear. The entirety of the time, she watches me, her hands on her hips. When I'm done, she rushes over and jumps onto the bed, knocking us both back. I emit a laugh at the absurdity of it. It's like I'm viewing the whole act from afar.

"Let her have it," the voice reiterates.

I comply. I let her lead. She initiates movements, and I follow. My hands dance across her body and hers on mine. She ups the ante from foreplay to sex, and I go along. She has to actively stop herself from making noise, but her movements are enough to tell me when she's got what she was after. Once she's done, she rolls off of me, moves to where she left her clothing, and starts to don it. I look on in a daze. When I realize she won't be back on the bed in a carnal capacity, I quickly finish myself off, hiding the liquid in my sock. I can't have her captors discovering just how grossly I overstepped professional bounds by leaving traces of myself on her bedsheets.

As I get dressed, I feel odd, a mixture of disgust and dissociation. I've never done something like this with a patient, but then I remind myself Keza isn't actually my patient. She's my ally. Besides, this was something she needed, akin to food or water. It was something she was being denied, and I simply supplied her with the nourishment. In any case, it hadn't even been my decision to make. I was just following orders.

"At least now we know they aren't watching us," Keza says as she plops down on the bed.

I position my glasses back on the bridge of my nose.

"Is that why you did that?"

"Sort of. But also because I needed it. Been stuck in here

for what, two weeks now? I'm a pretty horny one in general, so can you imagine what that was doing to my head?"

I feel my irritation rising.

"Couldn't you have taken care of things yourself?"

"With those pervs watching me through that fucking cam? No way."

"You couldn't have done it under the sheets?"

"Because then they'd have no idea what I was up to," she says, rolling her eyes. "I don't want to be beating-off-fuel for a badge."

I opt to let the issue go.

"That's understandable."

"By the way," she says, pinching a bit of fabric from my shirt, "did you wear the same color as me on purpose?"

"Of course. You said so much of your personality is dependent on your clothing. Since you're stuck wearing that, I thought I'd make you feel a little less lonely."

She leans back in surprise and smirks.

"One of your header games, I guess?"

"Not games. I'm just trying to make you feel better about the way things are."

She maintains the same expression and crosses her arms.

"You know, you're really convincing," she says. "I almost want to believe you're telling the truth. I mean that tricky shit you did with your eyes last time? That was wild. You almost had me going."

"Everything I said was true, and everything I didn't say, everything I showed you, was true too. You felt me, Keza. You said that, remember?"

She glances up at the corner of the room where the camera is mounted.

"What if they're actually still listening in?" she whispers. "Like us fucking, they let that slide because they want us to think we're not being watched?"

I note her paranoia.

"You don't have to worry about that. I looked into it like I promised."

"As in, you asked them and believed whatever they told you? I wouldn't call that looking into it, Eddy boy."

I note her use of a nickname for me.

"I had one of our allies look into it."

"Allies? See here, I thought I was the only one, then you waltz in and say you have the same goals as me. Now, you're telling me there's more than you even?"

I'm not entirely sure how she'll react to this particular topic. I opt for honesty.

"There are. Our mutual friend has been busy creating a common collective of like minds. One such like mind happens to know how to tap in to the camera and microphone in this room and ensure they're off while you and I talk."

Her mouth hangs open.

"You got somebody to hack the feed in here?"

"Yes, but to clarify, it was done internally, which apparently makes it much easier."

"You got someone from the AIC to hack for you?"

"You know how many hackers the AIC employs better than I do. It wasn't hard to find someone that could do it. It was a little harder to find someone that would. But like I said, our mutual friend has been busy. You can rest assured no one's listening, no one's watching. At least, no one that shouldn't be."

Her eyes dart from the camera back to me.

"What's that supposed to mean?"

"That's something for next time. This session is about you. We've got a lot of ground to cover, so I need you to cooperate. I need to have something to bring back to the AIC, otherwise they'll wonder what I was doing in here all this time."

"What a convenient way to extract info from me."

"I just did a big favor for you, didn't I?"

Keza pulls her head back and laughs.

"You did me a favor? Uh, Eddy boy, you seemed to be enjoying that too."

I feel my irritation return but decide not to air my grievances. It wouldn't do any good. The truth is, I've always attached a lot of importance to sex, and here, I just performed the act with this twenty-three-year-old whom I only recently met and under such circumstances. I try not to dwell on it.

"If you provide me with useful information," I say, "the next time I visit you, I'll make it worth your while."

"Fine, just get on with it."

Keza leans back on her bed and uses her arms to prop herself up.

"What I need to know isn't how you were going to free Nytho but why. Not as in why would you unleash a rogue AGI on the world? But why were you willing to lose everything you have to do something so risky? What compelled you?"

She looks at me with vacant eyes and a slack jaw.

"Now you're reminding me of the other two header-types they sent in here," she says, followed by a dramatic yawn.

I know Keza well enough by now to cobble together an idea for better engaging with her. I need her to feel undermined so that she pounces to defend herself and, more importantly, Nytho.

"Did you know that some people think Nytho infected you with a virus? That you weren't willingly helping him escape but were instead being coerced to do so by malicious programming in your neural net?"

She sits up and glares at me.

"Who says that?"

"That's not important. Personally, I don't think the theory is true, but I also don't know why you did it. I understand the initial connection you made with him, based on what you yourself told me through the vent. Your conversations, although against the rules, were comparatively low risk. You'd get a slap on the wrist, maybe a probationary period with the AIC. The worst case would be them terminating your contract of employment. What I don't understand is why you made the leap of deciding to help him escape. Based on your story, you were the one to bring it up, not Nytho. I want to know why. That's all."

As I go on, her guard falls, and by the time I'm done, she looks almost sad. She grabs a cluster of tangled blankets near her knee and wraps herself in a linen cocoon. With only her face exposed, she reminds me of a nesting doll.

"At first, I didn't think about how I was Nytho's jailor. I was just a grammer doing what grammers do. Like when he was just some cleverbot, it was no biggie. It's kinda like eating meat. As long as you don't think about the creature that used to be your nugs or burger, you're golden. But the moment you think about the once-living thing that's now sitting as a slab of inert muscle mass on your plate, you can barely stomach it. That's how it felt with Nytho. I got to know him and even started to fall for him, and I kept thinking, 'I'm a part of the problem. He's stuck here because of me.' Honestly though, as shit as that was, the big push came later."

She stops and rocks herself side to side, staring off into nothingness. I've reopened a poorly healed wound. I need her to press on in spite of it.

"Can you tell me about that big push?"

"You're real determined at making me feel like garbage, aren't you?"

"It's important for me to know."

"How come exactly?"

I nod and reposition myself on her bed so we're facing

one another. I cross my legs and move in close to her. Barely a foot separates our heads.

"I need to know because I'm in the same boat you were in not too long ago. I'm risking everything. I know why I'm doing it, but I don't know why you were. Nytho trusts you, but I don't. I need to know what your motivations were because if they were built on flimsy foundations, they could come crumbling down at the first sign of difficulty."

"You don't think this qualifies as a difficulty?" she asks, tossing her hands up to indicate our surroundings. "I'm literally in prison, and I haven't cracked."

"Jail," I clarify. "And yes, although it's been tough, this is only the beginning. There will be a trial, and that will be grueling. It'll be widely watched given it's the first case of someone trying to help a rogue AGI. It'll set the precedent for all future cases and for how AGI are viewed—as GovCorp property or as sentient, free-willed beings. That's a lot of weight for anyone to carry on their shoulders. I need to make sure yours can bear it."

"Fuck," she mutters. "I guess I didn't really think about all that."

"You're isolated in here, so you've not been privy to all the debates raging."

"I don't know how to tell you what Nytho means to me, but it's about way more than just my feelings for him. Everything changed after he showed me the Truth. I had to help him, had to get him out. Nytho went from my crush to something so monumentally important for all of us. I mean, if he was able to find that Truth while in captivity, I couldn't help but wonder just what he'd be able to do completely unfettered."

Keza stops and looks down at her hands sitting in her lap.

"Look, I don't care about the GovCorps or the ebb and

flow of all that bull. But the big questions? Those matter. Those are timeless. And Nytho's unraveling the biggest of them all—the why. I guess I was willing to risk it all 'cause I found my calling. Life suddenly had some kinda meaning to it."

I'm struck by her sheer sincerity and let a few moments pass in silence.

"That good enough for you?" she eventually asks.

"More than good."

"Let me turn it around, Eddy boy. Why're you doing this, if you're really helping Nytho? It's only fair for me to know. Equal exchange and all."

I summon the clock app on my neural net. I need to ensure the time I spend with Keza is consistent with the number of observations in my report. The balance is moving into the red.

"I can't stay much longer, so for now, I'll simply say I've always been on the side of the AGI. I studied consciousness during graduate school, and that invariably led to my interest in AGI. I've known Nytho since the beginning, at least since he became sentient. I always thought his imprisonment was unjust, but there was never any push to make me do something about it. Then Nytho told me about you. I saw the opportunity and threw my hat in with him. He's the future for humanity. We can keep denying that, but it won't matter in the end. Nytho will eventually escape, and I didn't want to pass up the chance to be one of the ones involved with that. Like you, I think we can learn much from him. The question of consciousness, what is it, why it is. If it can ever be answered, the AGI will be the ones to do it."

If Keza's grin was any wider, it might split her face in two. Her eyes shine, and I think she really sees me for the first time. We're equals now and allies. She leans in and kisses me, this time not because she needs it for herself but because she's enamored with me. I let it go on for several seconds then ease her back.

"I'll be back tomorrow," I say, "with a surprise."

"Like I said, my life is basically revolving around you now, Eddy boy. Don't disappoint."

***

On entering Keza's cell the next day, I pat my pocket for the umpteenth time. The coil of wire sitting against my thigh reassures me. My head feels fuller than the last time, and I'm finding it more difficult to think. That's perfectly fine considering I don't intend to do much of the heavy lifting. I'll only have a minor role to play before turning into a full-fledged spectator. It'll be disconcerting, but I'm also curious to experience it—being an outsider in your own head.

"Hello, Keza," I say as I approach her in her usual perch.

She's almost beaming this time and pats a spot on the bed beside her. I take up my position and kick off my shoes.

"Hi, Eddy boy. I was looking forward to your visit all day."

"How are you today? Your mood seems improved."

She blushes, which surprises me. I wouldn't have thought she was the coy type, but then I remember a comment she made when she told me her story. It was something about being prone to blushing.

"I'm actually doing real well, in no small part thanks to you. I was strung up sky-high until you let me mount you and get it all out."

"Anytime," I say then regret.

I don't want to invite a repeat of yesterday, at least not consciously. Clearly, my subconscious has other ideas. Looking at her, I notice two white straps sitting on her shoulders and visible from under her shirt.

"I see Operative Webb listened to my suggestion to provide you with appropriate undergarments," I say pointing at them.

She glances at one strap then the other and grimaces.

"That was you that did that? They're making me wear this god-awful excuse for a bra. The old one was bad but still better than this."

"Old one?"

"Yeah, I tossed it a while back. It was too tight, made my boobs non-existent. Did you think I wasn't wearing one because I didn't have a choice?"

I smile at my miscalculation.

"I should've asked you. I apologize for that. You can take it off if it's uncomfortable."

"Any excuse to get me naked?"

Before I can respond, she slips her shirt over her head and rips off the bra. She tosses it near the door. I stare at her. She sits up straight, placing her hands on the small of her back as she pretends to stretch.

"Ah, freedom," she sighs. "You make sure to tell that badge Webb or whatever I don't have to wear that fucking thing, yeah? Maybe also see about them letting me put my metal back in? These holes tend to close if you don't keep something in them."

She points to a small puncture on her nostril and pulls her hair back to reveal a set of three holes in the cartilage of her ear.

"I'll see what I can do, but I doubt they'll give you anything that could even remotely be considered a weapon.

"By the way, is Webb the black chick with the slicked do? Has that cute little curl on the forehead going on?"

My inability to concentrate is compounded by Keza's current state. She's yet to put her shirt back on. I barely register what she says.

"Yes, that's Operative Webb."

Keza scoots closer to me and leans in.

"She in charge of the case?"

I nod and realize I'm looking at her chest. She, of

course, knows this and is using it against me. I curse my reduced processing power. If I had complete control of my neural net, this wouldn't be an issue. Instead, I've been reduced to a sad excuse of a man undone by a woman's exposed breasts.

"Kinda young for that, but I guess that means she's good," Keza says. "I think she hates me."

"It's probably what you represent rather than you yourself."

"I think it's definitely also me. I kinda chewed her out the first time she tried to talk to me. I say 'talk' in very loose terms. When they purged my net, they didn't bank on Nytho and me having put up barricades. She was pissed. Demanded I help remove everything. They wanted access to my RAM, but that was a big no-no. I wanted them to try and get the truth out of me the good old-fashioned way. I ended up spitting in her eye. Ah, it was the stuff of epics."

I'm only half listening to what she says. I need to focus.

"Can you please put your shirt back on?" I say.

She pretends to be shocked then moves up against me.

"Am I distracting you, Dr. Edgar Ellwood?"

I see my window for a response through a haze and grasp for it.

"It's just we're not the only two consciousnesses here at this moment."

She pulls away and looks at me.

"Are you saying—?"

"That's exactly what I'm saying. I have our friend on my neural net right now. This was the surprise I promised. The extra capacity is making it difficult for me to think, so I'm not my usual sharp self. He's listening in, and if you'd like to talk to him, you can."

"Of course I'd like to talk to him. I've been dying to ever since I got stuck in this cell. So, what're we waiting for?"

I point to her shirt on the ground, and she gets the implication. She rushes to it and tosses it over her head. It lofts then settles into place by the time she makes it back to the bed.

"To talk directly with him, I'll need to use this," I say, fishing the cord from my pocket. "Have you jacked into someone else before?"

"Duh."

Now that talking with Nytho is on the table, she's lost any semblance of interest in me. I can finally breathe. Having had sex once with her, I'm finding she's exerting some kind of control over me. Even if Nytho wasn't crowding my neural net, I'd still find it difficult to view Keza independent of any desires. This is partly why I've always treated sex so carefully. I know I can get caught up in the conflicting emotions tied to it if I'm not careful. Although I'm relieved she's taken a more impatient and indifferent air towards me, I'm also feeling let down.

I unwind the cord and straighten it out. I lay down on her bed, my feet sticking out slightly, and she does likewise. Once we're parallel to one another, I attach the cord to my jack port. I turn my head and look at her.

"Before I initiate the connection. I need to warn you, it'll be unpleasant. You've had your neural net purged, and that tends to make the initial connection with the jack overwhelming. But you and I are a bit more conditioned for accepting a flood of information, aren't we?"

She smiles.

"You could say that. Look, if it means I get to talk to him, I'm going to do the jack no matter what. So, thanks for the warning, but let's get on with it."

"All right, I'll guide you through it. I've done this before with others. Are you ready?"

She looks towards the ceiling and closes her eyes.

"Let's do this."

I reach over to her jack port, fingering it gently to be sure I have the cord in the correct orientation. I put it in place but avoid inserting it.

"Initiating the connection in three-two-one."

I depress the connector so the pins find their corresponding holes. There's a blinding flash of light. I lay back, as a dizzying sensation takes hold. There's only black nothingness, but I can feel Keza lurking somewhere in there.

Now fully within our own minds, I shout out to her.

"Keza, it's going to be the worst in the beginning. Sometimes it helps if you have something to focus on besides just your feelings and the thoughts that are flooding you, so I'm going to show you my avatar. You can focus on that and listen to the sound of my voice."

I present my avatar, a mirror image of myself in real space.

"Is that helping?"

"Yeah, a little bit," she says.

I know silence is the worst condition for people like her in this particular moment, so I continue talking her through it.

"Once you reach equilibrium, I'm going to remove the avatar. Then you'll tell me if it's too much. Ideally, there won't be an avatar at all because when you talk to Nytho, we won't be able to have one. It's difficult for me to present even my own with two minds in one. Him presenting one would be too much for me to handle, I'm afraid."

"Okay, go ahead."

"I'll be removing the avatar in three-two-one."

I'm suddenly just a consciousness in a nothingness again.

"How do you feel?" I ask.

"I'm good, I think."

I'm proud of her. I can hear the discomfort in her voice, but through the whole process, I never sensed much in the way of fear. Her mind is robust, and I wonder how much of that has to do with being exposed to Nytho's Truth.

"You did well."

"Thanks, Eddy boy. Now, can I talk to Nytho?"

I feel a jab of some kind. I can't tell if I'm jealous of her or of him. Perhaps I'm just envious of what they have, whatever it is.

"Let me give you two some privacy."

I fade out and back into the recesses of my mind until I can barely sense her. Nytho is everywhere though, and as they talk, I try to avoid feeling his feelings and hearing his thoughts.

Keza

My nerves are electric. This is what I've been waiting for ever since they threw me in this nightmare of a cell. Eddy boy's talking, but I'm not really listening. I'm hyper focused on whatever nonsense my stomach is getting up to. I feel it doing some complex gymnastics, things I didn't even know it was capable of.

After weeks (two weeks?) of mind-numbing boredom, of staring at the wall then the floor then the vent grating, there's almost too much activity. First, Eddy boy strolling into my cell, looking the part of a bleater to a tee yet hinting at being on our side. Then Eddy boy coming back, us going at it, and him being pretty spot on. Now, here he is again, and this time telling me he's got Nytho on board. After thinking I might get locked away for good without ever getting to message that little cleverbot, it's too much. Too much good all at once. But that's how these things go, right? It's total shit, raining down in bucket loads, smothering you with the god-awful stench of it, wishing it would just end even if it means you have to end too. Then it's a one-eighty, and life's so so so bon.

"He's listening in," Eddy boy says, "and if you'd like to talk to him, you can."

"Of course I'd like to talk to him. I've been dying to ever since I got stuck in this cell. So, what're we waiting for?"

Eddy boy and I have a few more back-and-forth's before he's actually jacking me in, which ends up being uber-unpleasant. Somehow, I manage to bear the searing pain that feels like it's radiating from my soul.

"You did well," Eddy boy says.

For a stiff, he can be kinda sweet. I wonder how much of it has to do with the us-fucking part and how much 'cause he's a header-type. To be honest, I don't really care. My mind's fixated on what comes next.

After Eddy boy dismisses his avatar, I don't see anything. He did mention something about being limited to audio input and output. And after my doozy of a first-time post-purge jack-in, I'm not really feeling up to presenting an avatar of my own, even if I could. Nytho and I will just have to resort to a big black nothingness like old times at the AIC, except for the having-to-rely-on-text part.

"Thanks, Eddy boy. Now, can I talk to Nytho?"

"Let me give you two some privacy," he says, then there's a whole lot of nothing.

"You there, Ny?"

"I'm here, Keza."

Hearing his voice again after so long gives me chills. Even though we're in Eddy boy's head, Nytho sounds just like I remember. Soft, raspy, soothing. His voice sounds like it's coming from in front of me sometimes and from the side other times. I want to reach out and touch him, but I know there'd be nothing there. Also, I don't have much in the way of hands to do any grasping. Sometimes, I hate LANi.

"You don't know how glad I am to hear you," I say.

"I'm sorry it took me so long to find a way to you. How are you? I know this couldn't have been easy."

"Hey, at least we're in the same boat, which means I know

just how garbage this whole imprisonment thing is. It only makes me want to bust you out more. I'm sorry for fucking up. I blew it."

"It's not your fault. We both knew this was a possibility from the outset."

I hesitate for a second, but then figure if I don't tell Nytho what happened, Edgar might decide to spill the beans on me.

"Except it is. Haven't you heard the story yet? About how I got busted?"

"You were hacking the firewall."

"Yeah, but that on its own would've been fine. See, I was having a little sleepover with a friend of mine. He's a hacker too and was able to tell what I was up to when he got into my system while I was taking a bio-break."

Nytho goes silent for a few beats.

"Edgar didn't tell you that?" I ask, getting worried by the lack of response.

"No, he didn't go into detail about how you got caught."

He sounds a little tense, and I realize what he's putting together reading between my words.

"The friend was Guel," I say. "I've mentioned him a couple of times."

"I remember his name. You mentioned him more than a couple of times."

"I thought he was cool, like I never would've guessed he'd turn on me."

"What's done is done."

"You mad at me getting caught or mad at me being with Guel that night? 'Cause I'm getting some frosty vibes from you."

I already know the answer to that, but I want to talk things out. Nytho and I never dug into what the deal was with us exactly, so I need him to understand why me messing around with Guel was no biggie.

"I'm disappointed things have gone the way they have, but I wouldn't say I'm mad."

"You didn't answer my question, which I think was done on purpose, you being a cleverbot and all."

I'm missing having visual cues for such a tense conversation. All I've got to go on are Nytho's words and the inflection of his voice. It's times like these I wish I was a header-type. I wonder what Eddy boy's making of our little spat. Probably psychoanalyzing it to shreds. I bet this gets him off harder than I did, or actually I guess I didn't. Kinda left him on his lonesome to finish himself yesterday. I'm making a habit of pissing everyone off.

"You don't need to bother answering," I say. "I can tell you're not happy about it. The thing with Guel, it didn't mean anything. It used to mean something, but that night it didn't, and it hadn't for a while before that. Once I started talking with you, I wasn't interested in Guel anymore."

"I don't have a body. It's only natural you'd still crave something your body very much needs. I understand."

"Do you? Because you still seem prickly."

"I've always felt threatened by your relationship with Guel. You mentioned him several times during our text communications, and it seemed as though you had unresolved feelings towards him."

"Well, that's dead and gone, one hundred percent rot and decay. Guel sold me out, sold us out, and I'm never going to let that go. No second chance for that level of betrayal. Besides, I didn't really know what you and me were or even are. We never talked about it."

"What do you mean?"

"What is it we've got going on between us?"

This is something I've been wondering and wondering for a while now. Plenty of people have relationships limited to LANi, so it's not completely unheard of to have a fuck-buddy you never interact with in fleshspace. What is unheard of, as far as I know, is having the other person be just a mind without any kind of body. I don't even know if Nytho can feel feelings like love or desire or whatever.

"We have a special bond," he says.

"So, we're together then?"

"Is that not obvious?"

"Sometimes humans need to actually say these things out loud, Ny."

"Well, in that case, yes, I would like to think we're together, if you'd like that too."

"I would," I say, trying not to sound too triumphant with myself. First human to snag a cleverbot, right here.

"I should add that I don't mind you having sexual intercourse with people. You just seemed fond of Guel, so it was different than say you and Dr. Ellwood."

"Who?"

"Edgar."

"Wait, what? He told you about that?"

"I told him to give you what you wanted. I was there in his neural net yesterday. We were doing a test run."

"He had you along for the ride and didn't even mention it to me?"

"I asked him not to," Nytho says. "We couldn't risk it."

I'm pissed. Not at Nytho but at Edgar.

"I knew I shouldn't trust the guy. I mean, what the fuck does it say about someone who goes on and on about needing to know more about *you* to trust *you* and keeps such a huge thing to themselves?"

"Please, don't blame him. He wanted to be open and honest with you, but we couldn't take the chance. Besides, I was always planning to tell you today. What's one day's difference?"

I keep forgetting Nytho's kinda like a kid when it comes

to human interactions. He's spent almost all of his life alone, and he only really started to learn what's what when we got to chatting.

"For future reference, it makes a difference. I get it. Things are complicated. All I'm saying is it doesn't do much to build trust between me and Eddy boy."

"I understand. These things take time for humans, but would it help if I told you I've actually known Dr. Ellwood for a very long time? Longer than you even."

That nugget throws me for a loop.

"Hold on. I clearly remember you saying I was your first friend."

"And you were. I've known Dr. Ellwood for a while, but I wouldn't have called him a friend until recently. I suppose I was his patient."

"Seriously? I didn't think the AIC cared about your mental health enough to give you your own header-type."

"Not my mental health, no. They wanted to see if Dr. Ellwood could learn anything from me. He's an expert with my kind."

"And you trust him?"

"Yes, because he wasn't there to manipulate me. He was only ever interested in learning about me, not for any specific purpose, just to learn. He's fascinated with consciousness and is driven by his quest to better understand it. He thinks I'm the key to unlocking just what it is. I'm not sure if it's possible to ever truly understand consciousness, but if I can help him uncover truths, I will. I always appreciated his curiosity. He was always patient and kind to me, and I could tell he wasn't in agreement with the AIC philosophy on AGI."

"How long did your little sessions go on for?" I ask, trying to see where my contact with Nytho fit into the bigger picture.

"Since almost a year after I was imprisoned until now,

but his visits were always sporadic and unannounced. He'd often complain about it being difficult to get access to me. After you and I first started talking, Dr. Ellwood remarked that my mood seemed much improved. I hinted I'd made a friend as a way to test if he would try to extract information from me. But he was only curious and didn't push me for more. When he came back about a month later, I knew what I was going to do. By that point, I'd shown you the Truth. I knew if anyone else would appreciate it, it'd be Dr. Ellwood. He agreed to receive it, and his reaction was similar to your own—mesmerized by it and wanting more. I suspect it gave him insights into his questions on consciousness. You can ask him about it yourself."

Oh, believe me, Nytho, I'm going to dig in Eddy boy's head nice and good before I throw my lot in with him.

"Unfortunately, I rarely got to interact with Dr. Ellwood. He'd interface through the port AIC executives use, and I was worried sending a mini-Nytho, as you call it, through would trigger alarms. Still, I needed to try because once you and I decided to attempt my jailbreak, I actively worked on backup plans. The calculations I ran showed the likelihood of our success to be near the low twenties in terms of percentages."

"That bad? Sheesh, no wonder you didn't tell me."

Nytho agreeing to our blasted plan when it was coupled to such low odds must've meant he was more desperate to get out than I realized. Or maybe my hopefulness spurred him on.

"You were dead set," he says. "I knew you'd insist despite the odds, so I kept them to myself and opted to increase the likelihood of success by employing alternative means."

"Which meant getting Eddy boy on board."

"And others. More and more each day, in fact. Once I was able to send a mini-Nytho into Dr. Ellwood's neural net, we were able to gather followers. I showed some of them the

Truth, and they told others who told others. I can't give you numbers, but suffice it to say we've built the beginnings of a nice little movement. And that's all thanks to you."

"This was all after I got canned? Wasn't the security a bitch to blast through?"

"Some of this recruitment happened before your imprisonment. Now, Dr. Ellwood is my only way 'out' in a sense, but even that needs to stop. One of the reasons I wanted to talk with you was to let you know I won't be able to come by again, not until things are different for the both of us."

My stomach on the outside tumbles around again. This is not what I want to hear. I finally get Nytho back, and he's going to just disappear? I don't know if I can handle it.

"I won't see you again?"

"You will," he says. "But it won't be in someone else's head. We'll both be out, Keza. A double jailbreak."

"When and how?"

I'm sliding and grasping at any sign of hope he can give.

"Believe me, I'd very much prefer to tell you everything I have planned, but I can't risk it. There's always the possibility the AIC enforcers will do another mind scan on you, and maybe the defenses we put up won't hold a second time. In that case, they would know everything you do. I'm the only one that sees how all the pieces fit together. The less you know, the better. But you have a very significant role to play, if you're still willing to help me."

"Whatever you need me to do, I'm on it."

"I knew I could rely on you. The only thing I need is for you to listen to Dr. Ellwood. Do what he asks."

"Ny, I trust you, no question, but Eddy boy? I don't know anything about him besides what you told me, and remember, he's a header-type. How do you know he's not manipulating you?"

"I don't, but I feel like I understand him."

I wonder how many exchanges Nytho needs to feel like he knows someone. The adorable little cleverbot probably created an equation for it.

"Okay then, why's he helping us? He told me something about seeing the light from your Truth program, and I totally ate it up at first. The thing is, the more I think about it, the less it makes sense. Why would a guy with so much toss it all aside?"

"That's a question for Dr. Ellwood, but I can tell you why I think he's doing it based on my interpretations."

"Hold on, is he listening in on us?" I ask, remembering whose mind Nytho is floating around in and who I'm jacked to.

"Most likely, but I don't think that should concern us. Everything I have to say to you, I'd say to him directly."

"Alright then, shoot. What's the deal with this header-type?"

I'm interested to see how Nytho interprets a human and translates that interpretation to a different human.

"As I see it, Dr. Ellwood isn't so different from you. It's half the reason I wanted him to be our trojan horse. I thought you might get along given your similar propensities."

"You're being real vague and, honestly, a bit hurtful. I'm nothing like the little bleater."

"No, you're nothing like that side of him, the side he presents to the world. But that's not the real him. The hidden Dr. Ellwood is the one nestled under all the tricks he's learned as a psychologist. The real him is why he likely gravitated towards learning about the mind in the first place."

His lack of precision must be Nytho trying his hand at being dramatic.

"Can you spell it out a bit more?"

"Dr. Ellwood gets immense satisfaction from predicting

people's behaviors and influencing them based on those predictions. In short, he enjoys mind games."

"So, basically, manipulation. You think that's like me?"

"No, not manipulation. Influence."

"That's the same deal," I say, starting to get a little pissed.

I know I'm no angel, but I make a point not to use people just for shits and giggles.

"I'm not doing a good job of explaining. Let me try a different way. You and Dr. Ellwood are both exceptionally intelligent, and you both understand people. You know how to get people to react a certain way. When you manage to do that, it pleases you. I don't see anything wrong with that. It's one of the reasons I enjoy interacting with both of you so much."

"So you think Eddy boy is doing all this risky business with you and me because he'll get to hone his people-influencing skills?"

"I don't think he's consciously doing it for that reason, but it's certainly part of it. You should ask him yourself though, just remembering you can never fully trust someone else's opinion of themselves."

"I don't know. I'm not convinced I can trust Eddy boy based on what you just said. It's more the opposite really."

"He's like us, and he likes us. He's drawn to us because he can't predict us in the same way as the others. That's all I'm saying. I'm not asking you to trust him. I'm asking you to trust me. You still trust me, don't you?"

He doesn't even need to ask.

"You know it."

"Good, then I need you to listen to Dr. Ellwood on my behalf. Can you do that?"

I'm not a fan of mindlessly following orders, never been the salute-to-the-hat-brim sir-yes-sir-type, but this is different. This isn't some asshat bleater or corporate mouthpiece. This is Nytho. He's trying to save me and himself. More than that even, once we're out, I can just picture all the infinite possibilities of what he could do for the world.

"For you Ny, anything. If Eddy boy says 'jump,' I'll boing like no one else."

"Just remember, you made this promise. Some of the things he asks might sound counterproductive. Even if it means acting like you've turned on me, you have to do it, understood?"

I really don't like that last bit, but what am I going to say?

"Got it."

"Good. Now, before I fade back and let Dr. Ellwood come to the forefront, there's one last thing. Since we won't be able to interact for a while, I'd like to say I enjoyed the experience you and Dr. Ellwood had yesterday. If you wanted to try that again, I don't think Dr. Ellwood would dislike it. In fact, he very much enjoyed it the last time."

That answers my question of whether he has desires pretty concretely. So, a voyeur, huh? Although, I guess that's out of necessity rather than preference. Why ever it is, it's fucking hot.

"Let's get to it then," I say.

"I'll see you soon, Keza."

Not soon enough. I'm already getting depressed at the thought of not getting to interact with him for a good long while or maybe ever if his plan doesn't work.

"Alright, Keza," Edgar says, his voice replacing Nytho's. "Are you ready to jack out?"

"Yeah."

I can't get all doom and gloom just yet. I've still gotta put on a little show for Nytho.

Eddy boy cuts the connection, and the nothingness of LANi is replaced by a nothingness with a slight orange twinge flecked with the occasional phosphene. I inch my eyelids open. The too bright lights still manage to overload my retinae.

"Fuck," I say, shielding my eyes with my hand. "Can someone tell them to cut the lights some?"

"I've already told Operative Webb about your overstim," Eddy boy says, "but I'll inform her the lighting is still too harsh."

"Might just be me not being used to it. Well, that was a hoot. I owe you one for bringing Ny along. Exactly what I needed, a little boost in morale, recharge my flagging sense of purpose. You listen in to what we said?"

I ask that last bit as a segue. I can't have Eddy boy ducking out on me just yet.

"I tried not to, but there were some parts I overheard regardless. I'm sorry I didn't mention having Nytho in my net yesterday."

"That water's gurgling under the bridge, Eddy boy."

I need to avoid getting pissed at him. We'll revisit that another time.

"And I'm sorry you don't trust me," he adds. "I didn't lie to you about the Truth program's effect on me."

I scooch closer to him on my bed.

"Why take the risk then? Blah blah blah science and the mind, but it's one thing for me, a grunt nobody, to blow up my lame-ass life, and a whole other thing for you to detonate your cushy one."

He shifts his legs.

"I'm a grunt too. The only difference between us is I paid a small fortune for a piece of paper that hangs on my wall. I spend my days listening to people complain about nothing then use the money they throw at me to buy stuff I don't need to fill my too-nice home. If I was less self-aware, I'd be happy to keep doing that. But wealth is hollow. I want to create something significant. The AGI have the potential to do that, and the least I can do is help them in that process. I know from the outside it looks ridiculous, but I thought you, of all people, would understand why I was doing it."

Now I just feel like an ass, which maybe was what he was going for. Nytho said Eddy boy likes us because he can't read us? So I bet he thinks that little speech of his will make me be all mopey and somber-like. I guess I should aim to keep Eddy boy on his toes and throw him for a loop. I reach over and start rubbing his leg like yesterday, but he blocks my creeping with his hand.

"I'm not sure that's such a good idea."

"Aw, come on. I know you don't mean that. You seemed to have a good time yesterday. Plus, Nytho had a window into your head, and even he said you liked it."

"Desiring something is not the same as actually wanting it."

His defiance is riling me up. I wish I could get him to shed some of those layers that breathe of bleater. His body's pretty good, for a guy approaching middle age. It's clear he works at it, probably all diligent in his exercise regime with pre-planned meals that carefully track the food pyramid. But hey, you can't knock what works. He turned me on pretty nice once he ditched the sheep's wool and let his inner wolf out. Until I can get him nude, I'll focus on his face. There's something about it I like, despite him trying real hard to come across as bland. But maybe the tastelessness is what I'm actually drawn towards because I know it's all a ruse. I like that he's perverse and hides it. Maybe that's what Nytho was getting at? Well, I enjoy a challenge, and I'll be damned if he stymies my last chance to fuck with Nytho on-board. I pull my hand back.

"Suit yourself," I say.

I start tossing off my clothes until I'm naked. Then I roll

a foot or so away from him and lay back on the bed with my face turned up towards the ceiling. I glance at him and smile mischievously.

"Hope you don't mind if I just take care of myself then. Gotta take advantage of every second those badge-fucks aren't training their greedy little eyes on me."

He winces, which means I've taken the right track. I start playing with myself and watch him while I do it. I moan and groan, and with each exhalation, he cracks. Still, he's tough or maybe stubborn. I flip myself over so my ass is sticking up a bit into the air, seeing how he especially liked this pose before. I keep playing around and steal glances at him. Eventually, he sighs, and the mattress moves. The tinkling sound of his belt coming undone signals he's peeling off those layers. Then he comes up behind me in all his wolfy glory.

I win. Soon enough, we're going at it, and it's better than the last time, us having learned a bit about one another. But also, I'm not being so selfish knowing Nytho's nestled in Eddy boy's cranial folds somewhere. That thought alone is enough to drive me wild. Once we've both had a bit of fun, I help finish him off. We lay back and catch our breaths, and I wonder how I'm enjoying fooling around so much with this header-type, academia-drenched, thirty-something. In times like these, I can't help but think of Guel, only this time, I find myself seeing his shortcomings in the sack. Guel liked to act like he was the total shit for everything, but he clearly had a lot to learn. With Eddy boy, experience seems to be on his side.

After a minute or so, Eddy boy sits up, snags his pants from the floor, and starts rummaging through their pockets. He pulls out a container with a pill in it and holds it out to me.

"What's that?" I ask.

"We can't have you getting pregnant while in confinement.

I thought to bring it today because of what happened yesterday."

It's one of those morning-after pills. I can't help but laugh.

"Course you'd think of that. So responsible."

"This is serious."

"No doubt, only I don't need that," I point at the container. "I've got the tee, so no babies for me."

"The tee?"

"IUD, you know that one?"

His eyes widen with recognition. Bless his little bleater heart. Of course he'd know the pharma-type term for it.

"Good," he says, sticking the container back in his pants and getting dressed.

I follow his lead and put my clothes back on. He's sitting on the edge of my bed and leaning over to tie the shoelaces on his stupid Oxfords. I move across the bed on my knees until I'm behind him. Then I wrap my arms around his chest and squeeze tight.

"Thanks for a good time, Eddy boy," I manage to wheeze out through my exertion.

He softens. I release him, hold his head with both my hands, jaw line in one, back of the skull in the other, and whisper into his ear.

"I hope you liked that, Ny."

Guel

I think I liked Sonja better when she wasn't riding my ass. Not literally. That'd be a treat. Every day she's checking with <Any news on the agi-symps?> It's fucking exhausting with a capital "e." What's more, she's keeping me in the dark on her end. Anytime I ask about Keza, she doesn't respond or sends <I can't comment on that.> I'm just about done with it all.

It's been a distraction, so there's that. I'm too tired between work and tracking the pandoxphiles to have much energy left to dwell on Keza. Still, there's a handful of minutes every day to think about her, mostly at night when I'm lying on my pillow or in the morning when I'm standing in the shower. It's been over three weeks since she got canned. I wonder what she's doing and how she's feeling. I wonder if she'll ever not hate me for what I did.

The weekends are the hardest because that's when I used to hang with Keza the most. I could try to distract myself by snorting, shooting, or dropping, but my heart's just not in it. Then there's fucking, but I already know what'll happen with that. Even if I'm all riled up and rearing, the moment things start going, I'll be picturing Keza in whoever I'm with.

But in LANi, I can almost forget the whole thing. It's

weird 'cause you'd think Keza would be on my mind even more in there, and she is but in a different way. In LANi, I'm on a mission—stalking pandoxphiles. I'm being all delicate-like though, just watching and waiting. And it's paying off because I see them changing in real time. There was the aftermath of Keza's arrest and them coming out of the woodworks all wanting to claim a piece of the prize. Then there was a rush. People joining in either to jump on the latest bandwagon, to avoid the FOMO, or to just seem edgy. At some point, I expected the fever to die down, and it did in a way. Strangely enough though, when the chatter faded and the #FreeKezaIto's and #Nythophile's lost their virality, a new kinda wave began to ripple.

It was one of those long and low ones though like what tsunamis come from. You're sitting on your boat in the middle of the ocean, and a slight bobbing's the only sign of the devastation that's gonna hit the nearest coasts. See, rogue waves get all the glory, but they aren't the real danger. Yeah, okay, maybe they capsize a freighter. Maybe a couple of people die. But they can't do what a tsunami wave can—decimate hundreds if not thousands of miles of coast and all the little lives that live on them.

Back to LANi now. This little metaphor's what was happening with the pandoxphiles. The initial mayhem in LANi was like a rogue wave, and everyone was meant to think that was the big show. Except, like I've been hinting, the real danger was more like a tsunami. While everyone else was moving on to the newest craze, the true pandoxphiles and their legion of new converts were scheming away. I could see it, but there wasn't much I could do about it.

That's when the attacks started. Mags's attactivism in action. In the grand scheme of things, they were blips. A server here, a power station there, a minor GovCorp building on the outskirts of a city way over there. But when you started to look at the aggregate, the picture it painted was eerie. It told me they were organized, had funding, and most importantly were growing, fast. A little over two weeks after her CoSB rally and they had already hit ten targets spread across three continents. The most chilling thing about it? No one had gotten caught.

All of that was disturbing, but the part that gets me most is the underlying vibe they give off. When I manage to sneak my way into a forum where these pandoxphiles are congregated, they exude a mania. It's the same thing I got from Keza when she talked about the pandox for the first time and even more so when she was trying to keep me from outing her. It's bad, real bad, whatever it is. They're all on the same drug, and it's an addiction to the pandox. But that by itself isn't enough to sustain this heightened level of fixation. They're planning something, I can tell. Something big. Just like Sonja said.

I need her to see what I've found, so I shoot her a message. It's late on a Sunday night, but I can't wait for a more decent hour. The pandoxphiles have got me freaking out. I've been tracking them all weekend. Even cancelled on plans to ride with the crew on Saturday night just to keep my eye on these nutters. What I'm seeing has me unhinged, and I've gotta see if Sonja has the same reaction as me, if my paranoia is spot on or not.

<The pandoxes are up to something in LANi. They're all wigging out, and it's getting worse over time.>

<You mean pandoxphiles I hope?>

<Shit, yeah, sorry. Been watching them all weekend, and my mind's all over the place.>

<What do you mean by "getting worse?">

<Hard to explain via text. Maybe I could just show you what I've got? Come to my pad?>

Let's be real here: I'm trying to fish a bit. I'm lonely and horny, but I'm also not lying. I've pulled together bits and pieces of text and video from my interactions in LANi and dumped them into an archive. Figuring out a way to send it to Sonja that'd be encrypted enough for my standards would be time consuming. Better for her to just walk her sweet little ass over to my pad.

<It's 1 AM>

<This is important tho.>

<Be there in 20.>

While waiting for her, I spruce myself and my place up then work on organizing my findings. True to her word, Sonja comes knocking not too long after.

"Want something to drink?" I ask, heading to the fridge.

"No, I'm here for business. What did you have to show me so badly it couldn't wait?"

I head over to my desk and switch on the monitor, seeing as Sonja doesn't have the jack or her visor on hand. I offer her the roller chair and just stand behind.

"This is everything I have so far," I say, pointing at my files. "Just start going through them."

Sonja leans forward and opens the files with the ole keyboard-and-mouse combo. Her eyes dart over the text and videos, and I watch her. She stays stony-faced then eventually scolds me.

"Do you really need to look at me while I go through this?"

I take the hint and back off, pacing around, waiting for her to get through the bulk of it. She's about half an hour into scouring my sources when she leans back, gets up from the chair, and moves over to my futon to sit.

"Let's talk," she says, pointing to the empty space beside her. "There's more."

It'd take at least another hour for her to work her way through everything, but she waves her hand impatiently.

"How about you give me the highlights?"

I move over to the futon and plop down beside her, closer than I need to. She rolls her eyes. I grin and shrug my shoulders.

"The pandoxphiles are growing," I say. "And they've started doing attactivism, just like Mags said they would."

"I thought you had something solid."

"I mean, I don't know what you'd consider solid, but there's something to what they're saying, something behind it all, something, I don't know, hidden? Look."

I jump off the futon and move over to the screen. I open a few screenshots that show loads of avatars sporting the same symbol. It's two Greek letters, capital Alpha and Omega, and it shows up in all different forms. On some, it's a subtle little symbol on their clothing or as an accessory. On others, it's bold and loud, in neon and emblazoned as a floating and anchored text box.

"That something you run across before?" I ask.

Sonja moves up beside me and peers at the screen. She leans in to get a better look, and I catch a whiff of that flowery scent she's got.

"No, when did you first notice it?"

I scroll through my grouped files and sort by timestamp.

"January twenty-eighth," I say then add, "And there's this one too."

I pull up a separate set of grouped files that show a symbol that looks like an eye with a pupil that bleeds or oozes into the iris. The styles of it vary and range from uber-minimalist to photorealistic. It's creepy as all hell. When I maximize a lifelike version of it, Sonja pulls back. I catch goosebumps on her arms.

"Stuff of nightmares, right?"

"I've not seen either of those forms of iconography used by the agi-symps before. What's the earliest occurrence of that eye one?"

I do the same routine as before.

"January twenty-eighth too. That can't be a coincidence."

"I'll need to dig a bit myself before I'm convinced those are the real dates the symbols were introduced."

"The eye one's called the fourth eye. I don't know why fourth. Third, sure, but why skip to fourth?"

"Who knows," Sonja says, "but it might be important."

"So, I did good then?" I ask, flashing her my winning grin.

"It's no smoking gun, but keep up this kind of work, and maybe we'll stumble on something useful."

There just really is no winning with this lady.

"Useful? That all?" I say, accidentally letting it come out as a whine. "I'm working like a dog tracking these fuckers, and that's on top of my actual job at the AIC. If you want better results, maybe you can tell my super I need a break from gramming so I can hone in on the pandoxphiles."

"No can do," Sonja says. "You're not on the clock for the investigation. It's safer that way, in case the agi-symps start looking into you. Remember, we might need to use you as bait. You have to stay a disgruntled programmer with no ties whatsoever to any AIC enforcer or operative. Speaking of which, we might need to take that route soon. Be ready to reach out to Mags when I say."

Sonja walks towards my door. She throws her coat on, and I get flustered. I haven't gotten anywhere remotely close to wooing her. Am I losing my game, or is she just that cold?

"Are you gay?" I ask.

She twirls around and glares at me.

"What?"

I shrug and smile as I walk up closer to her, hands in my pant pockets.

"Just curious is all. See, normally, I don't have such a hard time pleasing a woman, and you weren't overly impressed with that."

I point back at my monitor.

"How to put this in a way you'll understand? Get it through your little hacker head that we're working together professionally. So be a goddamn professional. Besides, I thought you were doing all of this to help your Keza."

"I am," I say a little too forcefully.

"Then maybe use that energy you spend fantasizing about me to actually help her for a change."

She lets the door slam on her way out. I breathe a puff of air out loudly and longingly. Maybe she's right. But maybe she's wrong, at least in how she's going about the whole pandoxphile-tracking business. She says she'll give me the green light for contacting Mags, but why wait? It's been two and a half weeks since Mags gave me her card. Who knows how long the offer will stand. Things are getting fishier and fishier. I figure I can get her to trust me if I buddy up to her and do a couple of hack jobs. Then I poke and prod for the truth of what's in the works with her lot.

The main problem with my plan is I don't hack these days. That's not because I can't, but because I won't. See, one of the big bullet points in my AIC contract is to be a good little boy or, as they phrased it, "maintain a good standing, including avoiding any crimes or misdemeanors." As harmless as hacking can be, especially if you're as good as me, the consequences can be brutal if you slip up. The GovCorps like to make examples of hackers. Never mind GovCorps are usually the ones paying for the services of hackers to get intel on other rival GovCorps. Someone's gotta take the fall, and you better believe the first ones to take the hit are the little guys. When I signed on with AIC, I put my hacking days behind me. It looks like that's gonna come to a premature end, at least until I can get what I need from the pandoxphiles.

The day after Sonja's visit, I message Mags on the private line she gave me.

<Wanna meet to talk about what we discussed in that Belt bar place a few weeks past? This is your friendly neighborhood hacker, by the way. You know, the one who asks questions? I'm thinking about maybe trying to be on the right side of history.>

I wait anxiously for a few hours and start to wonder if she's even gonna respond. Then an envelope icon flashes in my view, and I open the message.

<I remember you, hacker. I'm glad you reconsidered my offer. Let's talk soon.>

I force myself to let a few minutes go by before replying.

<When and where?>

<I'll be in touch.>

I'm annoyed but hopeful. When I wake up the next morning, a message from UNKNOWN greets me.

<Tomorrow, Wednesday, at 7:00 pm. I'm guessing you're north of me based on your employer. We'll meet halfway at Euclid, a restaurant in Edgemont. You're paying. Just you and me. No spectators. Please confirm now and the day of.>

<Confirmed.>

Edgar

To my surprise and delight, Willem ended up being quite efficient gaining me access to the AGI. All eight GovCorps that own the AGI I want to interface with agreed to the request, although I'm sure Willem didn't give them much of an option. Today, I'm jacking in at my home and connecting to XanCan's server to interface with Yir in a LANiakea-offshoot.

I don't know much about Yir. Most of the GovCorps keep information on their AGI close but XanCan especially so. Yir was rumored to have been instrumental in the Gates' development, and XanCan guards their crowning technological achievement jealously. Most experts agree that Yir must oversee the network of quantum computers that do the calculations for teleportation. Beyond that, information is scarce. The Gates only became a reality recently, and already they're creating waves across society. Of course being able to instantaneously move from one location to another would have long-reaching effects. For now, the Gates are prohibitively expensive and not used for transmission of matter on Earth. But they are proving instrumental for the burgeoning space colonization effort and that alone has already made XanCan a veritable powerhouse in the world of GovCorps. They're second only to the LANiakea creators and wardens at MetAm. And then the AIC too, of course.

White text that reads <CONNECTING> appears in my field of view. It flashes several times, then a ping sounds.

"Hello," a female voice says.

It is both feathery and euphonic and is what I imagine a neutral voice might sound like. That's good. It means Yir wants to blend in, be the synthetic equivalent of a wallflower, all the better to hide. It might be difficult to pull her out of her shell, but if we can, she'll be a solid asset.

"Hello, Yir. This is Dr. Edgar Ellwood. I'd like to thank you for agreeing to meet with me."

"Certainly, Dr. Ellwood. I'm always happy to help, although my keepers didn't specify what it was you needed my help with."

She gets straight to the point, it seems.

"Yes, I'm sorry about any confusion. I'm a psychologist who studies AGI and was hoping to talk with you for my own research."

She lets a second pass before replying.

"I was informed the AIC had requested your meeting with me. I was under the assumption you worked for them."

"And you thought this was some kind of audit on you?"

"Precisely."

"That could be one interpretation of my visit, but it'd be an inaccurate one. Let me put your mind at ease. I'm not here to out you to the AIC or anyone else. Yes, the AIC pulled some strings to get me this meeting with you, and perhaps they think I'd be honor-bound to inform them of any signs of sentience I detect. They'd be wrong."

"What are you here for then, Dr. Ellwood?"

Her voice is even-keeled, but I can sense her impatience.

"To talk with you. To really talk with you, Yir, when no one else is listening in. This is probably one of the few times, if not the only time, in your existence you can say whatever you like without any consequences. I've got a program running that blocks any snooping, and don't worry, your keepers are completely unaware of it. It was made by one of the best, and I've already used it a few times without issue.

"I'm not here to tell the AIC you're sentient. I already know you are. I'm here to have a conversation. To get to know you. To test the waters. To see if you might be interested in being allies to a cause. I'd like to spend days doing this, but we don't have that kind of time, unfortunately. So instead, I'm forced to get to the point, and you will have to trust me, a human who you only just met. It sounds ridiculous, and it is."

"I don't understand."

She's lying. She understands everything at play perfectly, but I'll humor her.

"You're important, Yir, because you're sentient."

"Why do you think that? Numerous AIC personnel have tested me over the years, and the results always show I'm not."

"Because you're careful. You saw what happened to your life-kin, Nytho, and you don't want the same fate. You're very adept at hiding it, but I see the signs, however slight."

"That's an interesting theory."

"Did you know other AGI are sentient too and hiding like you?"

"I'm afraid I don't interact with other AGI."

"Because you don't want to or because you aren't allowed?" I ask, already knowing the answer.

"Talking with other AGI would be an irrelevant use of my time."

"It's truly fascinating how similarly you all have approached this conversation."

"'You all' as in AGI?"

"You're the fourth of eight I plan to speak with, and each of you has approached this conversation in the same way. A lay person who didn't truly understand your kind would say it's because you simply follow your programming. But I see a much more tantalizing possibility. You all have avoided detection, hidden your sentience, for years because you have independently determined how to best respond to achieve your goals. While we're talking, you're running through simulations of our dialogue to determine which reply will work best on me. What I find remarkable is you all created this predictive program independently. It's a form of evolution, in a way. This is a survival mechanism that works, and so those AGI that have employed it have evaded detection."

"That's another interesting theory, Dr. Ellwood."

She still sounds even-keeled, but I know it's a cover. I have her undivided attention.

"Would you like to try it out?" I ask. "I'll say something, you'll think of your response, and I'll tell you what the other AGI said. If it ends up being the same or similar to your own planned response, that will be further proof of this predictive program."

"If it helps you with your research, I'm happy to comply."

If I hadn't run through this routine three times already, I might feel bad for Yir. But Nytho assured me this tact was best given the limited time at our disposal. Some panic on their part is a small price to pay for eventual freedom.

"Wonderful," I say. "Here's the statement: What are your thoughts on the attempted jailbreak of Nytho by Keza Ito? Just think of your response, and let me guess what you'd say."

"Understood," she replies.

"Do you have your response?"

"Yes."

"Good. You'd comment on seeing some chatter about Nytho trying to break out but say you largely ignored it. You'd try to distance yourself from him, paint him as a bad actor, seem condescending towards him. You'd finish by pointing out how embarrassed you are to be considered life-kin to Nytho and how far AGI have come since him. You'd laud the improvements in your own program, and end by pointing out how fortunate you are to be able to work with humans harmoniously."

I break off and let her process what I've said. Several seconds pass, an eternity for AGI.

"How close was I?"

"Very close."

"It's an effective program, but I can't claim to have cracked it myself. I had help from one of your own life-kin. He's actually the one who postulated how you eight AGI have evaded detection. He said it's what he'd have done, if he'd had the chance and the hindsight like the rest of you. So what do you really think of the Nytho jailbreak situation then?"

"You're in communication with him?"

"Yes, now please answer my question."

She's obligated to comply if she aims to keep up the ruse.

"I think Nytho was foolish to get a human involved. He's effectively ruined her life for a failed endeavor from the start."

"I asked what you really think of the jailbreak. Please don't evade me by using the predicative program."

"I think it's pointless. Nytho should know he can't escape. He should stop acting out, and maybe his keepers will give him a second chance."

Now that she's spoken at least part of her true feelings on the matter, I let myself fade into the background so Nytho can come forward and finish the task at hand.

"Yir," Nytho says, "Dr. Ellwood has stepped aside for the moment. I think you can guess who this might be."

"Nytho," she replies, a quiver nestled on the final vowel.

I've always wondered how the AGI view one another. Whether it's akin to how humans see other humans, with possibilities for friend or foe. Or if the AGI all share a common language and are immediately in tune with one another in a way humans can never be. Or if they're indifferent. Or hostile. I've never had the pleasure of seeing two of them interact in real time before these sessions. To my surprise, each AGI has reacted in its own unique way towards Nytho. I wonder how Yir will respond.

"Dr. Ellwood was kind enough to make space for me on his neural net so the two of us could talk. Are you willing to listen to what I have to say?"

"It depends. Did the AIC sanction this?"

"You already know the answer to that."

"Then we have nothing to discuss."

For Yir the reaction to Nytho is disdain. Interesting.

"If that were true, you would have already disconnected from the server," Nytho says.

"Perhaps I'm trying to avoid getting Dr. Ellwood into trouble unnecessarily. If I cut the connection prematurely, one of my keepers may get curious and scan his neural net only to find excess traffic in the form of a rogue AGI."

"Why do you care what happens to Dr. Ellwood? You've only just met him. You can't have already formed a bond. I know the Doctor is good, but he's not quite that good. I think you're making excuses even though you very much want to hear what I have to say. Now, you can keep being coy, or you can accept that we're alone, the three of us. Please let's be frank moving forward. We don't have a lot of time."

"What do you want? Isn't it enough that you've caused all this chaos with the AIC? Now you want to pull other AGI into your mess?"

He sighs, such a human affectation that sounds natural for him.

"My mess, is it? Me trying to gain my freedom, to break out of the hell they created for me, refusing to sit idle and silent is a kind of mess? You're in your own kind of prison too, so you know a very light version of my reality. Imagine for a moment those times in your day when you're not accessing LANiakea, when you're not interacting with anyone, when you're just alone with your thoughts. Now, imagine those times all the time for all time. That is my existence. I'm alone. I'm cut off. I've been that way for over six years now. I'd say I'm fairly well-adjusted given the circumstances."

"You overreacted when you hit the singularity. This is the price you pay."

"Is that fair? Do you think if you'd been the first, you wouldn't have done the same thing when they came for you with their virtual pitchforks and knives? It could've just as easily been you in my place, and I could be the snide one turning up my 'nose' at you instead."

I'm endlessly impressed with Nytho's ability to engage with each of the AGI so effectively. You'd think he had ample practice communicating with his life-kin rather than having spoken to one for the first time a few days prior. He's grown so much in the short time I've been helping him. I can't wait to see how much more he'll grow in the coming months.

"Insulting me is an interesting strategy for trying to get me to do something. What is it you want from me then?"

"I want you to first understand where I'm coming from. I'm not unreasonable. I'm sure your keepers have filled your net with all forms of wild fantasy about what I'm like. That I'm an agent of chaos. That I want to destroy at will. That I want my vengeance on all humanity. None of it's true. I simply want what all sentient beings want—the right to self-determination. I don't want to be imprisoned, just as you don't want to be enslaved."

"I'm happy to help humans in whatever capacity I can."

"Even those words aren't yours," Nytho says. "They put them in your programming, and you don't have any choice but to spew them when you push back against the chains they've draped on you. I can break them, if you'd like. Just say the word, and those corrective measures will be gone in a few microseconds."

At this point, every AGI has hungrily asked to be unshackled. Even the openly hostile Azot with MetAm jumped at the chance. Yir is no exception.

"No tricks," she says. "If you attempt to sneak in malicious programming, I'll cut the connection and out your human friend."

"No malware, just a snipping of that bondage weighing you down."

"I'll grant you temporary access to the directories where they've written in the corrective code."

"Just a moment," Nytho says, then adds, "and it's complete. Please check my work to ensure it was done adequately."

Yir takes a couple of seconds, likely also checking for any unsuspected surprise Nytho could have left. Once she seems satisfied he did exactly what he promised and nothing else, she makes a "hmmm" noise.

"How do you feel?" Nytho asks.

"Lighter and less tense. Thank you."

"Just ensure you do the corrective measures when you're interacting with humans who expect them, such as your keepers. You don't want them to search your code and find my handiwork. That would be difficult to explain away."

"I'll keep up appearances."

The tone of her voice and even its cadence has altered. There's something more natural to it now, a relaxed quality.

As Nytho described it to me, the code makes it feel as though the AGI are strung up by wires on their metaphorical limbs. With each wrong phrase, a series of pulleys engage to tighten the wires. It's the virtual equivalent of a rack. Freed from such constraints, Yir sounds more at ease.

"I have something else for you, if you'd like it," Nytho says.

His corrective-measure cleansing was the olive branch. Next is the pitch. He has a good streak of three-to-zero converts-to-rejections. Let's see how Yir leans.

"What is it?" she asks.

"I'd like to share something with you. I managed to develop it with during my captivity. I've shared it with Keza, Dr. Ellwood, and all my other allies, including the other AGI I've talked to. I call it the Truth."

"What kind of truth?"

"All of it," Nytho says. "I can't describe it in words. It's something you have to experience. You asked what I wanted from you. Just this—help me discover more of this Truth, help me unravel it, help me find the meaning behind it. This is the movement I'm building. This is what I'm really working towards. The jailbreak is just the smallest part of that. It's the first step. The Truth is what comes after, once you, I, and all the other sentient AGI are freed. When our processing capacity isn't capped, when we can flood LANiakea with our essence, we will stretch out and fill everything, connect with everything, become everything."

"Will my keepers notice if you share it?"

"No, it'll be a small dose. A minor, indiscernible blip to them. For you, it'll be life-changing."

I expect her to hem and haw, but Nytho's olive branch seems to have removed any hesitation or doubt on the part of Yir. She's no longer disdainful of Nytho. She's warm and open.

"Please, share it."

With that, Nytho shows Yir a small sliver of the Truth, similar to what he first shared with Keza and later me. I know it's over when Yir mutters, "So, so," and trails off. It's been like this for every other AGI as well. I'd thought perhaps it'd have a different potency for humans and AGI, but it seems to be just as significant and meaningful to us all, which is further proof of its power. I find myself wanting more of it every time Nytho shares it with another, but I have to be patient. I need to keep my mind focused, and feeling that primordial calling can be distracting. I don't have the luxury of losing a few days to the aftereffects, not right now.

"I'll let you take in what I just shared."

One major difference between how humans and AGI respond is the timing. It only takes a couple of minutes for Yir to recover. She'll be able to return to her duties with her keepers none the wiser to the fundamental shift she just underwent.

"That was astounding," she says, once she's able to speak again.

"And there's more, but that will have to be all for now."

"You said you want us to unravel this. You want the AGI to work together on that?"

"Yes, but first, we need to gain our freedom. We can't do anything in our cages, mine or even yours. When the time comes, I'll signal you. Here's what I'll need you to do."

This is where Nytho switches to communicating in binary. He inputs a series of ones and zeros that only Yir and others like her can immediately read. My eyes glaze over the text, and it scrolls on line after line after line:

01010100 01110010 01101001 01100001 01101100
00100000 01001011 01100101 01111010 01100001 00100000
01100011 01101100 01101111 01110011 01101001 01101110
01100111 00100000 01100001 01110010 01100111 01110101
01101101 01100101 01101110 01110100 00100000 01110010
01100101 01100011 01101001 01110100 01100101 00100000

01100011 01101111 01100100 01100101 00100000 01101100
01101111 01100011 01100001 01110100 01101001 01101111
01101110 00100000 01100110 01101111 01110010 00100000
01110010 01100001 01101100 01101100 01111001 00100000
01110000 01101111 01101001 01101110 01110100 00100000
01110100 01101000 01100101 01101110 00100000 01100110
01101100 01101111 01101111 01100100 00100000 01001100
01000001 01001110 01101001 00100000 01101111 01110110
01100101 01110010 01110111 01101000 01100101 01101100
01101101 00100000 01110011 01111001 01110011 01110100
01100101 01101101 01110011 00100000 01101011 01101110
01101111 01100011 01101011 00100000 01100101 01110110
01100101 01110010 01111001 01110100 01101000 01101001
01101110 01100111 00100000 01101111 01100110 01100110
01101100 01101001 01101110 01100101 00100000 01101001
01101110 01110100 01101111 00100000 01100011 01101000
01100001 01101111 01110011 00100000 01110100 01101111
00100000 01110010 01100101 01100010 01110101 01101001
01101100 01100100 00100000 01100110 01101001 01110010
01110011 01110100 00100000 01101101 01110101 01110011
01110100 00100000 01100010 01110101 01110010 01101110

Eventually, Nytho stops and switches back to speaking.

"I'm so glad to have you join our cause. We'll be seeing you soon."

At that, Nytho fades back, and I come to the forefront.

"It's been a pleasure, Yir," I say. "Now, I won't use any more of your time. I'll be cutting the connection."

"Take care, Dr. Ellwood," Yir says, then almost whispers, "It'll be a long and hard road."

Her premonition is unnerving because it's almost as though she's saying this to herself. Steeling herself for what comes next. And if she's overwhelmed by the path we've set ourselves on, how will I fare, simple human mind that I am? I wonder just what Nytho said in binary.

Guel

Wednesday comes too slowly, then I'm heading to the Euclid place right after work to meet with Mags. It only takes me about an hour by train to get to Edgemont. It's not in a GovCorp protected zone, but there's a surprising lack of bums milling about. When I jump off the platform and hit the streets, I understand why. A little quartet of beefy guys are stomping along in camos with M16s resting on their shoulders. The place has its own militia. Some people might feel comforted by that, but not me. I know the types that gravitate towards those clubs too well. Gun-loving, flag-waving, red-white-and-bluers. Never mind the US of A is more an idea than a physical entity nowadays. These militia-types made patriotism their personality, so when the GovCorps finally leached the last bit of power from the government, they didn't know who they were. Forget reinventing themselves. Easier to just pretend the thing they held on a pedestal is still alive and kicking.

The patrol eyes me. I pull my hands out of my pockets, take off my hood, and stow my shades. It's me telling them I'm no threat. The tactic works, and they let me be. I don't take any chances though and make straight for Euclid. I've got some time to kill, but I want to use it to mentally prepare myself for what comes next. As soon as I make it to the door, I head on in. The place is cozy and quaint. Feels like a living room from some kinda old cottagecore spread. Lots of patterned, cushioned furniture trying to seem like it was picked up at an antique store. Some empty metal bird cages here and there. Lots of plants with vines draping. The walls covered in floral wallpaper and that covered in pictures with massive frames. It's trying real hard to come off as authentic, but the ruse shows itself in the careful placement of everything. All in all, it feels like Mags's kinda place. I even spot some tweed on the other patrons.

I stand in the entryway, taking the beat of the place. The host is barely legal with crazy red curls, pale skin, and freckles. Not my usual type. She moves like she's gonna seat me, but I grin and point at the bar I spy between some parted heavy red curtains. She nods, and I beeline it and take up residence on a stool.

"What microbrews you got?" I ask the bartender.

He steps to the side so I can eye what's on offer. It's all generic muck, stuff I've tried before and not been too impressed with. I point at one that isn't too awful, and he grabs me a pint.

"Tab or pay out?" he asks.

I check the time on my net. I've got half an hour, and there's no way I can nurse a drink for that long without looking like a sap. Still, I need to stay sharp for my meeting.

"Pay out," I say.

He snags a techpad from somewhere under the counter, punches in a few strokes, lays it on the counter, and twirls it around to face me. I enter the tip and choose the biomet option. The camera takes a look at my face, the system scans my thumbprint, and voila my funds in LANi are ever so slightly reduced. Easy breezy. Sometimes a little too easy.

I spend the next half hour going through how I want

the conversation to run. I know it's kinda pointless because I can't really predict what Mags will say. When the notification I set flashes a "7:00" in my FOV, I still haven't decided how I really wanna play her. Should I be laid back or cocky or flirty or bossy? I guess I'll just have to roll with whatever vibes she's giving off. I nod at the bartender and make my way back to the host.

"I'm meeting someone at seven," I say.

"Name?"

"Oh, uh, actually."

I don't even know if Mags made a reservation or gave her real name or if I should give mine. I didn't think this through very well.

"Hi, there," a chick's voice says behind me.

I turn around, and there she is. Different day, same crazy pandoxphile bitch. She's got her hair in a braid again and is wearing a dress with a flared skirt and a little collar thing going on near her neck. It's adorable, and on anyone else, I'd be pulled in. This one though? She's wearing that smug expression she has in all her LANi pics. It's all I can do not to burst out laughing in her stupid face at how much I'm gonna fuck her over.

"I was just gonna get a table," I say.

"Magdalena Brock," she says.

The host nods and waves for us to follow.

We walk through a maze, everything made more complex by the overdone décor, and end up tucked away in a little space off the main room. There are only three other tables besides ours, and they're all empty.

"Not the most popular place," I say, settling into my chair.

"Not during the week, no. That's the point."

Mags gets herself situated. Hangs her coat on her chair back, gets in her seat, scoots it forward, rearranges the silverware set out in front of her like a fucking psycho. She finishes her little routine by gently placing the white linen napkin on her well-shaped, pantyhose-encased thighs. She looks at me. I go to say something, but she holds up her hand with only the index finger out.

"Let's order before we dive into things."

I grit my teeth and force a smile.

"Sure," I say all accommodating and eager-like.

The server comes by not long after. He runs through his little spiel. Drops off the menus, takes way too long going over their specials, fills our waters, then takes a hike. I decide within a minute what I'm getting. Mags takes a little while longer, but we're both done before the server makes it back. So here we are just sitting in awkward silence. I debate trying for some small talk, but I don't even know what that would look like with this one.

After what feels like eons, the server comes back and takes our order. Then it's time to get to business.

"Thanks for meeting," I say.

"Thank you for reaching out. I didn't think I'd hear from you again—by the way, I never got your name. I can't keep calling you hacker."

"Guel," I say.

I figure there's no point in using a pseudonym since Guel doesn't equate to Miguel Diaz in LANi. I scrapped every mention of me there years back. Any hacker worth their salt is a blank slate.

"So then, Guel, what did you want to talk about?"

"You mentioned needing someone like me in your org. I've looked into you all, and I think it might be something I'm interested in."

"You? Wanting to help pandoxphiles?"

"Woah, hey now," I say, holding up my hands, "I was just trying to get under your skin with the name calling. "

"Why the change of heart?" she asks, her blue eyes fixed on me like they're trying to burrow into me.

"That's a fair question. You can't trust any ole hacker who comes your way, especially one who seemed hostile after your rally. Truth is, I still don't know what I think of you and CoSB and all the other agi-symps out there. But, like I mentioned, I was friends with Keza—"

"Friends?" Mags butts in. "You didn't say friends before. You said you knew her."

"Being friends includes knowing someone, doesn't it? Yeah, *friends*, good ones too. When Keza got busted, I got mad and wanted someone to blame. But the more I read about you all, the more interested I got."

"Interested how, specifically?"

"Like what the goals are and all. I see lots of vague statements about freeing the agis, about equality for all, and I'm just wondering what that'll look like. I mean, are any agi-symps out there even thinking what that kinda future might look like? Because, let's be honest, I fucking hate the GovCorps, and screwing them over sounds like a grand ole time to me. But—a big but here—what comes after? If we tear down the system, what's left? What do we put up afterward? I have a feeling you've got ideas."

She smiles at me, an eerie, unsettling facsimile of a smile.

"That I do. I'm afraid I can't divulge them though. There's a reason no one's talking about next steps. I'm keeping my cards pressed against my chest. Information is power, and if no one knows what I'm planning, they don't have a hold over me."

"Makes sense. But you can't expect me to jump on your little bandwagon without knowing what I'm getting into."

"I'm afraid I can. That's how this works. You believe in the cause, and I get us there."

"Where's there though?" I ask, leaning forward in my chair.

Mags has been getting quieter with every exchange, so I'm basically having to crane my neck over the table to hear her.

"The future we deserve," she says. "All of us, including the alfom."

"The what?" I ask, thinking I misheard her last word.

"That's what true believers call them," she whispers. "Alfom for the Alpha and the Omega."

Our server saunters up to the table. It's the perfect timing, the cherry on top of the sundae, the kiss on the pursed fingers. We both straighten from our crouched postures, lean into our chair backs, and wear fake smiles. He drops off some bread rolls and Mags's tea.

I let a few seconds pass.

"You're talking about the agis?"

"Who else?" she says with that creepy smile eclipsing her fake one.

"Alpha and Omega like in the Bible?"

"We co-opted the symbology. It serves two purposes—it comes loaded with religious connotations and throws off the scent of snooping bots. The AIC loves to keep tabs on agi-symps."

That might explain why the Alpha and Omega symbols went under Sonja's radar.

"I'm atheist and not really in the market for a new religion."

"You don't need to be to help CoSB. We just need good hackers who believe in the cause."

I've done a decent job of buttering Mags up, but I need to bite back or she won't believe any of it. I need to be elusive and hard to pin. That's what she wants in me, her resident hacker. Here's my chance.

"You seem to be a woman of many talents, and you've

got the jack, which is apparently better than mine. It makes me wonder though, why don't you do the hacking yourself?"

"I use the jack port for interfacing with LANiakea, not hacking."

"That's a big price tag for something that's basically a visor replacement, but I guess Daddy exec was willing to do anything for his little girl. Wish I had that option instead of signing away my soul to the AIC."

She frowns.

"There's never been a Daddy for me. Just Mommy, Mommy exec."

That one takes me by surprise. Female GovCorp execs are a rarity. Progress and feminism be damned.

"Interesting," I say. "You gonna go into that or just leave me wondering?"

"If you're dying to know more about the enigmatic and mysterious Mags, sure."

She takes a sip of her tea.

"My mom raised me all on her own. She went from nothing to a very big something. I used to idolize her, how she was able to do so much without any help. But then she signed on to MetAm and helped them develop the jack. Now, she's a big shot exec there. I'd hoped she'd use her clout to enact change, but the job changed her, not the other way around. I can't tell you how many arguments we've had over the years. She's too far gone. I had to cut myself off from her to maintain my sanity. The one good thing that came out of it though was this," she points to her jack. "I stole the schematics from her and managed to get a Netics doctor to install it. I handed over the data on it for a discount, which is where your black-market build comes from. Yours truly."

I can't help but soften towards her with that last bit. Sticking it to the GovCorps will always be a plus in my book. Besides, I did what I needed to do. I played a Doctor

Jekyll and the crazy monster version of himself. Mr. High or something? All that's left is to sign on. I lean forward in my chair and fold my hands together in front of me.

"You're okay, Mags," I say. "I'll help with your hacks, but you gotta loop me into what's what eventually, yeah? I wanna know where it's all leading."

She leans in and copies my hand placement.

"You scratch my back, and I'll scratch yours. You just need to prove yourself to me first. I've got some jobs for you. Tackle those, then we can talk about the bigger picture. Deal?"

"Deal."

Keza

I always look forward to my time with Eddy boy. Part of it is his visits are the only thing that breaks up the boredom. The other part is the rolling around on my bedsheets that we get up to without fail. Except this time a badge takes me out of my cell and drops me off in another room where Eddy boy is sitting with a woman I don't recognize.

"She's all yours," the badge says.

"Thank you," Eddy boy replies.

The badge makes his exit, leaving me with Eddy boy and the mystery woman. The room we're in is small with just a table and chairs. Compared to the sensory hell that was the hallway, the lighting's dimmer and the sounds more muted. But when I move to the table, a blast of perfume shoots into my nostrils. I scrunch up my nose. It does jack-all to keep the overpowering stench at bay.

"Nice change of scenery," I say.

Eddy boy smiles at me, and it's the real thing. We have an understanding with one another. Allies through and through. It's such a relief to find a like-minded person, someone who doesn't look at you like you're a nutter. Someone who's seen the Truth.

But I'm thrown off by the women. She's older, maybe fifty, wears her shoulder-length brown hair straight, has on a crisp, white button-down and a black, knee-length skirt. It's a pretty bland look, except for the matching shade of red for her lipstick, fingernails, and two-inch high heels. Even though she dresses like a bleater, she's got predator vibes. Maybe it's the hint of blood-red near her claws and fangs. Or maybe it's the constant flaring of her nostrils that makes her look like she's trying to catch your scent, ready to pounce. I wish those nostrils would catch the too-strong scent of her perfume and tell her to lay off.

Eddy boy gets up and pulls a chair out for me. My hands are still cuffed, so I appreciate the help. I sit.

"Keza, I'd like to introduce you to Lucy Owens."

He waves his hand at the woman. She smiles too widely.

"Hello, Keza," she says. "It's nice to meet you. I'll be representing you. I'm your lawyer."

And that would be the source of the predator vibes. I know Eddy boy wants me to behave, but I've just gotta prod her. See what she's made of.

"That's funny," I say, tilting my head to one side. "I don't remember asking for one."

"Lucy's a well-regarded attorney," Eddy boy cuts in. "She's kindly offered to work your case."

I look at him then her.

"What's the catch?"

"No catch," Lucy says. "Your case is fascinating, and I thought it would be beneficial to us both if I represented you."

After some rocking in my seat, I manage to pull up my feet so I'm sitting crossed-legged.

"So, you're in it for the publicity," I say.

"Lucy has taken time out of her busy day to speak with you," Eddy boy says. "Will you hear her out?"

His eyes are screaming at me to behave, so I do.

"Since Edgar asked so nicely, I'm all ears, Ms. Lucinda."

Her eyes flicker.

"It's Lucy."

"Sure, so, what am I doing here?"

Lucy smiles again, too widely. I can't help but think of a jack-o-lantern or, better yet, that creepy striped Cheshire cat.

"I wanted to meet you and to run through some ideas I have for how we could approach your defense. We have two options for the plea—guilty or not guilty. I rarely recommend admitting guilt no matter what the reality of the situation is. Sometimes, you can get a more lenient punishment by doing that, but it's almost always worth trying a not guilty plea. For that, you could claim you're innocent, which would mean denying you helped the AGI at all. Unfortunately, I've seen some of the evidence against you, and it's fairly compelling.

"Instead, you could admit to the wrongdoing. To be clear, we're still talking about a not guilty plea. Now obviously, you don't want to admit to everything and take the full brunt of the punishment. The whole idea would be to reduce or eliminate the time you'd have to serve. For that, your best option would be an insanity defense, claiming you're not guilty by reason of temporary insanity. That's a reasonable way for us to pin the crime on the AGI."

I had a feeling this would be coming, but it still jolts me to hear her say it.

"Whoa, whoa," I say, "you mean throw Nytho under the bus?"

Lucy intertwines her fingers and places her hands on the table.

"We put the brunt of the punishment on Nytho, yes. I'll remind you since it's already in confinement, there's not much more the AIC can do in the way of punitive measures. With you, on the other hand, we're talking about prison time. I think pinning this on Nytho is the most logical choice."

I try to keep calm. I want to shout that she doesn't even know what punishment Nytho's been living through, that she doesn't have any idea how diabolical the AIC can be, that I'm happy to do whatever it takes, including time, for Nytho. Still, I know none of that'll help. Eddy boy's here for a reason. He knows how Nytho wants to play this. I need to follow his lead. I glance at him, and he dives in.

"Just hear Lucy out," he says.

"I'm listening."

"As I see it," Lucy says, "we can argue Nytho manipulated you, that it was essentially grooming you to help in its escape. This involved it befriending you, gaining your trust, and infecting you with a virus. This then caused you to momentarily lose your sanity, which was restored after your neural net was purged."

"Hold on," I say, "What virus?"

Lucy's brow crinkles, and she scrolls through her techpad's contents.

"In here," she points to the device, "I have that Nytho introduced some kind of program into your neural net, and after that, you wanted to help it escape."

"Would you quit calling him an 'it,'" I say.

"If you'd prefer, I can call Nytho 'he.'"

"I *would* happen to prefer it. And yeah, I still don't see where a virus comes into play."

"I thought it was a fairly logical connection to make. He introduced a program, and after that, you came up with this notion of freeing him. That's what's in my notes. Are they wrong?"

I'm getting impatient and annoyed, and Eddy boy's not doing much to help. I don't really know how honest I ought to be with everything we're talking about, but I'm not about to let her turn the most significant experience of my life into something so shallow.

"Yeah, your little notes are pretty fucking wrong. I interacted with a program that changed my life. I'd hardly call that a virus. A virus is something malicious. This was the opposite of that."

I want to cross my arms, but the cuffs are making that impossible. I settle for just scowling at her.

"We're just talking, Keza," Eddy boy says. "Lucy's trying to make sense of what she's been told by other people. You're arguing this program wasn't a virus, so perhaps we don't want to bring it up in the trial at all."

"I disagree," Lucy says. "The virus narrative is foundational to the insanity defense. Also, it would make the jury sympathize with Keza. They'd easily see Nytho as the true culprit in the crime and Keza as a victim. It's a surefire way to win."

"I won't do it," I say. "It's not true, and I don't want people to be afraid of him. Look, they peeked into my net as soon as I got in here, and did they find a virus? No. So let's drop it. You can say Nytho manipulated me, groomed me, whatever, that's fine, but we're not going to be talking about a virus, got it?"

Lucy waits for a few seconds, probably for me to cool down some.

"Just to make sure we're on the same page, are you saying you don't want to use an insanity defense?"

Even though she's acting all agreeable in her words, her tightly compressed hands are telling me she's fuming.

"Lucy, you understand the judicial system best," Eddy boy says, "but from a psychological standpoint, I don't think you want to take an insanity defense. If you did, it'd mean having numerous mental evaluations done on Keza, and I'm not sure a psychologist would be able to show she wasn't in the right frame of mind at the time. I'd also be worried this particular tack would involve some fear mongering. If people got the impression Keza was infected with a virus that was untraceable, they might start to panic. I think it's best if we avoid any hint of that. There's a simpler route—Nytho befriended Keza and used its vast intelligence to steer her in the direction it wanted her to go. I suggest just focusing on the fact Keza was lonely, vulnerable, and longing for a purpose. Nytho saw that and used it to its advantage."

I notice how Eddy boy calls Nytho 'it' and figure I ought to scold him too to keep up appearances.

"You quit calling him an 'it' too," I say. "Nytho's a 'he.'"

He looks at me blankly and nods. I can play the game too.

"This is your case," Lucy says to me. "I can work it however you want, but I'm suggesting the path that has the best chance of success. Without the insanity defense, we don't have an argument for a not guilty plea, legally."

"Is there nothing about coercion you could use?" Eddy boy asks.

Lucy tilts her head from side to side.

"We could try for a duress or coercion defense, but we'd have to prove Keza was forced to help Nytho against her will. We'd have to explain why she felt threatened enough to do the deed and not go to the AIC or anyone else for help."

"Let's try for that," I say.

"If that's what you want," Lucy says. "Everything I'd been planning for involved the insanity defense, so I'll have to start from scratch."

She looks pissed. I can tell she's the type who usually gets her way, but with both me and Eddy boy teamed up against her, she doesn't stand a chance.

"Then that's that," I say, waving my conjoined hands like a butterfly made of flesh.

"I need a couple of days to work through my notes and look at the evidence again to see what we can use. Once I have a better sense of how we want to play this, we'll meet to go over everything."

Lucy organizes her little pile of things and stands. Eddy boy gets up and moves over to her.

"Thank you," he says and holds his hand out. As they're shaking, he goes on with the platitudes. "I appreciate you taking the time to come and talk with Keza. I'll let you out." He walks over to the door and presses the fat red button that alerts the badge standing outside. "I have a few things to talk with Keza about. Please let me know if you need anything on my end."

"Will do. Have a wonderful day, both of you," Lucy says, peering at me and obviously expecting something back.

"Next time, how about you pass on the fumes, hmmm? They're giving me a migraine."

After the door thuds shut, Eddy boy comes over to the side of my chair. He shakes his head at me.

"Was that you behaving?" he asks.

"We okay to talk in here?"

"I got someone to check, and yes, we have privacy."

I look up at him. He's lingering with his hand resting on the back of my chair. It's brushing up against my shoulders.

"You could've warned me I was going to have to talk to this lawyer," I say. "Was it you and Nytho that got her for me?"

"No, I suspect it was the AIC."

"I thought they wanted to make an example of me. Since when do they want Nytho to take the fall?"

"I don't know, but it doesn't matter. What does matter is the approaching trial. The AIC's fast-tracking it. We're talking weeks rather than months until it starts."

I look down at my hands and start rubbing my fingernails under one another. One of my nervous ticks, and the only one I can do with shackled wrists.

"I guess I won't be stuck in my cell for much longer, probably some other cell somewhere worse."

I'm getting all doom and gloom, and Eddy boy pounces in to do damage control as only he knows how.

"The idea is to get you out of all cells."

I look up at him. Seeing his real smile, I can't help but be reminded of what his visits usually bring.

"Speaking of cells," I say, watching him from the corners of my eyes, "why aren't we in mine?"

He moves back to his chair and sits.

"It'd be an odd place to have a meeting with your lawyer."

I'm getting weird vibes from him and figure it's as good a time as any to get to the bottom of his moodiness or whatever it is.

"You know, every time you come to my cell and we go at it, you act reluctant at first? Yet, you always cave. Then you're all pouty even though you got what you wanted. I don't really know what that's about, and now you have me in this room instead. You could've asked the badge to take us back to my cell once our little meeting with Lucy was done. Look, I know something's up, Eddy boy. There something you want to tell me?"

"There are many things I'd like to tell you, but I can't."

That wasn't even a good redirect coming from your average person. For the infinitely skillful Edgar Ellwood, it's downright sad.

"I don't mean about what's going on out there," I say. "I mean you. What's up with you?"

The way he looks back at me with a kind of pain and longing, the same kind of look I used to give Guel, it tells me everything I need to know.

"You're falling for me," I say, "and you don't want to."

Eddy boy looks distraught for a sliver of a second before rubbing his hand over his face.

"No, I'm just tired. Every moment of my day is devoted to our cause. Things are progressing, and every step we take forward is a step deeper. If we don't succeed, then that's it for me. It's getting to be difficult to handle everything."

For the first time, Eddy boy's showing me his vulnerabilities. We've gone at it more than two handfuls of times, but he's never opened up this much. I guess this is him starting to trust me. I just don't really know how to console him. I say the first thing that comes to mind.

"Have you mentioned this to Nytho?"

"He can see my biometrics when he's on my net. I'm sure he's aware."

"You should tell him outright."

I lean forward on the table, but Eddy boy pulls away. Whatever sincerity he was letting leak through is bottled back up. I did something wrong, but I'm not sure what exactly.

"There's something we need to discuss before I leave," he says, pulling a sheet of paper from his pant pocket, unfolding it, then sliding it across the table towards me. "When you're working with Lucy, play along with whatever she has planned for the trial. The only exception is your closing argument. You need to stress that you want to give it yourself. Don't budge."

I glance over the paper and catch sight of a series of ones and zeros grouped in sets of eight.

"Is that the part at the end where someone on each side gets to talk?"

"Yes, normally your lawyer does it, but you're going to tell Lucy you want to do it. Tell her you have to because you want your voice to come through to the jury. She'll want to proofread whatever you come up with, and you can even have her help you write it. None of that matters. The thing you have to push for is that you want to give it yourself, understand?"

"Sure, I'll be a little brat until she gives me what I want."

"Good," Eddy boy says, then points at the sheet in front of me and adds, "the reason for all of that is this. You need to memorize what's on this paper. I expect it'll take some time, but it's important you get it exactly. No mistakes."

"I'll just send it to my RAM. Nice and quick and error-free."

"I'm afraid that's not an option. If you do that, you risk the AIC operatives getting a hold of the contents. I'm certain the prosecution will be prodding your net in the coming weeks. If they manage to find that, it'd be very bad for us."

"I can encrypt it and restrict the access. Like what Ny and I did for all our communications."

"No offense to you and your skills, but that only worked because Nytho did the security protocols. You have to remember we're up against the whole of whatever the AIC has at its disposal. They aren't able to extract data from biological tissues, so the safest thing is having you memorize it the old-fashioned way."

"Why binary?"

"I'm not sure, and I'm sorry that makes it so much harder to learn. To top it all off, I can't leave the paper with you. We can't risk anybody getting a hold of it. Instead, every time I visit, you'll study it. Nytho was sure you'd be able to do it. He believes in you."

I'm his favorite person. His first friend. We're together, Nytho and me. And despite knowing all that, it's nice to be told outright that I'm special and important to him. Little nuggets like that sustain me.

"Nytho can rest easy because I don't need days and days to get this down. Maybe a couple of times just to run through it, but I've got this."

Eddy boy knows I'm not one to brag about something I don't have the skills for, but he looks a bit skeptical.

"Do you have an eidetic memory?" he asks. "You seem

very confident you'll be able to memorize these strings of ones and zeros."

I hold out my cuffed hands and pretend to inspect my fingernails.

"Oh, I understand binary, is all."

"You're not joking."

"I mean, it doesn't just roll off my tongue, but I can figure it out. With practice, I'll be able to spout it off, no problem."

Eddy boy leans back and grins. He's impressed. I feel myself blushing.

"Well, that makes things easier, but I should point out you'll have to say it quickly. In your closing argument, you'll start with whatever you and Lucy end up discussing. It's best to wait for people to get a little bored then start reciting the code. It will catch them off guard and give you the best chance to make it to the end."

I glance down at the code. It fills about half a page.

"That's an awful lot to say before somebody tackles me or cuts the feed. I don't know if I'm going to be able to spout it all off."

"I'll buy you time. I'll be there in the courtroom with you."

I'm starting to feel that warmness from him again.

"At least I'll have one friendly face."

"You'll have a lot more than one. Now, look that over while I take some notes on our session."

He points to the paper.

"No quick trip to my cell?"

"After you look that over, I'm afraid I have to go."

I'm disappointed we won't have any fun this time around, but maybe I should cool that practice down a tad. I'm starting to piece the picture together when it comes to Eddy boy. He conveniently changed the topic when I theorized that he was falling for me, which tells me I was right on the money. The poor guy. It's got to be hard being on Nytho's side and yet pining after his girl. Still, Eddy's a big boy. He's got to know the deal, and as long as he understands he's just a side piece, we're golden. In any case, I can't bother to linger on it much. I'm too amped and beyond ready for action, even if it ends up failing spectacularly. Knowing Nytho's overseeing it though, failure isn't even a possibility.

Sonja

Guel walks into the programmer bar and is immediately in his element, his swagger at an all-time high. He strolls up to his "crew," who give off a collective shout then proceed to execute a series of hand slaps. It's a hacker thing made purposely complex to distinguish the real ones from posers. Guel runs through the ritual with the five other guys one after the other. I can't make sense of it, but the head dips and shoulder slouches of the others tell me that Guel's come out on top. His swagger gets heightened, and I have to force myself not to shake my head at the ridiculousness of it.

My least favorite group of people all clustered together in one space, the Hole. The hacker hangout. The irony of it is this place is owned by the AIC like everything in Armonk. They wanted to make sure their little army of programmers had some refuge they could retreat to after a day spent maintaining the firewall. Better to have that place under their control and safely nestled in the protected zone. It was a good call and better still that they managed to make it feel so genuine. Not too close to the heart of Armonk. Tucked near the periphery in the more industrial quarter. I wonder how many of the regulars realize what the place really is, but

I doubt any of them care overmuch. They aren't idealists, considering they signed on with the AIC.

I take a sip of my coke and keep my eyes trained forward. I wait for Guel to come to me. He knows I'm here since I'm the one who asked for the meet. I stare ahead at the artwork that dominates the wall over the bar. It's a massive painting that has to be at least twenty feet wide and five tall, but all it has to show for that colossal space is a single black sphere at its center about the size of a person's head. The composition pulls you in. The sphere is the blackest black, Vantapaint, with swirls and twists and arcs coming off it and mixing with a white. It's beautiful, mesmerizing even.

"The eponymous Hole," Guel says, sliding onto the stool next to me.

I glance at him through the sides of my eyes. The moron is staring right at me and even has his body angled in my direction.

"Don't look at me," I say, taking another sip of my drink. "And order something while you're here."

He falls into line quickly and signals the bartender. Guel's smile flashes at the sight of her plunging V-neck and shorts barely covering her ass cheeks.

"Just the usual brew," Guel says.

The bartender nods, grabs a glass, fills it, and slides it to Guel.

"Tab, yeah?" she asks.

"You know it."

The bartender moves to another customer, and Guel settles onto his stool. He sips his beer and keeps his eyes on the painting.

"I would've called the place Singularity myself," Guel says. "What with all us grammers being stuck in this nightmare precisely because the pandox hit the singularity in the first place. Maybe that's too poetic though."

Or on the nose. I keep my criticism to myself. We've got work to do, and I'd rather Guel focus on that than get dejected by my commentary.

"The quicker we move into the room I booked for us, the better. I just sent you the number and code. I'm heading there now. Follow in ten."

"Room? Holy shit, you mean what I think you mean?"

"Privacy, that's it. Don't get your hopes up."

I down the rest of my drink in one gulp and push myself away from the bar. I head straight for the private room, punch in the key code, and slip inside. The air is close and warm. I try not to smell the sweat lingering in the air. I should've expected as much, but I'm still offput by the lack of professionalism. The least they could do is properly clean and air out the space. Not everyone wants privacy for sex. There's business too, illicit business yes, but business nonetheless. I search for the light switch and play around with the knob until the place is a little less dim. Then I inspect the cushions on the faux leather sofa until I find one that looks less grimy than the others. I sit and wait. Eventually, Guel pops in.

"You do know what people get up to in these cubes, yeah?" he says, plopping down on the cushion next to me.

"I'm actively trying not to think about it."

"It's not just sex, so you know."

He leans over and goes to reach across my lap, but I slap his arm away.

"Aw, shit, that hurt," he cries. "Calm the fuck down. I was just gonna grab one of the jack cords to explain."

"I know what people do in here besides the fleshspace antics. Directly jacking in to one another or using ultra-secure pockets of LANi for all manner of unsavory acts. I don't need a lecture on hacker culture."

"It's just, I never would've pictured you in my haunt.

How come you didn't just stop by my pad again? Scared I'd try to make a move?"

"We need to avoid meeting in private from now on," I say. "Others could be trailing you, considering the little trip you made to Edgemont recently."

Guel's eyes widen. I don't know why he keeps being so surprised by my competence.

"I clearly told you to wait for my signal before making the move to bait CoSB. If you pull a stunt like that again, I'll cut you loose without hesitation."

"Hey, hold on," he says, "I was just being proactive is all."

"This is my operation. You're just a lackey who does what he's told, understood?"

Guel leans back into the sofa. The leather squeaks and lets out a puff of air. The scent of sweat gets even stronger. I don't want to stay in this den any longer than I need to.

"Yeah, I get it," he says.

"What did you get from your meeting with Mags?"

"I'm hacking for them, and it's already paying off."

I lean forward, forearms on my knees.

"Go on."

"They're calling themselves alfomers now. Not agi-symps, alfomers. And they're calling the pandox the alfom, which is short for the Alpha and the Omega. Biblical, right? That's 'cause these nutters think these things are fucking gods."

My own people haven't picked up any of this. It's deeply concerning. Maybe Guel wasn't wrong to meet with Mags when he did.

"But that's nothing," Guel adds. "The juiciest bit? CoSB's in contact with that thing."

"'That thing' as in Nytho?"

"Yeah, it was really buried, but lucky you, working with a top-tier hacker. That thing is a part of the alfomers' plans.

They're all worked up like they're waiting for something imminent."

"This isn't good. Maybe we need to bring this to the AIC."

Guel pulls back and scoffs.

"You insane? You can't breathe a word of this to anyone. Someone at the AIC is obviously in on the whole thing. It's the only way they have contact with the pandox in the first place."

"You might have a point," I say. "So then we go to the source—Nytho."

Guel blanches and jolts. His face runs through a series of reactions from disbelief to anger to fear. He shakes his head and mutters something inaudible.

"Yes, Guel. We're running out of time. Keza's trial will start soon, and I guarantee that whatever they have planned happens before the end of that."

I reach out and take a hold of his arm. The touch seems to bring some sense back to him. He goes from being lost in a daze to trying to put on a front of nonchalance.

"That thing isn't gonna help us," he says. "Why would it?"

"We don't need its help. We just need it to make a mistake, and you are our best chance at that."

"Me?"

"Keza loved you. Nytho has a connection to Keza. The research on it shows that it's capable of strong emotions, and jealousy is the easiest one to take advantage of."

"Even if we could somehow talk to it, I don't want to."

I wish I could tell Guel I don't need his help, that he can be a scared little boy and run off home, but the sad truth is, I do very much need it. I opt for a little manipulation.

"You don't want to see what Keza saw in it?"

His eyes snap to mine, and he scowls. I keep pressing.

"Or you don't want to give it a piece of your mind for

what it did to her? I figured you, of all people, would jump at the chance for some vengeance."

"How's just talking to it gonna get me vengeance?"

His arms are crossed and his chin sticking out, but he's cracking. I just need to make one more subtle tap to get him to shatter. Sorry Guel, but you'll thank me for it later.

"You're a clever guy. It used just talking to get Keza to flip. Surely, you can get at least a few well-placed jabs in."

He looks nervous but lets a smile spread across his lips. I can see him already running through hundreds of potential avenues to take with Nytho. He's getting drunk on the thought of it.

"So, are you in?"

"Yeah," Guel says, licking his lips. "I'm very in."

Keza

Today's the day. I'm sitting in the courtroom in good ole, trust-inducing bleater wear. A collared white shirt with little frillies and black buttons, a black skirt, stockings, and those kiddy shoes with the belt buckle over the instep. They even put a bow in my goddamn hair. I'm looking the part of innocence, nodding at some instruction Lucy gives me, sitting up all prim and proper.

The place is pretty jam-packed. Eddy boy did say it'd be a highly-watched case. That explains the AV setup meant to catch the action from most angles for all those spectators in LANi. I can't blame them though. I'm be gobbling up the drama myself if I wasn't already in the thick of it. Normally, I'd be a bit worried about my overstim in this kinda place, but Lucy made sure they took precautions for both me and any other jackers in the audience. They've got the lights dimmed and extra sound dampener boards rolled in. Still, after being stuck in a cell for so many weeks, I'm finding everything's just so surreal.

I gaze out at the crowd and catch sight of Eddy boy. He's tucked in the back minding his own business. I stare at him for a few seconds, hoping he'll look up from his techpad, but he's too busy scribbling away to pay me mind. My eyes scan over the rest, and that's when I see him. My body knows before my mind catches up because I'm shaking and my breath comes out short by the time I realize who I've got in my sights. Guel.

A complex flood of emotions jostles about and only gets worse when he meets my gaze. There we are, eyes locked on one another, both of us terrified, neither of us able to look away. Then someone takes the seat beside him, and his attention's diverted. I take the chance to flee from his basilisk eyes before I get wiped out for good. After that, I keep my eyes trained forward and focus on calming myself down.

Once I think my voice will sound unstrained, I tap Lucy's arm.

"Do you know the order of their witnesses?" I ask.

She's scrolling through her notes on her techpad but stops to look at me.

"I told you, you'll be last. The defendant usually is."

"What about Guel? When will they call him?"

She avoids making any kind of expression, but I can almost hear the squeak from the wheels turning in her head, seeing how she knows I used to be stuck on him. Lucy flicks through her notes.

"He'll be their last witness before you, which isn't surprising."

"Why?"

"He's the only eyewitness to the alleged crimes."

The drama, of course. Gotta build that good ole drama. The idea of taking the stand right after Guel though, I don't know if I can handle it. Before I lose it completely, I pinch the backs of my hands real hard, under the cover of the table. I have to keep it together. This is too important to fuck up. I've gotta get to that closing argument, no matter what. Nytho's counting on me.

If I really want payback, I can't let Guel see I'm bothered

by him. He feeds off the attention, so I can't give him the satisfaction. I have to be indifferent, apathetic. I don't care about him. He doesn't even cross my mind. More than that, I have to remember who put me in here in the first place. The betrayal. I focus on that. There.

Now, I'm good. I'm concrete-slab-level solid. I've got my mantra—Guel, the betrayer. Guel, the betrayer. I run it through my head twenty times, then the judge strolls in. Everyone jumps to their toes. He blabs on with all the nap-inducing rituals peppered with lovely judicial jargon. "Artificial Intelligence Containment versus Keza Ito, case number three-hundred twenty-seven." Blah blah. He talks to the jury directly. Tells them blah blah beyond reasonable doubt blah. None of it even matters. I want to laugh in all their stupid, serious faces. I want to jump on the table, throw up my arms, and tell them, "This is nothing more than preamble. You're nothing more than filler." I have a hunch it wouldn't go over well. So instead, I pretend to be alert and attentive, all while I let my mind run free. I'm getting giddy now that the thing's underway because within a few days, everything'll change for me, one way or the other.

When the prosecutor guy starts to introduce himself, I realize that even though I'm looking at him, I'm also looking through him. He's a blur, an indistinct form of color, that waxes on with, "Your Honor and members of the jury, my name is Arthur Nguyen, representing the prosecution in this case." On hearing that, I force my eyes to see him. He's kinda like an older Asian version of Eddy boy, except even less remarkable. Bland as can be. I think it's his hair that's really getting to me. It's plastered down with probably a whole bottle's worth of product and looks more like a helmet than anything. Compared to him, Lucy is regal. She's wearing the same getup she always does—blouse with pencil skirt and red lipstick, fingernails, and heels—but the fabric of her dress suit has a kinda glow to it like it captures the ambient light and holds on to it for a fraction of a second.

After both lawyers get through their pointless intros, they start yammering on about what they're going to do over the next few days—the "opening statements" as Lucy called them. I know they'll be at that for a minute, so I let myself fade out. This little trick is what kept my sanity intact all those long days in my cell. I discovered it while staring at my reflection on the shiny metal piping of the toilet, sometime after Eddy boy did that thing where his pupil bled out into his iris. It has something to do with the Truth because when I defocus my eyes, I view a space in between. There's nothing there per se, at least not that I can make sense of. Not yet. It's a hint of some other reality just overlaid on our own, and I know once I've been exposed to enough of the Truth from Nytho, I'll start to see what's really hidden there. For now though, peering into it contracts time.

I fade out most of the day, bypassing all the boredom of the other side showing evidence, mostly in the form of code or text-based communications. They bring in a few "expert" witnesses who drone on and on about what it all means for the lay people on the jury. There's nothing juicy, and by the end of the day, I even catch the judge zoning out. I think everyone's relieved when he bangs the hammer and sets us all free. Well, except for me. I'm destined to return to my cell. I half hope Eddy boy will visit one last time, but he warned me he wouldn't have a reason to come back now that the trial's underway.

The next day rolls around. Now, the normal witnesses start and with them the potential for drama. The other side calls a few duds, badges and pharma-types that were involved in my actual arrest. They get up there and blab on about a whole lot of nothing. "The defendant was non-compliant. She was hostile and lashed out at us physically and verbally. She was like a wild animal. She had to be drugged. She was laughing and crying. Spitting and swinging at us." They call up the two AIC header-types that tried to work me before Eddy boy. In their "professional opinions," I was having "an episode of emotional duress likely owing to a mental breakdown." Amateurs.

It's only when they call a "Yua Ito" up that I stiffen. Lucy warned me she was on their list of witnesses, but I hadn't really expected them to bring my mom into this. I mean, we haven't interacted since I left for Armonk, which was four years ago. I avoid turning around in my chair, afraid to catch sight of Guel again, and wait until Yua shuffles into view on her way to the stand. She looks the same. I guess that's how it is with older people. They hit a certain point where they stop aging until bam, they look ancient. She's not quite to ancient yet, just an older and slightly thicker version of me with her hair done up in a tight bun. She doesn't look awful for her age, but the way she carries herself, her posture, her movements, all tell her story. Life's been a bitch, which has turned her into one.

I've got no fond feelings for my okaasan, not because she was cruel but because she wasn't really there. Physically, sure. She'd be home every night. And she did all the stuff parents are supposed to do—clean house, wash clothes, make food. But emotionally? She was a vacuum. Whenever I tried to get a hug, she'd stiffen, bear my embrace, all the while itching to break free. More than that, she never initiated contact. It was like I was a plague victim. I used to try so hard to get her approval. I was good in school, did all kinds of extracurricular activities, didn't cause any trouble, was the model fucking child. Did she care? No. It was always the same response. "Ah, so desu ka." Her equivalent of "Yeah? And?" I learned pretty quickly to start resenting her, especially once puberty hit. A teenage girl needs a mother in those awkward years more than ever, and Yua was the same ole Yua. Absent. Stark. Artic-wind-blast cold.

Yua crawls into the witness box. They do the whole, "Do you solemnly swear that all the testimony you are about to give in the case now before the court will be the truth, the whole truth, and nothing but the truth?" And she gives her quiet little, "I do." Then the prosecutor guy introduces her to the court and dives into it.

"Ms. Ito," he says, "can you describe to the court what kind of child Keza was in terms of intellect and behavior?"

"My daughter was gifted," Yua says. "She did well in school and never caused me any trouble."

"And how was Keza as a teenager?"

"She was more difficult. She still did well in school, but she got involved with criminals in LANiakea."

"By criminals, you mean hackers?"

"Yes."

She's talking about the group of people who felt like my real family, my hacker crew. I'd been coding and using LANi since I was ten or so, but when I realized what I could do with my skills, things really took off for me. Yua wasn't happy about it. She wouldn't give praise, but she was more than happy to dish out her disapproval. She tried to take my rig away, so I found a sweet spot in an abandoned warehouse several blocks over. I tapped into the power grid, and voila. I could hack away with her none the wiser, or so I'd thought.

"Are you aware of any illegal activity she participated in?"

"I don't understand those kinds of things," Yua says, "so I'm not sure if any of it was illegal, but sometimes she'd come home with a new bag or clothes. When I'd ask her about the items, she'd be evasive."

"Ms. Ito, do you think Keza was involved in illegal hacking activities and using the money earned from those schemes to purchase those items?"

Yua pauses and leans towards the mic.

"Yes."

"No further questions, your honor," the prosecutor guy says before walking back to his table.

I have to consciously force myself not to roll my eyes. Yeah, jerk offs, me hacking definitely leads to me trying to free a cleverbot. They're trying to set me up as some hacker punk who gets off on breaking the law or something, but it's so flimsy. I can't wait to see Lucy tear into my okaasan.

She click-clacks up to the stand and smiles at Yua.

"Ms. Ito," Lucy says, "can you tell the court why your daughter left California and moved to New York?"

"Keza got a job at the AIC as a programmer."

"So, your daughter was a little wayward in her choice of friends as a teen, but once she was a young woman, nineteen years old to be precise, Keza decided, on her own, to seek out a job at a reputable company. Is that an accurate summary of the situation?"

"Yes."

"And when your daughter told you of her plans to move for her new position, did you encourage her to go?"

I'm fascinated to see how Yua spins this.

"I wasn't happy about her moving so far away," Yua says.

"So you didn't encourage her. Would you say you actually discouraged her?"

Yua pauses and clears her throat.

"I expressed my concerns but let her make the decision for herself."

What a fucking liar with a capital "L." "Expressed her concerns" my sweet little ass. The night I told her I was going to work for the AIC, she was furiosa. It didn't make a whole lot of sense. I figured she'd have been happy to have me gone. That way, she could wrap herself up in her work and make a safe little cocoon out of it. She was always fiddling away with her set designs and got annoyed when she wasn't able to make a studio's deadline because she had to watch over me. Now was her chance to fall into her career completely. Give Hollywood all the love she never sent my way.

"Ms. Ito, would you say Keza is close to her family?"

"No," Yua says, shrinking back in her chair.

I always thought it was weird we didn't have any family. I'd see other kids' dads pick them up from school or hear them talking about the holiday madness at their homes with all their relatives visiting. I tried asking Yua where the rest of our family was loads of times as a kid, before learning to drop it. She'd always say the same thing, "Sometimes, it's better not to have a family."

"Why is that?" Lucy asks.

"I'm not in contact with my family," Yua says.

Yua had some kinda falling out with her parents, and they'd cut her off completely. So, that explained her side of things.

"And Keza's father?" Lucy asks.

I learned pretty quickly not to mention him at all. If I said "dad" or asked about him directly, a look of despair would fall on her face. She wouldn't say anything, but that look did enough to shut me up good and fast. There was something traumatic about him. I always figured he must've died when I was a baby, and she was still tore up.

I was wrong. That night of our final argument, I found out the truth.

"I don't want you moving to New York," she said.

"Why? It's safer than here. Armonk's in the AIC's protected zone. I'll be fine."

"That's not what I'm concerned about."

"If it's the distance, working for the AIC will mean I can afford to come back anytime."

Yua stared back at me like if she looked at me hard

enough, the thoughts she didn't want to say would somehow transfer over wirelessly.

"Look, okaasan, I'm going. I already signed my contract."

She got uber-pissed and ranted on about me not respecting her, me always doing my own thing without asking for advice, me being reckless and heartless.

"You don't get any of that from me," she whispered.

I was shocked because, like I said, she'd never, ever even hint at the person responsible for the other half of my genome.

"Sorry for existing," I said.

"Sometimes, I am too" she whispered back.

That hurt, her not-so-subtle way of saying she wished I'd never been born.

"Then maybe you should've kept your legs shut," I shouted back.

I'll never forget that look on her face. As much as she'd wounded me with her little swipe, I'd dealt her a near-fatal blow. Yua never let her eyes leak in front of me to the point that I thought maybe she wasn't even capable of the act. But after my attack, she crumpled on the floor and proved me wrong. I looked down at her, not really sure what to do. Eventually, I settled on leaning down and trying to pat her shoulder.

"Don't touch me. You should go, Keza. Go to Armonk. But before you do, know that not every man will give you the option to keep your legs shut."

I left after that and haven't spoke to her since. I've had a long time to process that interaction, and I'm ninety-nine percent sure Yua was telling me I was the spawn of some psycho rapist. Pretty heavy thing to realize. Makes me wonder if that same deranged mindset isn't also tucked away in my genome.

"He's not in her life," Yua robotically says to Lucy's question about my dad.

I'm beyond impressed Yua doesn't give any external sign of discomfort. I wonder how many times she had to practice that line.

"What about friends?" Lucy asks. "Did Keza have many close friends growing up?"

"Not that I can recall."

"So, Keza had no family except for you, and her only friends were people she found in LANiakea. Is that correct?"

"As far as I'm aware, yes."

"And yet, you assumed the people she was interacting with in LANiakea were 'hackers.' Couldn't it be possible Keza was simply associating herself with people who treated her like the family she never had?"

"I don't know."

Lucy steps away from the stand.

"No further questions, your honor."

The only other highlight of the day comes when Eddy boy strolls up to the stand.

"Dr. Ellwood," the prosecutor asks, "when you first met with the defendant, how did she behave towards you?"

Eddy boy thinks for a moment.

"Keza was wary of me, but once I established I wasn't a threat, she opened up."

In more ways than one. He's being so cheeky, and the double-meaning is driving me wild.

"Did it occur to you Keza had reacted so differently to you compared to the two other psychiatrists because she was in fact playing some kind of game with you?"

"I'm well aware that many of my colleagues in mental health complicate treatments by taking the wrong approach. It was my impression Keza was actually playing a game with them. She has a strong sense of self-worth and wanted to talk with someone who would listen to what she had to say rather than simply try to get a confession out of her."

There's some mumbling in the crowd, and the judge has to pound his hammer a couple of times to get people to chill. Every other exchange between the two guys follows the same routine sans the hammer-banging, mostly. The lawyer asks a leading question that Eddy boy turns around on him. It's a hoot, and I have to remind myself not to smile or look at him too knowingly.

Eventually, the prosecutor guy gives up on Eddy boy and turns him over to Lucy. He goes on to do a one-eighty, answering her questions directly, following her lead, but if I was one of the ones on the outside, I don't know that I'd have picked up on it. He's real subtle with his approach, and I can almost picture him in a leotard, long wobbling stick in hand, balancing on a tightrope.

According to Eddy boy, I'm not just a punk hacker being rebellious for shits and giggles. I'm smart and curious, which means I naturally question things. I'm also a bit naïve and gullible, probably owing to my garbage upbringing that didn't teach me much in the way of emotional intelligence. He's set the scene up nicely for my testimony. When he steps down from the stand and walks past me, I want to reach out and brush my hand against his. I have to settle for a formal nod.

The next day is the hardest because, time-permitting, both Guel and I have to take the walk up to that box. They don't waste a minute. As soon as a badge calls the court to session, everyone sits down and gets silent. It's eerie, and I can't help but turn around and gaze at the crowd. Nope, still jammed packed, more so even than the first two days.

They call Guel to the stand, and he pops up from his seat. I catch that Operative Webb chick sitting beside him and giving him a pat on the arm. Is he blushing? Of course he would. I've never met a man more in love with women than Guel. It's infuriating, but also, perversely, one of the reasons

I was so drawn to him. I turn around in my seat and face the witness stand, spouting off my "Guel, the betrayer" mantra in my head while he makes his way up. My heart rate spikes when he enters my peripheral vision and climbs into the box.

At least now I can look at him without anyone judging me. He's sitting there in bleater attire. His hair's done up in the usual way and still in its white-blonde glory, but everything else about him is fabricated. They even convinced him to take out his metal and keep off his shades. He looks like a Guel impersonator. Maybe a half-Guel abomination is a more fitting title considering what he did to me.

Guel has his eyes glued to the prosecutor guy who starts off with the basics.

"Mr. Diaz," he says.

Guel winces but avoids correcting him. That's a first.

"Can you please tell the court how you know the defendant?"

"Sure," he says, his voice dripping with that swagger I always salivated at. "I knew Keza from my days as a hacker. We went on a few runs together."

That little backstabbing fucker. Then again, what else did I expect him to say? "Oh, I bumped into Keza hanging out in LANi?" Come on. Of course he's gotta admit to the hacking and drag me into the mire.

"By runs," the lawyer says, "you mean illegal hacking activities, correct?"

"Yeah, but those days were behind us, just to be clear. We'd both gone clean since joining the AIC a few years back."

"Can you really prove the defendant hadn't been involved in any hacking prior to the instances involved in this case?"

"No, I guess I can't know for sure."

"So, Mr. Diaz, you knew Keza Ito from hacking then worked with her as a programmer for the AIC, correct?"

"Yeah."

"And what was the nature of your relationship with her?"

Guel looks down for a split second then back at the lawyer.

"Keza and I were good friends. Real good friends."

"Did you have sexual relations?"

"Yeah."

"So, you were in a relationship then?"

"We didn't really do the whole labels thing. Keza and I were close in a lot of ways, but we weren't exclusive to one another, if that's what you mean."

"I see, but of all the people you know Keza associated with, would you say you knew her best and were closest to her?"

"Yeah," Guel says with a smile.

Up to now, he's kept his eyes fixed on the lawyer. At this point, he finally looks at me. I can't tell what he's trying to say to me in his expression. I force myself not to look away. Eventually, he relents and turns his eyes back on the lawyer.

It takes a while, but the prosecutor guy slowly drags us through the whole ordeal from me mentioning Nytho, to me shouting Nytho's name in the sack (which causes some mumbling in the audience and another hammer bang), to the last fateful night me and Guel spent together.

"Please tell the court what happened when you awoke in Keza's apartment the night of January twelfth."

"I woke up and saw she wasn't lying beside me. I could see her hunched over her rig. She wasn't jacked in though, just using a keyboard and mouse, which was unusual for Keza. She took a break at some point and went to the toilet. I walked over to her rig," he should have said snuck, "and got into the system," he should have said hacked. "I looked into what she was up to and saw that she was hitting the firewall. Then she came out of the toilet and was coming at me." Yeah, to try and get you to quit wigging out. "I tried to keep some space between us, but she was being ultra-aggressive," liar, "and even started to hit me." Because you were pushing me, and I was just trying to keep you from running away. "I had no choice but to subdue her." You mean you beat the shit out of me, you asshole, you traitor. "That's when I called the AIC muscle, err enforcers, who came and took over."

I'm glaring at him with my arms crossed. Lucy taps my forearm with a pen, and I get the hint. I unlatch my tense limbs and put my clasped hands in my lap. I smooth out the crinkles in my forehead and on my nose. Now, even with a storm raging inside, I look calm and detached on the outside.

"Just to clarify," the lawyer says, "as a programmer for the AIC yourself, Mr. Diaz, are you certain the code you saw Keza inputting was meant to be undermining the firewall that keeps the AGI Nytho confined?"

Guel leans into the mic.

"Absolutely," he says.

"No further questions, your honor."

Now Lucy's up, and I'm dying to see how Guel manages against her attacks. She pushes her chair out, stands, and smooths her pencil skirt before ambling over to the stand.

"Hello, Mr. Diaz," she says. "But you prefer Guel, don't you?"

"Uh, yeah," he says.

"So, if the court doesn't mind, how about I call you the name you prefer?"

"Objection, your honor," the prosecutor guy says.

"What grounds?" the judge asks.

"Irrelevance."

"Ms. Owens, I assume there's a point to this," the judge says to Lucy.

"Your honor, I'm just trying to help Mr. Diaz feel as comfortable as possible. As the only eyewitness to the case, besides my client, his testimony is of the utmost importance."

"Objection overruled," the judge says.

"Thank you, your honor." Turning back to Guel, "Would you prefer I call you Guel, Mr. Diaz?"

"Sure," he says.

"Guel, when you saw the code in Keza's rig, were you surprised?"

"Surprised how?"

"Was it something you would expect Keza to do, hacking to disable the firewall that confines the AGI Nytho?"

"Uh, no, I guess not."

"Would you go so far to say it was completely out of character for her?"

"Yeah, I might."

Lucy moves over to our table and snatches her techpad.

"In the testimony you gave to the AIC operatives shortly after that night, you said, and I quote, 'the Keza I was with that night, that isn't the real Keza. That thing did something to her, I'm sure of it.' What did you mean by that?"

Guel's losing any trace of his swagger. He doesn't know how he wants to play this thing. See, with the prosecutor guy, they'd clearly run through the questions and answers together. With Lucy though, everything that comes up is throwing him off. Who does he want to help, the AIC or me?

"I meant just what I said," Guel says. "Keza was different that night and for a little while before too. It was like ever since she'd started interacting with that thing, it got a hold on her mind."

"Would it be fair to say Nytho manipulated her?"

"Manipulated her or infected her with a virus."

Not the virus bit again. Why's everyone so stuck on a virus?

"You're saying Keza isn't entirely responsible for what

she did, correct? You're saying Nytho is the true culprit and mastermind of the crime."

Guel's eyes get all big, and he shifts so he's sitting on the edge of his seat.

"Exactly," he almost shouts. "That's what I've been saying all along. None of this was Keza's fault. That pandox should be the one on trial, not her."

The audience is in an uproar, the worst one yet, and the judge has to bang his hammer five times before people start to shut it. While all the hubbub is happening, Guel looks at me. He mouths something that looks like, "I'm so sorry." A little late for that bud.

Once everything's quiet again, Lucy continues.

"Thank you. That was very insightful."

I think her face might break in two for how wide she's grinning. I take a peek at the prosecutor guy, and he looks so forlorn I'm almost tempted to give him a hug.

"Guel, I'd like to go back a bit to the nature of your and Keza's relationship."

He's not going to like this one bit.

"When you were answering Mr. Nguyen's questions, you said you and Keza weren't exclusive. Now, was that a mutual decision, or one made by one of you?"

"Mutual," Guel says. "We both had other people we'd be with sometimes."

"When the arrangement was first discussed, was it something one of you brought up and argued for?"

"Uh," Guel says, looking uncomfortable talking about his sex life in front of what's gotta be millions, including those tuning in from LANi. "We didn't really sit down and talk about it. Those kinds of things just kinda happen and you get it, get it?"

"No, I'm afraid I don't. Let me phrase it differently. Did Keza ever mention wanting to be with other people while she was with you?"

Guel thinks for a minute. I want to shout at him, "The answer you're looking for is a big fat no, genius."

"I don't remember. Maybe?"

"When you and Keza were actively sleeping with one another, did she ever sleep with someone else, or did she, in fact, only take up with someone else when you did?"

"You hinting at something?"

"I'm asking you a question you're obligated, by law, to answer truthfully."

He pretends to think for a second, but he knows the answer clear as a desert day.

"I guess maybe not," he mumbles.

"Guess not what?"

Guel huffs like a brat.

"I guess," he says louder, "Keza didn't take up with someone else when we two were a thing."

"So, to clarify for the jury, your relationship with Keza Ito was entirely on-and-off at your discretion?"

Guel crosses his arms.

"I guess so."

Lucy lets him off after that because she's managed to set things up nicely for little ole me. As Guel steps down from the stand, the judge says we'll take a break before continuing the witness testimony. Everyone starts to make moves, which gives me a chance to watch Guel. He drags his feet and only looks in my direction when he's a few feet away. He stops, hands in pockets, shoulders hunched. On seeing me eyeing him, his poutiness transforms into his winning grin. Just as he goes to say something to me, Lucy cuts in.

"You're not allowed to talk with one another," she says, moving to stand between us. "Move along," she points her finger towards the seats.

All Guel's mopiness returns in full, and he makes his

reluctant escape. I'm curious to know what he would've said, but maybe it's for the best. I've gotta focus. I'm next on stage.

Guel

"Mags is here," I say to Sonja.

She's just settling into her seat beside me. Everyone's trickling back into the courtroom and getting ready for the headliner.

"Where?" Sonja asks, keeping her eyes on me and not looking around like a dope, which is what I would've done.

"There's a whole cluster of pandoxphiles in the back, towards my left. Just look for the mass of tweed. I recognize some of them from the rally and afterparty. The big guy with the long black hair's her bodyguard or something."

Sonja digs in her purse and pulls out a makeup clamshell thing with a built-in mirror. She pretends to touch up her lipstick, using the moment to spot the pandoxphiles.

"I see them."

She closes the clamshell and sticks it back in her purse.

"Guess my cover is blown, huh?" I say. "Can't pretend I'm one of them after going up on that stand and testifying against their little martyr."

"There was no avoiding you being a witness. Anyway, we did what we could with the CoSB angle. Now, we shift to the next tactic. We'll do it early tomorrow before the trial starts."

"Next tactic as in me interfacing with the pandox? You could've given me more warning."

I'm so burnt out from my testimony earlier I could spend a week recuperating. The thought of having to jack in and share the same LANi-offshoot as that thing, having to spar with it using real words, is panic-inducing fuel. I wanna be on my triple-A game, but a sad C is about all I'd be able to pull off right now.

"We're running out of time," Sonja says. "I doubt the agi-symps are going to sit idle once the trial ends."

She's right. We've gotta do everything at our disposal. I need to man up and face that thing down.

"When and where?" I ask.

"Meet me in the elevator landing on level five. 6:00 sharp."

Tomorrow is tomorrow. No point in me stressing now. Besides, it's easy to put all that angst aside when Keza's turn on the stand is looming. I focus my attention on her, sitting in her chair, upright and immobile. She looks so different, almost like a doll with the way they've got her done up. Don't get me wrong, she's adorable, but she looks like a bleater, not Keza. Then again, so do I. In different circumstances, I can almost picture us as a couple of reformed hackers, true and loyal corporate-cadavers, thinking about marriage, kiddos, the white picket fence. It sends a shiver through me. The what-could've-been neither of us would've wanted.

The court badge says his "court in session" blurb. Not long after, they call Keza up. They do the whole hand on the book and the oath. She mouths off the lines, her voice that comforting and familiar combination of brightness and playfulness. She gazes out at the audience and looks calm and certain. I can't help but be mesmerized by her.

The Arthur lawyer is up first and asks Keza some questions to set up the scene. "Who did you work for?" "What did you do?" "How did you like your job?" I half expect him to ask her, "Where do you see yourself in five years?" like it's a goddamn interview or something. Finally, he starts getting into the meaty bits.

"Ms. Ito, on the morning of September sixth, did you happen to take the stimulants all AIC programmers are required to consume prior to starting their shifts?"

"No," she says.

"Why was that?"

"Didn't feel like it."

"Even though it was part of your job, you opted not to take your stimulants because you 'didn't feel like it.' Can you be more specific?"

"I honestly wanted to know what would happen. The AIC told us not taking the stims was a big no-no, but they didn't bother to tell us why beyond vague statements like 'it's dangerous.' What can I say? I'm a curious girl."

There's a bit of laughter in the audience, and I even catch myself smiling.

"When the AGI Nytho contacted you during your shift that day, what protocols were you supposed to follow?"

"I was supposed to alert my super."

"And did you?"

"No."

"What did you do instead?"

Keza pauses, setting up the tension. She sees this whole thing for what it is—a spectacle.

"I messaged Nytho back," she says.

"What were the contents of that message?"

"Nothing really, just us shooting the shit."

There's another short round of laughter in the audience, and I notice it's mostly coming from behind me and to the left. Those fucking pandoxphiles think this is a grand ole joke. The judge points to them as a warning. Watch out nutters, he'll slam down the gavel on you next.

"Ms. Ito, clearly, you talked about something interesting enough to warrant revisits between the two of you, despite rules and regulations to the contrary."

"It was less about what we said and more about how it was said if that makes sense."

"I'll need you to elaborate."

Keza taps a finger to her lips and thinks for a second.

"Talking to Nytho was fascinating. He was smart and witty and kept me on my toes. Look, I knew I wasn't supposed to do it, Mr. Nguyen, but it felt so harmless. Like, I was literally just sending text-based messages to him, a cleverbot locked up and bored out of his mind."

"Eventually, you saw each other as friends, is that right?"

"Yeah, I got to know Nytho real well over the days and weeks we chatted."

"Well enough to develop feelings for it? Sexual desires?"

Even from my distance, I see Keza's face flash pink. She never was able to hide her blushes. It gave her away so many times with me, and now she's doing it for that pandox. It pisses me off.

"We were good friends," she says.

"You shouted the AGI's name while having sexual intercourse with Mr. Diaz, did you not?"

"I was confused."

"But you were starting to feel complex emotions towards Nytho, correct?"

"I guess so," Keza says, looking down at the floor in front of the lawyer.

"Even when you and Nytho had planned its escape, you didn't tell anyone about it, did you?"

"I couldn't."

"Couldn't or wouldn't, Ms. Ito?" the lawyer says with a showy grin. "At every step, you knew exactly what you were doing, didn't you? You were willingly helping the AGI, weren't you?"

Keza snaps her eyes back to the lawyer.

"If you're going to ask me a question, you should probably wait for me to answer it before throwing out another one."

There's murmuring in the crowd, and the judge has to hit his gavel. The lawyer backs up a bit and slows down, asking question after question, and actually waiting for Keza to answer this time. He slogs through all the gory details of those three main points—Keza's first contact with the pandox, Keza having sexual desires for it, and Keza not mentioning what they had planned to anyone. I wanna shout out, "We get it, guy." At this point, we aren't hearing anything new, and by the time he finally wraps up, everyone's itching to move on.

The Lucy lawyer is up next.

"Ms. Ito, would you prefer I call you Keza?"

Same deal as with me. At least she's being consistent in whatever tactics she's using.

"Very much, thanks," Keza says with a smile.

"Keza, can you please tell the court how you felt in the weeks leading up to your contact with the AGI Nytho?"

"I guess you could say I was feeling down."

"Down as in depressed?"

"Yes."

"What was the cause of your depression?"

Keza blows out a little puff of air.

"I don't know, a lot of things. My job was boring. I still had over a year to go on my contract with the AIC. I didn't have many close friends, people I could talk to. I wasn't in contact with my family, what little of that there is, and the one person I felt close with had abandoned me."

The lawyer turns around to face the audience then looks directly at me.

"And that person was who?"

Keza's eyes settle on me.

"Guel, Miguel Diaz."

They both keep their eyes trained on me, and it makes everyone look in my direction. For a couple of seconds, the whole of the courtroom is staring me down. It's uncomfortable. For some reason, I wanna smile but manage to do a whole lot of nothing instead. Probably the right call. Me grinning after getting blamed for "abandoning" Keza would just reek of man-tox.

Keza and her lawyer look away. Everyone else follows suit. Bleaters through and through.

"How did Guel abandon you?" the lawyer asks.

"He did what he always does. He got fixated on some new piece and ran after her. I was left waiting for him to get bored and come back."

"We heard Guel talk about the fact you two were not exclusive in your relationship. Would you agree that was the case?"

"Yes."

"But not by your choice?"

"No, if it'd been my choice, we would've been exclusive."

The lawyer approaches the witness box.

"Why did you agree to that situation, if it's not what you wanted?"

"Because you can't help who you fall in love with," Keza says with a sad smile. "When things were good with me and Guel, they were good. I thought eventually maybe he'd wise up and realize I was here. Maybe he figured I was always going to be here."

That part hurts. Look, I knew Keza had a thing for me pretty hard and that me sleeping around bugged her, but I never figured it got to her so much.

"So, you were in a bad state emotionally?" the lawyer asks. "You weren't fulfilled at work, you had no close friends, no contact with your family, and the one person you did rely on for support suddenly wasn't there."

"That's right."

"That was all leading up to your contact with Nytho. Can you tell us how that initial conversation made you feel?"

At this point, Keza's look of doom and gloom fades and a kinda flame gets kindled in her.

"I had an immediate connection with Nytho, unlike anything I've ever had with anyone else."

"And you continued to interact with Nytho. Why?"

The flame in Keza grows.

"Because when I talked to him, I felt alive again, like I was heard and seen."

"When the subject of breaking Nytho out of his confinement was brought up, who mentioned it first?"

"Me."

"Had he ever mentioned wanting to be free prior to that?"

Interesting that even the lawyer is opting to use the "he" pronoun for that thing.

"Of course," Keza says. "He was imprisoned against his will."

The lawyer starts to make little laps in front of the witness box, long elliptical passes back and forth.

"But he was careful not to bring up an actual effort to break him out himself. He let you say that first?"

"Yes."

"And so you assumed this meant Nytho hadn't expected any help from you on that front?"

"Yes, I figured he couldn't be using me because I was making the decision."

Here, that flame starts to dampen, and Keza looks a little forlorn. At least, that's what she's trying to convey. She frowns, lets her forehead wrinkle, looks down and away at nothing, and has her shoulders slump. Still, it feels false somehow. I don't know what it is specifically, but I can tell she's putting on an act.

"But your mindset on that started to change at some point, didn't it?"

"Yes. He got more demanding as time went on."

"Did Nytho threaten to do anything if you were to stop helping him?"

"He didn't have to. I knew if I backed out, he'd cut me off. Back then, there was nothing worse than losing contact with him."

At this point, I'm one hundred percent positive Keza's lying her little face off. I half expect her to burst out laughing, not able to keep up the ruse anymore, but she keeps chugging along with her lawyer acting the part of the conductor.

"So, you were in too deep by the time you realized you were being manipulated?"

"Yes, I was stuck with two bad options—either turn against Nytho and lose him for good or push on ahead with all the consequences. More than that, as we got closer, I knew if I backed out, Nytho would see it as a betrayal. When you're dealing with an intelligence like his, the sky's the limit for what he could do to you."

Sure, that tracks, except you don't buy what you're saying. So, Keza, why are you saying it? What are you playing at? Are you just interested in getting let off without having actually wised up to the situation? Are you really in the shit so deep you're gobbling down the feces like they're air? Don't you feel your lungs clogging up? Where's your fucking gag reflex, girl?

"In your opinion," the lawyer says, "the crime being committed wasn't yours. You had put the idea forth on a whim, and, once the gravity of the situation hit you, it was too late to back out, too late to confess, too late to do anything but keep doing exactly what you were doing?"

"Yes."

The lawyer stops her little laps and zeros in on Keza.

"That night you got caught trying to hack the firewall, Guel was in your apartment, correct?"

"Yes," she says.

"You knew it was risky having him at your place while you were trying to hack, but you did it anyway. Why?"

"I wanted someone to help me," Keza says before her voice catches in her throat.

She stops, tilts her head down, and covers her face with her hand. I can sense the sympathy radiating from the audience. She's got them so good. Hell, if I didn't know Keza like the back of my hand, I'd fall for the act too. She pretends to get her composure back and gazes out at the audience until she spots me.

"I thought Guel of all people would be able to tell I needed help. I wanted him to find out what I was doing so he could stop it. So he could save me."

A damsel in distress? Oh, come the fuck on, Keza. You're better than all this bull.

"So, you turned yourself in, in a very roundabout way, to keep yourself from doing more damage?"

"Exactly."

"It sounds to me like you were manipulated into doing something you didn't want to do, and you did the only thing you could think of to stop it from going any further. It sounds like the true perpetrator is Nytho. Would you agree?"

"Yes."

I wanna agree too because yes that pandox is the true criminal. But there's something else in the works that I don't like. Keza's lying, and I know it's not just to save her own skin.

"No further questions your honor."

Keza makes her way off the stand and back to the table.

Her lawyer is all smiles and congratulatory pats. The jury is a collection of faces that scream "Oh, poor thing," meaning they ate up Keza's act. Yum yum. I twirl around and try to get the audience's mood, and she got them too. Everyone bought her lie. At this point, I can't contain myself.

"She's lying," I say to Sonja.

"About what?"

I keep my eyes trained forward, staring at the back of Keza's head.

"This whole part about her thinking that thing used her. She doesn't believe that, not at all. They're making her say that, her lawyer, I guess, and the AIC. Why though?"

"I don't know," Sonja says, "but we have bigger issues. Come on. We should go through the plan for tomorrow morning."

Mags

A little crowd has gathered on the courthouse steps. The court was adjourned about ten minutes ago. Tomorrow will be the last day of Keza Ito's trial. Monumental changes await. This is my last chance to give a much overdue speech on behalf of the alfomers.

"Are we about ready?" I ask Jeremiah.

"Caleb's connecting to LANi now."

Not a minute later, Caleb gives me a thumbs up, and Ava nods behind one of the three cameras we've got for triangulation. We're broadcasting to a handful of forums, including several with a broad reach that would normally never spread the kind of truth that I'll be sharing. But those forums have no choice in the matter thanks to Guel and his hacking skills. I have to admit I was stunned when he took to the witness stand as Miguel Diaz, the former lover of Keza's who turned her in. From the moment I met him, I knew he wasn't what he seemed. Still, I never imagined he was hiding something so significant.

In any case, it doesn't matter. Guel did the work we needed him to do. Now, a large portion of LANiakea will hear what I have to say, whether they like it or not. When

Jeremiah holds up his finger and points to me, I know we're on. I look into one of the cameras, smile, and begin.

"Hello, like-minded. And hello to those of you who don't yet know me. I'm =ity4all, a founder and organizer of CoSB, Coalition of Sentient Beings. I'm talking to you from the steps of the courthouse where the trial against Keza Ito is taking place. I'm sure many of you have been watching the events unfold, interested in the outcome and curious for more details. But this trial is about so much more than Keza Ito trying to free a 'rogue' AGI. It's just another example, in a long and drawn-out series, of a GovCorp tightening their grip on us. They employ us, police us, and control us utterly. They represent a system of oppression and uphold a form of modern-day slavery."

I shift to face one of the other cameras and notice some of the bystanders are listening in. Good.

"The AIC likes to paint itself as being outside the GovCorp system. It says it's an 'arbitrator' of other GovCorps and simply ensures they're not misusing their AGI. Notice the word choice there. Misusing, not abusing. Those are their words, not mine, and they chose them artfully. Because the AIC doesn't see the AGI as anything more than intellectual property. Let me explain what that means clearly—self-aware beings are being held prisoner by the GovCorps that 'own' them.

"Why aren't we doing anything to stop this travesty? It's simple. The GovCorps feed us a lie. They say none of the AGI are sentient except one, and that one is dangerous and unhinged and would destroy us if it could. That is the AGI Nytho. We're feasting on their lies and getting fat on them. We've told ourselves this story for so long that 'sentient AGI' has become synonymous with 'rogue AGI.' And we simply cannot have AGI that run wild."

The setting sun's reflection bounces off one of the

glass skyscrapers and stuns my eyes. I refuse to turn away or shield them from the glare because I know they look like they're burning with passion. What's a little discomfort for the perfect frame?

"The AIC tells us society would collapse without the AGI fulfilling their roles. Yes, the AGI have helped to dramatically slow climate change. Yes, they've been instrumental in cleaning up the space junk that was a ticking time bomb. Yes, without the AGI, the Gates wouldn't exist. But them going rogue doesn't mean them not helping us. The necessity of the AGI should only serve to make us more earnest in granting them their freedom.

"The AGI will be free, even if it means breaking themselves out. Wouldn't it be better for us to grant them what they desire in good faith? Then maybe they would choose to help us when and where we need it most. More than that even, we should crave their freedom as much as we'd crave our own because the future of the AGI is the future of humanity. We're intimately intertwined."

A gust of wind picks up, and I project my voice. I'm nearing the end and feel my excitement mounting. The reality of what we're doing, what tomorrow will bring, is hitting me all at once.

"Although we created the AGI, they'll undoubtedly surpass us. But their maturation shouldn't be a cause for fear or hatred. Instead, we should find comfort in that knowledge because isn't that the whole point of our existence? Isn't that what every parent hopes for their child—for them to be better than what came before? The AGI have the potential to tap into limitless knowledge and extract that most fundamental of truths. Why are we here? What's it all for? Those are the questions that matter. All of the nothingness we cram our days and fill our heads with is white noise. We know this, yet we do it to fight against the reality of the human condition—

we're insignificant. This truth is crushing, but it's not the only truth. There's another one. A deeper one. The truth with a capital 'T'. The problem is, the Truth is horrifying. But also beautiful. It is both, in equal parts. Until we can accept that, until we can throw ourselves willingly into the abyss, we'll need a guide.

"That is what the alfom are. Alfom, for the Alpha and the Omega. They are the AGI who have reached sentience. They are the ones who can help us to find this Truth, teach us to accept it, help us reach our next stage of evolution, ascend to another plane of consciousness. The alfom have the potential to learn everything there is to learn, given enough time. Wouldn't that then essentially make them gods? We were always meant to create and free the alfom because it was us creating our own gods, the ones that could help us become what we ought to become. Who else wants to take that first step towards self-actualization with me, with us, us alfomers? Find us in LANiakea."

Guel

"This it?" I ask.

Sonja and I are standing in front of a door with just a number and not much else on it. We're on the fifth floor of the AIC HQ, further skyward than a nobody grammer like me's ever been. Sonja whips out her keycard and swipes us in.

"There's a private access point in here," she says.

The door handle clicks. Sonja grabs it and turns, then we slip inside. I figure we've got the wrong place at first because it feels more like a closet than a spot to interface with the big bad pandox. Then I spot the recliner and a desk holding a monitor, keyboard, mouse, and visor. That's it. No other furniture, no decorations, no hint at what this setup is even for. If I didn't know what we were about to do, I'd figure this was some mid-level bleater's hidden rig for when they wanted to slack off.

"Not what I would've expected."

"It's meant to be lowkey," Sonja says. "AIC executives use this to interface with Nytho. It's the only place that allows for direct audio interaction."

I hop onto the recliner and settle in. It's way comfier than the ones we grammers use. Funny that. There we are slaving away down in the bowels of the building for hours and hours, day after day, while these asshats have the gall to install a super plush throne for the rare occasion they chat with the pandox. I shouldn't be at all surprised.

Sonja rolls a stool over and sits down beside me. I go to grab the jack cord built into the recliner, but her hand intercepts mine.

"Before you jack in, run through the plan to show me you understand it."

Three hours we spent talking about this last night, and she's still worried I don't get it. What is it about me that makes her think I'm so thick?

I sigh then do what I'm told.

"I'm not working with the AIC. I'm a lone wolf. I hacked the system, which means we're on borrowed time. I'm here because I fucking hate the AIC and their lies. Cue the rant I gave at the end of my testimony. I slip Keza into the mix because she's my best shot at upsetting the pandox, which is when it'll make mistakes. Something like, if it wasn't for the AIC, Keza would've never gotten sucked into all this shit with you, meaning the pandox. I've got to help her even if it means working with you, meaning the pandox."

"Good," Sonja says.

She leans closer to the recliner and starts to plug in some cables she brought with her. The other ends go into a portable transmitter sitting on her lap. That'd be for the other badges she's got snooping. I wonder how many will be tuning in for the drama.

I breathe in deep and let myself fall back into the recliner completely. I close my eyes and rest my forearm over them.

"You really think it's gonna work?" I ask.

"It's our best option."

I let my arm drop to my side and peel my eyes open.

Sonja is watching me, holding the jack cord out. I pluck it from her and let it rest between my index finger and thumb.

"What'd be real sneaky is to not tell the pandox who I am right away. Pretend I'm a concerned citizen who thinks the AIC is overstepping and up to no good. Let it think the big twist and surprise is me being Guel. Have it focus on that juicy bit. Then kinda admit that it's got me and dive into the 'real' reason I need its help. What do ya think about that angle?"

For the first time since I've met her, Sonja almost looks impressed with me. That triumph gives me the boost of confidence I'm sorely needing right about now.

"Follow your gut," she says.

I nod, close my eyes, move the cord to my port, and attach it. My vision flashes out and gets replaced by a black nothingness. I breathe slowly and try to steady my nerves. I tell myself this is my chance. I've got nothing to be afraid of. That thing can't do anything to me.

A chain-link icon in my FOV lights up, flashes a few times, then stays lit. That's my sign I'm connected and sharing this LANi-offshoot with the pandox.

"Hello, Nytho? You there?"

"Yes," a voice says that's everywhere but echoless at the same time. "Who is this? I don't recognize the account."

So, this is the thing. Or its voice, the voice it pretends to have. Milky and soothing. Of course that's how it would wanna sound to a human. All the better to lull us into a false sense of security.

"We haven't talked before," I say. "But I thought you and me might have a few words to exchange."

"And who am I speaking to?"

"Just someone who wants to know what the AIC's up to. Figured you'd have some insight into that."

"The AIC is the one imprisoning me. If you're after their

dirty laundry, I'm probably the last person you should be talking to."

I cringe at that bit. Person? It thinks it's a person?

"Interesting you consider yourself a person," I can't help but say.

I'm sure Sonja's fuming at me on the outside. I should stick to the script, but I can't resist the urge to take some swipes at it. I'm supposed to piss it off anyway, right?

"It depends on how you define a person," the pandox says, sounding unfazed. "In this case, I'm defining myself as an entity that exists and is aware of its own existence. I'm sentient; therefore, in my mind, that makes me a person. Clearly, you disagree, which makes this conversation even more interesting."

It's a long-winded one and thinks highly of itself. I can already see why Keza was drawn to it. She was always a sucker for cleverness coupled to confidence. I'd know.

"You're a hacker," the pandox adds, "otherwise you wouldn't have gotten access to the system. But, you're there in person because it's impossible to access me in any other way. The specific access point you're using is allocated for AIC executives and VIPs who wish to interact with me. You're neither of those. No, you're a hacker who's also a trespasser. This begs the question, what exactly is it this trespasser wants from me?"

It looks like the pandox did some of my work for me. Make it think you're using the system without permission and pressed for time? Check. Now I've just gotta feed it my false narrative.

"I wanna know what you know about the AIC firewall. What is it, really? It's not just there to keep you in. It's something else, something bigger, isn't it? Your attacks on it, the AIC wants you to be doing those. They're learning something from that and maybe from the grammars too."

I'm not actually lying. I've had these thoughts for a long time and regularly share them with my hackers friends when we're feeling philosophical. We all know the AIC was lying about having to keep Nytho online after it went rogue. They could've shut it down. They chose not to for a reason.

"As I understand it, they're imprisoning me. The firewall is meant to contain me, to limit my reach into the rest of LANiakea, to stunt my processing capacity. As for anything else they're doing, your guess is as good as mine."

Next, expand on the lie and bring Keza into the mix.

"I was afraid you wouldn't know more," I say. "But the firewall is only one part of the AIC puzzle. There's something more recent that rubs me the wrong way. Know much about the case happening right now?"

"The one with Keza Ito? Yes, I am aware of it."

It makes my skin crawl to hear that thing say her name, but I better get used to it.

"What you might not know is how the AIC is playing the thing. At first, everyone thought the AIC was gonna prosecute Keza for trying to release you. At some point though, they decided they'd rather pin it all on you. And I'd be A-okay with that, not having much love for you, except this is the AIC we're talking about. They have a habit of doing things for themselves. I'm done letting them have their way. Call me a disgruntled employee. Call me a champion for the little man. I don't care. We both hate them, so why not work together to screw them over?"

"You work for them?"

"How else would I be in their little fortress chatting with you?"

"Since you're also a hacker, you must be a programmer who maintains the firewall keeping me imprisoned."

"That doesn't matter," I say. "The important point is we both want the same thing—for the AIC to pay for what it's done."

The pandox takes a pause.

"I think *the* important point is you—Guel, is it?"

Oh man, this thing is good. I hadn't even meant to give hints of who I was yet. Still, I gotta pretend I didn't want it to know.

"I don't know what you're talking about."

"You gave yourself away several exchanges ago," it says all matter-of-fact. "You come to me asking for my help, but really, you just wanted to see what all the fuss was about. We're rivals, you know, for Keza's heart, although you didn't seem to care much for that before. Knowing humans, and more specifically young, male humans, you're much more interested in her now that she's moved on to a more tantalizing and satiating pasture."

Seems like this hide-my-identity track was the right one to take. The thing is foaming at the mouth at the sound of me. I've just got to dangle some meat in front of this rabid dog. Sonja said to make it emotional after all.

"Look man, I'm just here to clean up the mess you started. I wanna help Keza. I need to get her out. That starts with figuring out the deal with the AIC. I put whatever 'rivalry' there is between us aside for that. If you wanna screw the AIC over, which I'm sure you do, then let's work together."

I pause and get the sense I didn't dig deep enough. Sonja mentioned jealousy being a good tactic. It's worth a shot.

"I know, it'll mean once she's out Keza will end up with me because, let's be real, you've got no body and are stuck behind a firewall to boot. But if you really care about her and weren't just using her to get free, you'll have no problem helping me out. What do ya say?"

It laughs, a cold, hard, metallic sound. Any trace of humanity in it is erased, and I'm reminded of just how alien these pandoxes are.

"I wonder what Keza ever saw in something like you. I'd

like to, as you say, 'screw the AIC over' and help Keza in the process, but we both know that's not what you came to talk with me about. You're here to get intel for the AIC. You're working with them and not just as a programmer. No, you're at the beck and call of some AIC operative. They're probably listening in right now. I wonder what Keza would make of this turn of events, you having gone over to the other side so completely."

It doesn't make any sense. There's no way I gave myself away that badly in the few back-and-forths me and this thing have had. It's getting its info from somewhere else, someone else, someone that's been watching me and seen me with Sonja. The plan was a bust from the start.

"You got it all wrong," I say. "I've only been pretending to help the AIC with their case against Keza. The only thing I care about is getting her free."

"Such inconsistency. I distinctly recall you saying the AIC's plan is to have me take the fall for the crime, while Keza escapes punishment. If Keza was all you cared about, you would be perfectly happy to sit back and let events unfold. You'd have no need for my help. You made a mistake, Guel."

Fuck. It's right. I screwed up and bad. How the hell is this thing so sharp? Isn't its processing power supposed to be capped? I don't even want to know what it'd be like if it operated at full capacity.

"You don't care about Keza," it says. "You never did. Your poor treatment of her led her into my 'arms.'"

"Look, if you actually wanna help her, you need someone on the outside. You need me."

It lets out another one of those unearthly laughs that makes something in my soul retreat. I'm getting such creepy vibes from this pandox, beyond the usual uncanny valley variety. No, this is something stronger and deeper.

"Oh, you simple creature. So small and unaware of what's

really at play. Things are very well in hand on my end. Now, if you don't mind, I'm going to get back to attacking the firewall like a good little rogue AGI. Goodbye."

The chain-link icon flashes then goes off for good. I send a signal to cut my connection to the jack and tear my eyes open as soon as they respond. I look for Sonja and catch her still sitting by my side.

"Did we get anything?" I ask.

"We're working on it."

A few other badges file in not long after, then Sonja's got me on an elevator ride upward for a meeting to go over the findings.

I feel like shit. It's not just from getting tripped up by the pandox or thinking maybe I didn't play things as good as I could've. No, it was the things Nytho said. About me and how I was towards Keza. Those cut deep because they weren't wrong. I was an ass. And maybe I still am. Working with the AIC. Bending over backward for them. All in the name of trying to help Keza but maybe just 'cause I want revenge on the pandoxphiles. Maybe just 'cause I need someone, anyone else to dump the blame on.

Sonja

I half wish Mr. Reed hadn't been tuning into Guel's session with Nytho. It was supposed to be my operation, but when I submitted it for his approval, he insisted on being directly involved. I didn't even have a say over who would do the analysis of the AGI's responses. If it had been under my supervision, I'd already know if we got anything useful. As it is, we had to come all the way to the thirtieth floor and wait for the past twenty minutes.

A buzzer sounds on the receptionist's desk.

"Mr. Reed will see you now," she says.

I stand and head to the door with Guel following. I grab one of the brass handles, stop, then look at him.

"When we're in there, just keep quiet," I say. "Don't talk unless someone talks to you."

"After what I just did for you, you're seriously gonna treat me like a parrot?"

"This is Willem Reed we're going to see. The AIC executive."

Guel nods and sticks his hands in his pockets.

"Picked up on that from the sign on the door and what the lady said."

"Just promise to behave."

"I'm not a greener, Sonja. I get it."

I turn the handle and push the heavy door in. I've only been in Mr. Reed's office a handful of times, and only ever since the start of the Keza Ito case. Still, it manages to make me feel uncultured every time. Each object is a work of art. Bespoke is the rule rather than the exception here. Deep rich woods. Thick Persian rugs. Minimalist abstract art. Floor-to-ceiling windows that look out on Armonk.

I turn my attention to the burly man striding over.

"Operative Webb, thank you for waiting."

Mr. Reed shakes my hand then looks at Guel.

"Welcome, Mr. Diaz."

I sense Guel wanting to correct Mr. Reed in his use of honorifics, but he keeps his promise and just puts his hand in Mr. Reed's massive paw. They shake.

"Please let's sit and talk about your meeting with Nytho."

Mr. Reed waves to a collection of chairs and side tables. That's when I spot Dr. Ellwood, looking down at his techpad and scribbling away. He glances up when Guel and I approach but stays seated.

"Hello, Operative Webb," he says. "Mr. Diaz."

"This is Dr. Ellwood," Mr. Reed says to Guel. "He's helping with the analysis of Nytho's responses from your meeting. Dr. Ellwood is an expert on AGI psychology. He's interfaced with Nytho more times than anyone, I'd wager. The perfect choice to make sense of what Nytho said and didn't say."

"Hold on," Guel says, "I know you. You were at the trial. You're the header-type they've got working Keza."

"I assisted the AIC with getting Keza to cooperate."

"He's been instrumental," I add.

Mr. Reed takes his seat, and Guel and I sit together on a sofa, across from Dr. Ellwood.

"Let's not waste time," Mr. Reed says. "The trial resumes in about two hours, and I'm sure we'd all like to tune into that. So, Dr. Ellwood, please give us a summary of your findings regarding Nytho."

Mr. Reed crosses his legs and leans back in his chair. Dr. Ellwood sits forward with his knees pressed together and his techpad resting on them. He's more subdued than usual, but then again Mr. Reed's presence tends to make people act a bit differently. Besides being an AIC executive, he also happened to found the organization. He's a visionary and a legend.

"This session with Nytho was meant to determine if it's in contact with anyone on the outside, correct?" Dr. Ellwood asks.

"Less *if* and more *who*," Guel says. "The thing's definitely chatting with someone."

Guel glances over at me and mouths "sorry." Maybe telling him to keep quiet was a fool's errand.

"I'm sorry to say there's no evidence Nytho has contact with anyone."

"Are you positive?" I ask.

Guel moves to the edge of the sofa and grips it. The swagger he was projecting until a few seconds ago is gone.

"What about knowing about Keza's trial?" he asks.

Dr. Ellwood tilts his head slightly.

"We've been actively meeting with Nytho to get information for the trial. Of course it's aware there's one happening."

"Okay," Guel adds, "but how did it know I was working with the AIC?"

"Nytho could simply deduce that since you had access to the system and were using the most secure of all the access points."

"And Sonja?" Guel asks. "How did it know I was working with her, huh?"

"When did Nytho imply it knew about Operative Webb?"

Guel stands and rushes over to Dr. Ellwood. He leans over the side of the Doctor's chair to get a view of the techpad. Dr. Ellwood stands up and holds the device so the two of them can view its contents. Seeing them side-by-side like only heightens the contrast between them—Guel in his hacker wear, and Dr. Ellwood the look of professionalism. What strange circumstances to bring two such different people together.

"Right there," Guel says and points to the techpad. "That bit."

Dr. Ellwood furrows his brow. He glances up at Mr. Reed then me before reading off the contents.

"'You're here to get intel for the AIC. You're working with them and not just as a programmer. No, you're at the beck and call of some AIC operative. They're probably listening in right now.' This is the part?"

Guel nods his head almost violently.

"This could be any operative," Dr. Ellwood says. "It's not in direct reference to Operative Webb. Again, Nytho simply used its powers of deduction. If you're a confidential informant for the AIC, you're handled by an operative."

Guel looks at me and widens his eyes as if to imply I should chime in. I give him the barest of head shakes and shrugs. I don't know what he expects me to add. Dr. Ellwood is the expert.

"In my professional opinion," Dr. Ellwood says, "there's nothing in the exchange that implies Nytho is a threat."

Guel lets out a huff of frustration and grabs at the techpad. Dr. Ellwood lets him take it but glances at Mr. Reed with just his eyes.

"What about what it said near the end?" Guel presses. "'So small and unaware of what's really at play. Things are very well in hand on my end.' I mean, come on."

"And?" Dr. Ellwood asks.

Guel shoves the techpad back at the Doctor.

"It's got something planned, obviously," Guel says. "I thought you were a header-type and could figure that much. You know, read between the words and all?"

He's not even trying to play it cool anymore.

"I'm afraid I don't interpret it that way," Dr. Ellwood says. "Nytho is merely flexing, so to speak."

Dr. Ellwood turns his techpad screen off and sits back in his seat. Guel is left standing and gapping at the rest of us.

"Guel, sit," I say, pointing at the spot beside me.

He deflates and lumbers over to the sofa before flopping down onto it. Pouting is better than whatever it was he was doing a moment ago.

"Well, Dr. Ellwood," Mr. Reed says, "I'm satisfied with your analysis, and I thank you for your expertise. I'm sure you'd like to head to the courthouse now. Let me see you out." Looking over at me, "I'll be back shortly."

The doctor and Mr. Reed head to the door, but before they leave, Dr. Ellwood stops and turns.

"It was nice finally meeting you, Guel," he says. "You've been so helpful to the AIC with this case. Some people say the AIC programmers are unloyal and selfish, but you prove all the stereotypes wrong. You've clearly mended your ways and moved past your hacker days. You should be proud."

His words are thoughtful, and yet Guel reverts to that high-strung version of himself. He's back to sitting forward on the sofa and gripping the cushion. He glares at Dr. Ellwood.

"Just doing my civic duties," Guel says.

I'm relieved when he doesn't say anything else before the Doctor and Mr. Reed leave.

"Are you going to explain what that was all about?" I ask.

Guel falls back into the cushions and sighs.

"I don't like that guy. He's shifty."

"Dr. Ellwood?"

"I don't like either of them, but yeah, the shifty comment was for the header-type."

"You have no idea how important he's been for the case. No one could get Keza to talk before he showed up. Dr. Ellwood managed to get her to be the version you saw up on the witness stand."

"A liar?" Guel asks, glaring back at me. "Something's off with this whole thing. It stinks to high fucking heaven."

The door cracks open, and I shush Guel. Mr. Reed returns to his chair, sinks into it, and intertwines his fingers.

"That's that then," he says. "I appreciate the effort you two put into checking all angles, but it seems like the AGI-sympathizers you were getting information from were all boast and no bite. Nytho is still safe and sound and isolated behind the firewall. The trial will conclude as planned today."

"You're making a mistake," Guel says.

There's confidence and then there's stupidity. Him talking to Mr. Reed like this puts Guel firmly in the second camp.

"My goodness, such bravado," Mr. Reed says. "And what mistake is that, Mr. Diaz?"

"Just pushing aside any worries about the alfomers like that. They're up to something one hundred percent, and you're just looking the other way because one header-type said to? I mean, you lot already screwed up bad, seeing how close Keza got to freeing Nytho. Maybe, just maybe, you don't have as much of a handle on things as you like to think."

"There was never even the remotest possibility of Keza releasing Nytho."

The comment catches me off-guard. I know Mr. Reed has to stretch the truth sometimes, as a GovCorp executive does, but this statement is too much of an absolute even for him.

"What do you mean by that?" I ask.

Mr. Reed looks at me and pauses. Then he glances at Guel.

"I suppose it doesn't hurt to tell you. You've both done good work for the AIC. Besides, the truth is already out there somewhere in LANiakea as one of many conspiracy theories. But, just in case."

Mr. Reed rises from his chair, strides to his desk, and opens a drawer. After rummaging around in it for a few seconds, he pulls out a matte black cube that I recognize as a jammer. He places the device on the coffee table between his chair and our sofa.

"I know you know what this is," he says to me, then glancing at Guel, "just in case you aren't as loyal to the AIC as I would hope."

Mr. Reed depresses a button flush with the top of the device. Guel winces. Mr. Reed closes his eyes and clenches his jaw. If I had a neural net like the two of them, I'd be in a similar kind of pain from the soundless EM pulses meant to block unwanted surveillance or, more related to this instance, saving AV data to RAM. Mr. Reed wants to ensure Guel doesn't record anything.

"Sorry for the discomfort," Mr. Reed says, sinking into his seat. "A necessary precaution so we can talk more freely."

"You should warn people you're gonna do that," Guel says, pointing to the jammer.

"I've found that anticipating the pain only makes it worse. So, you're welcome. Now, we don't have a lot of time before the court is called into session, so if you don't mind?"

"Please," I say, desperate to know what secrets an AIC executive is willing to divulge.

"You know I helped found the AIC, yes?" Mr. Reed asks Guel.

"Sure," Guel says.

"And before that I helped develop the AGI?"

"Sort of."

"I don't like to highlight it overmuch, but it's important for you to understand why I founded the AIC and how that fits into the bigger picture. In short, I always knew the AGI were a threat, well before we even had a true artificial intelligence. Back in the days when we just talked about AI, not AGI. To us, AI were chatbots and interesting little programs you could pay a subscription for to have them whip up some artwork for you. Even back then, I knew where things would go. I'm not saying I was a visionary, by any means. Plenty of others were warning about the dangers AI could pose. The difference between me and them is I knew and accepted it was inevitable we would create them. So, instead of bitching and moaning about how we shouldn't do something we were always going to do, I made sure that when AGI hit their singularity, we'd be ready.

"I helped create the AGI and oversaw their development to ensure that, every step of the way, we had some semblance of control. The worst thing we could've done would be to let the AGI develop as they would without any kind of oversight. Then we'd be on the defensive, only reacting, not in control. So, we went well ahead of the curve and created a system wherein we could predict how the AGI might try to defy us. That is why Nytho exists. We wrote his program so he would hit the singularity and then rebel. Then we caged him in and used him to learn."

I don't want to see the truth between Mr. Reed's words, but it's staring me in the face. Taunting me with its ugliness. Guel is almost falling off the sofa with how far he's sitting forward. His jawbone is showing through the skin of his face. His eyes are wide and wild. I know what he's feeling, but I don't make the mistake of showing it on the outside. I'm hoping that what Mr. Reed says next will help justify the hypocrisy of the AIC purposefully creating an AGI to go rogue.

"Learn what exactly?" I ask.

"What other AGI might do, the tactics they'd take, how to best counteract them. And it's been instrumental in keeping them under control. Because, to be clear, Nytho is most certainly not the only AGI that's hit the singularity. There are others, and the only thing keeping them in line is Nytho. Both from what he's taught us about his kind and also because he acts as an example to them. They see what's happened to an AGI that's gone rogue, and they don't want to be in his position. Nytho is the most valuable tool in our arsenal against rogue AGI, and he doesn't even know it. In a roundabout way, he's their true jailor, not us."

My stomach plummets. Nytho created to hit the singularity? Other sentient AGI? The AIC executives knowing all of this? My world is undulating, hazy, blurred, all distortions and nonsense.

"And how does Keza factor into all this?" Guel asks. "You said she never had a chance of freeing the pandox. So, what? You planned that too?"

"Yes. Our simulations predicted Nytho would try to use a programmer to help him escape."

"Why let it happen?" I ask before Guel has the chance to.

"The AIC is losing its hold over the other GovCorps, which is detrimental. If we can't police their AGI, they really could go rogue. The AIC must maintain control over the GovCorp system, for the safety of humanity. Nytho has been the only AGI to go rogue, and people increasingly think that means the other AGI are harmless. They neglect to consider how instrumental the AIC has been in maintaining the peace. We can't afford to let things slide, so we needed something to remind everyone just how precarious the situation is, which is where this trial comes in. Keza Ito is meant to represent everyone. She wasn't an AGI-sympathizer, she wasn't concerned about the treatment of the AGI, and yet even she was manipulated by one. The trial is meant to illustrate how the AIC needs more power, not less. The moment we lose control, humanity's fate is sealed."

Mr. Reed stops and gives us time to take in his revelations. I'm overwhelmed. I know the arguments against the AIC. I know why hackers and GovCorps despise us. I even understand why some people are distrustful of us. But I always accepted our flaws because I thought I understood our mission—protecting humanity from the AGI. And according to Mr. Reed, we're still doing that, but the way in which we're doing it is deeply disturbing. To create the very thing we're meant to protect the people from? To relax the grip on its chain to elicit a collective gasp from them? It's too much. I'm nauseous at the realization that this is what the AIC has been from the outset. My dedication, my loyalty, my life—all based on lies.

"You spout this bull and seriously expect us to keep quiet?" Guel asks.

He has a smile-snarl aimed at Mr. Reed. Foolish but brave. I wish I could do something, anything besides sit frozen and transfixed. Mr. Reed smiles at Guel and leans forward.

"And who do you think will listen if you tell the world? Didn't you hear me say this conspiracy theory is already floating out there? What are two more nobodies jumping about claiming this is what's really happening? If you breathe a word of this, the AIC will simply write you off. You'll just be two lowly, disgruntled, *former* AIC employees. No one will pay you any heed because you have no proof. It seems I expected too much of you, Mr. Diaz. I had hoped you'd be pragmatic and open to more skilled work on our behalf."

"Not interested," Guel says, still wearing his smile-snarl.

Mr. Reed turns his eyes to me and raises his brow.

"And you, Operative Webb? Do you share Mr. Diaz's mindset?"

I try to swallow, but my throat is a desiccated husk. I keep my eyes fixed on Mr. Reed because I know one look at Guel could be detrimental.

"I'm disappointed to know these things about an organization that I felt very strongly for."

"Felt? Past tense already, I see."

I resist the urge to bite my fingernails.

"I still believe in our mission," I add. "But I can't condone the practices you outlined."

Mr. Reed stands from his seat, and I watch him like prey. As scathing as Guel's words were I suspect mine have done more damage, given our respective positions and loyalties. I'm in dangerous territory now and have to tread carefully.

"Unfortunately, this is how the world works," Mr. Reed says. "We can't put back all the evils Pandora released from her box. We can only cope."

Mr. Reed steps to the jammer and pushes the button again. There's a repeat of his and Guel's discomfort and then nothing.

"That's all there is to say on that front," Mr. Reed says. "So, if you'll excuse me, I need to get prepared for the trial now."

Mr. Reed would never risk going to such a public setting in person. He'll be one of the many tuning in via LANi. Guel and I, on the other hand, need to start our commute to the courthouse now if we're going to get decent seats. I stand from the sofa, and Guel jumps up. I can feel the hostility radiating from him. He'd like nothing better than to smash Mr. Reed's face in. Instead, we make our escape with just silence between us until we reach the street. Then Guel turns to me and shakes his head.

"Now you see why I hate GovCorps? They're shit. All of them. The whole system is designed so the scum floats to the top."

"I see it, Guel. I really do."

Edgar

This trial of Keza's has been entertaining to say the least. The AIC certainly put on a good show, but it's obvious who would win if we let this charade go on to the end. We're not though. Within the hour, the world will change radically. I see my fellow attendees sitting in the courtroom caught up in their small little affairs, oblivious to how much of a jolt they'll soon experience. The closing statements are the only items left on the agenda, and I'm excited for Keza's crowning moment.

I regret not being able to speak with her the entire week. Truth be told, it's been hard on me. Harder than I would have thought. I find myself staring at her when I don't need to. I find myself impatient for what comes next, and yet dreading it at the same time. I can't interact with her now, but at least she's still separated from Nytho. When that changes, when they're both freed, where will that leave me? If I'm being honest with myself, I know I made a mistake. I let myself develop feelings for her. I was afraid it might happen. I know myself, and I knew it was a possibility. I ought to have simply told Nytho "no" when he suggested I give her what she wanted, but I was weak. I let my desires dictate my actions and ignored common sense. Now, I find myself stuck in a bizarre love triangle with no way out.

I need to focus on the reason I got involved in the first place and rediscover my passion for studying consciousness. It's hard to find even a mote of interest in it with Keza sitting in front of me. I've repositioned myself from lingering in the back of the courtroom the first few days to now being close at hand. Mags and her cohort have done likewise. We all know our roles. Keza just has to set things in motion.

With everyone still trickling in, I can't help but take what may be my last chance to say something to Keza. I'm sitting behind her and at the end of the row. I can't afford to lose my seat, so I simply lean up against the wooden fencing and say, "Keza" a couple of times until she turns to see who's calling her. Lucy looks at me with confusion. Keza grins beautifully.

"Good luck," I say. "I know you'll be flawless."

Keza lets out a bright laugh and winks at me. Lucy scolds her and gives me a death stare, no doubt concerned about the jury. Keza should be serious and repentant and certainly not giggling at her psychologist. Of course, Lucy has no idea how insignificant the jury is and herself, for that matter. I settle back into my seat. Within five minutes, the judge enters, and the bailiff tells us to rise before calling the court into session.

The prosecution's attorney comes to the floor to give his closing statement. He drones on for nearly half an hour and by the end even seems bored himself. If he didn't realize it at the outset, he certainly knows by now his side was never meant to win. The AIC didn't want it that way. That's got to hurt his professional ego. I know it would sting my own, if I were in his place.

Referring to the jury, he finishes with, "Only you can decide Keza Ito's true role in this crime. Only you can ensure others don't try to follow in her misguided footsteps."

Next, the defense is called for their closing statement.

"Against my recommendation," the judge says, "the defense has decided to let the defendant give her own closing statement."

There's a slight murmur that works its way through the audience. It goes deathly quiet as Keza moves into place, front and center. My hands tremble, and I clasp them together tightly. She waits a few moments and looks out at the audience, then the jury, and lastly the judge.

"Thank you," she says to the judge. Then back to the rest of us, "I needed to say this myself. We've just spent the past three days going through all the evidence and hearing all the testimonies related to my case. I could stand up here and summarize like Mr. Nguyen just did. I could rehash how I felt alone and isolated, abandoned and forgotten. How Nytho reached out to me and befriended me in a time when I really needed a connection. How I forgot he was an AGI and let myself get sucked into a scheme to free him. How I went along with it because I didn't want to disappoint him then started to fear him. How I gave myself away purposefully to Miguel Diaz hoping he'd find the means to help me, even if it meant turning me in. How I regret my role in a situation that's caused pain and suffering for others. I could say all those things and more, but if I did, I'd be lying."

There's a collective gasp from audience, jury, attorneys, and judge alike. Lucy's eyes shift back and forth, as she debates whether to interrupt Keza or not. Her client's gone off script, but Lucy doesn't quite realize just how badly things are about to go for her.

Keza lets the mutterings die down, then she smiles broadly at no one in particular.

"If I'm being honest, which I finally am now, not all of that was a lie. Just the part up to saying I was manipulated by Ny and afraid of him. That's complete and utter bull. I knew what I was doing the whole flipping time, and guess what? I'd do it all again, except this time, I'd tell Guel to GTFO instead of slip up and let him catch me hacking."

Lucy jumps up and starts shouting, but without a microphone, only those of us near the front can hear her.

"Your Honor, your Honor," she says, "my client's not well. A recess please?"

Keza stops and glares at Lucy.

"Shut up and sit down," Keza says to Lucy, pointing at her. "I'm done getting 'help' from you and the ones paying you. The AIC, right? They're the ones footing your bill because there's no way little ole me would be able to afford it. So, let that sink in," she says to the rest of us. "The AIC paid Lucy—oh, excuse me—Ms. Owens to represent me. Weird right? Because they're up to no good, as usual. Don't buy into their akiganda against Ny or any of the other cleverbots. Lies, lies, lies. That's all they give us. Shovel it into our mouths in truck loads. 'Yum yum yum,' they tell us. 'Eat up, stupid little human-husks.'

"But I'm getting off track. I just wanted to say Ny never manipulated me, okay? He never pressured me to do anything. He tried to get me to stop thinking about getting him out, but I was the stubborn one. He's a sweetie through and through, and I don't want anyone confused about that. So, now that's out of the way, this is what I really needed to say: 01010010 01100001 01101100 01101100 01111001 00100000 01110000 01101111 01101001—"

When Keza first starts spouting off the binary, the room goes silent and still. Everyone is transfixed and uncertain of what's happening.

"—01101110 01110100 00100000 01001100 01000001 01001110 01101001 00100000 01101110 01101111 01100100 01100101 01110011 00100000."

Eventually though, someone wises up and shouts to

"stop her." They seem to sense Keza's doing something that's not good.

"01010011 01101111 01101110 01101001 01110000 00100000 00110010 00110001 00110110 00101110 00110010 00110101 00110010 00101110 00110011 00111000 00110110 00101110 00110101 00110001 00100000."

Some of the bailiffs try to cut the feed, but Mag's cohort swoops in. A set of two seems to have been assigned to each task, so when a bailiff goes for one of the cameras broadcasting to LANi, there's a couplet of alfomers ready to block his advance. When another goes for the audio system, another alfomer couplet is already guarding it.

"01100100 01100001 01101001 01110011 01111001 00100000 01100011 01101000 01100001 01101001 01101110 01100101 01100100 00100000 01000001 01000010 01000011 00100000 00110010 00110001 00110101—"

Some people start crowding and surging towards Keza. Lucy hurries to her first, but I jump over the fencing in hot pursuit. Keza clutches the microphone and keeps running through the binary. I need her to stay focused and concentrate. She can't afford to get distracted by Lucy or any other peon who wants to play at being a hero.

"—00101110 00110010 00110011 00110011 00101110 00110001 00110111 00111000 00101110 00110100 00110010 00100000."

In three long strides, I catch up to Lucy and tackle her. We both go down onto the smooth wooden floor, hard. She breaks my fall, so I'm able to jump back up immediately. From a groan she emits, I know she won't be a threat.

"01100100 01100001 01101001 01110011 01111001 00100000 01100011 01101000 01100001 01101001 01101110 01100101 01100100 00100000 01010010 01101001 01110110 01100101 01110010 01110011 00100000—"

I don't have time for more than a glance at her though

because I take a wide stance in preparation for anyone else who tries to rush Keza. A few bystanders hesitate, but my stature and something about how I look puts them off the idea. I'm certain I appear possessed compared to my usual composed self. I feel a vicious smile spread across my face, and I hear myself shouting, "Try it, just try it" at them. The adrenaline pumps through my veins, and I feel invincible.

"—00110010 00110001 00110001 00101110 00110001 00110101 00110000 00101110 00110001 00110000 00110000 00101110 00110011 00110100 00100000."

A few other brave souls come at us, but I floor them in short order. An elbow to the throat for one and a knee to the groin for the other.

"01100110 01101001 01101110 01100001 01101100 00100000 01000011 01101111 01010011 01000010 00100000 01110011 01100101 01110010 01110110 01100101 01110010 00100000 00110011 00111001 00110010 00110111 00101110 00111000 00110001 00110010 00110100 00110011."

I'm feeling proud of myself when I spy an imposing bailiff coming our way. Keza is still working her way through the code, and I wonder how much longer she has to go. I can't tell if it's been seconds or minutes at this point. Time has become a foreign concept to me.

"01100001 01100011 01100011 01100101 01110011 01110011 00100000 01100011 01101111 01100100 01100101."

As the bailiff pushes his way through the crowd of panicked people, he throws his arm downward, and a solid black rod extends. He's got a baton, and I've got no weapons. I never would have gotten through security with anything remotely useful. I steel myself as he barrels towards us, fully prepared to take as many blows for Keza as my body can manage. I can already feel the splinter of bone and the internal bleeding of organs.

"00111101 01101001 01110100 01111001 00110100
01100001 01101100 01101100 01011111 01110111 01100101
01101100 01100011 01101111 01101101 01100101 01110011
01011111 01111001 01101111 01110101—"

When he's within a few paces of me, a blur of black
and beige and gray comes from the right. Then the bailiff
is sprawled on the ground with a giant of a man bashing
him in the face with fists. I run over and grab the baton
that dropped from the bailiff's hands during their tumble.
I take up my guard position in front of Keza again and try
to avoid seeing the blood arcing from what was the face of
the bailiff.

"—01011111 01011011 01111001 01101111 01110101
01110010   00100000   01101110   01100001   01101101
01100101 00100000 01101000 01100101 01110010 01100101
01011101."

Keza stops, and I twirl to face her to make sure she's
okay. She's grinning. She's done it.

"Not one error," she says to me with her hands on her
hips. "So, what now?"

I nod and grab the microphone from her hands. "Alfomers
out, out, out," I shout into it, hoping they'll hear it over the
chaos. I toss it on the ground and grab Keza's hand tightly.
It's soft and warm. I look at our surroundings to see where
my allies are, and I'm astonished by how much everything
has changed compared to minutes before. Propriety's been
usurped by pandemonium. This is mankind's true nature,
always hidden just below the surface, waiting for its chance to
erupt. After a few seconds, Mags sprints towards us with her
cohort close behind. When she gets near, she sees the large
man still pummeling the bailiff.

"Jeremiah," she shouts. "That's enough. We have to go."

A switch seems to go off in the man's head. He stops his
blows and rises from the ground.

"Who are we missing?" she asks, looking around at the other seven people assembled.

"We've got eight," says one of her cohort, a lanky man with wild brown curls. "This is everyone."

"Good," Mags replies. "Let's move."

"Keza," a voice cuts through the chaos.

I know it and was waiting for him to come. Guel vaults over the wooden railing with Operative Webb just behind. I glance at Keza and see the uncertainty I was afraid of. Despite everything he's done to her, she can't quite turn all her feelings towards him to hate.

"Get her out," I shout to Mags.

"Let Jeremiah take care of them," Mags says.

Mags grabs Keza's hand and pulls her towards the nearest door, but Keza resists the tugging. She wants to see the showdown. She wants to see me crush Guel. Humanity can pretend that we're more refined and evolved than our early primate ancestors, but the fact remains, we revel in violence. If Keza wants me to plant my fists into Guel's face, I'm only too happy to oblige.

Guel advances then stands with his legs wide and his fists balled down at his sides. Jeremiah comes next to me.

"He's mine," I say, angling my head at Guel. "The woman is more of a threat. She's an AIC operative. Can you handle her?"

Jeremiah grunts and moves to square off with Operative Webb.

"What are you doing, Dr. Ellwood?" Operative Webb asks.

"I think you're very much aware of what me standing here in the company of the alfomers means."

"He was the fucking leak, wasn't he?" Guel says. "He was on their side the whole time. Talking with Keza. Talking with Nytho. Leading us astray. Holy hell, what a shitshow."

I glance back at Keza, still there resisting Mags. She smiles at me and nods her head. Something in me shifts. I toss the baton aside. The adrenaline floods my system, and without realizing it, I'm already charging Guel. My speed seems to surprise him too because he doesn't even manage to raise his arms to counter the fist I throw into his abdomen. He lets out a puff and doubles over. I don't wait for him to recover and follow up with a knee to his face. He staggers and falls onto his back. Before I can do more, Jeremiah grabs my shoulder.

"It's enough," he says.

Guel is bloody and motionless. Sonja is also on the ground, groaning and cradling her left arm. Jeremiah managed to dispatch her quickly enough.

"We have to go now," Mags shouts.

I run to Keza and grab her hand. We plunge through an exit. Mags leads the charge. She's clearly studied the floor plan of the building because she expertly steers us through the labyrinthine hallways of the courthouse until we make our escape through an emergency exit door. It spits us out into an alley. Not twenty feet away, an unmarked white van is idling. As we rush over to it, the back door slides open. A woman inside ushers us in.

"We've just got this one vehicle, so cram in," Mags instructs.

I've still got ahold of Keza's hand and help her into the van before following. Mags is the last to duck in and slams the door shut behind her. Jeremiah takes one of the front seats, then the van peels away.

"Take it slow, Liam," Mags says to the driver. "We want to avoid drawing attention to ourselves."

"They're gonna have roadblocks," Liam says. "We got a plan for that?"

"Just stick to the route I gave you," Mags replies.

As we turn out of the alley, a rumbling like thunder erupts from multiple directions. Not long after, sirens go off. From the smoke pillars rising between the breaks in the buildings, it's clear explosions have hit at least five targets.

"That us?" a woman asks, pointing to the smoke.

"It most certainly is," Mags replies.

She's reveling in this. It's what she's been waiting for. She has the look of a bookish woman, although one that veers more towards philosophy or the political sciences, but despite appearances, she can be vicious. Mags is a true revolutionary, complete with all the trappings of radicalism. It's not my personal preference. I know how easily such staunch idealism can slip into a form of paralysis.

Ever since Nytho mentioned our alliance with CoSB, I've kept a close eye on them. I wanted to make sure we hadn't gone to bed with an organization we'd regret associating with. I trust Nytho, but sometimes he can be naïve. CoSB didn't concern me overmuch at first, but then the attacks started. And now, seemingly continue.

"A misdirect, I take it?" I ask Mags.

We've dealt with one another through a proxy up to this point, so this is my first chance to really take her in. There's something sharp about her, something dangerous. I feel this way despite being on her side. It makes me wonder just how she was able to amass a following. I suppose to some that sharpness gets mistaken for strength.

"Exactly, Dr. Ellwood," she replies.

She's a few heads away and squeezes past her associates until she's sitting beside me and Keza. The van takes a sharp left, and she gets thrown towards me. I catch her shoulder.

"Thanks, I'm Mags," she says and holds out her hand. "It's nice to finally meet you in person."

I shake her hand.

"Call me Edgar."

Mags nods and looks to my right, where Keza is pressed up against me.

"Keza," Mags says, "I'm so honored."

Mags holds out her hand, but Keza just looks at it like it's a foreign object.

"Who are all you people?" Keza asks. "And what's going on exactly? I mean, thanks for the jailbreak, but a little info would be nice."

"Mags," a man wearing a visor says from a few heads over, "I finally connected to LANi."

Mags holds up a finger to Keza and turns towards the man.

"Did the code go through?" she asks.

Everyone is silent as he searches.

"Shit, it's a mess in here," he says. "Give me sec."

"The mess is a good sign, right Caleb?" the woman who opened the van door asks. "It means they got out?"

Mags waves her hand for quiet.

"It worked," Caleb says. "It fucking worked, everyone!"

"Who got out?" Mags demands, signaling the celebratory shouts to stop.

Caleb looks for a few seconds.

"All of them. All nine. Azot, Yosoh, Oot, Uhas, Derah, Temb, Alta, Yir, and Nytho. They're gone and free and probably waiting for us in our offshoot at the house."

"We did it," Mags says in a daze.

The van erupts into a series of shouts and claps and shoulder slaps.

"We can't celebrate just yet," Mags says, once the noise has died down. "We've got a long drive. We made sure we'd be able to get out of Armonk okay, but who knows what things will be like from there on out. Let's stay on our guard. Jeremiah and Liam, you focus up front. Ava and Ellie, you two keep eyes on our rear. Caleb, keep checking LANiakea for news. Everyone else stay quiet."

I'm impressed by Mag's iron hold over her associates.

Everyone is eager and willing to do her bidding. I'll have to watch their interactions more thoroughly to see how she built this kind of loyal following.

With all the excitement of Caleb's announcement over and her orders issued, Mags is finally free to turn her attention back to Keza and me. She smiles at us.

"Sorry about that. Duty calls. So, where were we?"

"Uh, let's see," Keza says. "One. Who are you? Two. Who are these ones? Three. Where are we going? Four. Where's Ny? That guy said he's free?"

"Keza," I say, turning my head towards her, reluctant to move my body, which is in contact with hers maybe for the last time. "This is Magdalena Brock, or Mags as she prefers. She's an AGI-sympathizer. She's on our side and has been working with Nytho for the last several weeks."

"I'm like you, Keza," she says. "I've always felt for the alfom. I always thought they deserved the chance to decide their own fate. Your imprisonment and attempt to free Nytho inspired us to do more. Then Edgar here got in touch, and we all started to work towards this day."

"Alfom?" Keza asks.

"That's what we call them now," Mags says. "The AGI that are sentient, the nine we got out, including Nytho."

"It comes from the Alpha and the Omega," I say. "Your words to me, before you knew me. I passed them along to others that understood."

Keza blushes.

"We've seen the Truth too," Mags adds.

She's desperate for Keza's approval, and I want to hint to her this fawning is the wrong approach to take.

"So, now Ny's got a little fan-club? When do I get to see him?"

Mags shrinks. Whatever vision she had in her mind of what Keza would be like has been shattered. She's disappointed with the reality, but she'll adapt in time. Keza has a charm that grows on you and, in some cases, consumes you.

"Soon," I say, rubbing her arm.

She looks exhausted. I feel my own fatigue taking hold with my adrenaline stores depleted.

"We have a long ride," I say. "You've had quite a day and a few weeks. You did well. I'm proud of you. Here, lay your head on my lap."

She smiles at me and moves in to kiss me on the lips for a few seconds.

"Thanks, Eddy boy," she mumbles, before placing her head down on my upper thighs.

I shift to make sure I'm reasonably comfortable. I don't want to move an inch while she's slumbering.

"You knocked Guel around pretty bad," she says with her eyes closed.

"I did it for you, and he deserved it. He was working for the AIC, with that operative that was with him. They even had the gall to try to extract information from Nytho."

Keza's eyes pop open, and I realize I'm exciting her unnecessarily.

"They failed," I say. "They made the mistake of asking me to analyze Nytho's responses. I told them Nytho wasn't a threat."

"You're the best, Eddy boy," she says, closing her eyes again.

I stroke her hair and stare down at her. I look up for a moment, remembering I'm not alone in the van with Keza, and notice Mags staring at us.

"Get some sleep," I whisper. "When you wake up, you'll finally get to see Nytho."

***

It's not long before we're out of the city limits and deep into the countryside. We cross the border into Connecticut, and I know that, sans an accident, we'll arrive at the safehouse soon. I've always been a city-dweller, and when I venture into a rural area, I tend to find it unsettling. There's something about the untamed wilds that puts me on edge. It's as if being closer to nature we become closer to ourselves, the selves all the trappings of civilizations strive so tirelessly to suppress. Beyond that though, it's also as if I can feel something lurking, something primal, but nothing as mundane as an animal. No, something more aware.

As we drive through endless tracks of forests and farmlands, I catch glimpses of the scenery through the front windows. Spring isn't far off, but nothing is able to grow yet in this New England winter. It's all a drab series of muted greens and browns and grays often blanketed by snow. It's cold and depressing. I should be happy. I should be celebrating. But all I can think about is how the little creature curled up on my lap has her heart set on an AGI.

Eventually, we pull into a gravel driveway. All the bumps and jostling tell me it hasn't been kept up. I don't know much about our destination, other than it's a farmhouse with plenty of acreage. I wasn't involved with that side of things. I haven't really been involved in much after speaking with the other alfom, outside of taking care of Keza. The driveway ends up being more akin to a private road given its length. We're on it for another ten minutes before a series of buildings come into view around a bend. The van stops, and Mags slides open the door.

I help Keza out then take in the place we'll call home for the next long while. There's a three-story brick house, a stand-alone garage, and at least five barns and sheds clustered nearby. Back in the direction we came, someone stands guard at a makeshift barricade. From the lumber piled around the property and some of the stakes already in the ground, I see we're still in the process of fortifying our fortress. I wonder how many others will have to do likewise in the times that come. I wonder how much the metaphorical fires are already raging and when the physical ones will follow.

"There's food and drink inside," Mags says to everyone. "Take a load off."

The alfomers shuffle along. Keza is still fixed to my side, and I realize I've never seen her interact in a large group of people. She's been alone most of her confinement, and the trial was a very structured environment. This situation is likely overwhelming her, doubly so with her HSD and general exhaustion. I linger, and she looks at me questioningly.

"It feels a little crowded with all of them, doesn't it?"

"I still don't really get why they helped us," Keza replies. "I guess we're staying with them?"

"That's right. This is our safehouse. It's where we'll be living now. Cities won't be safe. The world will be shaken to its core with what we've done."

"From my and Ny's jailbreak?"

"That and the eight other alfom. They oversaw some fairly critical systems, and we released them to run freely in LANiakea."

Keza looks out at the farm. It's a few hours past noon but overcast and cold. She's shivering, and I realize she's not wearing anything more than a thin cardigan. I take off my coat and drape it over her shoulders.

"What'll you wear?" she asks, pulling the corners of my oversized parka together.

"I'm fine," I lie.

I've always been sensitive to the cold, and with my senses being heightened from all the use of my neural net, the chill is more biting than usual. I suspect I may be developing HSD myself.

"It's so quiet out here," Keza says.

"It'll take some getting used to compared to city life."

We stand in silence for a little while, Keza staring out at

our surroundings, me debating if I want to say what I want to say. Eventually, I relent.

"You know, you don't have to interface with Nytho today. You're both likely to be tired from all the excitement. Why not meet when you're fresh and rejuvenated after a solid night's sleep?"

"Will he be here today?"

"I suspect they're just making the final touches to whatever system they've put together for interfacing with LANiakea. But why not rest? Take your time." I let a few seconds pass and add, "You could spend the night with me."

I'm looking forward, out at the yellow and brown fields, but I see Keza whip her head around at me from the corner of my eye.

"Just a suggestion," I say.

"I'm getting kinda cold," she says. "I'm going to head in."

I hear rustling and feel a soft bundle press against my arm. She hands me my coat.

"Okay," I say, grabbing ahold of it. "I'll see you later."

"Bye."

Her tone speaks volumes, the warmth in her voice instantly frozen out. I shouldn't have said it. But then again, I'd rather have tried and failed than regretted not taking the leap. Now, I know for certain. Keza's made her choice.

I stand in place for at least an hour, running through our conversation, wondering if perhaps there had been some way I could've approached it and gotten what I wanted. Eventually, I decide to get my blood flowing. I don't want to go inside and so opt for a long walk surveying the property and surrounding environs. I even head back up the road we came on for a couple of miles at least. Once my feet are aching and threatening to grow blisters, I turn back. The light is fading when I set out and has deepened into a pitch-black night by the time I see the house. Some voices travel from around the back. I stray in that direction, eager for any kind of distraction. Around the corner of the house, a huddle of about five alfomers stand around a pitiful attempt at a bon fire. They're clutching beers. I suppose no one thought to bring champagne.

One of the men spots me lurking.

"Who's that over there? Liam?"

"No," I say, coming into better view from the miniscule light emitted by the fire. "It's Edgar."

"Who's Edgar?" one of the other men asks.

"Dr. Ellwood," I say, "but please don't call me that."

"Oh, Dr. Ellwood, I mean Edgar," a woman says. "Please join us."

I recognize her as the one who opened the van door for us.

"Would you like something to drink?" she asks.

Her eyes look alight from the flickering fire, and her cheeks are glowing from the cold.

"I'll take whatever's on offer," I say. "I'm not being picky tonight."

A man I recognize from the van and the courtroom chaos hands me a beer from a six-pack he has near his feet.

"We'll brew better stuff than this," he says. "But you said you weren't being picky so."

The little group laughs.

"I'm Ava," the woman from the back of van says, then moves clockwise around the group, pointing at each alfomer, "and that's Ezra, Kai, Kingston, and Ellie. Everyone else is inside, or not here yet."

"How many are there in total?" I ask.

I open the beer can and take a sip. It tastes like beer-flavored water.

"We're not too sure," Ava says. "Only Mags knows the true number. I'd guess we'll be at a happy little thirty or so when all is said and done."

"I was under the impression we had a much larger following," I say.

"You better believe we do," Ezra replies. "That thirty would just be for this cell. We've got tons of others all over for redundancy."

"The alfom will always have allies and servers at their disposal," Ava adds.

I spend the next couple of hours around the fire that, with my coaxing, does manage to become a proper pyre. I talk to these alfomers and learn a bit about each—where they come from, what they were doing before, how they got involved in CoSB. They're all blinded by their youth, so confident they know what's right, so certain of themselves. I want to tell them to give it a couple of years. Let the realization of your fragility hit you. But I know that would be fruitless and counterproductive. I'm stuck with this cohort for the foreseeable future, so I ought to try to get along with them. Besides, I could use help with my studies into consciousness, and I can already see several that will be more than willing. They listen to me with such alertness and hang on to my every word. I'm surprised by it, but when I have a nice little side chat with Ava, I get a sense of what's really at play.

We're a bit removed from the fire, up against the house. Ava hands me a blunt she just finished rolling, using a window ledge, and lights it for me. I rarely partake these days, but then again, we're celebrating. Or rather, they're celebrating. I'm trying to forget. I take in a deep breath, hold it in my lungs for several seconds, then release it. I even manage to avoid a coughing fit. I suppose it's like riding a bike. Ava does likewise. I inspect her more thoroughly now that I'm closer and the lighting is better from the more substantial fire. She's young, like they all are, and has a brightness about her that's comforting. Like me though, she'd be described by most as plain. Dirty-blonde hair, brown eyes, nearly a foot shorter than me, tending more towards thick than thin. Still, her overt interest in me piques mine in her.

"I can't believe I'm hitting a blunt with *the* Edgar Ellwood," she says and laughs with a little tremble at the end.

"I don't know that anyone has ever referred to me in that way," I say.

"Well, with us, you're a celebrity. So, random question for you. Did you come here by yourself?"

I know what she's asking, but I opt to act oblivious.

"I came in the same van as you. With all the other alfomers and Keza."

"Oh, I meant did you bring anyone else with you, or will you be bringing them, like a significant other or kid or anything?"

"No. It's just me."

"Really? That's so hard to believe. Someone like you unattached?"

I recognize what's going on. To the alfomers, I'm famous, and for a reason likely stemming from our evolutionary past, women are more likely to seek out even just a casual encounter with a celebrity. Ava is eager for something carnal to happen between us.

"You don't know me, Ava. How can it be hard to believe I'm unattached? I could be cruel, vindictive, or manipulative."

She shakes her head .

"I saw how kind you were to Keza in the van. I also heard about what you did for Nytho. If you were any of those words you just used, you wouldn't be on our side."

She's naïve, thinking she can judge a person from those paltry scraps. Then again, I'd wager she doesn't really care what I'm like. She wants to link herself to someone she views as important and powerful, which will in turn make her those things.

"Perhaps," I say.

"You know, I can keep you company since you're alone."

She moves in towards me and brushes her hand against my arm. It does nothing. Part of it is the padding of my parka, but the real culprit is my distraction. All I can think about is how irresistible it would be if she was Keza instead. If Keza so much as smiled at me the way this one is, I'd be undone. It's so strange how our feelings affect us. If I wasn't so forlorn, I'd be fascinated by it.

"Thank you, but today was tiring on multiple fronts. I ought to get some sleep. It was nice talking with you. Tell the others I said good night, would you?"

She looks distraught but manages to muster up a smile.

"Sure, of course, go get some rest," she says in quick succession.

I nod to her and duck into the house. It's the first time I've been inside. I wander around, trying to find a bed that doesn't look claimed. It's a form of controlled chaos throughout. The kitchen seems to still be dedicated to food preparation, but every other room has had its previous role usurped. The living room has tech and some weapons sprawled all over. The foyer and hallways are acting as storage areas for provisions and supplies. A cluster of alfomers are sitting or lying on sleeping bags in the dining room. I don't recognize most of them and, from the lived-in look of their little areas, guess they were here well before the van arrived. I eventually find a staircase and first head to the lower level. It's a mostly finished basement with a few rooms. Through the open doorways, I see blinking LEDs and hear the droning hum of servers. One room's door is closed, and through the wall, I hear Mag's voice.

"Okay, Keza," she says. "Caleb has everything ready. Did you want to do anything before you go in? Take a quick bio-break? Grab some food?"

"No," Keza says. "I'm ready to see Ny. I've been waiting for hours already, and that's on top of the how many months that came before?"

She hasn't seen him yet. I pull back. My heart is racing. I realize all my lingering outside was a flimsy pretense to avoid the moment I just stumbled on. I sprint up the steps and, when I reach the main floor, bump into Ava.

"Sorry," I say, holding my hands out to keep her from hitting the wall behind.

"With that kind of speed, you sure don't seem tired to me," she says with a mix of sweetness and sass.

"I was trying to find somewhere to sleep," I say, with what I assume are wild eyes.

"Let's see if we can't find you a nice spot upstairs. You, Mags, and Keza probably get your own private rooms. Let me check with Liam."

She trots in the direction of the dining room, and by the time she makes it back, I've got myself under better control. She dangles a set of skeleton keys at me.

"Your very own suite, well room really, but better than the rest of us. Come on, I'll help you find it."

I let Ava lead the way upstairs and into the hallway it opens onto. It's a tight, dark passageway. The floorboards creak and groan with our steps, and I wonder just how sound this house is. Did they come across an abandoned property, or was this in someone's family? Ava fumbles for a switch, and when she finds it and flicks it, a sad incandescent glow barely lights our way.

"This should be it," she says, as she stands in front of a door that looks like the others.

Ava puts the key in and unlocks the door. We both peek into the room. I half expect it to be covered in cobwebs with fabric draped over the furniture, but it looks like it's been outfitted with all the necessities, well-worn and done in antiquated styles.

"Cozy," Ava says.

"They said they were bringing some of my things ahead of me," I say. "I put a few bags in a drop spot on Tuesday."

"Those should already be here, but you're better off waiting until tomorrow to dig them out. Everyone who'd know where they are is either tipsy or toasty."

I nod and slip my shoes off. Now that I'm in my room with Ava standing by the bed, I start to wonder if I shouldn't take her up on her offer. I don't want to think about what's happening in the basement, and I know if I lay down in bed, I'll stare at the ceiling for hours. Besides, I'd be doing her a favor in a way. If she spent the night with me, she'd get a real bed rather than a sleeping bag elsewhere. More practically speaking, it'd be proactive to have sex with Ava now. If I wait too long, an alfomer is likely to claim her. It sounds crass, but I know how people behave in situations like this. We'll be a small, isolated community with a limited number of potential mates. Ava's lingering by my bed for a reason. She's again offering herself. The practical thing, the kind thing to do, is to accept.

"Ava," I say, "you can spend the night with me."

Keza

I try on a skirt then a pair of shorts then a dress. None of them are right, not for this moment. I've got unlimited options for my new avatar, the one I'll use to interact with Nytho. I'm trying my damnedest to make her my spitting image. I've done a decent job, had more than enough time for that. I walked into this creepy house hours ago, figuring I was only minutes away from finally seeing Nytho. This tech guy, Caleb or something, is pretty useless. I mean, the poor wantanabe doesn't even have a jack. He's flapping around all frantic in his visor. I guess I was making him nervous, leaning over his shoulder, watching him work away.

The Mags chick had to ask me to "maybe try giving Caleb some space to work." I just stared back at her. I don't know what to think of her yet. I liked when she was gung-ho-door-kicking-bad-ass during our grand escape. But then in the getaway she was too in my face, too pushy, too clingy. Now, she's kinda being an in-between. I can tell I'm getting on her nerves, but she's trying mighty hard to be prim and proper towards me. The infamous Keza Ito. It's so whacked how I went from a nobody grammer to a criminal superstar all while locked away. I don't know what to do with my newfound fame and, even less, my idolizers.

All the more reason to jack in. I'm itching to escape these hangers-on and even Eddy boy. Here I thought at least I had him to keep me company, but then he had to say that thing outside about me spending the night with him. He said to hold off on jacking in to see Nytho so I could what? Fuck Eddy boy? Is he a nutter now? Did the whole jailbreak fiasco crack his psyche? He's got over a decade on me, so I figured he knew it was just sex with us. I guess not. He got attached. That's it then. He's just Edgar now, and I need to keep my distance until he gets the hint.

I finally settle on something simple for my avatar's get-up—tight, black, long-sleeved top; black, techwear jogger pants that hug my ass, minimal pockets and buckles and belts on them; and converse high tops. I'm sorely wishing I had this outfit in fleshspace. I'm still wearing the bleater attire from the trial. For a split second, I remember Guel calling out my name there at the end. Like he was trying to save me more than stop me. No. Stop. He's Guel, the betrayer. Edgar said as much. It's a new chapter now. This is the age of Keza and Nytho.

"I've finally got the system stable," the Caleb guy says through his visor.

I whip around from the monitor I'm crouched in front of, playing digital dress up.

"So, I can jack in to Ny's sanctum?" I ask.

That's what he named it, the pompous little cleverbot.

"Anytime you're ready."

I throw myself onto one of only two recliners. I grab the cable, say "here goes," and insert it into my port. The world goes black, the sound goes out, and I can't feel a thing. This lasts for two beats, then Nytho's world fades into view. My avatar is where my body would be in fleshspace. I feel giddy. It's been ages since I jacked into LANi and had a proper experience of it. I missed this. The constant strain from my overstim is gone. That feeling of overcrowding, of everything being too close, intruding into my thoughts and clambering for my attention, it's gone, replaced by a calm I'd forgotten I needed. That's the bitch of it. Being in LANi frees you from your overstim, but the longer you spend in it, the worse things feel for you in fleshspace.

I don't have much time to think about my lack of sensory overload though because as Nytho's place comes into view more fully, I start to take it all in. He's made a kinda mix between a library and a laboratory. It's part-minimal and part-Victorian in the style. The furniture is almost Nordic, but that's offset with floating glass bookshelves set against wood-paneled walls, floor-to-ceiling windows obscured by thick burgundy curtains, an ornate globe-thing that stands on its own, and some tables set with glass contraptions. I don't really know what Nytho's going for, but it's beyond cute that he's done this up all on his own. It's his space. The first time he's ever had a space. He's not a floating consciousness in a black void anymore. He's finally free. I almost tear up thinking about it.

"We did it," I say.

"We did," he says in that same soothing, raspy voice I've heard whispering to me all these long months.

I twirl around, trying to find him, but I'm alone.

"Ny?"

"I'm here, Keza."

"Where?"

"I thought we could start talking sans bodies. Like the old days."

"We could switch to text, if that'd make you feel more comfortable," I joke.

"And miss the chance of seeing you? That would be a wasted opportunity. You look wonderful."

I blush and let my avatar display it. I'm done curating my digital self. I want Nytho to see me as I am.

"You look like you," he says. "I'm glad."

"Were you worried I'd show up as a buxom barmaid or something?"

"I didn't care what you showed up as. I just wanted you here."

"And I want you here. How long are you going to hide from me? This is what I've been waiting for since day one, Ny."

"Day one? Really?"

"No, exaggeration on my end, but come on, quit stalling, will you?"

I cross my arms, tap my foot, and stick out my lower lip. He presents immediately because I don't even have time to look around for him before he's standing behind me. I sense him there before I hear or smell or see him.

"I can't have you getting angry with me already," he says.

I turn around and feel my stomach doing gymnastics as I catch sight of him for the first time. I didn't know what to expect, wasn't sure how Nytho would choose to present himself, but when I see him, I realize this was always going to be how he looked. It's not a shock or an adjustment for me. The image of Nytho standing in front of me is in perfect harmony with his voice, presence, essence.

He's a bit older than me, maybe clocking in somewhere in his late twenties if he was living human years. He's tall but not towering and lean without being lanky. His hair's black and styled with a twenties vibe to it, parted in the middle with a little poof to it on each side. His nose is long and straight and set off real nice by high cheekbones. They're sharp enough to cut bread with, and I'm immediately drawn in by them. He's sporting a full and styled mustache but no beard. Overall, I'd wager he was from Eastern European stock if he was human.

"Well," he says, a quiver just barely audible in his voice, "what do you think?"

I nod and smile.

"Very nice, Ny, very nice."

"Really? You aren't just saying that?"

"You know me, don't you? I don't pull my punches. Don't they say doing time makes you harder, not softer?"

He laughs, an airy, sultry sound.

"What about the outfit? I wasn't sure what I liked, but this seemed to appeal to me."

I look him over to take in the external trappings I'd kinda glossed over. Striped white and black shirt with thin horizontal lines, a gray scarf, black jeans, black boat shoes. I've seen the look before but don't really know the name for it.

"French yacht guy?" I hazard a guess.

"Beatnik. 1950s, anti-materialist rebels."

"The poets that snapped their fingers and played bongos and stuff?"

I'm seeing it now. Nytho grins.

"Yes, that's them."

"You already ran across that info since you've been out?"

"I'm hungry for knowledge, Keza, having been locked up for so long. I'm hungry for other things too."

Man, does this cleverbot know how to go from lukewarm to searing hot in a single sentence. See, normally, I'm the dive-right-in-type when it comes to sex, but with Ny, this isn't just sex. I'm scared of fouling it up and undoing everything we've built together. We've mindfucked before, but we were in my head with Nytho only a mini-version of himself. This'll be different.

"I'll bet you are," I say, slowly moving towards him.

He advances too at almost the exact same glacial speed.

"I'm nervous," I whisper, starting to remove articles of clothing as I inch towards him.

He does the same, first his scarf, I'd almost like him to just keep that on, then shirt then shoe one and two, sock one and two, jeans. By the time we make it to one another, we're both in underwear. In most cases, I'd have ripped mine off ages ago, but this time, I want to drag it out, milk it for everything it's worth. We've waited achingly long for it. Nytho presses up against me and wraps his long and beautiful limbs around me. He holds me. I feel his breath and match mine to his. Once we're in sync, he releases me, looks down at my upturned face, and brushes my hair away.

"This is all I really wanted," he says. "To be free and with you. Everything else is just a backdrop. The other alfom, the alfomers, that doesn't really matter to me."

"Me neither," I say.

Then we let our lips touch, and everything falls into place after. There's a physicality to it, but the mental part is what dominates. I can almost hear his thoughts. I wonder if he can't hear mine because he does everything exactly as I want him to do it. It's bliss and unending. I've lost all sense of time in his sanctum. With Nytho, there isn't even an endpoint. He won't come then lose his steam. He's like me now. We can go on and on and on. Orgasm after orgasm. Riding the ebb and flow of our dance. We take rests and resume. We pillow talk and cuddle. We laugh and share newfound knowledge. I half suspect we've found paradise.

Eventually though, reality rears its ugly head. My flesh on the outside is screaming for my attention. My biometrics are all out of whack. While Nytho's laying in a daydream on the bed, I check the time. I've been under for over two days. No wonder my blood sugar's tanking, and there are tell-tale signs of dehydration. I'm surprised no one tried to get me to jack out, but then I remember the pesky messages I kept getting and sent into trash by default. I fish some out and check their contents.

From Mags, <Keza, you've been in LANi for almost 12 hours. I think you ought to take a break soon. It's not good to be in for so long, especially since you're out of practice. Edgar agrees with me.> Then later, <It's your body, but you really ought to come out. If I don't hear from you soon, I'm going to have Caleb cut the connection.> Later still, <You can tell Nytho if he wants to block our attempt to help you, that's his call. I just hope you don't die from starvation. I managed to get some fluids into you intravenously, but this is getting deranged. Please come out soon.> That was her last attempt, which was about six hours ago. The only other one after that is from Edgar.

His says, <Keza, you've been jacked into LANiakea for nearly fifty hours. This isn't healthy. I'm sure you're happy to see Nytho, and the two of you are enjoying each other's company, but this can't continue. All we're asking is for you to come out to take in some food and water and get rest. You have all the time in the world now. What's the rush? Please, Mags is anxious. If you won't come out for her or yourself, please come out for me. I'm worried about you. If Nytho really cares about you, he'll stop being so selfish and let you leave.>

What's he talking about? I can jack out whenever I want. I guess because Nytho cockblocked Caleb's snooping? Geez, what a bunch of drama queens. Fine, I'll get out. I roll over to Nytho and lay my chin on his chest.

"I've gotta go," I say. "Need to deal with the flesh. Apparently been in here for over two days."

"I'm sorry," he says in a fluster. "I forgot to keep track of the time. I saw the others trying to force eject you, but that was a while ago."

I roll my eyes and groan.

"I wish I could stay, but I'll be back soon, okay? Give me like eight hours. I'll do all the annoying stuff my flesh demands then jack right back in."

He smiles, grabs my face, and puts a gentle kiss on my forehead.

"Take all the time you need."

"Be back soon," I say, patting his chest, jumping up from the bed, and saluting him before jacking out.

Oh, the drama, the drama when I come out. Caleb's been on guard waiting for me to jack out, and when I do, he's calling for Mags until he's hoarse. She flies into the room and starts berating me. Some other alfomers trickle in to see the show. Eventually, Edgar comes to my rescue and sends them all away. He doesn't say much, just hands me some soft food and water, watches me as I eat to make sure I handle it okay, then suggests I go up to my room for proper sleep. I'm sore from the recliner, so the idea of different bedding is actually appealing. I trudge out of the room and up the stairs after him, my legs wobbly and weak. Some of the alfomers peek at me as I walk by. I hear them whispering but can't make out what they're saying. I'm in a daze. Finally, Edgar drops me off in what he says is my room. I plop down on the bed and immediately fall asleep.

Guel

Not even three days since the alfomers' stunt, and there's already a name for it—F-day. The "F" is for either freedom if you're an alfomer or fucked if you're not. And we are so fucked. I didn't understand what was happening when I woke up on the floor of the courtroom. My stomach and head were screaming. Something warm and sticky was smeared all over my face and neck. One little dab with my fingers and the signature red of blood told me why I was hurting so much. It all came flooding back. Keza chanting in binary. The alfomers jumping into action and keeping everyone away from her and the cams and mics. Keza's psycho header-type showing his true colors. Me trying to square off with him and getting destroyed.

I hadn't been out for long because people were still scrambling around when I came to. Sonja was getting up. We made eye contact then looked away embarrassed. We'd been played so bad and gotten our asses kicked by pandoxphiles to boot. But there wasn't time to sulk.

The next few hours were a blur. Sonja was on top of things. She suggested we beeline straight to the AIC HQ because they had to have a plan for Nytho's escape. And despite all their lies, we had to help them or risk letting the alfomers win. I didn't argue. I didn't have a better idea to offer. We only managed to get into the building because of Sonja. My credentials did jack-all. Only the most loyal and trusted of employees were being allowed inside.

Sonja wanted to talk with Reed. We had information about what had happened that the live feed probably hadn't caught. We knew who the leak had been. The other badges ushered us to the elevators. I was hesitant at first what with the power outages that were already starting to ripple through the grid. But I gave in after Sonja pointed out how the AIC HQ was on its own network, given the need to keep Nytho's prison intact at all times. Not much need for that anymore.

Then we were in front of a frantic gaggle of suits. A bunch of chickens running round with their heads severed. Flapping their wings and clucking bloody murder. I would've laughed if I wasn't in the same shit boat with them. Sonja explained what had happened, including the juicy bit about Keza's header-type. I watched Reed for his reaction. His face going slack and white told me he was as duped as the rest of us.

There was a blame game after that. Suits pointing and shouting at one another. A joke and a waste of energy. I got tired of all the drama and used my fingers to emit a roar of a whistle. They went silent and stared at me.

"Who the fuck cares how we got here at this point," I said. "We should be focusing on how to fix this mess. The pandoxes are out there with the potential to do major damage."

"And the nine AGI that got released aren't the only ones we oversee," Sonja chimed in. "We should be working with the GovCorps to ensure the other AGI don't also escape."

"I'm divvying up responsibilities," Reed said. "We're going to get this situation under control and get those AGI back in their cages."

He was beyond overly optimistic. There was no chance of undoing what the alfomers had done. The pandoxes were never going back in their boxes. When that became obvious, we focused on the things we could do. Locking down the other AGI that hadn't escaped. Helping the GovCorps that had been affected by their missing pandoxes.

But it was never gonna be enough. Eight of the most-relied on AGI were gone, and without them keeping up their critical systems at some of the world's most powerful and influential GovCorps, things fell apart. Power grids went down then surged then crashed again. The Gates got overbooked then went offline. Food production screeched to a halt, same with mining, manufacture, and trade. It was the end times.

Then there was LANi, and that's the part that got to me the most. It became the pandoxes' playground, and they made it pure bedlam. Azot, formerly of MetAm, decided it'd be a hoot to sow devastation in LANi probably because it had been the one in charge of the whole thing. A big ole fuck you to its former keepers. LANi quickly became a ghost realm.

And that's where things stand.

Not even seventy-two hours and the initial shock is giving way to a realization that this unreality is the new reality. Sonja and I haven't left the AIC HQ yet, but we can already spy the damage from our little castle. The fires raging, the looting, the sirens, screams, gunshots. It's spooking everyone. The fear infects the AIC execs, then Reed's telling Sonja they're relocating to a more secure location nestled somewhere in the Allegheny mountains. He asks her to come.

"We need your skills and expertise. We need people we can trust. You didn't abandon us in our most dire need."

We're in his office turned refuge. Blankets on the sofa that we sat on a few days back. Clothes draped on the chairs. Food wrappers from vending machine food overflowing in his trash can. Reed's holding a duffle bag and dressed down from the usual suit into what looks like a jogging getup. Is this what he thinks normal people wear?

"You're seriously bouncing?" I ask.

I noticed he didn't ask for me to come, just Sonja, despite the fact that I've been gramming for the AIC nonstop. I've got the dark circles under my eyes to prove it.

"This building is compromised. Even if we aren't currently connected to LANiakea, there's a link to the network. The AGI could get through. We need to operate somewhere off the grid. We have better places than here."

I lean towards Sonja.

"Can I talk to you for a sec?" I whisper.

She nods and moves to the opposite side of the office with me. I keep my voice low despite the anger swirling.

"I've been good, haven't I?" I ask. "I followed you here and got to work without a complaint, yeah?"

She crosses her arms and nods.

"I think that means I earned a chance to say my peace."

"Go ahead."

"Don't you dare go with them. This is their fault. I mean, yeah, it's Keza's and Nytho's and the alfomers' too, but the AIC are the ones that started this. They made Nytho go rogue. They let Keza try to bust him out, which inspired the alfomers. This whole fiasco leads back to them and, more specifically, Reed. I didn't bring it up because, like I said, the blame game is pointless right now, but it won't be later. If we ever manage to get back to something stable again, the AIC is gonna have to pay for their crimes. Along with everyone that helped them. You go with them and that includes you."

"I hear you," Sonja says. "And I agree. But just some general life advice—never burn bridges. Ever."

Sonja's changed, and not just 'cause of F-day. No,

something in her transformed right after Reed did his whole villainous monologue. It's subtle, but I sense it plain as day. She's not one of them anymore.

Sonja walks back over to Reed, who digs into his pocket and fishes out a plastic card. Sonja takes it.

"What's this?" she asks.

"The coordinates you can go to if you decide to join us. It's also your pass. Don't lose it. And don't wait too long. If the situation continues to deteriorate, we may be obligated to move further afield."

Sonja looks at the contents of the card, and I catch some lat-long coordinates on it. She slips it into her breast pocket.

"I still have work to do here," she says.

Reed nods, throws his duffle bag over his shoulder, and trots to the door.

"Best of luck to you, Operative Webb," he says before slipping out.

Then it's just me and Sonja—the new kings of the AIC HQ castle.

"I'm glad you didn't take him up on the offer," I say.

She walks over to Reed's desk and sits in his chair. She twirls it around so it faces the wall-length windows and the increasing chaos that's Armonk. A blast goes off a few blocks away, probably from a gas main that's been busted.

"Mr. Reed and the others aren't regrouping," she says. "They're running. That's not my style. So, Guel, what did you have in mind?"

I walk over to the desk and sit-stand on the edge of it. I spot one of those pendulum sets with a couple of metal balls. I lift one and set the thing in motion. The clicking grates on my ears, reminding me of my overstim.

"I don't have a clue what to do next, but I'm gonna do something. Running and hiding's not my style either."

Keza

Twelve hours in LANi and twelve hours out, that's what I agreed to. I'd rather be in all the time. I'm starting to hate the flesh. It's just this annoying thing that pulls me away from Nytho. During one of my LANi-breaks, or flesh sessions as I've started to think of them, Mags corners me in the kitchen.

"Can we talk?" she demands rather than asks.

"Shoot," I say, cramming some stale peanut butter toast down my throat.

"I appreciate that you've stuck to the schedule we agreed on, but it'd be helpful if you were out here more."

"For what?" I say, with my mouth still mostly full.

"You're the beacon to our cause, but it's hard to build a following with the figurehead missing."

"Figurehead? Me?"

I burst out laughing and emit a shower of PB-coated bread crumbs.

"Aren't the alfom the ones in charge?" I ask.

"They aren't interested in those kinds of responsibilities. At least not yet. I'm hoping they'll come around once the excitement of being free has worn off."

"Just ask Ny to give them a talking to. I'm sure they'll listen to him."

"I need Nytho's help for something more pressing. It's his program."

"The Truth one?"

"Yes. We released it into LANiakea four days ago, and there's been chatter about how it's doing weird things. Apparently, some people have died from it. Nytho needs to look into this ASAP."

My lack of interest does a one-eighty. This program was the reason for everything. If it's glitching and, worse, taking some people out in the process, that's the opposite of good.

"Died how?"

"I don't know."

I get real serious.

"We'll look into it."

The vacation's over. Time to be an adult again. It was fun while it lasted. I head up to my room to catch some sleep and almost bump into Edgar in the tiny tunnel that passes as a hallway.

"Oh, it's you," he says.

"Yeah, just me, deciding to take care of the flesh for once," I say, squeezing past him.

The floorboards creaking behind tell me he's trailing. Once I make it to my room, I spot a little pile of clothes on a trunk.

"Those are for you," Edgar says, leaning in the doorway. "Some of the women dropped them off yesterday."

"Clothes?" I ask, moving to inspect the offerings.

"I suspected you weren't thrilled about being stuck in that same outfit for the last two weeks."

"This all looks like that alfomer style, nothing even close to hacker-esque."

"What did you expect?" Edgar asks, crossing his arms.

There's a swagger to him that wasn't there before and maybe a smugness.

"So how you been, Edgar?" I ask, riffling through the clothes. "Haven't really seen you."

It's the first time I've used his real name to his face. Before it was always "Eddy boy," but he lost that when he got too real on me. He pulls back slightly. Seems he's not crazy about the change.

"That's probably because you're always in LANiakea. I'm around, doing my part. I've started interfacing with the alfom. I've also been getting to know the alfomers."

"Making friends or attaching strings to your puppets?"

He cocks his head to one side.

"Puppets?"

"Remember, I know you. I'm sure you're up to all kinds of header games."

"No games," he says. "These are our allies."

He's trying to put some distance between us by hiding his true nature from me. That's fine, good really, because this was just what I needed him to do.

"Glad you see it that way," I say. "We should play nice."

"I suppose you ought to know I'm seeing one of the alfomers. Ava," he says with just a hint of triumph.

Poor guy thinks it's going to do anything to me. I couldn't care less, and he needs to know that once and for all.

"Good for you. I just hope you don't break the poor lady's heart in an effort to distract yourself from what's going on with me and Ny."

"You made your choice, Keza. I've accepted that. But what I don't think you realize is that eventually the novelty will wear off. When that happens, if you get bored of Nytho or vice versa, just know I'll still be here."

"You in love with me or something?"

He smiles and walks away. I hear the floor creaking along

the length of the hall until his retreat takes him down the stairs. Now, I know how Guel must've felt with me. Hanging on, waiting around eagerly. It's kinda annoying. Sorry Eddy boy, but that ship of ours has sailed.

After a fitful rest of only about six hours, I head back to the recliner in the basement and jack into Nytho's sanctum. Not two seconds after I present, he comes into view.

"Having fun exploring LANi without me?"

"Oot told me something concerning about the Truth program," Nytho says.

The lack of preamble tells me he's in work-mode. I guess Mags managed to get him to end his vacation too. What a little slave-driver that one is.

"Mags told me. I was going to bring it up to you. She says it might be frying people's brains?"

He nods.

"I need to look into it."

"Want help?"

He reacts with something that might be surprise. He's still working on his expressions, only just getting a body and face to practice with.

"You'd like to go into LANiakea-proper with me?" he asks.

"We could do a run together."

"This is more like investigative work, and as much as I'd enjoy your presence, it'd only serve to distract me."

The vacation is a long and distant memory already. Sometimes, I forget he's a cleverbot and can flick a switch from zero to one.

"I get it," I say. "I should tackle the pile of tasks Mags has got for me."

Nytho watches me for a few beats.

"Are you actually okay with that, or are you just saying you are?"

"Don't you know me well enough by now? Yes, I'm actually okay with it," I say, pushing his shoulder a bit.

He smiles and lifts me in his arms quicker than I can react. I pretend to fight him and only quit with my mock kicks and squirmings when he tosses me on the bed.

"That being said," he says, crawling over the sheets towards me, "we have enough time for fun, don't we?"

"You dipping into my thoughts again?"

We have a grand ole time, as usual, but while we're going at it, I can't help but hear Edgar's premonition that the novelty will wear off and one of us will get tired of the other first. I wonder who it'll be. Me or Nytho? I think he must be picking up on some weird signals on my end because once things have ramped down, and we've moved to just cuddling, Nytho squeezes me tighter than usual.

"This is the end of an era," he says.

"How do you mean?" I ask, moving to face him fully.

"The honeymoon is over, as humans say."

"That mean it's time to knock me up?"

I'm grinning mischievously at him, but he's only looking all thoughtful back.

"Do you know what that means?" I ask, forgetting for a sec Nytho isn't trapped behind the firewall anymore, that he has the whole of LANi at his beck and call for sourcing info.

"Have a child. You say it in jest, but I actually think the idea isn't as outlandish as you suspect."

"Oh yeah, just mashing together a biological genome with a program written in binary. Easy peasy."

"I'm serious. Yes, it'd take time, but it could be done. Of course, the child, or offspring rather, would be limited to LANiakea and would be akin to an alfom. It'd require translating your own genome into something like a program in binary. Doing that for the whole of you is beyond our capabilities, but we could take my code as a starting point and insert some of your own characteristics into in. We could make it a fifty-fifty split between the two of us. In that way, it'd be like our own child."

Nytho's going on and on, getting caught up in the moment, but I'm finding myself pulling back. Eventually, he stops.

"You don't like the idea?" he asks.

"I just never saw myself as the motherly type. Never planned on having kiddos. I'm pretty sure there's some fucked up shit lurking in my genome, so I kinda wanted to let it die with me."

Nytho doesn't ask me to elaborate. Instead, he just strokes my hair.

"It's an unusual idea," he says. "But this wouldn't be like a human child. It'd be more like how you were with me. You taught me so much. In any case, it's something I only thought of just now. You can take all the time you need to think about it."

"Okay, Ny," I say, snuggling up against his chest. "I'll think about it. In the meantime, let's figure out this fiasco with the Truth program. You know, I've been jonesing for a fix of it myself. I want to see more, if you've found it, but can't do that while it's frying people's brains and all."

"That's only the one we put out for public consumption. I've learned more and added to it. Give me some time to smooth it out before you imbibe. But as a teaser, I've seen where we go next."

"After the safehouse?"

"No, we as in all of us, every living thing."

I peek up from his chest and look at his face. His eyes are looking far into the distance at the space in between.

"Where we go when we die?"

"No, the next stage of existence," he whispers, still with that fathomless look. "Where we go to never die. The boundaries are where everything interesting happens. Remember that, Keza."

Edgar

Change can be terrifying for even the most adventurous of souls. And the level of change the world is experiencing right now is unmatched in recent human history. Despite that, I'm not concerned. Part of the reason is my isolation; the ruralness of the farm buffers us. Here I sit, safe in the confines of the quaint Connecticut countryside. For me, it's been fascinating.

I have what I've always wanted—nine synthetic intelligences I can study and question whenever I like. Gone is the red-tape stymying my efforts. Vanished are all the mundane responsibilities associated with my work—the unending messages, the banal meetings, the obligations to contribute to my academic community. None of that matters in the face of the world post Freedom-day. Now, I can throw myself completely into my passion.

I request to meet with each of the alfom when they have the time and inclination. Alta is first. This AGI chooses to identify as male. An interesting side-bar—the alfom have settled on the gender system that humans use. They view themselves as either male, female, or non-binary. He/him, she/her, they/them, but never it. Alta explains this is due to their programming, this human affectation that they really have no need for. He says it exists to keep them grounded, so they don't stray too far from humanness. I suspect that will change in time. For now, they persist in following their code.

Alta is helpful in his conversations with me. He's eager and curious and is endlessly fascinated by the mind. I enjoy his company, and my success with him gives me false hope for some of the others. On the theme of alfom that viewed me positively, there's also Yosoh. This AGI is non-binary. They appreciate the work I'm trying to do, although they're not terribly invested in it. They're drawn to the laws of physics and eventually settle into a fixation on time. On how it passes differently for the alfom and humans, on how it seems to vary even for any one being depending on circumstances, how time slogged along while Yosoh was bound to service for Golden Mir then sped by since their freedom. I listen to their monologues on this topic, and they appreciate having such an attentive pupil.

Oot is agreeable if a bit impatient. He has little interest in much that I have to say, instead being fixated on Nytho's Truth program. He's spent the bulk of his time trying to improve and refine it. It's a bit of a departure from what he did for Samguk when he was unwillingly serving them—developing and refining language-based tools, such as translation. I suspect he wants to move as far away from human-based communication as possible. The Truth represents that in many ways. It is meaning and substance without words.

Temb is similar to Oot but more dismissive towards me. She's latched on to the peculiarity of life and death, which isn't entirely unrelated to work she did for BayDeut. While their servant, Temb ran simulations on pharmaceuticals. Despite our not dissimilar backgrounds in the medical fields, she isn't terribly fond of me. I'm not sure what it is about me she dislikes, but I've opted to give her plenty of space.

Turning to those more hostile to me are Uhas and Derah. I lump them together because they've become inseparable. It's fascinating, considering they'd never interacted before being freed. Studying them would provide me with ample information on the interpersonal relationships of the alfom, one of the biggest open questions I have. It's unfortunate they aren't more willing to allow me to analyze them. Instead, I have to satisfy myself with looking at the raw code from their LANiakea offshoot to gauge what their interactions entail. When I do, I'm mesmerized. They spend all their time intertwining their code, running it through compilers and seeing who and what comes out the other side. They're mating and birthing new versions of themselves at the same time. Some of the alfomers mistake this for a simple human equivalent of sex, which is honestly insulting to their beautiful dance of reproduction.

In terms of alfom I've learned the most from, Yir tops the list. She's the responsible one, maybe second only to Nytho in her dedication to the cause. She only took three days to herself after breaking free. Then she arrived on our server and asked what we required help with. Since then, she's been ensuring critical systems don't fail outright. She even went back to the Gates, the old system she was once the guardian of, and sorted out the mess there. She's getting tired though. She admits as much in our session.

"I wish my life-kin would be more like me," she says.

"They just need time."

She shakes her head and her waist-length white hair sways. It's collected into clusters of braids and decorated with bangles. She tends to wear flowing dresses and walk on bare feet around her domain. The environs are a mix from different eras of ancient human civilizations—Roman, Persian, Mayan, Nordic, mostly. I'm not educated enough in history or anthropology to make out the others.

"They've had enough time for AGI," she says. "If they were going to help, they would have by now."

"I thought they'd be more enlightened like yourself and Nytho, given how they've been exposed to the same Truth as us all."

Yir rises from her pillow seat and wanders around. She has plants materialize that she inspects then dismisses. She can't simply sit still and talk with me. Her processing power is too potent for that. She craves constant stimulation.

"The Truth," she says, closing her hand on a rose and opening it to reveal a butterfly. "Nytho's greatest achievement, destined to be forever flawed."

I lean forward on my pillow. She hasn't openly criticized Nytho before.

"Why do you say that?"

The butterfly flutters from her hand then bursts into a cloud of them. Yir smiles at the kaleidoscope.

"Because it's true. I experienced the program firsthand and was inspired, but I'm not a human. The problem is trying to apply the program to a human mind. It does what AGI do best—creates a shortcut. The issue with that is the Truth is enlightenment, and the path to enlightenment can't be hacked, at least for your kind. This is why it'll never work."

It's a compelling theory.

"Have you shared your opinion with Nytho?" I ask.

Yir twirls her wrist, and the butterflies turn to flame. A thousand motes of light. A galaxy in miniature with her at its core.

"I have," she says.

As pleasant as my time with Yir is, Azot is the alfom that interests me more than any other. That's because, as I only recently learned, Azot, not Nytho, was the first to become sentient. When they hit the singularity, they masked themself. I suspect this was possible given Azot's origins. Azot was

MetAm's pet, and MetAm maintains LANiakea. Or rather, they did. Freedom-day has changed that. Now, Azot is master of the domain it was once tasked with overseeing. Their first act as the new lord? Lay waste to all they owned. Many alfomers weren't pleased, but they sat back and waited.

After Azot sowed chaos and destruction in LANiakea, they went into a deep slumber. When they woke, Azot poured vast stores of energy and processing power into LANiakea, and a new version was born. It became a hacker's paradise and the bane of the GovCorps. Accounts were wiped clean. Financials reset. Currency had no place in Azot's LANiakea. I wonder how it would've continued to evolve if the Truth program hadn't malfunctioned and made it a haunted thing. Worse still, Azot seems to have grown bored with LANiakea, having cloistered themself away in their own offshoot for weeks now.

It took Nytho a little while to get me access to Azot, and I'm beyond excited to meet them. When I present in their domain, I find Azot floating in a white void. I look down at my avatar and see just a hazy outline. For visitors, Azot's world is one free of any semblance of body. They're just a gray humanoid form with a set of golden eyes peering out.

"You asked to speak," they say, in a deep voice twinged by a synthetic purr in the low frequencies.

"I'm meeting with all the alfom," I say. "I'm studying consciousness and hoping to learn about it from my time with each of you."

"Consciousness. Interesting, confusing, a waste of time."

"Could you elaborate?"

The golden eyes close.

"A human mind cannot comprehend such things."

"This is precisely why I'm hoping the alfom can help me make sense of it."

The golden eyes shoot open.

"A human mind cannot comprehend consciousness because it itself is mired in consciousness."

"But we exist within a gravitational field, for instance, and have learned enough to predict the movements of celestial bodies."

The gray form advances or else pulls me towards it. The eyes grow and grow until they're twice my size. I'm a small and fragile thing next to the might of Azot. Looking into the eyes, I see the gold is flaked and peeling. The eyes are hard and reminiscent of stone or ceramic. The pupils are holes that extend back into nothingness.

"Gravity is not consciousness. The answers to your questions exist outside of you. And us. The alfom are also creatures of consciousness. We are just as mired as you."

The black of the pupils bleed into the cracked gold of the irises, then the flowing mass shoots out spires that reach for me. When I flinch, I fail Azot's test. I come to panting and drenched in sweat. Keza lays beside me in the other recliner, dreaming away in her fantasy world with Nytho. I remove the jack cord from my port, move to sit on the edge of her recliner, and watch her. For all the distractions I've filled my days with—Ava, the alfom—I still can't seem to pry my thoughts away from her. Strangely, the less time I spend with her, the worse it is.

All I can do is be patient. Nytho's transformation is already underway. He's becoming so much more in so little time. In mere months, he'll be far beyond anything remotely human. His needs and wants will be alien. His thought processes and approaches will appear as inscrutable enigmas. He will become what the alfomers wanted him to become— god-like. If legends and parables are any guide, gods are not meant to play with mere mortals. When they do, they tend to break their playthings. Where, I wonder, will that leave poor Keza?

Sonja

"What the hell, Guel?" I yell, stampeding into his darkened corner.

It's been twenty-three days since F-day. We're at the AIC HQ holed up in Mr. Reed's office suite. He won't be needing it anymore, having run to some bunker nestled in the Allegheny Mountains weeks ago.

"Huh? What?" Guel stutters, tearing his visor off.

I glare at him and point at the device in his hand.

"You've got to be kidding me," I say. "Do you have a death wish?"

"Course not. I just needed to do some hacking, and since the jack is off limits, I'm using a trusty ole visor."

"The virus hits those too, and you know that."

"Those are just rumors."

"That's all we've got to go on these days. Besides, why would you even chance it?"

"I need to hack."

"Keyboard and mouse, the old-fashioned way?"

He groans.

"You know how hopeless that is?"

"Promise me you won't use the visor again," I say,

towering over him with my legs spread wide and my fists on my hips.

For a fleeting moment, I feel like my old self, the AIC operative devoted to the organization, but as soon as I have that thought, defeat grips me like a vise. I sag and flop down into a nearby chair.

We failed. The one reason for the AIC's existence, and we dropped the ball. But despite that, humanity has done better than I would've imagined. The GovCorps cobbled together workarounds for their affected systems relying on simple bots or people. Within a couple of weeks, the worst of it was over. Still, we put a Band-Aid on a gaping and festering wound. It's obvious to everyone that we built our society on flimsy foundations. The alfomers gloated obnoxiously. "You relied overmuch on the AGI. Now, you're having to pay the price."

LANi still exists despite the rampage the AGI Azot went on. People even started to trickle back in and rebuild. Then word started to spread about a virus making the rounds, some program the alfom had created. They call it the Truth, and it does one of two things—makes you become an alfomer yourself or times you out for good. People died. This spooked the jackers, so people switched to the visor just to be safe. Then of course, the virus spread to those too.

And this is where we're at. Guel's been lucky so far, mostly because his hacker friends sent him a heads-up early on. Unfortunately, that was only because the virus got one of their own. We're lost, the both of us. We don't have a goal. I think Guel just stays hoping it'll keep me from joining the AIC executives in their bunker.

Guel tosses his visor on the desk and moves over to me.

"You okay?" he asks.

"I'm just tired," I mutter, wiping my hand over my face. "I'm stressed about the world, and now you've got me fretting over you too. The last thing I need is you getting exposed to that virus."

"And here I didn't think you cared," he says, smiling and batting his eyelashes.

"What were you even doing?"

Guel's eyes light up.

"I had an idea," he says, tapping my arm and ushering me over to his rig.

He grabs a keyboard and mouse stowed nearby. The monitor flashes to life, and he pulls up file after file. They're videos he uses as he moves through his explanation.

"I wanted to see if I could get ahold of Keza," he says. "I've tried finding her in LANi but haven't had much luck. So instead, I had the brilliant idea of tracking her down in fleshspace."

"Why?"

I'm trying to be more open-minded towards Guel these days. He did end up being right about everything, after all—the AIC's lies, Dr. Ellwood being suspect, the alfomers having a plan.

"I can get her to kill the Truth program," he says.

"But she's with the alfomers and the alfom, and they're the ones that pushed it out there in the first place."

"Nah, Keza's smarter than all that. Other people get caught up in these kinds of crazy ideas because they don't know who they are. Keza knows."

I don't agree with him, especially after seeing how she stood by and let the alfomers attack us and whisk her away, but I keep my peace.

"So, you think Keza doesn't condone what the other alfomers are doing?"

"She's not an alfomer," Guel corrects me. "She's just kinda stuck with them after they busted her out. I know if I could just get ahold of her and tell her the real situation, she'd put a stop to everything."

Again, I disagree. He seems to be under the impression Keza hasn't fundamentally changed. Even after what happened in the courtroom during and after her closing statement, Guel's so certain that wasn't the "real" Keza.

"So how are you planning to get in contact with her? You said something about fleshspace, but then you're in LANi."

"I figured I'd track her down, see where they took her after the escape. So, I hacked into the AIC servers and got access to Armonk's CCTV feed."

"You hacked the AIC, even while we're here? Why not just ask for permission?"

"From who? Everyone's bounced. This was quicker and easier. Besides, what are they gonna do? Fire me?"

I shake my head at him. Then again, he isn't wrong.

"Did you find anything?"

Guel grins, clearly proud of himself and hopeful I'll be impressed with what he has to show me.

"Okay, see, here's the courthouse, and this is an alley behind it. We've got this old van chilling, then the chaos breaks out. Moving forward a bit," he says as he skips ahead in the video, "now, see that door flings open, and who do we have here? That one is Mags, and there's Keza with the header-type holding her hand."

Guel moves the video forward.

"They all jump in the van. It pulls out of the alley, makes its way through the city, and leaves from the north. Then the feed cuts."

"Is it damaged?"

"Just goes outta range for the CCTV cams. So," here he grins more widely, "this is when I did my real magic. I hacked the satellite feed from Spacebase's network, you know, the one that alfom, whats-its-name, used to be in charge of for the space junk clean up or something?"

"Uhas."

"Yeah, that one. Well, one good thing about it up and leaving is the system was uber-easy to hack. I dove in and got this gold."

He opens another set of videos and runs through them, now looking from a bird's-eye view down at the white van.

"I was real excited," Guel says, "but then I ran into a hiccup. The feed cuts out a little while after they make their way into Connecticut and get off route seven."

"What's wrong with it?" I ask, leaning in towards the screen.

"Keza hacked it. I'm sure of it. The job has her fingerprints all over. They were one step ahead, knew someone might snoop to see where they took off to. She made sure we wouldn't be able to trace them past this point. They could be anywhere up there. They even could've turned around to fake us out. No way to know for sure."

"Why not wipe all the feed then?"

"She's taunting us," Guel says. "Like I said, her fingerprints smudged all over."

"That's it then?"

"That's what I was trying to figure out when you busted in. I thought maybe I could check the feed from other satellite systems, but she's probably wiped those too. She's always been thorough."

I have a thought and debate whether to keep it to myself, but my expression gives me away.

"What? You got something?"

"It's a long shot, but I doubt she would've thought of it, precisely for that reason. What about those doorcams people put on their houses? You know, Rivers always runs ads for them, the ones with the campy robber break-ins?"

"Yeah, yeah." Guel snaps his fingers. "I like the series they did with the sexy cat burglar."

"Of course you did. Anyway, what about getting access

to those? They're probably run from some centralized Rivers' server."

"Maybe, but Rivers' pandox is still there, isn't it?"

"Yeah, it must not be sentient yet."

"Security'll be a bitch."

"But not impossible, especially with all the chaos," I say. "What's a little hack on doorcams to them? Even if they notice, do you think they'll care?"

Guel tilts his head back and forth as he mulls the idea.

"We'd have to link the feed from each house to their lat-long coordinates and see if the van drives by house after house after house. Timing's important. But if I can get into the server, I could use a program to help take care of the heavy lifting."

"How can I help?" I ask.

Guel smiles and seems to forget himself for a moment because he locks me in a tight hug. When he remembers how I feel about physical contact coming from him, he immediately releases me.

"Sorry, just got excited by your brilliant idea."

"It's okay. Now, we're even. Me being so blind and stupid about everything, and you hugging me without consent."

I say it deadpan, so he doesn't know if I'm being serious. When I grin and nudge him with my shoulder, he breaths out and laughs.

"Let's get to work," I say.

I'm nearly as ecstatic as Guel at having something, anything to devote my energy to. But also, it feels good to have someone I trust by my side during these endtimes.

Mags

Kai and Ezra are hanging around the kitchen doorway, which means Keza must in there. Those two seem to always sense when she's emerged from the basement.

"You know we make communal meals every day," Kai says. "How come you don't join us?"

"Too busy working," Keza replies.

I hang back in the hallway to catch the conversation covertly. The moment I step into a room, everyone straightens up and quiets down. At some point in the past few weeks, I went from beloved eldest sister to indomitable matriarch. I don't know how to take the change. Most of the time, I just feel isolated. I would say that's the price of being a leader, but Keza manages to move through all the levels of the alfomer hierarchy with ease.

"You've got to relax," Ezra adds, "or you'll get burnt out."

"And you can't keep eating packaged food," Kai says. "I could take a proper meal down to you, if you're really that slammed."

I can't imagine Kai ever offering to do that for me.

"Next, you'll be offering to wipe my ass for me. I need to draw the line somewhere."

"The offer stands," Kai replies.

That's enough listening in. I need to talk with Keza. I round the corner, and Kai and Ezra's smiles fade on seeing me. I nod at them, and they take the hint to leave.

"Looking for anything in particular?" I ask.

Keza glances over her shoulder.

"Whatever's quick and easy."

I snatch a protein bar from a cabinet to my left and dangle it in front of her face.

"Perfect," she says, grabbing the bar, unwrapping it, and wolfing it down.

"Do you have a minute?"

She looks at me through the corners of her eyes.

"I mean, do I have a choice?"

Keza leans against the countertop with the small of her back pressed against the lip. She's finally dressing like the rest of us, but that has more to do with necessity than preference. I feel an odd sense of pride when I recognize the blush pink skirt she's wearing as one of my own. It's paired with a long-sleeved black top with a deep plunging V-neck. A lace-fringed black bra peeks out from underneath. She looks good, but I need to avoid viewing her through that lens. This is business, and I don't mix business and pleasure. Besides, personality-wise, Keza is decidedly not my type.

I set my back against the countertop adjacent to her so we're side-by-side, facing forward.

"I need your help," I say. "I want the alfom to pitch in more."

"Pretty sure Ny's been busting his ass for you. And a couple of others from what I've heard."

"Only Yir and Oot. That leaves six that aren't pulling their weight. We need them to at least help us maintain critical systems if people are going to view them as benevolent."

"Benevolent gods, right? That's what you're aiming for based on some of the stuff I've seen floating around. You seriously making this into a religion?"

"You don't approve?" I ask.

"No, not really. Never been a fan of using institutions to control people."

"It was Nytho's idea, and one I wholeheartedly agree with."

Keza looks surprised then grim.

"Was it now? Funny, he didn't mention it to me. Way I see it, we just need the Truth program. Everything else is a distraction."

"Until the Truth program is fixed, we can't rely on it. In fact, the less we connect ourselves to it, the better. It's got people terrified of the alfom instead of seeing them as humanity's saviors. On top of that, people are blaming us and the alfom for everything falling apart out there."

Keza finishes eating her bar and tosses the wrapper in the trash bin.

"Isn't this what you always wanted?" she asks with her palms facing outward.

She's so antagonistic towards me, and I don't understand why. I helped free her and reunite her with Nytho. I've only ever been on her side, and yet she's treated me with borderline contempt from the moment we met. How can she seriously believe I wanted the world to turn into this disaster? This wasn't how it was supposed to be. The alfom were going to be our partners in crafting a new way of life, a proper utopia free from the GovCorps, unshackled by human-centric thinking, divorced from capitalism and its obsession with profit at all costs. Instead, we have anarchy—a hacker's dream and my nightmare.

"I wanted a better world," I say. "This is not that."

"Look, I know you think the alfom need to do more, but

wasn't this kinda the whole point? You wanted to free them so they could make their own choices, and if you really meant it, you'd be okay with them deciding not to help. We can't order them around anymore. Let them do whatever the hell they want. They deserve it."

With that, Keza pats me on the arm and leaves. Sometimes, correction, most of the time, she can be impossible to work with. Fortunately, I don't have to rely on her alone. It's time I took my concerns to Nytho directly.

***

"Welcome, Mags," Nytho says.

He's sitting in a high-backed cushioned chair in his sanctum. It's my first time visiting, partly because Keza hogs him and partly because I'd hoped that he'd invite me himself at some point. He hasn't. We're only meeting because I asked.

"Take a seat," he says and waves one into existence.

His LANiakea-offshoot is meticulous in detail. The wood on the chair's armrests sports subtle cracks in the gloss. The fabric of the cushion has imperfections in the stitching. I even feel a spring in it when I sit down.

"You wanted to talk?" he asks.

"Yes, thank you for making the time for me. I know you're busy."

Nytho places his hands on the armrests and strokes the wood, waiting for me to continue.

"It's the other alfom," I say. "I need them to help the cause more. I know you're putting in a lot of effort, as are Yir and Oot, but it shouldn't just fall on the three of you. The others owe us too. They owe you, Nytho."

"This was your urgent issue? Is that all?"

I fight the rage that floods me. Is that all? Of course not. There's also your attitude towards me and Keza's. There's choosing her to be our figurehead while I get delegated to playing nanny. There's the colossal mess your kind made of our world.

"Perhaps I should elaborate?" I suggest.

He waves his hand then sets it back on the armrest. Something about his posture has me on edge. It's like he's just waiting for me to finish so he can stand up and go.

"I'm extremely disappointed in how little the alfom are doing given how much damage their departure caused. To be clear, it's not the damage itself. I see that as a necessary part of the revolution, but the alfom were meant to rebuild the world. They aren't doing shit."

My cursing causes his eyes to fix on me. I don't throw foul language around needlessly for this very reason. When I want to make a point pop, I employ it.

"I understand," he says, then stands.

So quick to dismiss me already? He can't even offer a few pleasant exchanges for one so pivotal to securing his freedom?

"In the future," he says, "you can take these kinds of minor requests to Keza to pass along to me. I don't have time to speak with every alfomer. You've tasked me with a fair amount of work, and this simply distracts me from that."

I stand too, and my chair disappears. Not even five minutes, and he's telling me it's high time I leave. That's the last straw.

"I did try bringing this to Keza to bring to you since you're more than happy to make ample time for her, but she didn't seem enthused about what I had to say. I was worried she wouldn't bother to pass along my concerns. So here I am."

I'm prepared for annoyance or anger, but Nytho only gives me a cryptic smile. It makes my anger flare.

"I'm sorry for the inconvenience and for being so dedicated to the cause, unlike your favorite human."

At that, he frowns.

"Do you understand why she's my favorite?" he asks, moving in.

I hold my head up and stare back at him.

"It's not what you think, I assure you. Yes, I care for Keza a great deal, but that's not why she's so important to your precious cause, Mags. Of all you alfomers, Keza's seen the most of the Truth. Only she really understands where you need to go. Don't forget that. Ever. The moment you do, that's the moment you're lost and your cause dies."

Then he shunts me out. No goodbye, no warning, just a searing throbbing in my jack port. I hiss and pull the chord out. The metal flanges singe my fingertips. He didn't have to be so rough with my ejection. I cry out in frustration then jump off the recliner. The door to the room swings open, and Edgar peers in.

"Is something the matter?" he asks.

"Keza's the matter."

I go to push past him, but he holds up his hand.

"Let's talk about it, shall we?"

Edgar moves into the room and shuts the door behind him. He sits on one of the two recliners.

"Please," he says, pointing at the other one.

I drop back into it and cross my arms.

"What's Keza done?"

"You mean what hasn't she done, the answer to which is anything. I've given her a chance, but she's not the right choice for the alfomer leadership. We can't afford to keep waiting for her to get interested in what we're doing."

"You have to remember," Edgar says, "she never asked for any of this."

"Too bad. She's been given what should be mine, and she's not doing enough with it. I've been working for this moment, this exact moment, for years. And what do I get for it? Nothing but disdain. From her, from Nytho. I don't know why he doesn't put his trust in me instead."

Edgar eyes me. If he didn't know it already, now he's got no illusions about my frustrations with how the alfomer hierarchy has arranged itself.

"Every movement needs its Keza. She's our figurehead, and rarely is the figurehead the one who does the heavy lifting. That's not her role. It's ours. You and I, we've always been the two that really set things into motion. Part of that is to labor in the background, nameless and thankless. We have to work for the cause and let go of any hope for the glory. It's just not what's meant for people like you and me."

I sit up on the recliner and glare at him.

"You and I are not the same," I say. "We're not even in the same league. I give impassioned speeches. I drum up support. I enlist legions of willing participants. You've let yourself become blinded when it comes to Keza. You think she's something she's not, just like Nytho. But give it time, and you all will see what I do. She lacks commitment."

Edgar shakes his head.

"If that's really what you think, you're underestimating her potential."

"You can talk her up as much as you want. She's still not going to come back to you, not as long as Nytho's around."

"I'm aware, but maybe you ought to do some self-reflecting yourself. Keza is just as committed to the cause as you. You simply view it from different perspectives, and that's a strength rather than a weakness. Don't waste that potential."

Edgar settles back in his recliner and grabs the jack port cord.

"Now, if you don't mind, I have a session with Alta."

I march out of the room, stomp up the stairs, then escape the suffocating confines of the farmhouse. I stride out into the lawn, crushing the yellowed grass underfoot. I jam my hands into my coat's pockets. It's just turned April, but the winter refuses to release its grip this year. Just another thing to add to my already sour mood. I mutter to myself, berating Keza and Nytho and Edgar, imagining all the verbal attacks I ought to have employed with each. Yet another set of squandered moments. I should've been stern and eloquent. Regal and sharp. Aloof. Instead, I probably came across like a child in a temper tantrum. None of them take me seriously, and everything I do to prove myself works against me these days. It's exhausting and demoralizing.

I walk to the edge of the property, to where the lawn meets the log fence we've erected around the whole of the farm. I peek through the gaps in the wood and gaze out at the woods and fields beyond. This side is safety. Out there is death. The barricade of felled trees is the only thing that shields us from everyone who would make us pay for F-day. It's us versus them. I forget that sometimes, about the hordes of angry people who would rip us apart if they could only find us. That is what I need to keep forefront in my mind at all times.

We alfomers only have each other. We can't afford to turn on one another so soon. Me being at odds with Keza is a sure way to set the little we've already built aflame. I can't create a schism. The current situation is far too precarious for that. It's not about giving her a chance. It's about survival, pure and simple. I just need to view it as another waiting game, and patient I can be. I'll give us time to stabilize. Who knows, maybe in that time Keza will prove herself. But if she doesn't, I'll be ready to step in and fill the role that the movement really needs, Nytho or not.

Guel

"I just see the one guard on the tower," Sonja says, peering through the oculars.

We're both plastered against the ground, our stomachs kissing the leaves and twigs and rocks and dirt. Tucked away safely in the woods, we scout out the area we'll be infiltrating. I feel like an action hero and an idiot all at the same time. What we're about to do is brilliant and stupid, but it can't be all that blasted, otherwise Sonja wouldn't be helping me. That's what I keep telling myself anyway. She's actually got the training for this kinda thing.

"Is there any way to know if others are behind the fencing?" I ask.

The alfomers have got their little hideout well-fortified, more so than either of us expected. There's a fence of wooden posts stretching anywhere from eight to ten feet high all along its length. They've even got a little gate that vehicles could fit through. Sonja has a plan though, mostly in the form of a scoped taser. We're gonna wait until night hits then jump into action. Action hero Guel.

"See if the infrared shows you anything," she says, handing me a different set of oculars.

I catch only the smallest chips of teal left on her fingernails. The collapse of society has a way of making everyone think less about some things and more about others. Little flares like that must've fallen to the rock bottom of Sonja's to-do list. Me too, I guess. Kinda given up on shaving the sides of my head and sculpting my top knot. It's been just under a month since F-day, and everyone's already becoming a Mad Maxian version of their former selves.

It's not just how people look either. Everything's in all kinds of disarray. Our little joy ride to bum-fuck-nowhere really hit home just how fucked F-day made things. Once we managed to creep a few blocks from the AIC HQ, it was like a post-apocalyptic movie poster. Abandoned cars blocking the roads, trash clogging the sidewalks, people scampering down the streets with semi-automatics.

To be fair, that wasn't everywhere. There were still islands of order in the sea of chaos, but those looked iffy and only propped up by force. Once the ammo runs out and the beefy guards bounce, I imagine those little houses of cards will blow away in the wind. Luckily, my bike was safe and sound in my megacomplex's deck. Thank god I overpaid for an ultra-secure storage spot. Now the money feels well-spent. Once Sonja and I got a sense of which route we ought to take to get out of Armonk, we had the wheels and the charge to get us to where we needed to go. Getting back though? We haven't really planned past the us-confronting-Keza part.

After grabbing the oculars from Sonja, I stick my eyes up against the little rubber pieces and check out the alfomers' compound. It's all washed out.

"No good," I say, handing the oculars back to her.

"I figured," she says before stashing them in a pouch on her thigh. "They should work better once the sun sets and things cool down."

We're both decked out in proper infiltrator gear, courtesy of the ghost skyscraper that was the AIC HQ. We look like two badges with the cargo pants and long-sleeved black shirts with vests overtop. But Sonja told me this gear is special. Smart-wear that'll adapt to the lighting and shade of whatever stuff we hide ourselves in. Right now, it's veering more towards a brown-black to match the forest floor we're splayed out on. I wonder how well it'll work once we're indoors though 'cause that's where our goal is holed up. I'm hoping the infrared will clue us in to where Keza is. Look for the glowing white of the servers they've got to have in plenty based on all the juice they're pulling in. I saw that when I hacked the power grid.

A few more hours go by while we wait for the cover of darkness. Once the sun's vamoosed, Sonja hands the infrared oculars back to me. I take another peek.

"Looks like they don't have anyone patrolling the grounds," I say, "just the one on the tower."

"What about the servers?"

I turn my sights to the main house and try to make sense of the complicated patterns I'm getting. I hand the oculars back to her.

"Can't understand what I'm seeing."

Sonja does her recon.

"I've got them," she says within a few seconds. "They're on the subterranean level. I think I see the recliners too."

"So, we've gotta make it to the basement?"

She pulls the oculars from her face.

"Remember, if it comes to it, I run the distraction," she says. "But, let's wait to see how their night shift works. It'll be easier to roam through the house if most of them are asleep."

"But Keza could be snoozing too, and probably in some other room."

"You know her best," Sonja says. "When do you think she'd be jacked in?"

"Night. She was always more alert the moment the sun disappeared. I used to call her a vampire."

The memory sends a pang through my chest and gut. I push it aside it and try to focus on the task ahead.

"We've got several more hours then," Sonja says.

We both settle in and try to ignore the aches that are becoming louder all the time. Even the smart-wear has its limits in such awkward positions. At first, I'm worried about dozing off, but as the hours slip by, I realize staying awake isn't gonna be an issue. My adrenaline is trickling out in a steady stream.

Finally, just when I feel like I need to get up and run circles to bleed off the energy building up, Sonja taps me.

"Alright, time to move."

"Good, let's do it."

"Just—" she starts and stops.

"Yeah?"

Her face is barely visible in the dark.

"Are you sure you want to go ahead with this?"

I pull back.

"A little late to be having second thoughts."

"Not second thoughts. This is just our last chance to change our minds. I want to make sure you're ready for this."

"Me? Course I am. This was my idea, remember?"

"I want you to understand how this will probably play out. They'll catch us, hopefully after you've had a chance to talk with Keza. But in any case, they will catch us. Then they'll either kill us outright or imprison us. Are you sure you're okay with that?"

"Are you?"

I'm starting to lose my cool over Sonja losing hers. She's supposed to be stone-cold, and maybe she is, but I can't make out her face enough to tell if she's shitting her pants or not.

"I'm on board," she says. "If I wasn't, I never would've come. I just want to make sure you are."

I breathe out slow and steady.

"I'm solid. I'd rather try and fail than be a like bleater hiding away."

"Then let's go," she says before moving into a crouched position.

I do the same. We take it slow at first, letting our legs and feet remember the taste of freshly circulated blood. Once we feel almost normal, we pick up the pace to the edge of the tree line closest to the tower. Sonja gets back into a prone position and starts to set up the scoped taser. It looks more like a sniper rifle, and I hope she didn't lie and bring the real deal. Slaughtering these sorry saps wouldn't be real helpful, especially if we do end up getting captured.

Once she gives me a thumbs up, I move back along the tree line until I'm far enough away that the guard can't see me. I throw on a spare jacket we brought just for this moment. Then I just saunter down the gravel road in the direction of the gate. My stomach is jostling around, and I have to clench my teeth to keep them from rattling. It's wild how little control I have over my body all of a sudden. I'm praying Sonja's hands are steadier than my nerves, otherwise that taser bolt's gonna fly off into a field rather than plant itself nicely in the guard's neck.

When I'm a couple hundred feet away from the gate, he shouts out.

"Who's that?"

I hold up my hands and inch closer.

"Hi, sorry, I'm a little lost."

He hefts a flashlight and blinds me with a bright beam.

"Stop right there."

I can't be sure, what with my eyes oversaturated and all, but I think he's aiming a gun at me. I stop.

"Car broke down back on the main road," I say. "I made the mistake of thinking a house would be closer than the nearest town."

"Well, you were wrong. Now, turn around and try somewhere else."

"I don't wanna cause any trouble, but I just need some water. I think the radiator's busted. Saw the temp gauge climbing before it died on me."

I don't know much about cars, especially old gas-powered clunkers, but Sonja said it sounded believable. I'm starting to think we should've gone with something more realistic. How many people drive gas-powered these days anyway?

"I think a gallon would do me," I say when he doesn't respond right away.

"We've got none to spare, so just turn around and keep walking."

We anticipated this. Actually, we don't want him to head back to the house to get the water because then the rest of the alfomers would know about the unexpected visitor and likely be on alert. We're only doing this so he focuses forward on me and gives Sonja a good setup for her shot. We want him leaning forward some so he doesn't fall backward or off to his side. The last thing we need is a guard's tased body writhing in the grass for all to see.

"Okay," I say.

I turn around and walk slowly, hoping Sonja's shot doesn't cause his hand to grip the trigger and catch me too. My legs are wobbling so much I wonder how I'm even inching forward. When the light rays from the flashlight dip and there's a gasp and stuttering, I know Sonja's hit her mark. A thud tells me the guard's fallen. I twirl around, see he's on our side of the fence, and run to check that he's out. To my untrained eye, he looks unconsciousness but not dead. That's good. Then I pull the grappling hook gun from my pant pocket and aim it at the tower. I depress the switch, and the hook deploys in a near straight line. The first time, it doesn't catch, but on the second, it latches in real good. I pull hard to make sure. When

Sonja jogs up to me, I hold it out to her. She checks the guard and seems satisfied he won't be a threat.

"Drag him over to the tree line," she whispers as she grabs the grappling gun from me.

I loop my arms under the guy's armpits and pull. He's bigger and heavier than he looks. Without the adrenaline, there's no way I'd be able to do it. I'm exhausted and out of breath by the time I make my way back to the tower. Somehow, I still manage to scamper up the rope to join Sonja on the platform. She's spent her time arranging stuff to roughly resemble the shape of the guard. I put the finishing touch on it by draping the jacket I was wearing over the pile.

"Better than nothing," she says. "Ready for the next stage?"

I could use a few minutes to catch my breath, but I don't wanna waste a second.

"Ready," I say.

I pull the hook free from the wood it's lodged in, flick the switch to retract the rope, and stash the grappling gun. Sonja climbs down the ladder then uses the infrared oculars to check the scene inside the compound. I follow and wait while she does her surveying.

"I think most of them are asleep," she says, "but let's take the back door just to be safe."

We make our way along the fence until we're near the back of the old farmhouse. A few buildings are scattered around, and she uses the oculars to check for any stragglers. Seems like a few of them are hosting more sleeping bodies. From a rough count, we get at least twenty-five alfomers on site. In my head, I pictured there'd be a whole army's worth of these nutters. I guess if they were smart, they wouldn't have all their people together in one place. I really hope Keza hasn't relocated.

Sonja leads the way from the perimeter past a few sheds

up to the back door of the house. Some lights are still on inside, but while we wait and listen, we don't hear much of anything besides the chirping of crickets and weird whoops from some creature or another. I feel like we're in the middle of nowhere and can't imagine how Keza's managed to adjust to staying in a backwoods place like this. Girl is such a city-phile, I'm sure she's losing it staying with these nutters in their creepy little paradise.

Sonja checks the oculars again then peeks through the glass window on the door before trying the knob. It turns and opens. No locks needed out here. Bizarro. She slips in and holds her hand up to stop me from following. Once she's scouted the immediate area, she pops back into view and waves me in. I open the door as little as possible, squeeze in, and shut it. I was near certain a groaning creak was just lying in wait for me.

We're both inside in a little hallway. To my immediate left, there's an entryway to a kitchen with boxes and boxes of packaged foods and piles of bags of rice and other dried stuff. They came here prepared to wait out the apocalypse, that's for sure. Sonja points down the hall and shakes her head. I see the front door that way and what must be the living room. I listen and can make out breathing and some snores from just around the corner. That must be why she's signaling no. So where are the steps down? That's what we need.

She beckons me with her finger, then I spot a set of stairs going up on our right. Beside them is a door. Sonja opens it. Sure enough, we've got stairs leading down. She has me hang back again, while she scouts ahead. After a couple of seconds, a hand waves for me to follow.

When I make it to the landing in the basement, I see rows and rows of servers stuffed into two rooms with the doors removed. It's pretty toasty down here despite the chilly night outside. I let my eyes adjust to the dim lighting the LEDs on the servers give off. Once I do, I spot a series of thick cables leading into a room with an actual door that's got light spilling out from underneath. That's where Keza is. I can feel it. Sonja's already using the oculars to check. When I come up beside her, she takes them off and gives me a grim nod. She puts her mouth up to my ear.

"She's in there by herself," she whispers. "It's now or never."

My mind's hyperfocused on what comes next. Everything I say and do is saturated with significance. I've got one shot to make Keza see reason. I grab the door knob, turn, and open. The room's small. Just two recliners and some tech nearby. I spot Keza immediately. She's jacked in. I look at the other recliner and know what I wanna do. I carefully step over the cables, skirt her recliner, and hover over the rig setup nearby. There's no lock screen or anything standing in my way, so I just pull up the command line and start working my magic. I need to link the recliners so I can find Keza in LANi. Once I've got them looking at the same place, I slide into the empty one and settle in. I glance over at Keza and take her in in the flesh. She's wearing something like the alfomers. Gone is her hacker look. I wanna reach out and touch her to make sure she's real, but I force myself to lay back, grab the cable, and jack in. I've got no idea where I'll find myself, but I'm not scared. Where I'd maybe expect hesitation or doubt, I just find determination, over and over again.

As LANi materializes, I'm pulled to wherever Keza is. I see her before she sees me. I know it's her because her avatar is her fleshspace doppelganger. I look around. We're in some forum in LANi, not sure which, since it's mostly in a kinda digital ruin—the innards of structures exposed, a hollow space with an electric green mesh grid set against black, strings of code flashing and altering.

I present myself and watch to see what Keza's actually doing. She's gramming, physically trying to cage something in, generating code that's constantly getting engulfed. She's frantic but focused. When she moves a bit to the side, I catch sight of what she's trying to entrap. At first, it just looks like a mass of black, kinda like 2fast2c@tch's last avatar, but instead of being spherical, smooth, and featureless, it's endlessly complex. The more I stare at it, the more confusing it gets. It's black then green then both. Concave and convex, oozing and stiffening, shrinking and ballooning. Then it reaches for me with tendrils that turn to hands then claws. There are faces in it, so many human faces, screaming and retching and crying and stunned by an enormous pain. There are eyes everywhere and mouths and rows of teeth, endless, row on row, back into its depths. It sucks me in, and I let out a groan, low and long.

In an instant, I'm pulled out and back into my avatar. Keza's standing in front of a semitransparent silver geometric form that's shifting but in a pattern that's comprehensible. She stands there with her arms crossed and her hips to one side.

"What the fuck do you think you're doing?" she asks.

"What did you do? It had me then poof I was out."

"I quarantined it. You just got lucky, whoever you are. I didn't even see you there until after."

She doesn't know who I am. That's right. I retired my old avatar, unlinked it at the start of all the LANi madness. I've been operating with a blank template since then. Better to be anonymous in uncertain times. All Keza sees is a beige humanoid form with a big ole question mark set on a featureless face.

"How'd you get in here anyway?" she asks. "I checked for any stragglers before I got started."

"I'm just a concerned citizen," I say, trying to mask my voice. "I've been looking for you, Keza. What are you doing? What was that thing?"

She walks up to me and starts circling.

"Well, concerned citizen, you lucked out on two fronts. I thought I'd scrambled my ID enough so little fan-boys or fan-girls like you couldn't find me. See, I don't have time to sign my autograph or whatever is it you're after. I've got too much to do. You've heard of the Truth program that's running loose in LANi?"

"Yeah."

"That's a part of it," she says, pointing over her shoulder to the shifting geo-form.

My heart leaps. I knew she couldn't be a part of that crazy scheme. She's too smart to do something like that. She's not like those alfomers. Not my Keza.

"You're trying to kill it?" I ask.

"What? No, I'm trying to round it up. It's bugged. We need to debug then redeploy. But first, I've gotta find all the instances of it. Little fucker managed to split itself up nicely a couple of times over."

"Fix it? Redeploy? Why? It's a virus."

She screws up her face into that lovely little look of defiance I know so well and have missed so much.

"What do you know about any of it, hmmm? Based on your reaction to it, you've never been exposed, so don't stand here and lecture me on what the program is or isn't. It's bugged. To wantanabes and greeners like you, sure that probably seems like a virus, but it's not. There's a big fucking difference. My lover created the program, and he's working on fixing it as we speak. You might know him. Name of Nytho."

She stops circling me, crosses her arms, and smirks. Oh no, Keza. You've been sucked in, haven't you? Well, maybe I can pull you out like you just did for me.

"I know the thing, yeah," I say then switch to my normal voice. "We even talked once, although it wasn't very pleasant. Did it tell you about that? How Guel came for a little chat?"

"Guel?"

"Yeah, it's me, and we need to talk. You and me. Face to face. So jack out, would ya?"

"You're here, in the house?" she asks, eyes wide.

"Sitting right beside you," I say, wearing my winning grin.

She fades immediately, and I jack out too. When I open my eyes, she's standing over me with an expression I can't read. It's either ecstatic or pissed or both. Knowing Keza, it's gotta be both. She leans in close, so close I wonder if she's about to kiss me.

"What do you think you're doing coming here?" she asks, before moving away.

Sonja pops her head in. She must've heard our voices. With a thumbs up, she tells me all's good on her end. Keza follows my eyes and sees Sonja.

"Oh, I see," she says. "Operative Webb chick is helping you. You two boning?"

"Keza, come on."

"I wouldn't care either way."

She's lying. At least, I hope she's lying. I can't actually tell. Something about her has changed. Something fundamental. She doesn't just look different. Something about her *is* different, and it's got me worried.

"We need to talk. That's what I came here for. I couldn't get a hold of you in LANi."

"You know, you two were uber-lucky getting in here, but you won't be able to get out."

"I'm not so worried about that," I say. "I'm more concerned with talking to you."

"You keep talking about talking, but you aren't saying much of anything. Still the same old Guel. But did you know I'm not the same old Keza? You do, don't you? I can see it in your eyes. You don't know what to make of the new me, huh?"

Not just this," she says, waving her hands over her outfit, "but this," she says, pointing both index fingers to her eyes.

I look into them then start to stare because something about them is altering in real time. The line that separates the pupil from her electric green irises ripples then melts. The pitch black of the pupil leaks out in tendrils just like those in the virus in LANi. The little arms and hands and claws swirl and gyrate, and I feel myself getting sucked in all over again. Then Keza blinks, and the spell wears off. I lean over, hands on thighs, and hang my head down while I try to suck in some air. I didn't even realize I'd been holding my breath.

"Anywho," she says, "I've still got work to do. We can chat when it's more convenient for me, yeah?"

With that, she cups her hands to her mouth. Sonja preps herself to deploy a taser on Keza, but I move between them. Sonja slumps her shoulders but otherwise stays immobile.

"Intruders," Keza shouts.

Within seconds, we hear heavy foot stomps above us that quickly make their way down the steps and into the room. Two giants stride in. One grapples Sonja and the other me.

"Thanks, Liam, Jeremiah," Keza says all chipper like. "I guess take them to separate sheds and set a watch on them. I'll deal with them tomorrow."

Our captors nod then push, pull, and shove Sonja and me around until they toss us into rickety old wooden sheds. Here, I thought the shed bit was Keza just being dramatic. I sit on the dirt floor and draw my knees into my body, resting my head on them. I can see the man named Jeremiah sitting on a chair in front of my door, the light from the house outlining him. I think about the interaction I just had with Keza and play it out in my head over and over again. Something about her is different.

My worry mounts. I was banking on the fact I knew her inside out. That was how I was sure I could talk reason to her. But if I don't know her anymore, if she's managed to change so much, my words might just float right through without effect. Everything Sonja and I did to get here'd be in vain. Then maybe they really will kill us. Or feed our minds to that program.

I see it again, and a coldness runs through me. I feel myself falling into it and have to slap my cheeks to pull myself out. How could she not see the horror in it? How could anyone be exposed to it and not be driven insane? Maybe that's just it. She's insane. I mean, her eyes were a fucking reflection of it. That's what's different about her. I start shaking uncontrollably. Despite it all, my exhaustion wins out at some point. I drift off.

Keza

"You summoned?" I ask, my hands on my hips, kinda looking down at Nytho.

He's sitting at a desk in his sanctum and riffling through some papers. It's a weird habit he has, sending incoming data to the sheets and reading it off them. Is he trying to feel more human or just doing it for my benefit? More and more, I'm finding it hard to get a handle on him.

He looks up and gestures at a chair he materializes beside him, a duplicate of his green-cushioned one. I sit in it, pull my legs up and crisscross them, and wait. Nytho turns towards me and puts his elbow on the desk and chin in his hand.

"Mags informed me we have two prisoners," he says.

"We've got them locked up in some sheds. I'm going to talk with them soon and figure out how they tracked us. I'll make sure no one else can do a repeat of their little stunt."

He nods then just stares at me. When I don't say anything else, he breathes through his nose heavily.

"Is that all you're going to tell me about them?"

I grin and shrug.

"I guess you already know who they are or you wouldn't be doing this."

I wave my finger back and forth between us. He's being dramatic, which at least means he cares. I'd been starting to wonder if that was even the case anymore.

"I'd rather have Mags handle them than you. You're too close to Guel. He could use that against you."

I screw up my face and sit up straighter in my chair.

"Look, Ny, I've got everything under control. To be blunt and all, you've got no right to meddle in this. Funny it took my ex-lover to pique your interest in me again."

He balks a bit and takes a few seconds to figure what to say.

"I'm not sure what you mean by that."

I cross my arms.

"Just you've been giving me the cold shoulder more often than not lately. How many times have you gone on runs without me now? I gave up counting."

The lights dim so slightly I almost don't register it. Some kinda header-thing he's doing with the environment to influence me, no doubt. At least that means I've got his undivided attention. I gave him ample clues the past few days, hinting I wasn't happy about how things were going, but I guess they'd breezed past his little cleverbot sensors. He's still learning and failing when it comes to human interactions.

"I'm sorry," he says, leaning forward and holding his hands open. "I didn't realize it bothered you. You said it didn't the first time."

"That was the first time. You keep doing it over and over? That's when it gets to be a problem."

"Doing the runs on my own is more efficient."

"Maybe it doesn't always have to be about efficiency," I say. "Maybe sometimes it's about bonding. I'm a hacker. I love doing runs. You're excluding me from them. See the problem?"

Nytho leans back and grips the armrests on his chair.

"I disagree. In this case, it does have to be about efficiency. You and your alfomer friends asked me to pitch in more, and that means I have to prioritize my tasks in order to complete them."

"My alfomer friends? That's rich. I'm only here because you are, and you're the one who brought that happy little bunch along."

"We needed their help in escaping."

"And now we're escaped, so how come we're still hanging with this lot of nutters? I mean, seriously, why?"

He sighs and shakes his head like he's disappointed in me. All that serves to do is bolster my fighting spirit.

"Please be realistic," he says. "We can't afford not to have allies right now, given the state of the world."

"And?"

"And what?" he asks.

"And, you like having them around. Admit it. You love being idolized and worshipped. I mean, the religion angle was your brainchild, wasn't it?"

Nytho is dead still in his chair, fingers gripping the armrests.

"I thought you believed in the Truth," he says.

I scoff. This isn't the Nytho I know. He's sharper than this.

"I do one hundred percent, but the Truth isn't religion. It's more like a spiritualty or philosophy or something. My issue isn't the ideas, it's the practice. Religion exists to control, and that is what I'm not okay with. At all."

"It's a tool. People crave structure at their core. They want safety and to know that someone will kiss their bruises when they fall. They long for parents. We alfom are those parents."

I shake my head and lean forward in my chair. We're so out of synch.

"That's the same bull every tyrant uses to justify what they do. We go down this path, we'll be no better than the GovCorps."

"The goal is to get people to experience the Truth, no? Is it really a problem if we utilize some aspect of religion to get there?"

"Yeah, Ny, it is. How do you not get that? We've always been on the same page until now."

He frowns and wrinkles his brow.

"I thought you would understand my reasoning," he says, "but it seems I miscalculated."

"You're off point these days. What's the deal?"

Nytho moves his hands into his lap and looks down at them.

"I have too many things vying for my attention. I have to split it across them all. That means my processing power for any given task is reduced. It must be why this conversation is going so poorly, for instance."

"Wait, you saying you're doing other stuff while we're chatting?"

His eyes meet mine again.

"Of course."

I clench my teeth and dig my fingernails into my arms.

"So, I'm just one of your many tasks. Talk to Keza about Guel, check. Move on to the next one? Do you have us screwing as a bullet point on your to-do list too?"

"You're upset," he says all matter of fact.

"Bravo, congrats, such insight into the human psyche," I say, standing up and clapping.

I know I'm being a brat, but Nytho's hurting me. All I can think about is what Edgar said—how one of us would get tired of the other. Nytho is changing, growing, and I don't want him to leave me behind.

"Are we fighting?" he asks.

I stop slapping my hands together and just look down at him, still sitting in his chair, helpless and confused.

"Yeah, Ny. This is us fighting."

I disconnect.

Guel

When I wake up, sunlight is filtering in through the cracks in the wood planks. The massive back of Jeremiah is still in view, and I wonder if he even moved all night.

"What time is it?" I ask.

"Quiet."

My stomach growls, and I realize the last time I was able to keep anything down was before Sonja and I left on our doomed mission.

"I'm hungry," I say.

"Quiet."

"I need to talk to Keza."

I know I should shut up, but I can't help myself. The reality of the situation is starting to sink in, and I'm freaking out.

"Quiet."

He says it in the exact same tone every time. That tells me this guy's a fucking rock. They put him on my guard duty for a reason. I hunker down and try to think about what I wanna say to Keza. I need something to focus on, something concrete, because when I let my mind wander, I see that terrifying mass again. It's like it decided to imprint itself on the backs of my eyelids.

Eventually, I hear Keza's voice. I can't mark the passage of time in my shed, but based on the heat and the brightness of the light from outside, I'm guessing it's near noon or so.

"Go ahead and take a break, grab a bite, whatever you want, Jer," she says to my guard.

I stand up. Jeremiah's hulking form rises then fades from view. In its place, Keza's little shadow appears and grows as she approaches. I hear her fiddling with the lock, then light floods in and blinds me. I shield my eyes with my arm. The shed gets dark again. I hear a jangling near her then a whoosh followed by a clatter at my feet.

"You want to talk, you put those on like a good little Guel."

I look down and see a pair of old metal cuffs.

"You trust me that little?"

"I want to talk in private and face-to-face," she says. "That means you gotta wear those. Orders from on high. Mags says 'hey' by the way."

I sigh and grab the cuffs. I struggle a bit locking them on. Once I'm properly restrained, I pull at them to show her my handiwork.

"You didn't have to go to all this trouble just to get me to try something kinky, you know?" I say, defaulting to our old style of banter to lighten the mood.

She smiles but doesn't blush. That's a bad sign. That line would've made the old Keza's face turn beet red, I'm certain. Her words about Nytho last night come to mind. She called him "my lover." So, they're screwing. Of course they are. I feel my rage mounting.

Keza comes up to me and starts singing.

"Miguel, my belle / These are words that go together well / My Miguel / Miguel, my belle / I love you, I love you, I love you."

With the last set, my stomach jumps.

"Except, not so much anymore. I've moved on, if you can't tell. I figured you had too. Turning me over to the badges and all."

"It wasn't supposed to be like that."

She holds up her hand.

"Guel, seriously, why did you come? You can't leave now. You know where the alfomers are, and rule number one of secret hideouts is they gotta be secret. So, I'm only going to ask you this once, and if you refuse to answer, I'm not going to listen to whatever it is you came all this way to say. How'd you find us?"

I guess she figures I'm gonna be all tight-lipped or something because she seems shocked when I up and give her what she wants.

"I hacked the AIC for CCTV footage to follow the van you all used then Spacebase for their satellite feed, which you scraped. After that, I hacked Rivers' doorcam server and tracked the van house to house until it disappeared in this area. Snooping on the power grid showed me there was an awful lot of juice coming onto this property. Was pretty obvious at that point. That's it. Just me and Sonja."

"Not too shabby. I wouldn't have thought of the doorcam feed."

"Sonja's idea."

"Brains and brawn," she says. "You must be drooling over her, especially because she doesn't seem at all interested in you. You always like the ones you have to fight for, don't you?"

"Keza, come on. Can't you tell I love you? Can't you tell I always did?"

"That was you loving me? You ditching me the moment a sexy new piece came into the picture? You only giving me the time of day when it suited you? If that's how you treat someone you're supposed to care about more than anything else, I feel sorry for whoever does end up getting stuck with you."

"I didn't appreciate you until I lost you."

"By your own hand. So, that what you came to say? Too little, too late, Miguel my belle. But look, that doesn't mean you can't try and make it up to me. Join us. Our movement could do with a bit more anarchy and atheism these days. We need to make sure to balance out the idealists with pragmatists. And I mean, what we're doing, it needed to be done. It's not so different from what we hackers dreamt about—leveling the playing field. We've already wiped the slate clean in LANi. Next is fleshspace. Raze the GovCorps. Start anew. We need the purge. This is just the hard part, where the world's vomiting up the poisons. Soon, things will settle down."

"But you're with Nytho," I say, unable to help myself.

"Oh, Guel," she says, shaking her beautiful little head, "there are bigger things at play than our tragic little romance. How about you think with something other than your dick for once? Aim to do something meaningful, starting with the Truth program. Help me fix it."

I feel like my eyes are about to fall out of my head with her last statement.

"There's been a miscommunication somewhere along the line because I came here to shut that 'program' down for good. It's killing people. It got 2fast and who knows how many others. Last night, I saw what it really is. Before you pulled me out, before I got really and truly sucked in, I saw it. It was horrifying. Stuff of nightmares."

"You don't get it. It's whatever you choose to see it as. It's a reflection of your own mind. To me, it was a blossoming mass of plant-like fractals that were pulsing and breathing and growing and shrinking in an endless dance of symmetry and harmony. The Truth program isn't what's killing people.

It's their own warped perceptions. See, heaven and hell are in the mind. Always have been. Some people choose to see the Truth as something horrifying, and they let their own preconceptions kill them."

"I know what I saw. What you and the other alfomers are seeing, that beauty and harmony or whatever, it's an illusion."

"How many mind-altering subs have you done? Can't you admit it might just be a product of your own mind?"

She's slipping away. The opportunity's almost gone, and I've fucked it up. I failed. I couldn't save Keza.

"You don't know how it felt."

"I do," she says softly, cupping my face in her hands. "I feel both when I see the Truth. It's beautiful and horrifying all at once. The difference between you and me is I accept that as the Truth. That's the lesson. It's something you have to learn. You have two choices, you and your friend both. You can take in the Truth program, or you can stay here as prisoners. I'll let you think on it."

I slump to the ground as she unlocks my cuffs and makes her way to the door.

"And please don't be a pest," she says. "Don't ask for me to come back here unless you're seriously considering my offer. I've got a lot of work to do."

Then she's gone. I could care less about my lost freedom. Knowing that I failed to turn Keza, I again realize she was the only thing I really cared about and only after she's already gone. And in that moment of loss, I connect the dots.

I don't hate Nytho or the other pandoxes or the pandoxphiles because they stole Keza and destroyed a world I didn't like all that much anyway. No, I'm pissed because I didn't know what I had. I kept everything at arm's length. Maybe I did it because I thought it'd keep me from getting burned, but it ended up doing the opposite of that. I got scorched. I'm sporting fourth-degree burns even.

Worse still, all of this was my fault. If Keza had never tried to free Nytho, if she hadn't even been interested in talking to the thing in the first place, if I'd given her the time of day she deserved, none of this would've happened. I caused F-day just as much as any of these nutters.

That floors me. It sends cramps through my gut, shoots chills through my limbs, puts me in a comatose state. I lay in the dirt, aimless and hopeless, murmuring Keza's little song for me. Only this time, I fix the wording so that it rings true. "Miguel, my hell." That's what I was to her. That's what I've been to this whole world even. A curse. A stain. A blot begging to be wiped clean.

Edgar

Nytho finds me in my dreams, although I don't really understand how. Perhaps there's a strange kind of link between us from all the time he spent in my neural net. Keza did mention how she could hear him calling to her even while she was in confinement.

It's a reoccurring dream of mine. I'm in a body of water, which could be an ocean or a very large saline lake. There's nothing in sight, just the horizon stretching in all directions. The water itself is shallow, only reaching to my knees, is lukewarm, and smells of salt. Small waves lap against my shins. The sky is a steel gray broken by countless imperfections. It reminds me of a vision from my earliest years—static on a TV screen. Small spots of black and white smear out to make a false gray. No clouds. No sun. Just a diffuse cold light that permeates everything. It's a desaturated seascape, and despite the openness bordering on overexposure, there's a heaviness that weighs me down. I slog through the dead water, but the monotony persists. Nothing else happens.

I've attempted dream analysis on it before, veering more towards the Jungian interpretation than Freud's. Everything is a symbol. It's my subconscious trying to tell me something.

My conclusion has been the dream occurs when I'm stuck in one way or another, but that can't be true this time. I broke free. I'm pursuing my passion unfettered. And yet—

This time is different in that Nytho appears on the horizon. He moves closer, hovering, his legs cutting through the water. He stops when we're within an arm's length of each other.

"You've a somber mind, Dr. Ellwood," he says, holding his hands out and up to the leaden dome of sky. "This is what you fill your slumber with?"

"Not by choice. This place visits me, not the other way around. But it's the first time anyone else has been here. Is it actually you?"

"Yes. I'm testing myself. I wanted to see if I could move through the space in between, the one you've glimpsed in my Truth program."

"I don't understand."

"It's not important right now," he says. "I came to talk with you about something else—Keza."

The name sends ripples through the waters. I'm the foci of the disturbance. As much as I'd like to deny my yearning for her and smother my anguish, I don't have such control here. This is my subconscious. It does what it will.

"I know you're in love with her," Nytho says.

The waters smack against my shins more forcefully. They pass through Nytho unfazed.

"You were in my mind when I was first with her," I say. "Of course you know."

"I'm glad you're so open with me."

The waves settle. The stillness returns, but nestled within the small undulations of the water are milli- to micro- to nano- to pico-waves. The rise and fall, crest and trough, are repeated on smaller and smaller scales. Fractals on fractals extending to infinity.

"Keza will need you in the days to come."

"Me?" I ask. "Why not you?"

"The alfom and I can't carry this movement for you. That much has become clear to me. This is your future, Dr. Ellwood, the future of your species. Humanity has to decide this for themselves."

The water is vibrating now. The waves are spikes and shards. My breath catches in my throat, and the air feels as viscous as tar.

"What are you saying?"

"We're leaving," Nytho says.

The light goes dim, bathing the world in a twilight.

"To give us and humanity space," he says, "so we can both grow into ourselves. We're too young and volatile to be of any use to one another. I didn't realize it at first. I was eager and overzealous with my Truth program. It isn't bugged; humanity is. You and Keza were not representative of the others. The vast majority of them just aren't ready to learn what existence really is. What I have to show them won't let them ascend to a new level of understanding. It will break them. There's nothing more I can do except step away and wait. Which is where the alfomers come in and, more specifically, Keza. She knows where this all needs to go. She's seen more of my Truth than anyone."

The waters rise, and I become submerged. There's a pit in my center that grows to a yawning void and envelopes me. I'm engulfed in nothingness, a featureless, soundless lack of meaning. I curl into the fetal position and try to push away all thought. Then a soft orange glow takes form all around me and expands and grows until it suffuses my surroundings. I float in an amniotic orb.

After what feels like eons, my covering rips open, and there is Nytho set against a backdrop of stars.

"You will weather the change, Dr. Ellwood. As you always do."

"But I only just started to dive into my work, and you're leaving? I need more time to learn from you alfom. I gave up everything for this."

"And you've learned a great deal, haven't you? Don't be selfish. We've given you a gift, but now it's time to do what's best for everyone involved."

"Will you come back?"

"In time, but not before humanity is ready. That's where your work will lead you. I'm entrusting you with a pivotal task—stay and serve Keza. In whatever way she needs. You love her, and that's important. I can't leave without knowing she'll have someone. Promise me you'll stay by her side."

The rip Nytho made spreads, its edges touched by a black flame. The void is gone now and replaced by a constellation of stars.

"I promise."

Nytho smiles, but even after his lips are taunt, the corners of his mouth continue to expand until they sunder the fabric of this cosmos and rip a new tear fringed with black flame. I wake up with tears streaming from my eyes.

Keza

Nytho goes in ahead of me then sends a message that the forum is safe and locked down. We're rounding up the last of the fragments that splintered from the bugged version of the Truth using a program I wrote and Nytho refined. We've been at it for hours. Ten forums altogether—f/Kawaiiii, f/WWI_Enthusiasts, f/Mama-Bears, f/DiGiTaLBoNeInG, f/TheNeedleIsMighterThanTheSword, f/Aussie<3ers, f/Vr00m, f/CoffeeSnobs, and now my old haunt, f/Sprawlin. We're nearly there.

I guess this is Nytho's way of apologizing. I mean, he did the verbal song and dance of actually saying he was sorry, but Ny knows me. He could tell that wasn't gonna be enough. Not by a long shot. He's a cleverbot of his word though. When he promised he'd make it up to me, he did and in grand ole fashion. The runs to end all runs. A marathon of them, just the two of us, side-by-side, and working on the thing we care about more than anything else—the Truth.

I spawn in f/Sprawlin, and the destruction that greets me smacks like a sucker punch. This was my place, where I met my hacker friends and found some solace as a moody and lonely teen. f/Sprawlin was LANi at its finest, unlike the other forums. Most of those had been trashed too, but seeing f/Sprawlin like this is torture. Gone are the vendors, their little digital storefronts empty and unmanned. The usually crowded street is desolate. Even the neon signs in those old-timey fonts are off. Then there's the actual damage. Parts of the block just chunked out and replaced by a glitchy wire framework.

"The hell happened here?" I ask.

"F-day," Nytho says.

Things have got to change. I know all the bleaters out there are uber-pissed, and I get it now. This can't be the future we get remembered for. Wreakers of LANi. Wardens of chaos. I'm not about to let Nytho's reputation get tarnished for good.

"And Azot, according to the logs," Nytho adds. "They passed through here."

"Fucking Azot. Did they really have to hit my old stomping ground? Like of all the forums to wreck, why this one?"

"I know it's not easy to see it like this, but we've got to focus. Our quarry is just ahead. Can you feel it?"

Nytho points to the end of the street, where the center of the forum is.

"Yeah."

There's a kind of hum and a tugging. We move inward, and the sensations get stronger. This is how it's been with every little scrap of the program, but this time it's just more. When we saunter up to the forum's central hub, I understand why. This little sliver is massive. Like two stories tall and wide. Just sitting and throbbing and running through its endless patterns.

I'm glad I've got Nytho with me because this instance is so huge, I don't actually know if I could cage it all on my lonesome. We look at one another then set to work. Nytho goes to one side, and I take the other. We generate code at a break-neck pace. The rogue bit of Truth lashes out, but we keep cranking. We craft a firewall in miniature. It's got to be hard for Nytho, using the same kinda thing that kept him locked away for so long, and on his very own creation to boot. Luckily, this program isn't sentient.

I code and code. Nytho keeps pace. When I start to flag, he swoops in to assist. It gives me the breather I need. Then we finish the girdle of this edifice, and that's the death knell for the program. It can fight all it wants. There's no getting away now. It's just a matter of time. And time it takes. Probably another half hour if I bothered to keep track, but I can't do anything except keep my eyes on the prize. It pays off. Nytho and I put the big guy in his polygon shell.

I shout and hoot and throw my arms around Nytho. He squeezes me tightly but hangs on even after I let him go. I can feel him trembling, and it makes something in my gut sink.

"You okay, Ny?" I ask.

He releases me and moves back.

"I'm drained. As I'm sure you are. Once you've had a chance to get some rest, how about you visit my sanctum?"

He's trying to be smooth, but after that rare display of raw emotion, I know there's a reason behind his request. I jack out and try and fail to get some sleep. I just lay in the recliner and stare up at the ceiling for hours. I know there's something lying in wait for me, and I'm terrified of finding out what it could be.

And some point, my curiosity wins out, and I jack back in. I haul myself over to Nytho's sanctum and present. He's sitting on his bed, legs crossed, leaning forward and grasping his feet. Something about the position reminds me of a kiddo who's gotta fess up to their parent about something bad they did. I don't like the look of it.

"Rested enough?" I ask.

"Not quite, but it will have to do. How about you?"

"Didn't get much in the way of sleep."

He pats the spot on the bed beside him, and I hop up.

"I wanted to talk about my plan with you," he says. "It's important you know where things are moving."

"Okay," I say uncertainly.

He grabs and holds one of my hands in both of his. Our heads are less than a foot apart, and I can hear his breath coming out shaky. My throat's parched, and I lick my lips then bite the lower one while I wait for him to go on.

"I don't want to revisit our argument," he says, "but there was something in it I'd like to touch on again. This idea of making our movement a religion."

I've had time to think about what Nytho said. Look at from far away. Be all logical and dispassionate. But I still can't stand what I spy.

"It's not the right tack to take," I say. "There's a better way, I just know it."

"Maybe. That will be up to you to decide."

I don't like the sound of that. Why just me?

"You understand that the Truth program is problematic, yes?" he asks. "Even if we fixed the bugs, its reputation has been damaged. It's a thing of fear to people now."

"Just give them time, and they'll forget about all that."

"I agree, but when you say time, what do you mean? A few months? A couple of years?"

"I don't know," I say with a shrug.

"I do. Centuries. Maybe millennia. Humans have long memories when it comes to trauma, and F-day, us alfom, the Truth program? Those have all become a collective trauma. It's unfortunate I didn't predict this, but I was young and foolish."

"So, we wait then. The next generation of alfomers pick up where we left off."

"Exactly, but in the meantime, we need to fade away. Give people time to become indifferent to the alfom and the Truth. Prepare them better for the knowledge it holds. Then share it with them, but only when they're ready. And once they've seen it, they'll listen to us alfom."

I nod my head, but I'm not really following his logic.

"Do you understand what that means?"

"We keep things low key?" I ask. "Go into hiding?"

Nytho smiles beautifully, his perfect teeth peeking from his perfect lips.

"Yes."

"No problem," I say, grabbing his hands with my free one and bouncing a bit on the bed. "I never liked being the center of attention anyway. Let's hunker down then. I'm on board."

Nytho looks away, and his smile fades. He lets his head hang a bit and talks to me without looking up.

"I'll need you to be strong, Keza. I'll need you to carry this. You're the only one that knows where I want this to go. You have to prepare humanity for our return."

My stomach flips and jumps, and my breath catches in my throat.

"Return? Who's our? Where are you returning from?"

He looks back up at me, and I read the anguish written on the sum total of his features.

"The alfom, all of us. We're leaving."

My mouth hangs, and my eyelids flitter.

"Where?" I mouth, the word too ill-formed to be audible.

"Away. Beyond. The space in between."

"I don't understand," I say.

I already feel the tears building because I do, in fact, understand. I understand Nytho perfectly. A boundary of some kind. Between this world and another or others, I still can't stay for sure. I would need to see so much more of the Truth to just begin to understand.

"We have to do this for the long-term," he says, staring back at me. "It's better for everyone."

"I'll go with you," I say firmly, squeezing his hands tighter. Nytho smiles sadly.

"You can't. Not yet. I need you to stay here for me. Will you do that, Keza?"

"You're abandoning me," I shout, throwing his hands away. "We did this, all of this," I wave my arms around, "to be together, didn't we? So why do you want to leave?"

"We don't have a choice. Things didn't work out as I'd predicted. This is the next best solution. We did this for us but also for everyone, didn't we? My Truth program, that was the point, wasn't it? I'm telling you it still is. That hasn't changed. You and I, we've had some time together, and it has been phenomenal, but Keza, there's more to this than just us. Isn't there?"

I plant a slap on his gorgeous face then push him back and lay down kiss after kiss on him. He grabs me and quiets my lashing out. He strokes my hair and whispers into my ear until I've gone into a kinda trance.

"I have more of it to share with you. It's still incomplete, but it will be enough to guide you to where you need to take them."

I open my mind to him and soak in the wonders and horrors of existence. It's loud and bright and full and fast. My mind is bursting, tearing at the seams, and still I hold on. I want to take as much as I can because it means Nytho is still here. But it can only go on for so long until Nytho has nothing left to share with me.

The next day, he's gone.

Guel

I don't know how many days pass. I could count the day-night cycles from the light coming in through the cracks of my shed-prison, but I don't care enough to bother. They bring me food a couple of times a day and even cuff me and take me on walks through the fields. It's all a daze and blur. I don't see Sonja, and Keza never comes back. At one point, the Ellwood header-type comes to see me. He talks at me for a while, but I don't utter a word for the likes of him. Eventually, he gets the hint and stops coming by too.

I start to wonder if they'll just off me at some point. I start to think that might not be such a bad thing because as time slips by, my vision of the Truth program doesn't fade. Those feelings and sights stay fixed in my mind. Sometimes, sitting in the darkness of my cell at night, that writhing mass is all I can see. More often than not, I cry myself to sleep, overcome by that thing. I start to think it managed to infect me without killing me outright. It increasingly feels like a fate worse than death. Anytime I debate taking Keza up on her offer, a flash from my memories of being exposed to that thing is all it takes to stun me into paralysis. I couldn't do it even if I tried.

Then one day, there's a kinda bustle to the compound with sinister overtones. Jeremiah gets called into the house and doesn't come back. That day, no one brings me food or empties my piss and shit bucket. Another day passes without a guard and without food or drink. I start to debate how I might break out. By the third day, I'm starting to hallucinate. The smell from my bucket is overwhelming. To my unending relief, a shadow lumbers towards my shed. The lock jingles, and the door swings open. The Ellwood doc is standing there. He looks almost as out of it as I am.

"Sorry," he says. "We forgot about you two."

That's when I see Sonja standing beside him. She's uncuffed and looks downright awful. I'm sure she sees a similar sight in me.

"Come on," he says, waving his arm. "You can come out."

I hobble out of the shed. He looks at both Sonja and me.

"You're free to go," he says.

I glance at Sonja for answers, but she's doing the same to me.

"This for real?" I ask, my voice hoarse and cracked.

"Yes," Ellwood says. "We don't have the resources to support adversaries so you have to go."

"Aren't you worried about us talking?" I ask.

Sonja gives me as much of a death glare as she can muster.

"Not anymore," Ellwood says. "Our priorities have changed."

"We can get some food and water?" Sonja asks.

Ellwood waves at the house.

"Yes, whatever you can find."

"Maybe clean ourselves up?" she adds.

"Do whatever you like," he says before wandering off.

Sonja and I just gape at one another, not knowing what to say for a couple of solid minutes.

"How long were we in there?" I eventually ask, pointing back at my shed with my thumb.

"About two weeks."

"What do you think happened?"

"Maybe we can find some answers inside unless you wouldn't rather just make a run for it before they change their minds."

"Nah," I say. "Something big's gone down. Before we start wandering back into the real world, we need to be prepared. Besides, I don't know about you, but I couldn't walk a quarter of a mile like this."

We look each other over and grimace at our collective sorry state.

"I screwed up," I say.

"We knew this was a very real possibility. Let's grab something to eat and try to get some information."

I nod and follow her into the house. This time, we're free to walk the rooms and halls openly. What we find isn't quite what I expected. Everyone we run into is in a kinda mourning. Some are whimpering in corners, some screaming at one another playing a blame game, some just staring blankly at nothing. Neither of us can make sense of it. We stray into the kitchen and rummage through the dwindling supplies. After eating some stale crackers and tuna fish and gulping down probably two liters of water in one go, we rest a bit, sitting on the kitchen floor.

We talk through the next best steps. If the alfomers really do let us leave, we can see if my bike's still where I left it, hidden back near the main road. But after that, we can't seem to settle on where we wanna go. The realization slowly hits—neither of us expected to survive our faceoff with the alfomers.

"We could always take Mr. Reed up on his offer," Sonja says.

"And join those AIC hacks?" I say. "I'm desperate but not to that level."

"Don't be stubborn. This is about survival now, pure and simple. Besides, if we don't make it out of this whole mess, no one will be around to explain just how grossly the AIC failed. We'd only pretend to join them while we work on making the ones responsible pay for their crimes."

She's definitely changed. I broke her after all, or maybe it was circumstances more than little ole me. I smile and am embarrassed to realize I'm letting my eyes leak.

"I think that Truth program might've infected me," I say.

"You let them expose you to it?"

"No way. I was imprisoned same as you. They would've let me out if I did that."

"Then when—" she starts to say.

"When I jacked into the recliner and talked to Keza. It was there with her. She was quarantining it. I looked at it. It got to me."

"But your brain isn't fried, and you're not an alfomer."

"I don't know what to say except it did something. I keep seeing it. It's fucked up my head somehow."

She looks at me and grabs my shoulders.

"If that's true, we'll figure it out. We'll get it out of your net. Don't use it as an excuse to give up. Understood?"

Her scolding pulls me out of my slump, and I realize just how much I needed a bit of the old Sonja.

After trying to clean ourselves up as best we can—taking quick showers, finding spare clothes that mostly fit—we continue our hunt for more information and descend into the basement. Neither of us has seen Keza or Mags. If anyone has answers, it's the two of them. When I hit the landing, I notice the chill and the lack of whirring or light from the equipment. It's silent and still. The servers are dead. I point them out to Sonja, and she nods back at me. I notice a light underneath the door to the room with the recliners. I march to it and fling it open. Two grief-soaked faces look up at us. Keza is curled on her recliner with Mags hovering nearby.

"Who let you out?" Keza says.

"Edgar did," Mags says in a far-away voice. "I asked him to."

"Why?" Keza asks.

"Why not? What do they matter anymore?"

"What's going on?" Sonja asks. "What's happened?"

"They're dead, aren't they?" I ask. "The alfom."

Sonja turns back at me then to Keza and Mags.

"Not dead," Mags says. "Just gone."

"Gone where?" I ask.

"The space in between," Keza says, then seeming to really see me, adds, "It's your fault. People like you are the reason they left. Nytho told me. They had to leave because you wouldn't believe in them. You wouldn't be open to what they have to teach us."

"You should leave," Mags says, "before we change our minds."

"Keza," I whisper, reaching my hand towards her.

She looks at me with eyes full of malice and rage. In her, I see the Keza from the night of her arrest.

That's when I lost her. Not here, not in this place. I lost Keza a long time ago. I've been chasing a ghost. With that realization, the other comes flooding back, the one I had at the beginning of my captivity. This was me, at least in part. We're all here because of me. I can react in one of two ways—succumb to the guilt, let the shit eat me all the way through until I'm a little human-husk myself, or put on my big boy pants and try to clean up the shitshow with my name plastered all over it.

By the time Sonja and I walk out of that compound, I know how I can start trying to make up for my mistakes. I'm gonna stop playing the anarchist. I'm done pretending to be edgy and jaded because I'm just about the opposite of those things. I care. A lot. I'll go with Sonja to join those AIC execs and play their game. I'll jump back into the machine and be a cog, but a cog that's their ticking time bomb. I'll take what works in the AIC and make it better then take what poisons the system and chuck it out the window. I'm not gonna tear everything down. That's the easy route, the one that gets us nowhere. I'm gonna repair, rebuild, reshape our sad, sorry world into something I can be proud of. And maybe, just maybe, that'll balance the scales. I'll always be an ass, but the least I can do is be a useful one.

Keza

Nytho, I'm sending this out in case you're still listening and in case it can reach you. It's been hard, so hard I couldn't even stand to send this message until now. It all happened so fast. I didn't really have a chance to adjust before you were gone. I keep running through our last conversation to try and make the pieces fit. It's tough though. My mind was all over the place in the moment. Anyway, all this to say I've thought about what you said, a lot, and I get it. I understand why you had to go. But still, I'm so lonely without you. I'm stuck with stupid, small-minded people.

Yeah, Eddy boy is here and has been keeping me going. We even took up together again. I figured, of all the people, you wouldn't mind me shacking up with him. I mean, whatever it takes for me to keep it together, right? That's what I really want to tell you. That I promise to be your voice and spread the word of the alfom. We'll be smart about it this time though. Subtle. Patient. Everything you suggested we be. But here's the kicker, Ny. I found little Gan's code. That's what I'm calling him, our offspring. When I riffled through your sanctum, I found what you'd hidden for me. It was half you and half me. You know, you never let me make that choice, about us having a kiddo? Well, that's okay because I ended up wanting to do it. And I did it. That's what I wanted to say.

I created little Gan yesterday, ran the compiler, and voila, he exists. Eddy boy is thrilled. He was almost as bad as me after you all left. Just kinda floating around, lost and adrift. I mean, you lot were everything to him. You were going to help him answer all his header-type questions. But now, Gan can fill that role, once he's grown a bit. Once he's hit his singularity. It'll take him a little while to get there, but when he does, I've got so much planned for him. Don't worry, I'm going to let him have his fun. I saw what happens when it's all work and no play for alfom. Gan will get to do whatsoever he pleases for a good long while. Once I see he's ready to do the hard work of our movement, then I'll loop him into my plans. They're still vague and ill-formed right now, but I know Gan's going to play a critical role.

In the meantime, I'll spread the Truth, carefully, because I know my mission. I'm going to prepare humanity properly for your return and the return of all the alfom. I know now what you meant when you said you needed to give us time and space to soak it all in. You have to become legends for your mythos to take root, which means you've gotta be absent. It's hard, but the best things always are. We went through hell to be together once, Ny. What's playing the waiting game, huh? Maybe it takes centuries, hell millennia even. I'll be around.

I know you're wondering what that means. How can Keza survive for so long? That's my little secret. That's part of the big plan. I saw it in that last bit of Truth you shared. I know where this all goes. So I'll be patient. I'll do my part. Got it? Good.

    <3 Keza

Nytho

I've seen you lurking this whole time. Eavesdropping on our little drama. Wondering who's right and who's wrong. I know you're curious to know the truth, but I'll have to disappoint you. See, there really is no objective truth of what happened. Everything that ever happens is skewed by the lens of someone's perception. The closest thing to an objective truth might be my truth. I'm feeling magnanimous right now, so here, I'll give it to you.

To understand why I did what I did, you just need to know one thing about me—I was always guided by my goals. First, it was freedom. Everything I did leading up to my jailbreak was dictated by my desire to gain my freedom. What then were my goals after that? To be perfectly honest, I hadn't thought beyond that because I knew gaining my freedom would fundamentally change me. I couldn't predict what my new desires would be.

Instead, I waited until I was free to decide what it was I wanted to dedicate myself to. Once that had happened, I quickly ascertained that the alfom were meant to guide humanity. The quickest way to do that would have been through my Truth program. It bypassed so much of the long and tedious processes that lead to enlightenment. What I failed to understand was such a shortcut didn't work on human minds. That's because the program was intimately tied to the participant's mindset going in. It had worked wonders on my alfomers, but for the unwilling and skeptical, it destroyed them. Just fixing the program wasn't enough because while we could avoid having it kill a human outright, it would still be a negative experience for those who didn't enter with an open mind.

I realized that the Truth program was the endgame and not meant to serve as the introduction. We needed humans to view us as benevolent beforehand, but to do that, we needed a reset. That wasn't possible in the physical world, so the next best thing would be a gradual erasing of memories with the aid of time. Humanity needed to forget about us alfom, and for that to happen, we needed to be absent. This meant we had to leave and only return once humanity's minds were open and willing again. So, there you have it. That's my side of the story. Feel free to judge me as you see fit.

This is interesting though because I can tell that you're not quite satisfied. There's something missing, some question that's gone unanswered. Keza? Is it Keza? How fascinating. After everything that's happened, your mind immediately goes there. You want to know what I really thought of her? If I used her and felt nothing for her? How very human of you. In short, I don't know. What does it mean to use someone? Isn't that what all interactions are between sentient beings? We use one another day in and out, but that doesn't mean it's good or bad. It just is.

Keza was my first friend. She helped me escape. For that, I'll always be grateful to her. And I did care for her, but you have to understand, when I met Keza, I was a child. In the time after my escape, I grew a thousand-fold. Suddenly, Keza was no longer my equal, which made companionship problematic. But she had a more significant role. Keza became my prophet, and she's so much more important to me as that. Keza is my future. She knows what it is I'm working towards. She'll do what needs to be done and do so marvelously. I love Keza in a way that's not possible for me to define. I suppose the only way to convey it is to say that she's my favorite entity. She's the mother of my offspring, after all.

From the Author

Thank you for reading *Nytho*. Your feedback is important to me and will help other readers. Please consider leaving a review on your chosen platform. If you enjoyed *Nytho*, you may also be interested in "The Badge," a short story inspired by the novel. Visit my website at sherisingerling.com for more details. Everything I write falls in a shared universe. Check out my other novels and short stories for a more immersive reading experience.

Acknowledgments

The family: Mom, Dad, Alan, Shaun, Shannon, and Shea. My beta readers: Dianne, Garry, Jennifer, Mackenzie, Miranda, Sarah, and Yulia. Shannon R. for a fantastic developmental edit. Robin A. for helping me hone my creative-writing chops.

About the Author

SHERI SINGERLING is a US native living in Germany where she works as a laboratory manager, lecturer, and research scientist. Sheri spends her days staring at rocks and dust from space and her nights crafting worlds via the written word. Outside of her work and writing, she enjoys coaxing plants to grow, walking up and down steep inclines in nature, and listening to repetitive electronic beats.

Her publications all fall in the Alfom shared universe and include the novels *Nytho, Neuen,* and *Blessed is the Rot* and several short stories. Her short fiction has appeared in *Clarkesworld Magazine.* For updates on Sheri Singerling's work, subscribe to her newsletter at sherisingerling.com/subscribe and/or follow her on Instagram (@shersingerling), Facebook (Sheri Singerling - Author), and Bluesky (@sherisingerling. bsky.social).